PRAISE FOR
JEANETTE BAKER
AND
LEGACY

"[FOUR STARS]. . . . A fascinating time-travel yarn. Jeanette Baker has woven history and fantasy into a tale about the Murray clan, and about four women of the clan connected through the centuries by a curse first uttered in 1298. . . ."

—Helen Holzer, *Atlantic Journal*

"Fans of rich and unusual novels are in for a treat and should not miss this truly unique and mesmerizing tale. . . . A marvelous book that is as riveting as it is haunting."

—Jill M. Šmith, *Romantic Times*

"Tantalizing. . . . Ms. Baker is a talented writer. . . . [she kept] me intrigued and enthralled. . . . A thought-provoking novel not to be missed."

—*Rendezvous*

D0802700

Books by Jeanette Baker

Legacy
Catriona

Published by POCKET BOOKS

JEANETTE BAKER

Catriona

POCKET BOOKS

New York   London   Toronto   Sydney   Tokyo   Singapore

This book is a work of fiction. Names, characters, places and incidents are products of the author's imagination or are used fictitiously. Any resemblance to actual events or locales or persons, living or dead, is entirely coincidental.

An *Original* Publication of POCKET BOOKS

POCKET BOOKS, a division of Simon & Schuster Inc.
1230 Avenue of the Americas, New York, NY 10020

Copyright © 1997 by Jeanette Baker

ISBN: 1-4165-0170-3

This Pocket Books paperback printing May 2004

10   9   8   7   6   5   4   3   2   1

POCKET and colophon are registered trademarks of Simon & Schuster Inc.

Cover art by Mitzura Salgian

Printed in the U.S.A.

Catriona

❧ PROLOGUE ❧

Cait Ness, Scotland

Leaving her with Bonnie Sutherland was clearly the most difficult thing I'd ever done. She was so very small, her skin milky sweet, her features yet unformed, her stare the vacant opaque gray of the netherworld. She was the reason I'd kept in touch with Bonnie and Ken across thousands of miles, the reason I sent for them from halfway across the world.

We were all Sutherlands, of course, but the connection was too distant to call us family. Yet, because of who I was and what I saw, I knew Bonnie would come. I knew she would take her, raise her, love her and send her back to me when the time was right. I knew also that she would never betray me. What I didn't know, what I couldn't possibly imagine, was the pain I felt when it came time to let her go.

She was born of my flesh and blood, but there was little of me, nor of the isle of Cait Ness, in her, neither hair nor eyes nor temperament. She was all Hunter, from the wispy black hair sprouting from her small, perfectly shaped skull to the odd Celtic slant of her eyes. I took some small comfort in that. But when a woman carries a child beneath her heart for nine long months, feels the fluttering lifeforce quicken and turn within her, suffers the agony of childbirth, hears the first faint wail heralding life and knows the age-old, insistent pull of a tiny mouth against her breast, somehow lineage pales in significance.

I knew from the beginning how it must be. The vision was clear enough, although, not being one of the twice-born, I never knew why I was the one selected to see what others could not, to bear the burden and the wonder of the Sight. I was taught that it wasn't suitable for mere mortals to question the web destiny chose to weave for those of us caught in her silken strands. It was a gift handed down to

1

the very few. For that gift, I would pay the price of obedience.

Most of the time it is enough for me to understand that every small cog in the windmill of life has its singular purpose, that we are here not once but many times, on a journey that ends quite differently than we could ever imagine. Occasionally there is a moment of doubt, a flash of awareness, a diamond-edged moment when duty gives way to a pain so acute, so all-consuming, that I cannot help but cry out in anguish, pleading for answers, for release, for the blessed peace of the sightless. The answers come, but not soon enough, not nearly soon enough.

She was born, as I was, here on Cait Ness, one of the islands in the far North Country called the Shetlands. Here, where legend tells us Morgawse was queen to King Lot, mists hover like blankets of smoke over stark hillsides and barren shorelines. Waves of cerulean blue pound coarse-sand beaches and gulls circle and shriek beneath a leaden sky. On Cait Ness, land of the Sutherlands, the old ways of the Druids mingle with the teachings of Christ in a jumble of sacred confusion. Here, where the Picts ruled for centuries, tracing their lineage through matrilineal bloodlines, Christianity came late and, to many, not at all.

To the Catach, the worshipers of sun and moon, of fire and water and earth and wind, the concept of woman and her role in original sin was met with great skepticism. Women were lifegivers, harbingers of mystery, their bodies carrying the secrets of immortality. Men honored, revered and served them. It was here, on Cait Ness, that I learned my craft.

It is not for me to question why infants are fed spoonfuls of dirt to cement their partnership with the land, or why salt and rock and sea and air are given the same regard as sheep and cow and human child. It is, I was taught, as it always was.

I came soon to the understanding that I would be a seer of the Pectiwita as my mother was before me and her mother before her and her mother before that. I knew that I would be alone, forbidden to share my life with another, and that I would know what others would not. All this and more I was prepared for.

CATRIONA

Although the followers of the Goddess are greatly maligned in the more civilized parts of the world, there was never a time when witchcraft was not practiced among the Celtic people who populate the islands known as Britain. Wicca— or wise ones, as we are called—rarely live up to the expectations of outsiders. White witchcraft is nothing more than to work magick for the benefit of others, to use herbs for healing and to look into the future.

We do not, as our persecutors proclaim, worship the devil. Indeed, we do not admit to the existence of Satan. He is a biblical fabrication. Our beliefs are older than the Bible, older than Satan. I have often thought that men need a devil to justify the evil that exists in their hearts, but that has nothing to do with us. We worship the Goddess, Mother Earth, the sun and moon, and we use our magick to practice only good. Occasionally we are called to a cause we do not understand. And so it was with me.

If I had known then what I know now it would have made little difference. I could no more have changed the path of my future than I could command away the mists separating the summerlands from the Isle of Cait Ness. Nor did I wish to. It is not often that the chosen of the Pectiwita may follow their hearts. In that I was more fortunate than most. The ways of the star-born are not our ways, although they often work through us. That year the Beltane fires would hold their own special magick for me.

It was the second of February in the year nineteen hundred and sixty-five when Hunter Sutherland came back to the island. Until then, I remembered him only as the son of the laird, nemesis of my youth, a grinning black-haired villain, intent on pulling my plaits, copying my lessons and stealing criachan from the manor kitchen. He left, a mere boy, to further his education in London as all the nobility did, and returned a man, a light-eyed, sharp-cheeked, strong-jawed man with the lean grace of a Celtic warrior and a smile that dazzled white in a face as bronzed and chiseled as a Roman coin.

From the beginning I knew it was impossible. But Hunter knew nothing of the sort, and all my good intentions were lost beside the banked heat in his moss-colored eyes and the dark blood that rose within me at the touch of his hands on my skin.

There were those who warned me against him. "He is the laird," they would say. "Nothing can come of this."

They were wrong. I had seen my future, and no one knew better than I what would come of my passion for the future chief of Clan Sutherland.

For three months I denied him, stirring the embers of the flame he carried for me into a raging inferno. It was on the eve of Beltane, the fifteenth of May, when the faithful celebrate the pagan rites of fertility as they have done since the days of the Picts, before the summerlands could no longer be summoned from the mists, that I held back no longer. The prophecy would be fulfilled. And even though I knew the pain that would follow, I was as helpless against the pull of destiny as a twig sucked down by a mighty current.

It was an icy spring. Except for a few thin patches in shady glens, the snow had melted from valleys and flatlands, and purple heather shadowed the hillsides. But the air was still cold enough to burn nasal passages raw if one was foolish enough to draw a deep breath. Peat fires burned day and night, and linens left to dry overnight on rocks and shrubs were frozen stiff the following morning.

Preparations for the festival were nearly complete. A huge tree trunk, stripped of branches and decorated with ribbons, was erected on Lleaneach Mound near Scalloway. Hot usquebaugh, brewed in ale houses and sealed into barrels, had been rolled to the foot of the mound, awaiting the moment when merrymakers with hot pokers would puncture the seals and distribute the fiery liquid to all.

Throughout the day a steady procession of families from all over the islands bore steaming, cloth-covered dishes of poacher's stew, haggis, skirlie, stove tatties, fried quail and rabbit, pirr, bloaters and drammock to crofts near the mound. Fire pits were dug and laid in circles. Cait Ness's barren summits and rocky slopes, chiseled by glaciers and centuries of rain, supported few trees. Before dawn and on through the dim light of late afternoon, the men of Lerwick and West Burra lugged thick squares of peat to the tip of the mound where the sacred fires would be lit, the rites of

Beltane consummated and the twentieth century left behind for a brief twelve hours.

Through it all I waited, fasting and praying, preparing myself for the ceremony to come. Initiates of the Pectiwita laid out my clothing, a long white dress with a loose belt. Dipping their fingers in woad, they painted a blue crescent moon on my forehead and below my navel. My hair, straight, thick and red as flame, hung unbound to my knees. Golden torques were clasped around my neck and forearms, and a mixture of pounded damiana and saw palmetto berries was dabbed behind my ears, between my breasts and thighs, the purpose to deepen sexual desire.

Through the hunger haze clouding my brain, I heard the laughter and calling of merrymakers. Soon I would be with them, carrying the sacred torch. The Goddess would speak through me, and the valleys would be fertile for the season to come. Calves and new lambs would roam the hillocks and more than one wedding would be hastily arranged in expectation of the child conceived at the Feast of Beltane.

For me, it would be different. There would be no wedding for the child conceived amidst the heat of the sacred flame. There would only be the night and the long, lonely months to follow and the birthing and then all the years of not knowing until a woman seeking answers found her way back to me. Until then I would wait and in the waiting learn the reason for my own existence.

At first, it was as I thought it would be. Flanked by women in long robes, I carried the flaming torch to the tip of the summit and thrust it into the dry kindling. A piece of wood smoked, then one by one the branches caught and a crackling flame as high as a croft lit the sky. I stood close enough for the heat to singe my cheeks and led the chant, asking for purity of air, for hostilities to disappear and for man, beast and vegetation to thrive and multiply. Food and usquebaugh passed from hand to hand. Pipers took up their pipes and the wild eerie keening of the notes mixed with the moaning wind, the crackling fire and the hypnotizing mantra on the lips of the faithful.

I danced around the fire, pulling men and women into a ring around the leaping flames. We were all Sutherlands, Gunns and MacKays, remotely related through an ancient clan system that was no longer practical in the modern world, and we knew each other well.

Around and around we circled and clapped and drank and swayed and sang. Couples broke away and, with arms wrapped around each other, disappeared into the darkness. Minutes passed—or was it hours? Still I danced. Masculine forms appeared before me, holding out their hands. I shook my head, waiting for the one I knew would come. When he did, I was ready. I think perhaps I had always been ready for him.

Without warning, he appeared before me like a spirit of the night. My breath caught, and once again I wondered how one could doubt that Viking raiders had sown their seed on our islands. Hunter Sutherland was the tallest man on Cait Ness. His skin was darkly tanned, although winter was still upon us, and his eyes were a curious gray-green that spoke of ice-stilled tarns and distant shorelines. There was a presence about him that was more than unusual height and strength of jaw. It was a wildness, an unconscious masculine grace, a complete disregard for conventional wisdom. Hunter Sutherland knew nothing of fear. I was twenty years old and had never known anyone like him. He drew me, inexorably, toward him.

His hands reached out, pulling me into the circle of his arms. I was tall for a woman of Celtic ancestry, but nothing compared to his great height. A current surged from his eyes to mine. He pressed my face against the wool covering his chest. Before a hundred island families, he wove his fingers in my loose hair, pulled my head back and set his mouth on mine, hard.

I had been kissed before, but not like this. The earth turned under my feet and a strange roaring sounded in my ears. A boneless sensation began in my ankles and climbed up my legs, claiming my entire body. Weak-kneed, I leaned into Hunter's embrace, clinging to his shoulders. His mouth softened and moved against mine. Suddenly it was very warm. The fire disappeared, along with the crowd behind me. I no longer heard the whistles and ribald catcalls. The wind was soft against my face, and the hands moving along my skin were warm and sure and sensuous. Strong arms lifted me from the ground and carried me to a place I had never been before. It was soft and very dark and smelled of sage and clover and summer herbs. Careful fingers fluttered against my cheeks and lashes, and warm hands moved across my body, caressing my shoulders, my waist, my hips, lingering on my breasts.

I moaned softly and he waited no longer, claiming me as powerfully and completely as ever I had seen in my vision. Only it was so much more than that. With the first surge of rigid flesh, his mouth came down on mine and I forgot the pain. My face flamed with shame and joy. This was not the laird of Cait Ness mating with the Goddess of Fertility. It was Hunter Sutherland claiming the woman he loved. I rejoiced in the knowledge, even though I knew that the roads the two of us were destined to travel did not lie together.

When Hunter Sutherland left Cait Ness, I thought I knew everything there was to know about heartbreak. But when he returned, two years later with his new bride and he never looked my way again, an entirely new dimension of pain was born within me. I left Cait Ness for the tiny, westernmost island of Foula and, from then on, made my way alone.

❧ 1 ❧

Salem, Massachusetts, December 1995

So this was Salem. Kate Sutherland looked up at the leaden
sky. It was late afternoon, and the air was sharp and heavy
with the promise of snow. She breathed in deeply, smelling
salt and fish and the gray, cold scent of the sea. Shivering,
she pulled her glove off with her teeth and dug down into
her coat pocket for the address she had stuffed into it
earlier. Smoothing out the crumpled paper, she glanced at
the bold writing and looked up, checking the numbers on
the small building before her.

Kate frowned. This must be the place, but it certainly
wasn't what she had expected. A Cape Cod saltbox with
peeling white clapboards, wooden steps and two feet of
unshoveled snow around the doorjamb did not reflect the
lifestyle of a woman who could afford a high-priced California law firm. Why Celia Ward of Salem would choose
Barrett and MacKenzie, a firm on the other side of the
country, to handle a simple tax problem was a mystery Kate
wasn't paid to question.

But then Lillian had referred this woman to Kate, and
Lillian was full of surprises. Kate hadn't wanted the case.
She didn't like traveling and New England in winter didn't
appeal to her. It wasn't until Lillian Spencer, Kate's therapist, had explained that Celia was a clairvoyant that Kate's
interest was piqued. She had never met a clairvoyant.
Something inside of her, something emotional and carefully
repressed, broke free and demanded attention. Kate had
buzzed her secretary, telling her to place an order for a café
latte from the Express House across the street and to book
her on a flight to Massachusetts.

At first she considered Celia Ward and the idea of
witchcraft laughable. But Salem, Massachusetts, with its

9

street signs in the shape of witches on broomsticks, its Cotton Mather museum and Nathaniel Hawthorne's House of the Seven Gables, conjured up ghostly images of a time when it wasn't laughable at all.

Kate shivered. She had completely discounted the snow, something easy to do in the seventy-degree comfort of a Southern California winter. She shivered again, chastising herself for the wild goose chase that had led her to the coast of Massachusetts in the windchill of late December.

She hesitated in front of the door. It was nearly Christmas, and last-minute shoppers, breathless and red-cheeked, hurried down the narrow streets to lighted doorways and apple-log fires. Pine wreaths decorated the doors, and windows were glazed with flocking and holiday greetings. Kate expelled her breath in a cloud of mist. Why was she so reluctant to meet the woman now that she was actually here? Her plane left Logan Airport at nine the next morning. It was now or never. She resolutely pulled the bell.

A cheery voice called out, "Come in."

Wiping the snow from her boots, Kate stepped inside and looked around. A counter reminiscent of a fifties' diner ran the entire length of the room. Glass jars of every shape and size filled with powders, liquids, shells, flakes and feathers were side by side. Dried herbs hung from the open-beamed ceiling and chintz-covered pillows beckoned invitingly from two loveseats in the corner. A fire blazed in the fireplace, and a long-haired white cat slept on a braided rug in front of the hearth.

On her knees, rummaging in the drawer of an antique dresser, was a small woman wearing jeans and an enormous red sweatshirt. Her profile—all Kate could see from her place near the door—revealed a tip-tilted nose, round metal-framed glasses and the longest blond braid she had ever seen on an adult woman. The woman looked up and grinned. "Have a seat."

She wasn't as young as Kate had first thought. Despite the braid, the youthful clothing and unlined skin, there was something about the woman's eyes that spoke of experience, wisdom and a deep, unshakable compassion.

Kate smiled tentatively, walked across the room to the

loveseat and sat down. If this was Lillian's witch, there was certainly nothing intimidating about her. "Are you Celia Ward?" she asked.

"In the flesh," the blonde replied, standing up, flipping the braid over her shoulder and closing the drawer with her foot. "What can I do for you?"

Kate hesitated. For a moment it seemed as if their roles were reversed and Celia Ward really could do something for her. She shook off the feeling and stretched out her hand. "I'm Kate Sutherland, the attorney from Barrett and Mac-Kenzie. We have an appointment. I'm sorry that I didn't call from the airport."

"Oh yes. Kate Sutherland." Celia's forehead wrinkled as she shook Kate's hand. "You look very familiar to me. Have we met before?"

Kate shook her head. "I don't think so. I rarely come to Boston."

Celia Ward stared into the wide, expressionless eyes of the woman before her. She really was quite lovely, decided Celia, or she would be without that tight look drawing down her face. Kate Sutherland exuded a dignified sort of beauty, the kind that came from long bones and straight teeth and thick, shining hair.

"I'll make some tea," Celia said softly, rising to her feet, "and then I'll explain my legal problem. There's no hurry. Take off your coat and relax."

Gratefully, Kate shed her coat and gloves and leaned back against the pillows. She had what was left of the day and night. The fire was pleasant, the woman friendly. Maybe this anxiety she felt was nothing at all.

Celia returned with a tea tray, china teapot, matching cream and sugar bowl, two delicate porcelain cups and sterling-silver teaspoons. "I normally use mugs," she explained, positioning the tray on the floor beside the loveseat, "but you look like the cup-and-saucer type."

Kate picked up a cup, refusing lemon and sugar, and cut to the quick. "What kind of legal troubles are you having, Ms. Ward?"

Celia stirred milk into her teacup and sipped it. "I'm a member of the Wicca religion. The word means 'wise one.'

We follow the practices of the ancient Druids. The government has audited me and decided that I owe nearly fifty thousand dollars in back taxes."

Kate's voice was firm, crisp. "Do you have receipts, check stubs, a log?"

"I have everything," Celia insisted. "It isn't a question of proving expenses. The problem is the Internal Revenue Service has decided that I'm not a legitimate business."

"You don't have to be. The law clearly states that expenses for the purpose of maintaining and upholding religious institutions are deductible. You are a religious institution, aren't you?"

"Yes, we are," Celia said softly, "one of the oldest religions in the world, with a great many practitioners."

Kate rubbed the delicate edge of her cup with the tip of her finger. "You're not what I imagined."

Blue eyes twinkled back at her. "What did you expect? A black robe and a broomstick?"

For the first time, Kate laughed, liked the sound and laughed again. "Not exactly. I did think you'd be more mysterious, maybe a little frightening, certainly older."

Celia Ward looked down at her tea. When she looked up again, there was nothing of warmth or sympathy in her eyes. "I can be frightening, Kate," she said quietly. "But not today and not to you. Now, tell me why Lillian Spencer sent you to me."

"To help you with your tax problem. Why else?"

Celia shook her head. "I don't think so. I don't have the Sight, but I know Lillian. Your being here is no accident. Lillian knows a lot of lawyers—there are several firms that have offices in Los Angeles and Boston besides Barrett and MacKenzie. There's no logic in asking you to fly all the way out from Los Angeles unless she had a specific reason."

"Federal problems have no jurisdiction and I am licensed to practice in Massachusetts," Kate explained. "Besides, I'm only here to advise you on your case. If, after reviewing the facts, I think you have one, I can refer you to a litigations attorney in our Boston office."

"That doesn't explain why Lillian chose you."

"I'm very good at what I do, Miss Ward."

Celia sighed. "I wish you would take off those contact lenses. I can't see anything through them."

Kate gasped. No one had ever guessed that she wore contacts. With the colored lenses in, her eyes were nothing like the vivid aquas and turquoise colors worn by those who wanted to be noticed. Kate had deliberately chosen an innocuous blue-gray, a color typical of ninety percent of the light-eyed population. "How did you know?" she asked.

"Your eyes tell me nothing at all," said Celia matter-of-factly. "That's the first clue. Please take them off. I'll be much more comfortable if you do."

Kate hesitated. Somehow their positions had been reversed and she wasn't sure she wanted it that way. Then she reached down for her bag and opened the zippered pocket, pulling out a small plastic case and a bottle of saline. She squeezed several drops of the liquid into each side of the case and self-consciously removed first her right contact lens, then her left, dropping them into the container. Slowly, she raised her eyes to the other woman's expectant gaze.

Celia Ward's eyes widened and she went very still. She had never imagined it would make such a difference. Kate Sutherland, with her true coloring, was vividly, hauntingly beautiful. Celia could remember only one other person with eyes like that. A thought occurred to her, and this time she looked more carefully at the younger woman's face. Sweet heaven! Could it possibly be? She repressed a tremor of delight. It had been such a very long time.

She decided to begin slowly. "We can't do this over tea and polite conversation," she explained. "It takes much more. Why don't you tell me something about yourself?"

"What did you mean by not having the Sight?"

"I think you know the answer to that."

Kate swallowed and lifted the teacup to her lips. Her hands shook, but she craved the heat and warmth of the liquid. "I'm not sure that I know what you're talking about."

"Of course you do, or you wouldn't have come here at all." Celia stood up and held out her hand. "Will you let me show you?"

Kate hedged. "Well, we've got to take care of your tax problem and I have a plane to catch in the morning."

"I need at least three days."

"Impossible." Kate was emphatic.

"Why?"

"It's my mother. She's alone now and her health is poor. I can't leave her alone at Christmastime. My sister lives in Florida. She'll be celebrating the holidays with her husband's family."

Celia tilted her head, considered telling her and decided against it. Kate was very resistant. Perhaps it wasn't yet her time. If Celia had learned anything in her forty-eight years, it was that certain things couldn't be rushed. "All right," she conceded. "Perhaps you should go home. You can always come back."

Kate set down her cup and reached for her briefcase. "Let's get to your taxes, shall we?"

Four hours later, Celia stretched out her legs and yawned. "It's late. Why don't I see what's in the refrigerator. We can finish up after we eat."

Kate checked her watch: It was after ten. "I should get going. I think I have enough information. I'll call if I need anything else."

Celia looked startled. "You can't possibly think I'd allow you to leave on a night like this. It's snowing and you're from California. The spare room is all made up. I insist that you spend the night."

In the end Kate agreed. Negotiating the streets of Salem in an unfamiliar automobile didn't appeal to her, and Celia was more than welcoming.

The guest room was old-fashioned and lovely, with daisy-studded wallpaper, matching curtains and a down-filled comforter, hardly Kate's idea of a witch's bedroom. One of the doors led to a modern bathroom with thick lemon-colored towels.

Kate washed her face, brushed her teeth and pulled a flannel nightgown over her head. She was exhausted. Leaving the bathroom light on, she pulled back the comforter, climbed into the double bed and fell asleep.

Immediately they claimed her, images she neither recognized nor understood. A land surrounded on all sides by water and gray mist. Grass, a brilliant, shocking green. Sheep grazing on hillsides before cottages with thatched roofs and whitewashed walls. Red-cheeked children racing down unpaved roads shaped like question marks and, high on a bluff, an attractive red-haired woman approaching middle age stood wrapped in a plaid shawl facing the sea.

Then suddenly the scene changed, and along with it she felt a weightless turning and the loss of all sense of direction. Once again she was in a place she didn't recognize. It was dark, and torches licked the dampness from hissing stone walls. A turreted castle dominated the landscape, and people dressed in period clothing appeared to be in the middle of a historical reenactment.

Kate was moving faster now, across the drawbridge and courtyard, through the huge oak doors into the great hall. The room was lit with thousands of candles, and elegantly dressed men and women were seated at long banquet tables. The handsome black-haired man with the dazzling smile was the king. Kate was sure of it, although he wore no crown. She recognized the redheaded woman by his side. Someone else should be here. Someone very important, but who?

The door to a small antechamber opened, and a man stepped out and walked across the floor toward his king. He was tall and lean and he moved with a predatory, catlike grace. His hair, shorn close to his head, was a rich mahogany, and the third finger on his left hand was missing.

Suddenly Kate found it difficult to breathe. Pain and joy warred with each other in her subconscious. She reached up to touch her cheek. It was wet with tears. This man was no stranger. She knew him as well as she knew herself. His smile, his strength, the warmth of his hands, the ice in his eyes, were as familiar to her as her own face. "Patrick," she whispered. "Patrick MacKendrick."

A voice she recognized as Celia's broke through her vision. *"Enough, Kate. Time is running short. You've seen enough for now. Concentrate and go back."*

Kate's mind screamed with frustration. She needed more time, just a little more time. Someone else should be here, someone very important, someone who held the key to her locked memories. A woman stood near the fire, her face in the shadows. A woman with long black hair and a red gown. Who was she, why wouldn't she come forward? Kate struggled to pull away from the hand that held hers in a grip of steel.

"Let me go," she shouted. *"I want to stay. Please, let me go."*

"I can't, Kate," Celia's reasonable voice answered. *"This isn't your place. You would be lost forever. Concentrate. Come back now."*

A hand tugged insistently at her arm. A warm wind rushed at her, whipping back her hair and burning her eyes. Again she lost all sense of space and time. The terrifying, frantic feeling left her and the weightless peace returned. Her eyes opened briefly, focused on the daisy wallpaper and closed again. The dream was over. She would sleep until morning.

❧ 2 ❧

Hunger woke her. At first she was disoriented, but the frost on the windows brought back her memory. A soft tap sounded on the door. "Come in," she called out.

It was Celia, carrying a breakfast tray complete with French toast, bacon, juice and coffee. "I thought you might be hungry," she said, positioning the tray on the bed.

"I'm starved," Kate admitted, "but you didn't have to bring me breakfast in bed."

Celia smiled. "There's enough for two. I thought we could eat before you left for the airport." She climbed on the bed, folded her legs under her and reached for a piece of bacon. "Did you have a restful night?"

Kate poured syrup on her toast. "Don't you know?" she stalled. "I thought you were a witch."

"You don't believe it, do you?" the older woman asked, staring at her thoughtfully.

"Don't take it personally. I'm just not into the occult."

Celia smiled briefly. "All right then: Who is Patrick MacKendrick?"

Kate gasped. How could she know? *Patrick MacKendrick.* The name evoked sensations of flame and heat and a piercing sweetness. White teeth and a flashing smile, eyes clear, measuring and honest, like water over sacred stones, and a searing, throat-tightening tenderness that came only from deep within him and only for her. She would never deny him. "I don't know," she answered truthfully.

"But you dreamed about him," Celia persisted.

Again Kate nodded. "Yes. I must have heard of him. But I can't remember." She looked at Celia. "How did you know about my dream?"

Celia hesitated and shrugged. "There are things I know, that's all. I know that your dream belongs to another place and time and that I need direction before I can advise you. Do you want my help, Kate?"

This time Kate was sure. "Yes, I do."

"Your visions take place in Scotland. There is someone I think you should see. Her name is Maura Sutherland and she lives on Cait Ness, one of the Shetland Islands. She's a high priestess of the Pectiwita, an ancient form of Wicca. I feel a connection between the two of you. I believe Cait Ness is the ancestral seat of Clan Sutherland. Most likely your family has roots there."

Kate opened her mouth to speak, but Celia held up her hand. "I don't know what it is. I do know that she's a descendant of the Picts, an extinct tribe of people who lived in the waterless mountains of the Highlands and followed the practices of the ancient Druids. They originally came from Ireland and ruled Scotland for hundreds of years, until Kenneth MacAlpin, half-Pict and half-Celt, united Scotland under one king." She hesitated. "They were a pastoral people with a unique culture. Some of the Pectiwita still practice the old ways."

"What do you mean?"

Celia fixed her eyes on Kate's face. "Their practice includes the use of natural herbs. The Goddess and the horned stag come alive at their festivals and ancient fertility rites are practiced."

"In other words, they use drugs, hallucinate and have orgies."

"Not quite," replied Celia coolly. "I'm saying that their magic is very powerful, and Maura Sutherland's is the most powerful of all."

"How can that possibly help me?" Kate demanded. "I'm certainly not going to travel to the Shetland Islands."

Celia sipped her coffee. "That's up to you. However, I wouldn't discount it so quickly. Obviously money isn't a problem for you, or Lillian Spencer wouldn't be your therapist."

Kate flushed. "It isn't money," she muttered.

"Then what? There doesn't appear to be anything more important going on in your life right now."

"That's an understatement." Kate's laugh was brittle.

Celia reached out and rested her hand on Kate's knee. "This isn't going to be easy for you to accept, Kate, but you need to see Maura. There's more I can tell you, but you wouldn't believe it. You're very troubled and it isn't going to get better." She glanced toward the bathroom. "Do you always leave a light on all night?"

Kate refused to answer, but the wave of red staining her face was answer enough.

"Go home for Christmas and think about it," Celia urged her.

Kate smiled. "Thank you for being so patient with me."

"My pleasure."

"Do you know this Maura Sutherland, Celia?"

"I've met her, once."

"Can you tell me anything about her?"

Celia wet her lips and turned away. "No."

She was lying. Kate sighed. It was one of the things she wished she couldn't tell so easily. "What does she look like?" she asked.

"She must be about fifty by now, but I imagine she's still lovely."

"Can you be more specific?"

Celia sighed. "You can be difficult. Oh, all right. There is something about her that I specifically remember."

Kate leaned forward. "What is it?"

A cloud swept across the lemony winter sun, darkening the room. Celia was looking at her strangely. She never blinked, and her words were slow and deliberate. "Maura Sutherland reminds me of you. In certain ways the resemblance is uncanny. There's something about your eyes."

A chill began at the base of Kate's spine and spread throughout her body. "I've never seen anyone with eyes like mine," she whispered.

Celia rubbed her arms. "Until now, neither had I."

Celia was about to speak when the ringing phone interrupted them. She picked it up and, after a terse monosyllabic response, handed it to Kate. "It's your sister, dear. She sounds upset."

Laguna Beach, California, 1995

Kate pulled the keys from her purse, inserted them into the lock and turned. The door opened easily and she stepped into the cool, sun-dappled elegance of the marble-tiled entry. For a brief moment the quiet startled her. She had expected to hear Bonnie Sutherland's predictable "Katie, is that you?" calling to her from down the hall. Then she remembered and her throat tightened. She would never hear her mother's voice again.

Dropping her purse, Kate reached for the wealth of envelopes on the sideboard and sorted through another mass of sympathy cards.

Replacing the mail, she kicked off her shoes and stepped down into the expensive plush of her mother's silver-beige carpet. Only it was no longer her mother's. Now it was hers—hers and Megan's. She pressed the button on the answering machine. Megan's husband, Steve, his voice tinged with concern, asked his wife to call him back.

Her mother's lawyer was due in less than an hour to discuss the disposition of the trust. There would be no surprises. Bonnie Sutherland hadn't believed in surprises.

She had been predictable as the dawn and completely organized. There would be no frenzied scrambling for funds to cover her expenses, no concerns that last wishes would not be met, no lengthy waiting period for the trust to kick in. Everything would be evenly divided between her two living daughters, with a small bequest for Jason, her twelve-month-old grandson.

It was dusk, and the panoramic view from the wall-to-wall glass living room was incomparable. The Pacific, stained from the melting sun, was a tide of serene, molten gold. Colorful flecks gleamed from the sand, and the tracks of a thousand scurrying creatures, rushing away from the retreating tide toward survival, were outlined in bright relief. Above the water, streaked with pink and peach and silver, filled with the silhouettes of a thousand gulls and the slender promise of a pale moon, the darkening sky stretched out, farther than the eye could see, as far as the mind could soar.

Kate sank down into the comfort of a twin sofa and stretched her legs across the glass coffee table, feasting her eyes on the view. This, at least, never disappointed her.

She heard steps in the entry and the familiar husky tones of her sister's voice. "Hello? Where are you, Kate?"

"In the living room."

From the elegant marbled entry, she felt her sister's eyes on her, worried, watchful, hurting. "How was your trip back?" Megan asked in a careful voice.

Sighing, Kate tore her gaze from the window and focused on the baby sleeping in Megan's arms. She rose, motioned her sister into the room and held out her arms for her nephew.

Gratefully, Megan handed him over and sat down on the opposite couch. Once again, Kate was struck by the differences between them. Megan was a soft, golden, fluffy woman, with rosy skin and a rounded, petite figure. She had passed down her coloring to her son, now sleeping peacefully on Kate's shoulder.

Kate breathed in the downy scent of her nephew, and the erratic beating of her heart slowed. Jason always had this effect on her. There was something sweetly soothing about this damp, warm, powdery bundle of life, something so important, so purposeful, so worth it all that the world seemed to right itself when she held him close to her chest. The fact that he faced a risky operation to correct his impaired hearing made him all the more precious.

Megan's heart melted at the picture of her son snuggled in Kate's arms. Kate needed to meet someone wonderful and have children of her own. After all, she was already thirty. But then, Kate had always done everything on her own time. When she did have children, Megan wondered who they would resemble. She imagined a little girl with Kate's green eyes and dark hair and sighed enviously.

Breathtaking was the only word to describe Kate. There was simply no other adjective that did her justice. By the time she was twelve, she had already topped Megan's five feet and gone on to grow another seven inches. It wasn't an unusual height, but people thought she was taller, mostly because of her legs. They were long and very slender. Too skinny, Kate always said, until she was eighteen and it became quite obvious that her legs had turned out to be an asset after all.

Megan always wondered why her sister never appreciated her own appearance. She couldn't be sure, but she was halfway convinced that the reason Kate chose to use her law degree for research rather than litigation had something to do with a lack of confidence.

Kate noticed the tightly clenched hands in her sister's lap and smiled gently. "Don't worry, Meg. I know you can't travel now, not with Jason's operation coming up. It never crossed my mind to ask you to come with me."

Megan released her breath and ran her hands through her short, curly hair. "I just can't risk traveling with him. We've postponed the operation twice already. If he should catch another cold—and with the new business starting up, Steve can't take the time."

Kate turned to look out over the ocean and forced her voice to remain normal. "Mom would want you to do what's right for the baby. I'll go to Cait Ness."

"When will you leave?"

"I don't know." Kate gently laid the baby on the couch

beside her. "I'll decide after the funeral." She didn't mention her other, far more bewildering, reason for visiting Scotland. Looking around the room, she assessed the changes of the past few days. "You've decorated the Christmas tree. That was nice of you."

"I wanted it to look the way it usually does this time of year."

Kate stared at the vision of sparkling white lights and red bows. The silence was thick and cloying. Nausea gripped her stomach. "We're orphans," she whispered.

"What?"

Kate shook her head. "Never mind. People die, Meggie. That's what Mom always said. It's the price we pay for life."

Megan's face worked. "She was young."

Kate reached across the table and squeezed her sister's hand. "Not really. After Dad died, she wasn't the same."

Megan sniffed and rubbed her eyes.

Kate checked the baby, tucked the blanket around him and and stood up. "I think I will go to Scotland, but not now. I don't think I could stand anything colder than seventy degrees. Do we have anything to eat? I'm hungry, and Bill will probably want food." Bill Brockman, her mother's lawyer, had a standing invitation for dinner every Wednesday night.

Megan stared at the slender loveliness of the woman before her. Kate was never hungry. Food didn't appeal to her. She ate for survival, nothing more. In fact, she was as unconcerned about her eating habits as she was about everything else in her life. Megan couldn't remember a time when Kate had actually shown a passion for anything. "I went grocery shopping today," she offered. "Would you like me to make something, or would you like to forget Bill altogether and go out after he leaves?"

"I'm too tired to go out but I'll fix my own dinner. Steve called. He sounded worried."

"I'll call him now." Megan picked up the phone. "Why don't you put Jason to sleep upstairs for me and take a nap yourself. I'll make dinner after I tell Steve about the funeral arrangements. It's been a long time since we've eaten together. Even with Bill, it'll be a nice change. I'll call you when it's ready."

An hour later, after a long shower and a change of clothing, Kate pulled her hair back into a sleek ponytail that revealed the clean, uncluttered purity of her jaw and walked down the stairs.

Bill Brockman was in the kitchen with Megan, leaning against the counter, a glass of wine in his hand. He raised the glass and nodded at Kate. "You look lovely," he said, nodding at her silky, wide-legged pants and long red sweater.

"Thanks." Kate dismissed the compliment. She respected Bill as a lawyer and colleague, but that was as far as it went. Just because he'd won her mother's approval as a prospective son-in-law didn't mean that he was any closer to winning hers. "Can I set the table?" she asked Megan.

"I already did. We're eating in the dining room tonight. You can pour the wine."

Kate looked at the bottle. "Are we celebrating something?"

"Your homecoming."

"I was only gone overnight."

Megan carried the salad bowl into the dining room. "It's still a good excuse. Come and sit down. I made something you'll like."

Kate's eyes widened when she saw the table. "Homemade lasagna? How did you do this in an hour?"

"I made extra a few days ago and froze it. I hope you'll eat more than your usual two bites. They don't make lasagna in Scotland."

"Scotland?" Bill's eyebrows rose. "What's this about?"

Kate sat down and helped herself to the salad. "I'm going to Scotland to scatter my mother's ashes. Megan can't go. She's got the baby and Steve."

"Isn't this rather sudden?"

Kate's fork halted in midair. There was an edge of panic beneath the calm tones of the lawyer's voice. "Do you have a problem with my leaving, Bill?" she asked softly.

"Of course not."

"Is there something you're not telling us?"

He sighed. "Can't we just have a relaxing dinner before business?"

Megan watched the exchange in interested silence. She had lost all interest in food.

Kate resumed chewing. "All right. Tell me about Scotland. I know you've been there. How long has it been?"

"Seventeen years. What would you like to know?

"Have you ever been to the Shetland Islands?"

Bill kept his eyes on his food. "Yes. It's where your parents come from."

"What is it like?"

"Remote and very lovely. There are green hills and valleys, lots of water in the Lowlands, very little up high. It's surrounded in mist all year round. Legend has it King Arthur's son, Mordred, was raised there. The people live very much as their ancestors did, in small crofts, making their living from sheep. Or at least they did," he amended. "It's been a long time."

"I imagined it that way: the green of the land and roads shaped like question marks." Kate's voice sounded very far away.

Bill looked at her curiously. "Yes. It looks just like that." He swallowed his last bite of lasagna, set down his fork, drew a deep breath and looked directly into Kate's eyes. He couldn't wait any longer. There would never be a better time. "You were born there too, Kate. Bonnie and Ken adopted you, thirty years ago. Bonnie knew she would have to tell you someday, but it never seemed the right time, and then *her* time ran out. It still doesn't seem right, but I can't let you go there without knowing."

Kate's eyes, clear and green as new grass, never left his face. There was no way of knowing what went on behind her expressionless gaze.

"Do you know who my birth parents are?" she asked carefully.

Bill shook his head. "Bonnie never said. She told me that you were a miracle, that she and Ken had tried to have a child for ten years. Bringing a baby back into the United States wasn't as difficult as they thought. You were too young for a passport. No one thought twice about it."

"Are you saying that I'm not legally adopted?"

"Of course not. All the required paperwork is accounted for. Everything is perfectly legal."

"But they never went back."

Bill's cheeks were an uncomfortable red. "No."

"Is there anything else I should know?" Kate persisted, refusing to allow the emotions gathering at both temples free rein until she was out of this room, away from this man who uttered impossible words.

"Yes. The name on the adoption certificate is *Megan,* not *Kate.*"

Megan. Kate had forgotten Megan. She turned to look at the woman who was not really her sister. Her pink mouth was a perfect circle and her cheeks were very pale.

Megan cleared her throat. "Are you saying that I'm adopted too?"

Bill Brockman took a fortifying sip of wine. "No. I'm saying that your parents intended to name Kate *Megan.* But, for some reason, Bonnie didn't think the name fit Kate. She never told me why. But the name-change documentation is there and it's all legal."

"Is *Katherine* my legal name?"

"No." Bill frowned. "Your legal name is a Scottish name. *Katherine* is the Americanized version. The name on the certificate is *Catriona.*"

A strange pounding began in Kate's temple, as if the syllables of the name were taken apart and set to the beat of a heavy drum. Louder and louder, the name pounded against her brain until it drowned out Bill's words. *Cat-ri-o-na, Cat-ri-o-na, Cat-ri-o-na.* She pressed her hands against her ears and moaned.

Immediately, Megan was by her side. "Are you all right, Katie?"

Kate dropped her hands. Her face was the color of bleached ivory. The noise in her head had stopped as suddenly as it started, leaving her weak and shaking. She reached for her sister's hand. "It's nothing, really," she reassured her. "I'm just more tired than I realized. I think I'll go upstairs to bed."

Megan squeezed Kate's shoulder and returned to her chair. "Just eat a few more bites," she said in motherly fashion, "and I won't say another word."

To appease her sister, Kate ate another bite of lasagna and

most of her salad before standing up. "The jet lag must be affecting me." She came around the table and kissed Meggie's soft cheek. She felt closer to her sister now that their mother was gone. "Don't worry, Meg. I'm not going into a deep depression or anything over this. Sleep well. I'll see you in the morning."

Tears misted in the younger woman's eyes. Kate rarely indulged in displays of affection. "Goodnight, Katie," she said softly.

Four hours later, Kate sat at her window seat, wide awake, staring through her window at the moon. It was a crescent, unusually white and very large—a Cinderella moon, her mother used to tell her when she was small enough to still believe in fairy tales. Tonight, it wasn't insomnia or disillusionment that prevented her from sleeping. It was fear. Fear of her own future and the odd, out-of-body experiences that she had deliberately ignored but had continued to plague her for most of her life.

Had there ever been a time when life felt completely normal? Had there ever been one moment when she didn't dread the darkness, when her mouth didn't dry at the thought of a closed-in place? Kate didn't think so. The feelings of separation, of standing apart, the painful isolation, the wondering how she had come to be here among these people, this family who loved her desperately, yet could never hope to understand the turmoil within her, had always been there, like the way the hair grew back from the widow's peak on her forehead and the odd, light-struck green of her eyes.

Kate had always suspected that the family she called her own was not the one she'd started with. The fit had never been quite right. There were differences, too many that could not be explained. But she'd brushed her suspicions away just as she brushed away everything that didn't fit into the predictable life she'd molded for herself.

Late at night, she dreamed of leaving her body, rising above the bed and looking down at her sleeping form. Sometimes the world spun so quickly she would grasp at whatever stability was at hand, lurching dizzily until her stomach righted itself again. At other times, moments passed so slowly she suffered agonies of frustration and wondered if she would survive the boredom.

The most terrifying phenomenon of all, the one people feared most—the one *she* feared most—was her clarity of vision. There were moments when she looked into the eyes of a stranger and knew him to the depths of his soul. Terrified, he would look away. Kate understood that terror and struggled against her power, but she rarely had enough control to extinguish it completely.

It all became too much for her, and three years before, when her father died unexpectedly and she continued to cry for months after his funeral, Megan convinced her to try grief counseling, which had led to Lillian Spencer and something else entirely.

At first the thought of anyone having access to the innermost workings of her mind terrified Kate. But gradually, Lillian, a chic Beverly Hills psychologist, gained her trust. All of which led to absolutely nothing unusual, no repressed sexual experiences, no molestations, no psychosis, nothing other than a normal, somewhat indulged childhood.

Lillian Spencer had no answers. But someone did, and Kate was willing to bet that the someone was somewhere on the island of Cait Ness. Maybe it was time to ask the right questions.

She walked into the bathroom, removed her contact lenses and stared into the mirror, framing her face with her hands as she looked at her reflection. It was still her face, the same high-boned, sharp-cheeked, slanted cat's eyes and pouting mouth, the same dark mole at the corner of her lip, emphasized by the delicate ivory of her skin. But there was a difference. Kate could see it, just as she always saw what others couldn't. This time it was something she couldn't pinpoint, something half formed and surrounded by the cobwebs in her brain, something that waited patiently, in the darkness, for its long-overdue release.

Lifting the toilet seat, she opened first the right side of her contact lens case, then the left, and dropped the blue-gray ovals into the bowl. Then she flushed the toilet.

❧ 3 ❧

It was the middle of April before Kate boarded British Airways Flight 546 to Edinburgh. At the urging of her travel agent, she had arranged to spend four weeks seeing the sights of Scotland. But after twelve hours in the air and a two-hour layover in Newfoundland, she was angry with herself for even considering it. Flying didn't agree with her. It upset her stomach and made her sluggish. By the time she'd collected her luggage and cleared customs, it was nearly midnight.

Kate was tired and discouraged. She had expected to feel something when the plane landed, a kinship, a jarring of memory, a flash of recognition, anything that indicated this was the country of her birth. But it hadn't happened. She felt more unsettled than ever. For the first time, the reality of traveling alone in a foreign country overwhelmed her. She was frightened, self-conscious and very alone. The idea of renting a car with the steering wheel on the wrong side and venturing out into the streets of Edinburgh looking for the George Hotel was unthinkable. Besides, it was raining, and Kate hated to drive in the rain.

A row of antique-looking cars with their doors open were lined up along the curb. Assuming they were taxis, she approached a friendly looking driver. Instantly the man's hat was in his hand.

"I'll be happy to take you to the George, lass," he said in a brogue almost too thick to understand. "It's a lovely hotel in the heart of New Town. I'll see to your luggage and we'll be on our way."

Thirty minutes later Kate was following a red-cheeked porter, who appeared to be no more than twenty, up the stairs of an elegantly refurbished seventeenth-century hotel.

Her room was lovely, with a massive four-poster, an antique armoire and a dressing table.

"Breakfast is served between seven-thirty and ten in the morning room," announced the youthful porter after hanging up the clothing in her garment bag. "Is there anything else you need tonight?"

"No, thank you. Nothing, except a wake-up call at nine." Kate fished in her purse for a pound note, smiled warmly and held it out to him.

His eyes widened and a tide of red washed over his face. "I'll arrange for it immediately, miss," he stammered, backing out of the room and stumbling over the seam on the threshold. Blushing furiously, he turned and fled to the stairs, completely ignoring the tip in her outstretched hand.

Shrugging, she locked the door after him and left the bill on the dresser. She spoke to her reflection in the beveled mirror: "If I have this effect on every schoolboy in Scotland, I'll certainly save a great deal of money." Suddenly it was all very amusing. The woman in the mirror with the jewel-bright eyes and pouting mouth laughed. Kate laughed with her. Pulling off her sweater and leggings, she found her flannel nightgown, then walked into the bathroom to brush her teeth and wash her face. Leaving the light on, she closed the door slightly, climbed into the four-poster and slept.

Eight hours later, the phone startled her. Through a haze of exhaustion, Kate realized that the persistent ringing must be her wake-up call. If she didn't want to miss breakfast she couldn't ignore it.

In Scotland, breakfast appeared to be an elegant affair, with white linen tablecloths, delicate china and gleaming silver. After glancing hesitantly about to see how it was done, Kate seated herself at one of the smaller tables. Immediately, an apple-cheeked woman in a starched apron brought out a teapot and a tray of preserves. "Help yourself, Miss Sutherland," she said, pointing to the array of chafing dishes on the sideboard. "We've scrambled eggs with bacon and sausage. The haggis and kippers are cook's specialty. If you prefer, there is dry cereal and oatmeal in the kitchen. Your toast will be out shortly."

Despite the fact that she never ate more than a piece of fruit in the morning, Kate did a creditable job on her breakfast. She had just finished her pot of tea and was spreading Golden Shred on her fourth piece of toast when the acute sensitivity she had come to despise registered that someone was watching her.

Without appearing obvious, Kate allowed her gaze to sweep the room. It was nearly empty. The two tables within her range of vision were occupied by couples deep in conversation with one another. No one appeared interested in her at all, but the tingling feeling in her fingers and toes hadn't disappeared. Someone was definitely watching her with more than cursory interest.

Giving up all pretense of politeness, Kate turned and looked back at the door. Her heart stopped and, for a full minute, under the impact of his gaze, she forgot to breathe. The man in the doorway was tall and leanly muscled, with Celtic cheekbones, sun-darkened skin and a squared-off jaw with deep, shadowed hollows. His brown-black hair gleamed with rich highlights and his eyes, hard and gray and curiously light, were fixed unmistakably on her face.

Her breath returned in a rush. Unable to look away, she watched him cross the room toward her, the controlled grace of an athlete in his step. Who was he? Frustration hammered at the locked ports of her memory. Why couldn't she ever remember when it mattered? He stopped, as she knew he would, at her table.

"I beg your pardon." His voice was rich, the brogue strong but cultured. "My name is Niall MacCormack. Have we met before?"

"I don't know." She could barely manage the words.

He frowned. "You're an American."

"Yes."

"I've never been there."

"And I've never been here before now."

He smiled, a flash of white teeth and lethal charm. Her stomach flipped.

He shook his head. "I could have sworn—"

"I'm sorry," she interrupted him.

"It's I who should be sorry. I've disturbed your breakfast. Forgive me."

Kate smiled. "Of course."

He seemed reluctant to leave. "Have you been in Scotland long?"

"Only since last night. I plan to see the city today. Can you recommend a place to start?"

"High Street," he said mechanically, distracted by the flashing green of her eyes. His head spun. Where had he seen eyes that color before? "Everything worth seeing in Edinburgh is located on High Street, except the shops. You'll find those on Princes Street."

Kate stood up. "Thank you. I'll keep that in mind."

He watched her walk away, admiring her leggy slenderness and the fall of straight black hair. It wasn't often that one saw hair that color coupled with such fair skin. Niall had noticed her the minute he walked into the room. All he could see was the back of her head and a glimpse of her profile when she looked out the window. But it was enough. He couldn't turn away. Something about her called out to him. She had felt it as well. It was almost as if she'd known he was staring at her, the way she turned around and looked directly at him. And those eyes, cat's eyes, not just the color—that startling green that assaulted him from across the the room—but the odd, provocative tilt at each corner that reminded him of the golden-eyed felines on the Isle of Man. For an instant, fleeting and over too quickly, the void within him had leapt into life.

He shrugged, walked over to a table by the window and sat down. The waitress brought him tea and toast and the poached eggs he preferred to the scrambled version filling the chafing dishes on the sideboard. Absentmindedly, he lifted the cup to his lips. The woman returned to his thoughts. She was young, probably midtwenties or so, and her speech was cultured, formal, of the private-school variety. The absence of all jewelry except for the diamond solitaires in her ears spoke of good taste, old money and a lack of ostentation.

Niall was not a people person. Not that he couldn't summon up the considerable charm he was born with and, when necessary, persuade almost anyone to contribute to the several large grants required to continue his excavation of Celtic burial sites.

In fact, it wasn't unusual for Harry Farmington, the

director of operations at the University of Edinburgh, to insist that Niall pull his tuxedo out of mothballs and make his biannual appearance at the Galashiels Ball, an event known for its tedium, its boring conversation and its wealthy patrons of the divorced female persuasion. Niall, with his lean good looks, boyish grin, Old World manners and the thick straight lock of hair that inevitably fell over his forehead, was an unqualified success.

It wasn't that he couldn't sustain a social life, it was simply that he didn't need one on the same level that others appeared to require. He was an introvert, one of that rare breed who prefers his own company over anyone else's, choosing long nights alone in his study before a comfortable fire with an untranslated excerpt from *The Annals of the Four Masters,* or a communication from Charles Howard at Trinity University, describing the latest theory on why the hominid found in Africa's Great Rift Valley could not possibly be the missing link between man and ape.

Women had a place in his life, of course. They were excellent dinner and theater companions, compassionate, clever, intelligent, sensitive. But he'd learned long before that women could not maintain an intimate relationship without the promise of permanence. And permanence was something he could not, as yet, bring himself to offer. Eventually he wanted to marry. Niall liked the idea of marriage. The huge country house left to him by his parents was ideal for children. Niall saw himself as a husband and father. What he couldn't see was the woman who would be his wife.

His eggs were cold but he didn't care. His thoughts kept returning to green eyes: green eyes and black hair and a mouth made for—abruptly, Niall pushed back his chair, dug into his pocket for a tip and left the breakfast room. It was obvious she wasn't interested in him, and his time in Edinburgh was too limited for him to be concerning himself over a woman who hadn't even offered up her name.

Kate was nearly at the top of High Street before she slowed down enough to notice her surroundings. The encounter in the morning room of the George had shaken her completely. It was terrifying to recognize someone without

32

knowing him. In retrospect she realized that she should
have made an effort to find out more about him. After all,
she was in Scotland to confront her past. Running away
wouldn't solve anything. A thought occurred to her and she
brightened. He was obviously staying at the George and he
had told her his name.

It was cold, the damp cold of a water-locked city in the
throes of early spring. Clouds danced across a gray-blue sky
and the wind blew an occasional gust of rain into her face.
Edinburgh Castle hovered over the city like a slumbering
giant, dark and brooding in its magnificence. Men and
women clutching shopping bags and briefcases hurried
about, carrying out their lives in the shadow of its ancient
presence.

Kate walked slowly across the cobblestoned esplanade,
bought her ticket and proceeded through the gates into the
courtyard. From the battlements she could see Edinburgh,
the Firth of Forth that separated the Highlands from the
rest of Scotland, and all of High Street where the nobles had
their town houses. She frowned and looked at her map.
High Street was filled with shops offering tea and gifts.
There was a museum, a wealth of historical sites and
buildings, including Holyrood Palace at the other end of the
Royal Mile. There were no residences on High Street.
Where, then, had her thought come from?

She looked out over the city. The half light of late
morning, a muted yellow that bathed even the seamier side
of the city in a euphoric glow, blinded her. She closed her
eyes. The quality of the street noises changed. Cabbies'
horns and the sound of engines died away, as did the sharp
click of heels hitting the pavement. Horses blew out their
breaths in soft snorts and carriage wheels turned on dirt
roads. Dust lingered on the air, and irritated noses sneezed.
Vendors cried out their wares and the sharp "Gardyloo!"
warning was followed by the sound of water and slops flung
into overflowing gutters. The smells of ripe garbage, rank
sweat and urine were overwhelming. Kate breathed deeply.
She reached out and her fingers tightened on the stone wall.
It was all so dreadfully, achingly familiar.

A voice that did not belong intruded. "Are you all right,
miss?"

Embarrassed, Kate opened her eyes to find an elderly white-haired gentleman staring at her.

"I'm fine. Thank you," she mumbled.

The man hesitated, nodded briefly and walked away.

She drew a ragged breath. Perspiration beaded her upper lip and the hollow between her breasts. Awareness had come so close. Sinking down onto the red bench in front of the battlements, she looked around. It looked like a small city built inside the castle walls. Buildings with separate entrances joined one another. Round turrets topped with brightly colored flags bearing the royal crest of Scotland identified the oldest structures of the castle.

Kate had no need of her map. At the highest point of the rock summit, lit by large windows on its south side, would be the castle's great hall. She stood up and walked across the slate-paved courtyard. Two massively carved doors on the west end bore the royal arms of Scotland with the words NEMO: ME: IMPUNE: LA ESSIT. Brass handles adorned the doors, but Kate ignored them and pushed at an eye-level rose carving.

The door swung open and she stepped inside. Dust-streamed light filtered through the windows illuminating the rectangular room and the elaborate hammered-beam ceiling. She blinked and looked around, confused momentarily by the light and the golden oak planking covering the floor. There should be timber screens separating the main body of the hall from the doors. Where were the screens and the long banquet tables and the rush-strewn floors?

A group of tourists had stopped below a framed portrait, listening intently to a slender woman in a plaid skirt. Kate crossed the room in time to hear the docent's last words. "This is said to be an excellent likeness of James the Fourth of Scotland, architect of this very room. The painting was commissioned at the end of the fifteenth century, upon his marriage to Margaret Tudor. Notice the squareness of the chin and the large, heavy-lidded black eyes. James was an enlightened king, handsome, educated, compassionate. Historians believe him to be the best of the Stewart monarchs."

He most certainly was not. Kate clapped her hand over her mouth, certain she had shouted the words. Her heart pounded. Good Lord. What was she thinking of? Surreptitiously, she glanced at the people around her. No one so much as turned in her direction. She waited until the group had moved on before positioning herself in front of the picture. Was there a mocking glint in the dark eyes staring down at her? She stepped closer.

The room dipped and swayed. She kept her eyes on the portrait. The features appeared to change, the nose lengthening, the features hardening, becoming fleshier, handsomer, less stylized. The hair darkened and the colors of the tunic deepened into rich, jewel-like hues. The mouth lost its sternness and assumed a rakish, familiar grin. *Catriona.* The name pounded in her temples. *Catriona. Catriona.*

She touched the smiling lips of the portrait. Words formed in her mind and reached out across the centuries. "You were handsome, Jamie," she whispered in a voice that sounded nothing like her own. "I'll give you that. Perhaps you were enlightened and educated as well, but they know nothing of you when they label you compassionate, and even you must agree that Mary was the best of us all."

A lute sounded behind her. She turned, her heart in her throat, praying that what she was about to see was exactly as she remembered. Tears burned her eyelids and she leaned against the wall for support. Men in tunics and hose and women in long gowns surrounded banquet tables piled high with trenchers of bread and meat. Dogs lay on the rush-strewn floor gnawing at discarded bones. Torches flickered against blackened stone walls and a bard played a haunting ballad of the borders.

On a trestle, several feet above the other tables, was an elegantly dressed company of ladies and gentlemen seated on benches. Directly in the center sat James IV of Scotland. He raised his goblet. "A toast," he cried, "a toast to Patrick MacKendrick, my new lord admiral of Scotland."

One by one the party took up the cry. "To Patrick, Patrick MacKendrick."

The king looked around. "Speak up, Patrick. Where the devil are you and where is Catriona Wells?"

Responding instinctively to the name, Kate reached down to lift her skirt away from the dirt and the dogs and step forward, but instead of the soft velvet she'd expected, her hands brushed against the rough denim of her jeans. Again the room swayed. She stumbled and sagged against the wall, blinking her eyes.

"I'm sorry, miss," a tentative voice interrupted. "It's after five. The castle closed ten minutes ago."

Slowly, Kate turned. Her neck felt stiff, as if she had held it rigidly in one position for a very long time. Without speaking, she nodded and walked slowly toward the door. The portcullis gate stood open and a guard watched her from the exit. "Watch your step," he said. "The esplanade isn't lit at night."

"Thank you," Kate whispered, and she turned in the direction of George Street. Where had the time gone? It wasn't even noon when she stepped through the great hall doors.

Somehow, she made it back to her room at the George. Still shaking, she ordered soup and a glass of Scots whiskey from room service. What possible explanation could there be for the events of the day? Had she really lost her mind? The sooner she found Maura Sutherland, the better.

At breakfast, there was no sign of the man she had seen the day before. She ate quickly and hurried to the bellman's desk to find that the only cars available had standard transmissions.

"But I've never driven a stick shift," she explained.

"There's nothing to it, lass," the bellman assured her. "Just let up on the clutch slowly and give it the petrol. You'll manage."

Surprisingly she did, with only a minimum amount of stalling through the traffic lights of the city. It took every ounce of concentration she possessed to remember to look right when turning left and left when turning right. Her confidence restored, Kate entered the roundabout and followed the directional toward Peebles and Hermitage Castle, ancient home of the earls of Bothwell.

Yesterday nothing short of a death threat would have convinced her to drive a car with manual transmission and the steering wheel on the passenger side for forty-five miles down a twisting country road. But since then, she'd read her guidebook and found an interesting bit of information. The first earldom of Bothwell was bestowed by James IV of Scotland upon a commoner named Patrick MacKendrick.

Stopping once in Hawick for precise directions, Kate turned on to the B6399 for the last fifteen miles of her journey. The brilliant blue of the sky, the emptiness of the road and the sun's reflection on the untinted window lulled her into a dreamlike complacency. Her fears were completely unfounded. It really wasn't all that difficult to negotiate the roads in Scotland.

Then it happened, the small twist of fate that set into motion events leading to the fulfillment of a five-centuries-old destiny. Later, Kate would marvel at the randomness of it and wonder how it all would have turned out if she had left Edinburgh ten minutes later or if the day had been cloudy and the sun had not glinted on her window, momentarily distracting her. What would have happened if a long-haired sheep had not stepped out of a trench and into the center of the road? How would it have ended had she not come out of the bend too quickly, twisting the wheel and skidding off the road into an igloo-shaped haystack?

Heart thundering in her chest, she rested her forehead against the wheel, waiting for the pain she was sure would follow. A minute passed and then another and still another. She raised her head. The silence was suffocating, but that was all. Apparently she was unhurt. Hooking her purse over her shoulder, she opened the car door and pushed through the hay, brushing the golden bits of straw from her hair and arms. She looked around. The field where she landed was deserted. The sheep she had narrowly missed hitting was still on the road, along with two others. They stood close together, their black-faced, round bodies smug and motionless. "Probably waiting for the demise of another driver," Kate muttered, picking her way across the field.

There was no sign of human life. She looked at her watch. If the map key was accurate, it was less than twelve miles to Hermitage and a telephone. With a resigned sigh she began hiking toward the castle. Moments later, she heard the steady purr of an automobile engine. She hesitated briefly, made her decision and stepped out into the middle of the highway to flag down the car. This wasn't America, and she really had no choice.

The Land Rover slowed and then stopped. Kate ran toward the car just as the driver opened the door and stepped out. Words of thanks froze on her lips. It was the man from the George and he was staring at her as if he couldn't believe she was real.

"It is you, isn't it?" he asked.

Kate nodded.

He looked around. "How did you get here? The nearest town is almost fifteen kilometers back."

Kate pointed to the haystack. "My car is in there. I had an accident and ran off the road."

A look of concern crossed his face. "Are you hurt?"

"Not a bit. But I do need a ride to the nearest phone. Do you think it's all right to leave the car?"

"Wait here and I'll see exactly what's wrong with it."

She watched him cross the field to the oddly elongated haystack and decided that she liked the way he moved. Within minutes he was back, carrying a rod-shaped coil.

"Your car isn't going anywhere for a while," he announced, opening the passenger door and helping her climb into the Land Rover. "We'll have to call a garage."

"Is there one nearby?"

"You can use the phone at Hermitage. We're nearly there."

He climbed behind the wheel and turned the key. The engine roared to life. "Where were you going, anyway? The last time we spoke you were set to tour Edinburgh."

Kate stared straight ahead through the windshield. "I decided to visit Hermitage Castle instead. You know, Sir Walter Scott and all."

"As a matter of fact, I do. Is he a favorite of yours?"

"Not really." She felt him looking at her.

"I see. You decided to take a mere fifty-kilometer jaunt into the country to see the favorite castle of a man whose work doesn't inspire you. Is that it?"

He was not only an expert driver, he was quick and completely without that British reserve Bill Brockman had warned her about.

"There's more to the castle than Walter Scott, isn't there?" she asked, turning her eyes away from the window to rest on his profile.

"Most definitely. Hermitage is one of the oldest and most controverial castles in all of Scotland. It belonged to the Douglas clan until the fifteenth century."

"Then what happened?"

"It changed hands. The MacKendrick of Hailes became the earl of Bothwell."

Patrick MacKendrick. The name called out to her.

"I beg your pardon. Did you say something?"

"No." She turned back to the window.

Niall frowned. If she wasn't interested, why had she asked? And why did he feel so bloody awkward and tongue-tied around her? He was thirty-four years old, for Christ's sake. Too old to be playing peek-a-boo with a woman across the bench seat of his car.

He tried again. "I don't believe I caught your name."

"Kate Sutherland. And yours is Niall MacCormack. I remembered from the hotel."

He was enormously flattered, and it disconcerted him even more. "Are you interested in castles, Miss Sutherland?"

"I don't know." She hesitated. "I came to find out if one of my ancestors had anything to do with this one."

He glanced at her curiously. "Why would you think that?"

She shrugged. "It's just something someone said. I don't have any real proof."

"The Orkneys and Shetlands are Sutherland country. You'll find most of your ancestors on the isle of Cait Ness, not here in the Lowlands."

"People married out of their clans, didn't they?"

"Of course, but not far from them."

She tilted her head, sweeping the curtain of dark hair across her cheek. Her eyes met his, and for an instant his breath caught. He had seen that look before. But where? Who was this woman? He racked his brain, frustrated at his unusual memory lapse.

"Is everyone in Scotland a history buff, Mr. MacCormack?"

"Most of us know our history, Miss Sutherland."

"But you know it especially well."

He grinned. "Has anyone ever told you that you lack subtlety?"

She thought for a minute, considering his question seriously. "I don't think so."

"I see." He choked back the laughter rising in his throat. "Far be it for me to be the first to do so. I'm a historian, on leave from the university to research my book. My specialty is artifacts. I know a great deal about Hermitage, more than anywhere else, because my home is on land that once belonged to the estate. The MacCormacks are a sept of the MacKendricks, all of which means we're distantly related."

She stared at him, her eyes wide and green on his face. "Are you telling me you're related to Patrick MacKendrick, the first earl of Bothwell?"

"In a manner of speaking."

"What can you tell me about him?"

He shrugged. "Not a great deal, I'm afraid. He was a commoner without title until Sauchieburn."

"Sauchieburn?"

"The site where James the Fourth engaged his father's troops in battle and won. Some see Patrick MacKendrick as an opportunist seeking a title. The only way he could do it was to change the established order."

Kate was disappointed. "Do you see him that way?"

Niall shook his head. "No. I believe his motives were true. He was a border lord who had experienced firsthand the bitterness and brutality that characterized the relationship between England and Scotland for hundreds of years. He was the laird of Hailes, which meant a great deal more to those born north of the border than an English title. He wanted a king who was more of a man and a leader than James the Third."

She hung on every word until it was clear he had finished. "What happened to him after Sauchieburn?"

"Next to the king, he became the most powerful man in Scotland."

The words came back to her as clearly as if they had been whispered into her ear. *A toast. A toast to Patrick MacKen-*

drick, lord high admiral of Scotland. Where the devil is he and where is Catriona Wells?

"Was there a woman in his life?"

Niall's eyes glinted with amusement. "Most likely several. Jamie Stewart hardly led a monastic life, and I imagine he couldn't tolerate anyone who did."

"What about a woman named Catriona Wells?" she persisted. "Have you ever heard of her?"

For an instant he looked confused, and then the confusion changed to shock. His hand came down heavily on the steering wheel. The Land Rover careened precariously, tires screeching, around a bend in the highway. Pulling over to the side of the road, he left the engine running and turned to Kate, his eyes moving over her face, verifying what he saw. "I knew I'd seen you before," he said at last. "Now I know the reason I couldn't remember."

"I beg your pardon?"

His face appeared lit from within. Kate couldn't look away.

"The portrait of Catriona Wells in the gallery at Holyrood Palace. It's you. Who would expect someone in the breakfast room of a five-star hotel to be the image of a woman who died five hundred years ago?"

She breathed in carefully. "What are you saying?"

He laughed out loud and reached for her hands. As naturally as if she'd done it every day of her life, her fingers returned his grip.

"The resemblance is incredible. What I'm saying, Kate Sutherland, is that your face is hanging in the royal portrait gallery at Holyrood Palace. The woman's name was Catriona Wells and she was the first countess of Bothwell."

"You're joking." But somehow she knew he was not.

Niall shook his head. "I'll show it to you."

"I'm leaving Edinburgh tomorrow."

"Will you be back?"

Kate pulled her hands away. "Yes, but not for four more weeks. I'm traveling north, to the Shetlands. I won't be back until my plane leaves for home."

"I see." His face was expressionless as he maneuvered the car back out on the road.

She bit her lip. Aggressiveness was not her style, but she was too close to let it go. "Maybe we can see it later today or early tomorrow before I go."

He smiled encouragingly, turned down a gravel path and pulled into an empty lot. "We'll work it out."

Kate looked around. "Are we here?"

He pointed to a knoll where long-haired sheep grazed on green grass. "Just over that rise is Hermitage. It's not nearly as spectacular as some of the restored castles, but I like it better this way. Seeing it the way it was gives me a sense of perspective." He held out his hand. "I'll show you what I mean."

So this is what it's like to feel comfortable with a man, she thought as the warmth of his palm pressed against hers, to share an easy camaraderie, to fall into step beside him without having to search for words that refused to come, words that would keep him interested, amused and challenged, brittle sophisticated words to assure that he would call again. Niall MacCormack didn't need words. She knew it instinctively. It was enough for him that she walked beside him, her hand resting in his, their thoughts anticipating the same end.

They climbed to the top of the knoll and looked down. Kate caught her breath, unprepared for the tears crowding her throat. Somehow she had known it would look like this: the golden bricks, the small high windows, the H-shaped architecture with its great central block and powerful corner towers.

Together they walked down the hill. Kate walked into the deserted courtyard while Niall paid for their tickets at the guard gate. She looked around, wondering why the inside walls hadn't inspired the same feeling of déjà vu as the outside structure. Hermitage Castle was indeed a ruin, with roughly hewn stone walls, dark, damp hallways and no floors or ceiling separating its three stories from the sky.

She shivered, zipped up her jacket and climbed the precarious staircase to the second floor. A thick, creeping mist had settled over the sun. She closed her eyes and leaned against a piling. Suddenly she was no longer cold. Colors leapt against her eyelids and laughter mixed with anticipation hovered at the edge of her consciousness. Slowly, she opened her eyes.

This time she wasn't surprised to find herself in a room filled with people. Banquet tables groaned with food and dancers in transparent costumes stood on their hands, or juggled golden balls and teased a huge chained bear. Again Jamie Stewart raised his goblet and pronounced a toast. Again the guests took up the cry. But this time she heard none of it. Her attention was fixed on a man, lithe and leanly muscled, a man with light eyes and mahogany-streaked hair, a man who raised his goblet with only three fingers instead of four. But it was the woman beside him who caused her mouth to go dry, who forced her hand to lift and press against her chest, who made her breathing rasp and go shallow and her lungs gasp for air.

She was lovely, her skin startlingly pale against the dark frame of her hair, nearly as pale as her white gown. Her eyes were light and very green, and she was trembling. The man by her side lowered his head and spoke into her ear. She nodded, moistened her lips and stood up, her hand in his. A loud cheering filled the hall. The woman lifted her skirts and ran through a small door, followed by a throng of breathless, laughing women.

"Kate?" A firm hand grasped her shoulder. "You're shaking. Are you cold?"

From a place deep inside herself, she recognized Niall's voice. Forcing herself to concentrate, she pushed the images away. Her eyelids fluttered, and his chiseled nose and hollow cheeks came into focus. She shook her head. "I'm not cold. Where have you been?"

"Downstairs, looking for you. I've found something. I think you'll find it interesting."

Kate followed him down the steep stairs to a low-ceilinged chamber where blackened niches had been cut into the stone walls.

"Where are we?" she whispered.

"I believe it's a burial chamber. Look over here." Resting on his haunches, he pointed to a darkened corner where the wall had been cut away. A woman's face had been skillfully carved into the stone. Kate knelt beside him, her fingers running over the sculpted features. As she tested the lines of the oval face, the straight nose, the definite skin and the wide, heavy-lidded eyes of the death mask, her hand began to shake. *This can't be happening. Dear God, this just can't be happening.*

❧ 4 ❧

The silence she could bear, soul-effacing though it was. She closed herself against it, murmuring a cadence she had learned from someone in the woods, someone whose name she could no longer remember. It mattered not at all. Silence was not her enemy. It was the darkness, the darkness and the man she knew would come, even though she prayed to the blessed Virgin that he would not.

Please help me. Her mind formed the words even as the door opened and the darkness was swallowed by the licking flames of the torch.

"Catriona." He spoke softly, seductively, the smoky tones of his voice meant to reassure, to calm, to break . . . to seduce. She knew what he wanted even before she saw his face, leached of color by the dance and gutter of the evil-smelling torch. *"Catriona,"* he said again, his eyes searching the darkness. *"I would have it go differently between us."*

Still she said nothing, waiting for the black points in the center of his eyes to widen and find her huddled form, a lump beneath the bedclothes.

"Are you fearful, Catriona? There is nothing to fear from me." He held the torch aloft and searched the room, the bed. Smoke circled his head. He found her. *"Must we always go through this, Cat? I would have thought, by now, you would welcome me."*

It was too much. She sat up and scooted back, her spine pressed against the stone wall. *"Welcome you!"* Her voice was clear and low, the line of her teeth straight and white against her lower lip.

"Accept it then?"

The question inflamed her. She was Catriona Wells. Acceptance was an impossible condition. *"Never."*

He walked over to the bed, flanked by shadows thrown by the torch. Reaching out with his free hand, he twisted a strand of her hair around his finger. *"Do you know what I want, Cat? What I've always wanted?"*

"Aye." She jerked her head away, leaving behind black strands, prisoners in his fist. She knew only too well what he wanted. *That* she would never give him. What he got, he must take. It gave her small satisfaction, but it was all she had, the one tiny rebellion that kept her sane and whole through the nightmare of her life.

"You are so beautiful," he whispered reverently. *"My God, how can you do this? Do you know how I despise myself?"*

She shrugged a bare shoulder. *"Not nearly as much as I do."*

"You are cold, Cat. I burn for you."

She stared at him, wondering once again what he saw when he looked at her. Could he have forgotten the untamed, leggy girl, the awkward, over-long limbs, the mouth smeared with blackberries and wild honey, the tangled hair, the sullen face, the nuisance that stood between him and Ravenswood?

"What would your mother say if she could see you now?"

The flame sputtered, throwing out light, bathing his hair and eyes with shards of gold.

"She would ask herself if she had been well served in her choice of husband."

"She was older than I."

"By five years only, nearer your years than you are to mine."

"I was fond of her, but I never loved, not as I love you."

His eyes pleaded with her. William Neville was born a gentleman. She knew rape did not suit him. But rape it would be. There was no other name for it. *"Do you think to plead your cause by telling me you had no love for my mother?"*

He flushed at the contempt in her voice. *"You always were*

a hellion and well named. By God, I should beat you for making me beg like a peasant."

"You have a choice. I have none."

Again he reached out for her hair. She moved her head. He forced her chin into his palm and moved his thumb along her jaw. She felt him tremble.

"Wed with me, Catriona. I would give you much."

"You offer what is not yours. Ravenswood belongs to Richard."

His thumb moved across her face, caressing her cheek, her lips. *"Richard can have Ravenswood. He'll not begrudge the rest of the holdings to his sister and her husband."*

She clenched her teeth. *"I'll never call you husband, William. I will die first."*

He mocked her. *"Brave Catriona, spirited Catriona. Would you have your brother die with you?"*

It was always the same, this scene between them. He would lock her in the darkness for hours, until her flesh crawled and her mind was no longer hers. Then he would come, offering love and light and life for Richard. When she refused, he would leave again and she would try to sleep, pushing out the terrifying images of fire and sickness and ashes, the smell of burning flesh and the age-old keening of mourning women. Hours passed and still she endured. The walls seemed closer now, and with every agonizing minute, closer still. She closed her eyes, praying for deliverance, for her mother, for a servant brave enough to withstand Neville's wrath.

None came, save William. He came as her savior, murmuring words of comfort, stroking her hair, his mouth and hands lingering on her breasts, tasting her skin, pushing aside the bedclothes, moving over her, his breath heavy and shallow, parting her legs, claiming possession, until he spent himself. When it was over, he would rise, unable to look at her, pulling on his clothing as he departed, leaving the door unlocked.

When she no longer heard his footsteps in the hall, she would search for her shift, wrap a blanket around her trembling body and creep back to the warmth and light of her own bedchamber, until the next time. There was no help for it. She knew that now. No help from the servants, nor from Richard—the boy of twelve years who was her brother—no help from the king, her protector. Jamie Stewart was the only man in all the world who could help her. But to go to him would mean selling her honor. A thought occurred to her and she laughed humorlessly, bitterly. She no longer had anything left of honor.

With new resolve, she rose and walked to her chamber. It was night and very late. William always timed it so. He would leave for Whitehall in the morning. In his absence she would think and scheme. Father Thomas had told her more than once that her mind moved as quickly as a boy's—nay, more quickly even. Perhaps she could play both sides of the same coin. Jamie had killed his father at Sauchiburn. To spy on a murderer was not such a terrible thing, after all.

Kate lifted her hand to brush away the cold drops wetting her face. It must be raining. She opened her eyes to find Niall MacCormack staring down at her, a concerned expression on his face. She tried her voice. "Where am I?"

"On a bench in the courtyard at Hermitage Castle. You fainted and scared me half to death. How do you feel?"

"I don't know." She sat up and rubbed her forehead. "Did you show me a death mask?"

Niall nodded. "It looks like sixteenth-century markings. Are you all right?"

"I think I dreamed. It was so strange."

He interrupted her. "You can tell me later. Just now I want to feed you, call a doctor and a garage, in that order. Can you walk?"

She nodded.

Niall slipped his arm around her waist and together they managed the walk to the Land Rover before the first onslaught of heavy rain.

"Where are we going?" she asked, pulling her damp hair back away from her face.

Niall hesitated. "I live close by. You can rest and use the phone in complete privacy."

Kate's back teeth locked. "I don't think that's a very good idea."

Incredibly, he laughed. "This isn't America, Kate. It's not

what you think. My housekeeper is expecting me, and I'm sure she can produce some dry clothes and a hot meal for you as well. Besides, unless you're pregnant or you faint often, you probably should see a doctor."

"I'm definitely not pregnant and I don't faint often, but I don't think it's anything serious."

"How can you be sure?"

She frowned, twisting her hair behind her head, holding it up off her neck. "Something frightened me. It was dark and the walls were close together. I've always been claustrophobic." She didn't mention her fear of the dark. More than anything else, it made her feel inadequate somehow, less than she was.

He changed the subject. "You were going to tell me about your dream."

Kate wrinkled her forehead. "I can't. All I remember is that I was somewhere else." She laughed self-consciously. "I'm sorry. Usually I remember my dreams."

"Dream recollection is the sign of a healthy person."

She tilted her head. The dark curtain of hair swung forward, concealing her face. "I thought you were a historian."

"I am."

"You sound like a psychologist."

"Good lord, I hope not."

"Do you have something against psychology?"

He looked at her curiously, considering her question. "Not the field itself. But I've found there aren't a great many competent people practicing it. The few talented ones command enormous sums of money. The majority are ineffective."

"That's a strong statement."

"I'll stand by it—that is, unless you're a psychologist. If so, I'll apologize immediately."

Kate bit her lip and stared out the window at the intense green of a Scottish spring. She wondered into which category he would pigeonhole Lillian Spencer and her obvious metaphysical preferences. "I'm a lawyer."

"Good lord, I never would have placed that one." He seemed genuinely astonished.

"Why not?"

"For one thing, you don't look old enough, and for another—"

"I'm thirty. Old enough, I think."

He shook his head. "Never mind. The stereotype doesn't fit, that's all. I stand corrected."

The car slowed to a stop in front of an enormous three-storied brick home set back on grounds as green and wide as a golf course.

"My goodness." Kate stared in disbelief at the gabled roof, the double oak doors and the manicured beauty of the plush grass. "Teachers must earn a lot more in Scotland than they do in the States."

He laughed. "I don't think anything in Scotland is bigger than it is in America, especially salaries. The house has been in my family for generations. I moved in after my father died. Except for the taxes, it's all paid for."

"Does your mother live with you?"

"No. She died when I was a child."

"I'm sorry."

He lifted his hand, brushing aside her sympathy. "It was a long time ago. Shall we go inside?"

With Niall's hand under her arm, she walked up the front steps. The door opened and an ageless, stern-faced woman wearing a tweed skirt and black stockings ushered them inside. Not by so much as the dip of an eyelash did she indicate surprise at the arrival of an unexpected guest.

Niall introduced her. "Mrs. Frasier, this is Miss Kate Sutherland. She'll be having tea with us. We were caught in the rain. Have we anything for her to wear?"

"How do you do, Miss Sutherland?" the housekeeper replied, measuring Kate with her eyes, assessing the cost of the expensive blazer, the cashmere sweater and designer jeans. "I'm sure we can find something for you if you aren't terribly fussy."

"I'm cold and wet, Mrs. Frasier. Anything would be fine, even a bathrobe."

The housekeeper's stern expression melted and she tucked her hand inside Kate's arm. "Come along then. I'll take you to one of the bedrooms. You can change and rest before tea."

"I hope this isn't inconvenient for you," Kate said as she allowed herself to be led up the stairs. "Having a stranger turn up at the last minute can be difficult."

Niall grinned. Kate Sutherland certainly had a knack for public relations. He walked into the drawing room to phone the garage.

Kate's eyes widened with appreciation when she saw the bedroom. She loved antiques. There was something about a hand-carved armoire that brought to mind perfumed silks, sepia-toned photos, satin fans edged in lace, corsets and panniers, relics of a richer, more gallant age.

She crossed the gleaming wood floor to the long, diamond-paned bay window and looked out. The view faced east toward a small lake and a copse of trees, shrouded in menacing shadows. Apparently, sunlight was a precious commodity in Scotland. The gloom darkened her mood. She had read about people who suffered tremendous bouts of depression when deprived of sunlight. Strange, it had never affected her before.

"Would you like me to draw you a bath?" Mrs. Frasier called out from the adjoining room.

"No, thank you." She had trespassed enough on Niall MacCormack's time and hospitality. Bathing in his guest bathroom was an intimacy she did not intend to explore.

The housekeeper materialized in the doorway. "I've found a robe and mules. When your clothing is dry, I'll call you for tea." She smiled encouragingly. "Have a rest, Miss Sutherland. You look as if you've had a very long day. I'll wait outside for your clothing while you change."

Kate undressed and pulled on the robe, belting it snugly around her waist. It was warm, very soft, and large enough to wrap around her several times. Slipping her feet into the mules, she gathered her clothes and opened the door. True to her word, Mrs. Frasier waited outside. Removing the clothing from Kate's arms, she moved silently down the hallway.

Alone in the antique-filled bedroom, Kate tested the mattress. Tempted by the softness of a down-filled comforter, she stretched out on top of the covers and closed her eyes. She thought of Lillian Spencer. What would Lillian say about her unsettling dreams? She concentrated, willing her mind to conjure up the image of a round, heavily made-up face. But it wasn't Lillian's face that materialized. It was her own. Or was it? The woman's hair was longer, darker, the cheeks rounder, the eyebrows more naturally shaped.

Kate sniffed. Roses. She smelled roses. Not the odorless, hothouse variation with their thorns removed and their necks flaccid and drooping after a single day. These were real roses, gloriously thorned, red and pink and yellow and white, their proud postures the result of wild seed and sweet rain and pearl-filled mist blowing in from the sea.

Kate tried to open her eyes, to find the source of the smell, but her lids were too heavy. She mumbled something under her breath, then tucked one hand beneath her cheek and dozed. Images swirled like smoke inside her brain, blurry at first and then sharpening, as if tiny focus buttons were fine-tuning the details.

The moon shone silver-bright. Shadows flickered against manor gates. Catriona Wells, dressed in breeks and a leather jack, her hair plaited into a single black braid as thick as a man's hand, leaned over her brother's sleeping form and shook him awake. "Richard," she said, her voice low, "wake up."

Drowsy with sleep, twelve-year-old Richard Wells sat up and rubbed his eyes. "Is it time?"

"Aye," answered his sister. "You must help me."

Richard nodded. Without a word, he followed her down the long hall, the stairs, through the receiving room and out the door leading to the garden and the gates. The stone steps and flagstone were icy cold on his bare feet. Cat stopped at the wall and turned to him. Lacing his fingers together, he held his hands steady as she stepped into them and boosted herself to the top.

"God speed, Cat." His voice quavered. "Hurry back."

Cat hesitated. She would give anything in the world to take him with her, but it was impossible. Besides, Neville wouldn't harm Richard. The boy was his only claim to the estate. Until he had a better one, Richard would be safe.

"Everything will be all right, love," she promised. "Jamie

will help us." Better to lie than to have him worry. Tears burned beneath her eyelids. He looked small and helpless standing there, staring up at her with a frightened expression. She hated to leave him. "Send word if you need me. I'll come. I promise."

The boy lifted his hand. "Farewell, Cat. I shall miss you."

Catriona turned, breathed deeply and leapt to the ground. She lost her balance and fell, knocking the wind from her lungs.

"Catriona?" A low voice called from the trees. "Are you hurt?" A slender, youthful form ran to where she lay and knelt by her side. "You should have waited for me."

Gritting her teeth, Cat sat up. "Find the horses, Andrew," she ordered. "'Tis late. If we miss the passage we'll not find another ship to take us."

Sir Andrew Percy hesitated, his protective instincts alerted. If Cat was hurt she would be unable to travel. "Surely this secrecy is unnecessary," he argued. "If the king knows—"

She interrupted. "Everything must look as if we've run away. 'Tis for naught if Jamie finds out our true purpose is to unmask the Pretender." Impatience sharpened her tone. She rose to her feet. "Hurry. We've no time to lose."

"The mounts are tethered beyond the trees." Andrew pointed to two dark shapes in the distance. "Come, I'll take you to them." Slipping his arm around her waist, he helped her to the clearing where the horses grazed.

Cat breathed more easily when she was mounted. "Did you find someone to carry our trunks to the ship?"

Andrew grinned. Catriona was ever practical. "I did, and it was no small task. You brought enough trunks for a year."

"We'll be guests of the king of Scotland," she reminded him. "Jamie's court is not like Henry's. We will need them all." She did not mention that they would very likely be in Scotland for a long time.

The night was mild. Stars studded the sky like diamond chips. Cat inhaled the sweet scent of clover and blinked back tears. Damn William Neville's greed and damn Henry Tudor's icy soul. How long before she walked through the gates of Ravenswood again? Uttering a quick prayer to keep her brother safe, she urged her mount to greater speed. Hope lay ahead, to the north, in the person of one Perkin Warbeck, the one man in all the world whose name alone made Henry Tudor lose his color and his calm.

Jamie Stewart, once a mere cousin, was now James IV of Scotland. They had been close as children. Scotland's new king was a fearless warrior not likely to be intimidated by the might of England. Catriona frowned. If only she dared tell him the truth. But Richard's future was at stake, his future and his life.

She remembered the fierce, dark-eyed prince who had been her childhood champion and felt a twinge of regret. After all, they shared the same blood. They were Stewarts—he from his father, she from her mother. Perhaps he would save her from the unspeakable atrocity that Neville suggested and save Richard's inheritance as well. She would wait and bide her time. Meanwhile she would pacify Henry, feeding him tiny morsels of information to keep his curiosity satisfied.

A knock startled her. Groggily, Kate slid off the bed and answered the door.

Mrs. Frasier stared at her curiously. "I thought you'd left us without telling anyone." She held out Kate's clothing. "I pressed them for you."

"Thank you," she said, accepting the hangers and praying that her cashmere sweater had survived the ordeal. "I must have been more tired than I thought."

"When you've dressed, I'll be back to take you down to the drawing room for tea."

Kate smiled. "Thank you, Mrs. Frasier. I appreciate it. I really do. You don't have to wait. I know the way."

"Very well, then. I'll set it out in fifteen minutes."

Kate dressed quickly and walked over to the mirror, searching through her purse for a brush. Bending over, she brushed her hair vigorously from crown to ends and flipped it back over her head. Thick and full, it waved back from the widow's peak on her forehead down to the middle of her back. Her cheeks were flushed from her upside-down position and her eyes were exceptionally green above the maroon of her sweater. She stared at her reflection for a long time. Experimentally, she pushed aside the wispy bangs framing her forehead and tucked the layers behind her ears, pulling the long blunt-cut ends back into a braid. Blood throbbed against her temples and the color left her face. This time she hadn't forgotten her dream. This time she remembered the woman who was cousin to James IV of Scotland. Her name was Catriona. But why was she important and why were the events of her life unfolding in such crystalline clarity in Kate's mind? Most disturbing of all, why was the woman's face identical to her own?

Kate made her way back down the stairs to the drawing room. Niall stood by the window, hands in the pockets of his trousers, staring out at the acres of green hills rolling into the Firth of Forth. He was deep in thought and she hesitated to disturb him. There was something different about him, something she had recognized that first day in the breakfast room of the George, something that hadn't been there when he picked her up in his car this morning. She tilted her head, resting it against the door frame, and watched him.

The bones of his cheeks were very pronounced, sharp blades shadowing the hollows beneath. His brow was furrowed, his nose narrow and slightly beaked, his mouth tight and troubled. He looked vulnerable and alone. Without warning, her eyes filled with tears. Hastily, she scrubbed them away. What was it about this man that affected her so?

The movement of her hand roused him. From across the room, he turned and looked at her. Gray eyes met green. Tension stretched between them, heightening the already suffocating stillness. Kate drew a deep quivering breath and straightened, waiting.

He walked toward her slowly, inexorably, his movements smooth, dreamlike, his purpose unmistakable. She met him halfway, her inches fragile beside his greater height. Her head fell back at the same time his hands touched her face. He lowered his head. She closed her eyes and felt his mouth move against hers.

Niall felt as if he'd always known this woman: the shape of her mouth, the feel of her hair, the taste of her skin, the way she fit in his arms, the sweep of black lashes framing eyes as clear and green as the shallows of the North Sea. She was warm and soft and incredibly sweet. Their lips merged without the usual awkwardness of first encounters. His fingers sifted through her hair, stroking the back of her neck, testing the delicate bones of her spine, the dip of her waist, sliding underneath the wool of her sweater to the soft skin beneath. He felt her stillness, the slight intake of breath that was a question.

Need, deep and searing, consumed him. Tightening his embrace, he parted the seam of her lips, felt the long, slow rise of her response and lost himself in the swirling, heat-filled mist that erased the room, the hills, the darkening sky, everything but a sweet mouth, long legs and cool hands sliding through the hair against the back of his neck.

The whisper of thick-soled shoes on wood floors intruded. Simultaneously, they pulled away, their faces flaming. When Mrs. Frasier entered the room with the tea tray, they were on opposite sides of the room, Niall at the window, Kate seated on a low couch in front of a card table.

Her eyes widened at the salmon and watercress sandwiches, the meat pies, the scones with clotted cream, the lemon cake and chocolate truffles. "Is this what you usually have for tea?" she asked, surprised out of her embarrassment.

"You both look like you need sustenance," answered Mrs. Frasier. "Will there be anything else before I leave?"

Niall found his voice. "No, thank you, Mrs. Frasier. You may have the rest of the night to yourself. I'll manage with the tray and dishes."

"Very well, then. It's my night off," she explained to Kate. "My sister is expecting me. See you in the morning, Mr. MacCormack." Too soon, her comfortable figure and even more comfortable conversation left the room, and they were alone.

Niall smiled ruefully. "I'm not sorry, so I won't apologize."

Kate poured milk into the cups and added tea. "Sugar?" she asked, holding up the tongs.

He noticed that her hand shook. "Two, please." He crossed the room to sit down beside her. "The salmon is local and delicious. You really should try it." He filled a plate and handed it to her, brushing her fingers with his own.

Kate looked up. "You did that on purpose."

"Of course." He grinned disarmingly. "Can you blame me?"

"You promised me food and a garage, that's all."

"That was before I kissed you. Has anyone ever told you that you're shockingly responsive?"

"Not lately." She'd been told quite the contrary, but she didn't see any reason to divulge that piece of information to someone who was little more than a stranger.

"I'm glad." Niall was no longer smiling. Removing Kate's plate from her hands, he set it on the table. Then he reached for her, bending his head to her lips.

"Please don't." Her faint protest stopped him.

He lifted his head. "Don't what?"

"What you were going to do."

He moved away. When he spoke, his voice was distinctly cool. "I was under the impression that we both wanted the same thing."

Kate shook her head and brushed back her disheveled hair. "I won't deny that I'm attracted to you, but I can't,"—she corrected herself—"I don't want this."

"Why not?" he asked baldly.

She hesitated. The truth was a stretch even for her, and she'd lived with it all her life. He would never believe it. "I'm not free to pursue a relationship right now."

"Were we speaking of pursuing a relationship?"

Her face flamed. "No, we weren't. I apologize for being presumptuous. If you'll call a cab, I'll pass on this wonderful tea and go back to Edinburgh immediately."

Niall cursed himself silently and picked up the phone. It never occurred to him that she might be spoken for, even married, for Christ's sake. Wishful thinking on his part. A woman who looked like that probably had to endure unwelcome advances all the time. He was a fool, and worse, he'd behaved badly.

Carefully, he spoke into the phone, replaced it and turned back to look at Kate. "Your cab will be here shortly."

She was very still, her eyes the only color in the pale oval of her face. "Thank you."

He released a breath. "Listen, Kate, I've been unforgivably rude and my only excuse is embarrassment. Will you accept my apology?"

She smiled shakily and took his hand. "If you'll accept mine."

"For what?"

She pulled her hand away. "Leading you on."

His eyes glinted. All of a sudden he felt much better. "Is that what you were doing?"

Kate nodded, secure again. She felt very unlike herself. "You're much too attractive, you know. I couldn't help myself." Good lord! Had she really said that out loud?

Niall's throat went dry. He swallowed. "Perhaps I'd better wait in another room."

"Why?"

He stepped closer and stopped. "Because I'm having the hardest time remembering that I'm a gentleman."

Her voice was smoky soft. "I like you very much, Niall."

He wondered how he would stand it when she walked out the door. It would help matters if he knew exactly what "not free to pursue a relationship" meant.

"You'll think this is completely absurd, but I feel as if I've known you forever." He lifted her chin. "Kate, are you crying? Don't cry, darling. We'll work something out. I promise."

She shook her head. "I'm not crying. I never cry. I'm just tired and hungry and confused, which isn't at all unusual because I've spent most of my life confused." She laughed hysterically. "Don't even attempt to understand. No one ever has, and why I'm babbling away like a complete fool is beyond even my understanding." She sniffed and looked around for the backpack that served as her purse.

Niall's eyes twinkled. Anticipating her need, he reached into his pocket and pulled out a handkerchief.

Gratefully, Kate took it, pausing to look dubiously at the monogram stitched into the immaculate linen. "Don't you have any tissue? It seems a shame to use this."

"I'm sure Mrs. Frasier knows where we keep tissue, but I don't. Do you have something against cloth?"

Kate blew her nose and handed it back to him. "Not at all. I'm sure you have dozens exactly like it."

Niall had never before considered the piles of snowy linen in the top drawer of his clothes chest. "As a matter of fact, I do," he replied.

"I knew it," Kate muttered.

"Excuse me?"

"Nothing. How long do you think it will take for the cab to get here?"

Niall sat down and helped himself to some food. "Twenty minutes or so. Please eat something. Mrs. Frasier will assume you don't like her cooking."

"I'm not particularly hungry."

He bit into his sandwich. "You just said you were," he reminded her between mouthfuls.

And you called me darling, which proves that people often say what they don't mean. "I changed my mind."

"Has anyone ever mentioned that you have the most interesting face?"

Kate completely forgot the morsel of salmon she had attempted to extricate from between the slices of bread on her plate. " 'Interesting'? What exactly does that mean?"

"Unusual. Out of the common way." His voice was careful, preoccupied, as if he were speaking of a fascinating specimen. "You look like a Sutherland, and yet there is something different about you."

She could feel the slow, erratic rhythm of her heart. "What do you mean by 'different'?"

Niall considered her face, the small haughty chin and thin aquiline nose, the pouting mouth and clearly defined bone structure. He would stake his reputation that she had little Viking or Celtic blood in her. Cait Ness was bordered by the Atlantic on the west, the North Sea on the east. Inhabited for generations by the Picts, invaded by the Norse during the tenth century, no Sutherland alive had escaped the merging of those two gene pools. Despite her clear cat's eyes, Kate Sutherland did not look like a Scot.

He chose his words carefully. "The Sutherlands hail from Cait Ness, and although there are quite a few now living on the mainland, they've interbred for centuries. Certain characteristics are hard to miss."

"Such as?"

A loud horn sounded from the driveway. Niall stood up to look out the window. "Apparently this discussion will have to wait for another day. Your taxi is here."

"I must have left my bag upstairs. Please tell him I'll be right down. I don't want him to leave without me."

Niall looked astonished. "He'll do nothing of the sort."

"Please."

"There's really no need, Kate," he explained. "He'll wait for as long as you like. Fares to Edinburgh don't turn up every day. But if it makes you feel better, I'll go out and talk to him."

"Thank you." She hurried out of the room and Niall walked outside to confer with the driver.

Minutes later she ran down the steps and climbed into the back seat of the cab. Niall tapped on the window. She rolled it down.

"I'll let the George know about the car."

"Thank you."

"Kate?"

"Yes?"

"Will you call me when you're back in Edinburgh?"

She hesitated.

"Please say yes."

"There's no point, Niall. Even if there weren't extenuating circumstances, we live eleven thousand miles apart."

"I'll take you to Holyrood Palace."

She laughed. "Are you trying to bribe me?"

"If it works."

"I'm not sure when I'll be back."

"Where will you be staying?"

Kate shook her head. "I'd rather not say. My chances for success aren't very good, but it started a long time ago and I can't give up until I've exhausted all options."

Disappointment tightened his chest. He was a fool to persist. Whatever relationship she was trying to resurrect obviously meant a great deal to her.

He reached for her hand. "If your circumstances change, I would very much like to see you again."

"I'll remember that," she said softly, pulling her hand away.

Kate's last night at the George was restless, and although she couldn't remember anything specific, she was sure she had dreamed. Heavy-eyed and silent, she sat down on a bench to wait for the train to Aberdeen. From there a ferry would take her over one hundred miles of water, across the Pentland Firth and the North Sea to Cait Ness, the future and final resting place of Bonnie Sutherland.

The day began as dark and bone-chillingly cold as the previous one had been brilliant. Huddled in the warmth of her down-filled parka, Kate marveled at the hardiness of a people who endured endless months of fog-filled mornings, afternoons of cool milky sunlight and nights that lasted fifteen hours.

The train pulled into the station directly in front of her and screeched to a stop, snorting and puffing like a temperamental racehorse. She downed her tepid tea, crumpled the paper cup and climbed aboard, pulling her luggage behind her. Most of the compartments were empty.

She lifted her suitcase to the rack above her seat and, with a sigh of relief, leaned her head against the upholstered back. It was sixty miles to Aberdeen. The man at the ticket booth said it would take nearly two hours, enough time to nap and rid herself of the exhausting lethargy sapping her strength. The train whistle blew and her car lurched forward. She looked out the window. A thick fog had settled over the city. She was alone in the compartment. The bench seat tempted her. With a contented sigh, she stretched out her legs, pillowed her cheek on her hands and closed her eyes.

The gray behind her lids darkened and the hum of the rails disappeared. The quiet was hushed and reverent. She felt curiously warm. A voice spoke to her. She strained to hear and then, suddenly, everything was very clear.

Someone else was in the room. She was sure of it. She had always seen what others could not. Catriona Wells did not question the instincts warning her that she was not alone with the king in his private sanctuary. Over the years her gift had been strengthened. It did not fail her now. Somewhere, concealed in the well-appointed chamber, the eyes of a hidden presence followed her every movement.

Her eyes narrowed to slits of brilliant green. So be it. Straightening her shoulders, she crossed the room with a swinging, graceful gait and knelt at the feet of James IV of Scotland.

"Thank you for receiving me, Your Grace," she said, her voice clear and confident.

Jamie Stewart looked down at the girl before him. Annoyance warred with the normal appreciation of a man suddenly confronted by a beautiful woman. Appreciation won. Childhood memories prevailed and his lips twitched.

"Rise, Cousin," he said, motioning for her to stand. "Tell me how it is that Scotland has the unexpected honor of your presence."

Cat rose to her feet and looked around the room. Without asking permission, she pulled a low stool from the corner and sat down arranging her skirts.

James bit back a smile. Apparently his lovely young cousin knew the measure of her worth. The fact that she was in the presence of royalty didn't awe her in the least. He sat back in his chair and waited.

"My father died five years ago," she began.

James nodded his head. "I know. I heard also that your mother remarried Sir William Neville."

Cat's lip curled contemptuously. "Therein lies the problem. She died six months ago. Neville lays claim to Ravenswood until Richard's majority." Her eyes flashed. "The king has granted it."

James's brow puckered. He searched his memory. "Richard?"

"My brother," Cat reminded him.

"How old is the lad?"

"Twelve years, Your Grace."

The king braced his elbow on the chair, weighing her words, judging her sincerity. For the first time Cat realized just how much he had changed. He was no longer a lad, her adored older cousin who had rescued her, time after time, from the consequences of her childish pranks.

She looked at his dark skin and heavy-lidded eyes, at the muscles bulging under the fur-lined jacket and the powerful legs folded beneath him. He was a king, a powerful adversary, and he had wrested the throne, not three months before, from his weak, ineffectual father. His eyes were very dark as they lingered on her face. The color rose in her cheeks. He was also unnervingly handsome. Why had she never noticed that before?

Cat held her breath, thankful that her story, except for one small detail, was true. Her skin prickled. The Sight was strong. Once again she felt a presence somewhere behind her. Without blinking, she allowed the night-black eyes of Scotland's new king to look their fill. For a brief moment, she wondered if she had made a mistake. Perhaps she should have taken her chances with the blunt, capricious Henry Tudor of England.

Instinctively she knew the man before her could not be managed by fluttering eyelashes and forced tears. Cat felt a moment's regret for her kindly, aging uncle who had been Scotland's king. Henry Tudor had a right to be worried. Jamie would be a formidable opponent. He was a Stewart, decreed by God and royal birth to be king. Unlike Henry's claim to England, there was no question of his right to the succession.

He interrupted her thoughts. "Neville's claim is not an unusual one. A twelve-year-old lad needs a guardian."

He did not miss the slight motion of Cat's hands as they clenched in her lap.

"Richard will not live to his majority, Your Grace. Neville will see to that."

"How do you know?" The black eyes held her own, demanding the truth.

She looked down at her white knuckles and frowned. Forcing her hands open, she stretched out her fingers, allowing them to relax against the velvet of her gown. "He seeks my hand in marriage," she said at last. "King Henry has already sent to Rome for the papal dispensation. There is no blood tie between us. It will surely be granted." Her words were bitter. "What man will step aside for his stepson when he has hope of his own heirs? Ravenswood is an estate of great wealth. My brother's untimely death will assure Neville of the largest fortune in England."

"Does Henry command you?" asked James, his interest caught.

Cat lifted her head to meet his gaze. His eyes were very bright, very intent, as he waited for her answer.

"The guardianship will go to Neville," she replied. "Because of the friendship he bore my father, Henry will not force my hand." Her cheeks reddened. Begging did not come easily, but desperation forced her to continue. "Until I reach my majority the inheritance is controlled by my stepfather. I am penniless, Your Grace." She lifted her chin proudly. "I will not become the wife of my mother's husband. That is why I come to you. There is nowhere else for me to go."

He looked at her for a long moment, assessing the rich fabric of her gown. A ruby pendant rested between her breasts. "You don't look like a pauper, Cousin," he remarked casually.

Cat lifted her chin. "As long as I do Neville's bidding, he is a generous man."

"Does he know you are here?"

She shrugged. "By now, he surely must."

"What manner of man is William Neville?"

Cat spit out the words: "He is a swine!"

James laughed, lighting up his dark features. He suddenly looked very young, much like the cousin Cat remembered. She smiled back at him.

"You may stay, Cousin," he said, his eyes glinting with amusement. "If Neville's suit is unwelcome to you, I cannot, in good conscience, send you back to him. For the affection I bore you in my youth, I will make you an allowance of one hundred and twelve pounds a month."

She gasped.

"Is it not enough?" James demanded.

"Certainly, Your Grace," she stammered. "I had not imagined you would be so generous."

"Be sure it is put to good use. You will be a welcome addition to my court. God knows I need some amusing diversions." He grinned again. "Do you still introduce monkeys into the royal dining hall, Lady Catriona?"

She laughed, a low musical sound. "Nay, Your Grace," she protested. "I've grown up since then."

"A pity." He stood up, every inch a king. The audience was over.

"Go now to your apartments. I shall look for you at court this evening."

Cat spread her skirts in a deep curtsy and, with practiced ease, backed out of the room. She stepped outside. The guards were gone. Deliberately, she did not force the door, allowing it to hang open slightly. Dropping to her knees, she pressed her face against the opening and narrowed one eye.

Immediately a man stepped from behind the tapestries. Out of the shadows and into the candlelight, he moved with the smooth, predatory grace of a panther. It was too dark to see clearly. Frustrated, she shifted her position and cupped one hand behind her ear. She could no longer see, but she could hear perfectly.

James smiled, disarmed, as always, by the incredible charm of the man he trusted with his life.

Patrick MacKendrick grinned. "A credible performance, Your Grace."

James looked startled. "You didn't believe her? She seemed most sincere."

"Where a bonny woman is concerned, your instincts are not always to be trusted."

James sighed. "She did take me by surprise. I had no idea Catriona would look like that. Many years have passed since we've met." He looked up, an arrested expression on his face. "What say you, Patrick? Can we use her to our advantage? She's by far the loveliest woman at court."

She was the loveliest woman he'd ever seen, Patrick MacKendrick thought privately. But he wasn't about to voice his opinion. The effect her slim, high-breasted figure and green eyes had on his pulse rate would remain a well-kept secret until he knew what the king intended. Jamie Stewart favored beautiful women. He was also a possessive man. Patrick wanted no argument with his king, especially over a woman, even a woman as lovely as the Lady Catriona Wells. The English beauty was hiding something, he was sure of it. When he found out what it was, perhaps he could use it to his advantage.

"I would know this English cousin of yours better, Your Grace," he said at last. "Perhaps, whatever she hides has naught to do with kings and countries. It is possible she harbors a more personal secret."

James grinned, his teeth even and white against the dark olive of his skin. "You have my leave to find out. If Cat is anything like she was as a child, she will lead you a merry chase." He laughed out loud and rubbed his hands together. "What I wouldn't give to see the mighty Patrick MacKendrick dance to a fair lady's demands."

"You'll wait in vain." The silky voice sounded amused. "There isn't a woman in the world worth that aggravation."

James considered his friend. "What of marriage and heirs, Patrick? Surely you want to see your line continue."

Patrick MacKendrick crossed his arms and leaned back against the mantel, his thoughts filled with the image of Catriona Wells. Cat, James had called her. Eyes, the green of sunlight on pond water, flashed through his mind. The name suited her. She was like a cat, slim and graceful and cautious. She was also the daughter of a Stewart princess and an English earl, her rank as far above a simple border lord as a king was above a kitchen maid. Deliberately, he wiped her image from his mind and considered the king's question.

"I have no need of heirs," he said at last. "Let any man in the borders with the strength to take what is mine, have it."

Without knowing it, he voiced the very words that convinced James of his unquestioning loyalty. So had Jamie Stewart taken the kingdom of Scotland, not by right, but by the strength of his sword arm.

The king stood up and reached for the hilt of a great sword that hung on the wall. It was the blade of Robert the Bruce from the Battle of Bannockburn. "Kneel," he commanded.

Patrick MacKendrick knelt. James looked down on the mahogany-dark head. Emotion choked his words. Collecting himself, he touched the sword to Patrick's broad, velvet-clad shoulder.

"May your courage and loyalty live in the blood of your sons," he said gruffly. "Rise, my lord."

Patrick stood up and James replaced the sword. Neither man spoke. Finally the king growled, "Enough," as though many words had passed between them. "I've created an earldom for you, Patrick. Perhaps now you'll agree to a wife."

Patrick grinned, the chiseled features suddenly young and boyish. "Give me time, Sire. How will I know if a woman wants me for my title or for myself?"

"Enough women have made it plain they want you without a title," said James wryly. "Someday, perhaps, you'll reveal the secret of your charm with the lassies." He waved a golden goblet encrusted with jewels in front of his friend. "Come. We'll drink a toast."

Patrick took the cup and raised it in the air. "Shall we drink to Scotland?"

"Aye," the king agreed, "and to women." He lifted his cup above his head. "To the bonniest lass in Edinburgh."

A green-eyed face, its features indistinct, flashed through Patrick's mind. He was now an earl. Lifting the goblet to his lips, he drained it. The future was suddenly filled with possibilities.

⭑ 6 ⭑

Ashen-faced, Kate stood at the railing of the ferry and stared at the mist-shrouded island looming larger by the minute. A desperate anticipation held her in its grip. She was afraid to relax, to sleep, to allow her thoughts to wander freely. Maintaining rigid control was her only solution. Coming here had been a mistake, one she intended to correct as soon as she distributed her mother's ashes.

Hunching her shoulders against the wind, she tightened the muscles around her eyes, forcing them open, refusing to blink, terrified that the moment she closed them she would sleep and, with the slide into dark unconsciousness, dream those terrifying, lifelike dreams that weren't dreams at all but a different kind of reality, a reality so three-dimensional, so real, that mere living and breathing seemed flat in comparison.

Kate had dreamed regularly and frequently for as long as she could remember, but not like this, not with such clarity and color, not with her senses alive and quivering. She could smell and feel and hear and speak and touch with an intensity she had never experienced in her waking hours. Yet she had no defined role in these fabrications of her mind. She watched as if she were a movie director with the cast of a feature film unfolding before her, her part nonexistent, her omniscient presence necessary for rhythm and order.

The dense fog muffled all sound except for the lapping waves and the purring of the ferry motor. The island was all around them now, the boat cutting a path into the silent harbor. Tall masts, hung with mist, attached to wooden-hulled fishing boats, dipped and rose with the steady current. Kate could barely make out the outline of a bait shack and a wooden dock fifty yards ahead. She tightened her grip on the railing as the ferry surged forward into its mooring.

The wizened ferry captain helped her from the boat and tipped his hat. "We don't have many visitors here in Cait Ness. Is someone coming to meet you, lass?"

Kate shook her head. "I've reservations in a bed and breakfast in town. Is there a taxi?"

He smiled. "If you'll wait a bit, I'll shut down the boat and take you myself."

"Please don't trouble yourself," she protested. "I'm sure I can find a way."

He stared at her curiously. "No trouble, miss. This is the last ferry of the day and I live down the road from the only bed and breakfast on the island. You're goin' my way."

Helpless against such logic, Kate waited for the man to secure the ropes and empty his cash box. When he wheeled out a rusted bicycle from behind the bait shack and motioned her to the bar in front of him, she managed a weak smile and did as he suggested. Clutching her suitcase with one hand and the bar with the other, she closed her eyes and prayed silently for safe deliverance as her chauffeur pushed the creaking bike forward. Amazingly, he managed to hop on the seat, work the pedals and keep them both upright and moving forward at a steady clip.

Kate summoned her courage, opened her eyes and looked around. Cait Ness was exactly as Bill Brockman had described it. The countryside was very green, with paths that looked like question marks ending in front of whitewashed cottages with thatched roofs. Long-haired sheep grazed on the hillsides, and occasionally she saw cows and clusters of very small ponies munching on marsh grass. "Those are the smallest horses I've ever seen," she announced.

"Aye." Her chauffeur was pedaling furiously now, and Kate noticed they were traveling uphill. "Shetland ponies, they are. We export them."

"Of course, I'd forgotten." These were the Shetland Islands, after all.

Their steady ascent worried Kate. The ferry captain was not a young man and the ride would have made anyone breathe heavily, even without the extra weight of another person. She glanced around and saw that he was barely winded.

He grinned at her. "We're nearly there, lass. It wasn't such a bad ride, was it?"

She laughed, her fears a distant memory. "Not at all. Thank you for your generous offer."

"Mrs. MacLean runs a neat room and a tidy breakfast. You'll do well there," he assured her, dragging his foot along the ground to brake the bike. "Tell her I said so."

Tenderly, Kate lifted herself off the bar. She was sore all over. "I'll do that," she promised, waving as he rode away into the rising mist.

She turned to the neatly painted white house set close to the street. A wooden fence surrounded a postcard-sized green lawn bordered by flower beds still brown from winter. Kate opened the gate, walked up the brick path to the door and rang the bell.

"Come in. The door's open," a lilting voice called out.

Kate stepped inside and looked around in surprised pleasure. The walls were very white, with blue stencils and wood-framed sea prints. Oak tables and wingback chairs were tastefully arranged on the gleaming wood floors, and a fire crackled in the stone fireplace. Kate had never seen a room so warm and welcoming, so completely suited to her own tastes. She knelt down by the fire to warm her hands.

A small, round woman with graying hair and almond-shaped brown eyes came into the room carrying a teapot and a tray of pastries. "Do sit down, my dear. I've been expecting you." She set the tray down on a low table. "These are fresh from the oven."

Kate rose and smiled. "I'm Kate Sutherland, Mrs. MacLean, and I'm starving, but I didn't expect anything other than breakfast."

Glennis MacLean beamed. "You've had a long day and it's late. I couldn't live with myself if I sent you out to find a meal when you've only just arrived. The meat pie and pudding won't be ready for another hour. These should hold you until then." She sat down in a chair and poured the tea. "Was the ride calm?"

Kate took the cup of steaming liquid and sat down in the

chair opposite Mrs. MacLean. "Very. The captain was very complimentary. He told me to tell you that he was sure I'd like it here." She looked around admiringly. "This is a lovely room."

Two red spots of color stained the woman's cheeks. "I'm so glad you approve. I like it very much myself. Does it remind you of your home, Miss Sutherland?"

Kate thought of the glass and chrome living room her mother had preferred. "I'm afraid not," she said. "I moved back in with my mother before she died and her taste was nothing like mine. If I could, I'd change everything to look exactly like this."

Mrs. MacLean smiled. "Thank you, dear. Drink your tea and have some of these biscuits. They're delicious, even if I did make them myself."

Plied with pastries and tea and Mrs. MacLean's obvious approval, Kate began to unwind. "This is delicious," she said, "just what I needed."

"Is your visit to Cait Ness for business or pleasure, Miss Sutherland?"

Kate hesitated. Not everyone approved of cremation. Still, the woman deserved something of the truth. "I'm here to find someone, a friend of my mother's. I don't know her name, but the last time they saw each other was thirty years ago. Someone told me Maura Sutherland might help me."

Glennis MacLean's nut-brown eyes widened for the briefest of seconds. Had her lips tightened imperceptibly? Kate couldn't be sure, but she knew something had changed. Her heightened senses, never far from the surface of her consciousness, leapt into full alert.

Sighing with pleasure, Kate turned down the lamp, kicked off her shoes, snuggled into the corner of the couch and pulled the knitted afghan up to her chin. It wasn't late by California standards, but she was exhausted. The fire snapped and sizzled in the brick hearth, and outside a soft rain pelted the windows. The fire threw an arc of light across the ceiling. Shadows, larger than life, flitted across the walls. She yawned. Her body was tired, but her mind refused to give up the day. Her senses were particularly sharp, honed by a curious sense of anticipation. Falling asleep meant dreaming unsettling dreams. But for some reason, here on Cait Ness, in this room, she was ready for them.

Cat opened the door to her apartments in Edinburgh Castle. Her women, gathered before the fire in the sitting room, immediately stopped their conversation. With a wave of her hand, she dismissed them and walked over to a slender youth leaning against a high trestle seat. A quill was in his hand and an open bottle of ink sat on the desk before him. She waited until the last woman exited the room before speaking.

"It is as I thought," she said, her voice low. "My cousin is no fool. He suspects me for what I am, an English spy. We shall have to tread carefully."

"Henry won't wait forever," the young man answered. "You must convince Jamie to trust you."

"I know that, Andrew." Cat sighed impatiently and rubbed her arms against the chill. "It may take more time than we thought."

Sir Andrew Percy glanced with distaste at the ink stain on his finger. "The sooner we are done with this pretense the better. One of the women remarked that my figures are not clear enough to warrant my position as your secretary. As soon as someone realizes you can read and write better than I, there will be questions. Jamie will wonder why you brought me with you."

Cat frowned. "You must practice. I'll help you. If anyone suspects you are noble, we are done for." She shivered and walked over to the blazing hearthfire. "I would much rather trust Jamie than Henry," she admitted. "When I was a child, he showed me great kindness."

" 'Tis not kindness to murder your father for a kingdom," Percy retorted.

The green eyes glinted. "Did not Henry do the same? By marrying Elizabeth and murdering every legitimate York heir, he secured his own claim."

"Richard killed the York princes," he reminded her.

Cat stared into the flames, the flickering light mesmerizing her for several moments. "I wonder," she said at last, "if Richard or Henry had more to gain. Perhaps this Pretender is really who he claims to be: our rightful king."

Percy threw down the quill and strode to the fire. Grasping her shoulders, he turned her to face him. "Enough of this," he said, his boyish features unusually impatient. "Henry holds our future in his hands. Prove this Pretender false and Neville loses." His hands tightened on her shoulders. "Think of it, Cat! You'll be free and Richard will have Ravenswood."

His glance moved over her face, noting the brilliant eyes, the haughty high-bridged nose and prominent cheekbones. It was a beautiful face but one unlike any he had ever seen before. There was something vital and primitive about her. Something definitely not English. With a sigh, he folded her gently into his arms. Cat's vulnerability pulled at him. It was the reason he'd left the comfort of Whitehall to journey hundreds of miles north to play a role for which he was completely unsuited.

Cat stood quietly in his embrace thinking of the evening ahead.

The court of King James of Scotland was licentious, immoral and extravagant, everything Cat had expected it to be. Accustomed to the frugality of the Tudor regime, she was shocked at first, and later delighted. The great room was filled with throngs of people speaking several languages. Servants poured glasses of ale and spiced wine while others offered platters filled with fruit and tempting morsels of roasted meat. Jewels gleamed on brightly gowned women and winked from the folds of exquisite tunics. The use of fur was lavish, from the darkest mink to the snowiest of ermine.

A great fire burned in the center of the room, reflecting off the glittering eyes of masks, both animal and human, mounted on stone corbels supporting the hammered-beam roof. Oil-drenched torches flickered and smoked, blackening the granite walls, giving light to the large rectangular tables laden with food and arranged in an open square around the fire.

The court jester, clad in a striped suit, moved among the guests, juggling an array of golden balls. Cat recognized the mincing figure of Pedro de Ayala, the Spanish ambassador. She smiled as the Danes, huge men with pale eyes and golden hair, astonished everyone by consuming enormous quantities of liquor.

There were rumors of an alliance with Denmark. Cat wondered who she could approach for more news. She stood alone, close to the fire, unaware of the openly admiring looks leveled in her direction. Her dress was of white velvet. Because of her rank, she was entitled to wear white ermine. More than a foot of the fur swirled at the bottom of the long gown and around the edges of the sleeves that partly covered her hands. The bodice was tight; it set off the shoulders, the swell of her breasts evident above the deep square neck. The costly velvet fit tightly below her narrow waist, hugging her hips and falling in soft folds to the floor.

She wore a pendant, a giant emerald that hung between her breasts, and her black hair, unbound as Scottish tradition ordered, fell in shining waves to her knees. Her nails were polished and her mouth slightly reddened, but the deep rose of her cheeks and the lovely dark eyebrows and eyelashes were her own.

Patrick MacKendrick, deep in conversation with the Spanish ambassador, didn't notice her arrival. He stood in a corner of the room, thumbs hooked through his belt, his foot propped against the fender. It was several moments before he noticed the man wasn't listening to him. Turning to see what it was that had captured his attention, he immediately recognized the slender, black-haired woman standing alone by the fire. He sucked in his breath.

"Sweet Mary," he swore softly, the blood pounding in his temples. From his hiding place in the king's apartments, he clearly recalled her slim, graceful lines. Before she turned her back to him he had caught the briefest glimpse of striking features and slanted green eyes. Patrick knew she would be lovely, but not in his wildest dreams had he imagined she would look like this. Ignoring the warning signals ringing in his brain, he left the ambassador without a word and shouldered his way toward her.

Cat watched him cross the room, his stride long and purposeful. She smiled as he parried questions and brushed aside the feminine hands reaching out to delay him. He was straightforward and uncompromising, his walk unhurried, even and measured.

Catriona knew, without question, that he was a man of importance. Like an aura, he carried his authority about him. *Hard* was the word that leapt instantly to her mind. His face, harsh planes and sharp edges, was the kind women longed for and feared. Nothing would sway this man from his purpose.

His eyes met hers, narrowed and intent, as he came ever nearer. Cat shivered with a delicious sense of anticipation. Whom did he seek with such conviction? Her tension increased as he continued his pace, bypassing one figure after another. Awareness of him drained her mind of everything but his presence. Incredibly, he stopped directly before her.

Cat racked her brain. She knew she had never seen him before. He was not a man easily forgotten. Tall and lean, dark as a Romany knight, he stood with a sense of harnessed strength, his mouth proud, his lips thin. The slate-colored eyes in his brown face were the iron gray of a Highland loch, and his hair, dark brown with streaks of red, gleamed like burnished mahogany under the torchlight. Beneath his crimson tunic, he wore a saffron shirt, its pale color accentuating the leathery hue of his skin drawn tightly across high cheekbones. His smile was a blade of white in the bronze of his face.

He was smiling now as he lifted her hand to his mouth. His fingers were firm and cool, but where his lips touched her skin, she felt heat. Straightening her shoulders, she kept her eyes on his.

He was silent for a long moment as his gaze moved boldly over her face and figure.

Cat flushed and bit her lip. She would not be the first to speak. He had come to her.

"Welcome to Scotland, Lady Catriona," he said at last.

Her eyes widened in surprise. The unmistakable burr of the borders was evident in his speech. It couldn't be! And yet she had heard that voice before. There was only one man in all of Scotland who hailed from the borders and sat at the right hand of Jamie Stewart.

She wet her lips. She had to be sure. "How do you know me, sir?"

He smiled again, a blinding flash of white against dark skin. "You've the look of a Stewart. It would be useless to deny it."

Cat lifted her chin. "Your eyes are keener than most, m'lord. No one else has ever said as much."

He stared into the light-struck green of her eyes. It was no wonder her resemblance to the Stewarts had gone unnoticed in England. The face before him was not a Celtic face. Not an ounce of Viking blood was evident in the small, haughty chin and thin, aquiline nose. Nor was she of Saxon blood. Only those familiar with the tale of Walter Fitzalan, the first high steward of Scotland, knew the Stewarts hailed from Norman stock. When the sixth high steward married the daughter of Robert the Bruce after the Battle of Bannockburn, the Royal House of Stewart was established.

To Scots born north of the Grampians, the Somerleds were the real kings of Scotland, or perhaps the MacDonalds of the Isles had a stronger claim. To the MacKendrick it made little difference. The Stewarts were usurpers. Clever, greedy, selfish and strong, they rose from obscurity, stepping on the backs of the weak, taking what they wanted, until an entire kingdom bowed to their demands.

For those very reasons, Patrick MacKendrick had pledged his sword to James. In the frustrated son of James III he had recognized a kindred spirit. Scotland cowered in fear of an English invasion and bled from the drain of English tariffs on desperately needed imports. Nowhere was the strain greater than on the borders, where, day after day, centuries of enmity blazed to bitter hatred. It was English against Scot, England against Scotland. Torture, betrayal, murder, Patrick had seen them all. Scotland needed a king who would not retreat before the might of England. In young Jamie, Patrick MacKendrick had found that king. He had used his power, the strength of the borders, and his incredible magnetism to secure the throne for him.

Patrick MacKendrick was born eight and twenty years ago. He had hacked out his fortunes with his wits and his own two arms, asking favors from no one. For a long time his power had gone unquestioned in the borders. Now, thanks to Jamie, he had the rest of Scotland as well.

He considered the lovely face before him. Neither in war nor politics had he experienced the taste of defeat. He wondered, for a brief moment, if he might suffer it at the hands of an English lass.

"You've lived too long in England," he said at last, breaking the lengthy silence. "Has no one ever remarked that you've the look of your mother?"

"Many times," Cat replied shortly. The wound of her mother's death was still fresh. She would not speak of it to this stranger. "Who are you?" She was almost completely sure, but she wanted to hear it from his lips.

"Patrick MacKendrick."

The name hung between them for an endless moment. Cat was unprepared for the surge of anger raging through her at his open admission.

"You!" she cried. "I know you! Everyone knows of you! You are the MacKendrick of Hailes!"

His eyes were remote, guarded against her. "Aye." He nodded.

Her voice shook in a furious whisper. "You whoreson traitor!"

Patrick MacKendrick said nothing. A muscle worked in his tight jaw, and those who knew him well would long since have backed away.

"You are a peasant attempting the impossible," she railed at him. "Do you imagine you'll keep your position? Jamie is wise enough to know if you betrayed one king, you'll betray another."

He seized her arm and pulled her against him, his eyes glittering dangerously. "Pull in your claws, Lady Cat." His voice was as smooth and soft as polished satin. "I would like a private word with you."

"You may not have it," she panted, attempting to struggle against the arms that bound her like bands of steel.

"You have no choice," he murmured against her ear. "'Tis undignified to struggle. Do you wish the entire court to witness your display of temper?" He twisted her arm until she winced at the pain. "Jamie dislikes scenes. Submit or I will persuade him to send you back to England."

She smiled sweetly and relaxed, her voice as cloying as

warm honey. "Very well, I'll go with you." Under the veiled lashes, her eyes glittered and her whisper cut like the lash of a whip. "But understand this, you arrogant bastard: If you manhandle me again, you'll live to regret it."

Patrick's mouth twitched. "Make all the threats you wish, m'lady, but refrain from maligning my mother. She was lawfully married to my father, and 'tis a sin to speak ill of the dead."

Cat glared at him. The laughter in his voice enraged her. She would not dignify his comment with a reply. Coldly, she withdrew her arm from his grasp. Head held high, she preceded him out of the room into a recessed antechamber furnished with a small table and a single chair.

Only when she heard the door close did she turn to face him. "Say what you must and then release me. I tire of your presence."

His face looked grim and very dangerous in the light of the flickering torches. Cat was suddenly afraid. She stepped back and felt the wall behind her.

A tight smile crossed his lips and then vanished immediately. He leaned against the door and crossed his arms. "Are you afraid, mistress?" His voice was velvety smooth, but she could hear the anger beneath the mild words.

"I fear no man," she retorted, lifting her chin.

"Then you are a fool." He pushed away from the door and came toward her until his face was inches from her own.

His breath fanned her cheek. She could smell the scent of soap-root that clung to him. His cheeks were very hollow under the high, jutting bones, and once again, Cat noticed the remarkable color of his eyes. They were a deep, unrelieved gray, the gray of rain and mist and tempered steel. She held her breath, but he made no move to touch her. She was oddly disappointed.

"Jamie Stewart is yet an uncrowned king," he warned her. "The slightest hint that he is undeserving could mean death."

"I've no quarrel with Jamie," she whispered, "nor do I question his right to the throne. After all, my uncle is dead."

He reached out for a lock of shining hair, tugging at it to

bring her closer. "You spoke of murder and traitors, lass. Is your quarrel only with me?" Her eyes were as green as the emerald resting in the hollow between her breasts.

"My cousin would never have committed his foul act without the likes of you!"

"Nay, you are wrong." His denial was swift and forceful. " 'Tis true, I wanted a strong king for Scotland, but never doubt that Jamie always intended to rule. He sought me out, lass, although I must admit, neither of us needed a great deal of persuasion."

"I don't believe you!"

The MacKendrick was silent. He was aware that she continued to rail at him, but her words ceased to hold meaning. Her hair felt like black silk in his hand. In the shadows, in the firelight, everywhere he saw her face, she was beautiful. The pure curve of her cheek, the line of her throat, the odd slant of her eyes, the very scent of her stirred his blood.

"Are you betrothed?" he asked, interrupting her.

Her eyes widened. "How dare you?" she breathed. The rise and fall of her breasts was very pronounced. "The blood of kings runs through my veins, MacKendrick." She lifted her head proudly. "When I wed, it will be to a man of my own order."

His eyes danced with amusement. "Are you always so presumptuous?"

Cat flushed. "Why would you ask such a question?" she muttered, ashamed of her lack of composure.

His hands slid under her sleeves and gently gripped her elbows. The very presence of him threatened to overpower her. She could feel her knees weaken. Swaying, she braced herself against his chest for balance.

"Look at me, Cat," he ordered.

As if she had no will of her own, she lifted her head. She met his burning glance with heavy-lidded eyes.

"There is more that binds a man and woman than holy vows," he murmured, his breath tickling her ear. "I've no inclination for marriage. When the time is right, I'll see to it." His lips brushed the hollow of her cheek. "Meanwhile, I took no vow of celibacy. Would you have me live like a monk?"

Reacting to the warmth of his chest and the persuasive seduction of his words, her eyelids closed. Every instinct clamored to accept his invitation, to lay down her guard and melt against him, succumbing to the magic of his touch.

He chuckled. Immediately her eyes flew open. He sounded amused and much too sure of himself. Cat blinked, struggling to rid herself of the bone-weakening spell his lips and arms evoked.

"Release me, MacKendrick," she demanded.

Immediately, he dropped his arms.

She met his gaze steadily, without embarrassment. "If you burn, 'tis your own fault. There are women enough who would gladly warm your bed."

He grinned, his eyes resting on the arrogant tilt of her chin. Holy God, she was a woman worth having. "I'm flattered you noticed."

"I could scarcely help it," she retorted. "They practically fall at your feet."

"But not you." His voice was almost a whisper. "You will not fall at my feet, will you, Cat?"

She bit her lip. "I'll not go spoiled to my marriage bed." Even as she said the words, a shadow hovered on the edge of her memory and disappeared.

He smiled, a warm, engaging smile. Cat forgot to breathe. By the blessed Virgin, no wonder the women hung on him. Never had she met a man with such charm. Without even touching her, he raised the goose bumps on her arms.

"How old are you, lass?" he asked abruptly.

"Twenty."

He whistled softly. "All of twenty and not yet betrothed. Are the English fools that such beauty is left untouched? Or is it your shrewish tongue they fear?"

"I never said I wasn't betrothed," she replied defensively, rubbing her arms.

"Say it now. I want no innocent man's murder on my hands."

Her eyes were huge against the clear porcelain of her skin. "You wouldn't," she whispered.

"Aye, I would." Reaching out, he pulled her against the wall of his chest.

Her heart pounded against his ribs.

"I speak too quickly, perhaps," he admitted. "Another man would woo you properly. But 'tis not always wise to delay these things." Brushing his mouth quickly against hers, he set her away from him and walked to the door. Holding it open, he looked back and grinned. "I put no value on maidenhood. 'Tis a messy process deflowering a woman. But it pleases me you have known no man." His voice was an intimate caress. "When I take you, Lady Catriona, you won't be spoiled, you will be awakened."

Cat released the breath she had been holding for an endless moment and leaned weakly against the wall. There was no peace for her in all the world. Not even Ravenswood was worth this. She thought of her brother. Before leaving England, she had seen the strut of approaching manhood in his step. His voice had deepened, and a full year ago, his cheeks had been flushed with the excitement of bringing down his first stag.

Her eyes filled with tears. Ashamed, she brushed them away. Richard's life was more important than her own unsettled emotions. What did it matter if Catriona Wells lost her virtue? As long as her brother stayed alive and well at Ravenswood, her purpose would be served. Taking a deep breath, she straightened her shoulders and walked out of the small retiring room into the great hall.

On the other side of the room, Patrick MacKendrick threw back his head and shouted with laughter. The woman at his side smiled triumphantly. Cat could see that she was beautiful. She was dressed in pink satin, with tiny strips of fur across each sleeve, and her dark blond hair under the matching cap was parted in the middle and piled high on her head.

She was married, Cat realized with an irrational shock of delight. In Scotland, only married women bound their hair. Her satisfaction dissolved as the woman leaned closer to Patrick and rested her hand on his arm. It was a languorous movement, designed for only one purpose. Cat watched as his arm reached up to lightly caress her back. He bent his head and whispered something into the woman's ear.

Abruptly, Cat turned away. She would not watch him make a fool of himself with a married woman.

"Cat?" A shy, sweet voice intruded upon her thoughts. "Catriona Wells, is it truly you?"

A vision in blue velvet stood before her. The girl was tall and very slim, with eyes so blue they looked almost purple. Her hair was as black as Catriona's own, but it hung straight and shining as a crow's wing down her back. She looked vaguely familiar.

Cat frowned. "I'm sorry, mistress, but I don't remember you."

Color flooded the girl's pale cheeks. "'Tis Mary Katherine Gordon, your cousin. Have I changed so much?"

"Mary?" Cat's mouth dropped open in astonishment. Could this willowy beauty be shy, scrawny Mary Gordon?

"Where is George?" Cat looked around. "Is Janet with you?"

"Nay." Mary laughed. "Janet likes to make an entrance."

"And George?" Cat persisted. "Does he like to make an entrance as well?"

The smile left Mary's face. "George is banished for three years. The charge is treason, for fighting against Jamie at Sauchieburn."

"God's wounds!" The masculine curse burst from Cat's lips. "How can George be charged with treason when he was fighting for the rightful king?" The injustice of it was hard to bear.

"You must watch what you say, Cat," Mary warned. "Our uncle is no longer king."

They were silent, lost for a moment in their private memories of a graying kindly uncle who was also the late king of Scotland. The Stewarts had been a large and loving family when James III was alive. His younger sister had wed the chief of Clan Gordon and borne him three children. George came first, and then Janet, who was exactly Catriona's age. Mary was two years younger. Although they spent most of the year in their Highland stronghold of Strathbogie, they managed to travel to Edinburgh when Catriona's mother, another sister, visited from England, bringing her own two children to her brother's court. After the two women died, the familial ties were broken and the cousins had drifted apart.

"If your family is in disfavor, why are you here?" Cat asked at last.

"There was nowhere else to go," Mary replied. "We are deprived of all revenues from our estates until George returns." She dropped her eyes. "Glenkirk has asked for Janet's hand in marriage. He wishes to have her here at court."

Cat gasped. "Does Janet agree? After Kennedy left her widowed, I would have thought—"

"In Scotland even a widow has little choice."

In all her memories of Janet Gordon Kennedy, there was none of passive acceptance. "Has she changed so much then?" Cat wondered.

A commotion at the entrance of the room drew their attention.

"See for yourself," Mary whispered.

At first Cat could see nothing at all for the cluster of men that surrounded the door. She noticed a brawny redheaded nobleman shouldering his way through the crowd. Men and women cleared a path before his tall figure. When he reached the door he frowned and held out his arm.

It was then that Cat saw her. Suddenly it seemed as if a rush of clean wind swept through the dank, cloying hall of Edinburgh Castle. Smiling with relief, she knew that her cousin was the same as always.

For the rest of her life, Cat would remember the image of Janet Gordon as she stood before the gathered assembly, slim and straight and proud, her hair a curtain of molten gold rippling to her waist. Her dress was of rustling silk, the bodice black with a deep decolletage. The outer skirt was cut open to the waist in a narrow vee, and the satin underskirt, a brilliant shocking red, was so tight it clung to her slender curves like a second skin. A priceless emerald brooch was all that held the fabric together over her breasts. Janet's golden eyes, brimming with defiance, reminded Cat of an angry lioness. She looked exotic and extremely sensual.

Stifling her laughter, Cat looked at Mary. "She hasn't changed a bit. How can she possibly walk in such a gown?"

Mary grinned back at her. "She'll be very glad to see you.

I'm much too lacking in spirit to be a fit companion for Janet. I think I'll sit back and watch the two of you wreak havoc on Holyrood House."

Cat kept her eyes on Janet, holding the smile on her lips until her mouth ached with the effort. If it were only that simple. What she wouldn't give to be a child again with nothing more on her mind than the mischief she could brew with Janie Gordon.

❧ 7 ❧

"Breakfast was delicious, Mrs. MacLean, but I'm really not a big eater." Kate pushed back her chair and stood up. "Some of these delicious scones and tea will be fine for tomorrow."

"That won't be enough food for weather like ours, Miss Sutherland. Hot food fuels the body."

Kate gave up. Obviously the woman preferred her ritual of cooking more food for a single meal than one person could eat in a week. "How can I contact the ferry captain?" she asked.

"Ferris?" Mrs. MacLean cleared the table, expertly piling plates one on top of another. "I rang him up an hour ago. Just wait outside and he'll come." She looked approvingly at Kate's jeans, parka, backpack and sensible shoes. "You've dressed warmly. Good girl. Foula is a cold, dismal place. You'll need gloves. I have a pair if you haven't any."

Kate patted the pocket of her jacket. "They're here. All the guidebooks warn you about the weather."

"Do you have any family here on the islands, Miss Sutherland?"

"I don't really know." Kate's brow wrinkled and she leaned against the table. "My mother didn't mention anyone."

"Maybe they're not here anymore. Most of our young people emigrate to the mainland. There's not much of a living here on Cait Ness."

"I suppose." Kate was not convinced. "I've no idea what time I'll be back. Please don't wait up for me."

Glennis MacLean smiled. "You'll see the finest scenery in the islands, my dear. Take all the time you need."

The ride down the hill was considerably more treacherous than the ride up had been. Kate clung to the handlebars of Ferris Sinclair's bicycle and closed her eyes until she felt the ground level out. The sea was very close. She drew a deep restoring breath and opened her eyes. Strange how the ocean always smelled the same whether it was pounding the California shoreline or lapping against fishing boat hulls on Cait Ness Island.

Once again she was the only passenger on the ferry. Ferris munched on a bun and drank from a mug of tea while steering the boat confidently into a thick wall of fog. It was cold. Kate realized for the first time in her life that she finally knew what the word meant. Cold was not the sixty-degree temperature of a winter night in California, nor was it Boston at Christmas and the frosty tingling of skin under soft wool. Cold was bone-chilling numbness, wet fog against one's face and the curious, paralytic set of lips that had long since lost their ability to move. The mist stung her face like icy needles and twisted the fine wisps of hair against her forehead. The boat had left the shelter of the harbor only minutes before. She would never make it to Foula.

Something heavy and warm fell across her shoulders. It was a large plaid blanket. Gratefully, she pulled it around her. The fog was so thick she couldn't see her own hands. The captain's voice called to her through the mist. "There's a bit of a chill to the air. The tartan should help. Nothing like it to stop the wet and the wind from getting through."

"Thank you," she managed through stiff lips. It was May. Somewhere people were warm. Somewhere skies were clear and Santa Ana winds blew across a cracked earth scorched by drought. Somewhere dust particles danced on planes of light, a blazing sun rode across a cobalt sky, barefoot joggers ran across warm sand beaches and striped umbrellas shielded sensitive noses from ultraviolet rays. Somewhere else, people who had the sense to leave the North Sea and its islands to mammals with thick layers of fat went about the normal business of living. Kate set her teeth and burrowed down into the thick plaid until her face was completely concealed. She would never eat ice cream again.

"We're nearly there," Ferris announced. "Ten minutes more and you'll see land."

She felt marginally warmer. The plaid had done the trick, driving the worst of the cold from her arms and legs. She narrowed her eyes, straining to see through the mist. Suddenly the fog lifted and she caught her breath. The shoreline was bathed in sunlight.

"Happens every time," Ferris whispered reverently. "Just like the legend says."

Kate walked to the back of the boat to stand beside him. "What legend?"

He looked at her, astonishment etched across his homely features. "Surely you've heard of King Arthur?"

"Of course I have. But what does Foula have to do with King Arthur?"

"There are some who believe his son, Mordred, was raised here. His foster mother was Morgawse, who ruled these islands with King Lot."

Kate had done some research of her own. "Lot and Morgawse ruled the Orkneys. These are the Shetlands."

Ferris shrugged. "Boundaries weren't so firmly drawn back then. The Northern Isles is what they were called." He changed the subject. "Does Maura expect you?"

Kate shook her head. "Not unless Mrs. MacLean called her."

Ferris grinned. "She wouldn't be doing that."

"Why not?"

"Glennis MacLean is recently come up from Edinburgh. She doesn't hold with the likes of Maura."

"I don't understand."

Ferris chuckled and expertly maneuvered the boat into the ferry slip, looping the line over a post and pulling the knot taut. "You will, lass, soon enough."

Kate watched as he unlatched the door and rolled his bicycle out onto the dock. Bracing herself for another bumpy ride, she followed him.

"Can you manage a bicycle, Miss Sutherland?"

"Of course."

He smiled. "Good girl. There's lodging two miles up the road. Call Glennis if you decide to stay the night."

"You're leaving me?" Kate asked incredulously.

"Aye." He smiled. "Don't worry. There's only one road. You can't get lost."

Kate watched mutely as her one link to civilization motored out of the slip and disappeared into the mist. Her eyes blurred. Angrily, she wiped them with the back of her hand. She was thirty years old, for heaven's sake. Too old to cry over being left to fend for herself. If Foula had guest lodgings it couldn't be as unpopulated as it looked.

She found her balance and pedaled in the direction Ferris had pointed out. The sharp air burned the delicate tissue inside of her nose. Kate altered her breathing pattern, substituting small shallow breaths for deep long ones. Riding uphill for two miles on a bicycle took longer than she had expected. It was nearly noon when she pulled into the tiny village that was the capital of Foula.

"Maura Sutherland?" The woman behind the counter of the convenience store raised her eyebrows. Her hands and apron were dusted with flour. "Maura doesn't see strangers, lass. What would you be wanting with her?"

"I'd like to talk to her. Can you tell me where she is?"

"Now that I think of it, you've the look of someone familiar," the woman said slowly. "Do you have family on the islands?"

Kate shook her head. "I don't think so."

Wiping her hands on a towel, the woman came out from behind the counter. "Come with me. I'll point out the way."

Kate followed her out the door and stood on the stone steps. "Follow the main road to the fork," the woman said, pointing to the single lane in front of the store. "It isn't paved. Take the path to the right and walk for nearly a mile. You'll come to a clearing. Maura's croft is there."

"Thank you very much." Kate climbed back on the bike and began to pedal.

"Will you be wanting lodging for the night?" the woman called after her.

Kate stopped the bicycle by dragging her feet and turned her head. "I nearly forgot to ask. Would you have room for me?"

The woman laughed. "Of course. We haven't had guests in Foula since last September."

Eight months. It had been eight months since anyone from the outside had come to the island. Goose bumps rose on Kate's arms. Why did Maura Sutherland live in the most secluded spot on an island that no one visited? Why would anyone live here? The question on her mind, Kate almost missed the fork in the road. Swerving to the right, she continued up the steep dirt path. The earth was rich with moisture and very dark. It grabbed the tires of the bicycle until Kate could no longer pedal. Winded, she stopped and climbed off the bike. Her stomach growled. Why hadn't she thought to ask Mrs. MacLean to pack a lunch? Removing her gloves, she stuffed them into her pocket and trudged on. The sky was very blue and flocks of gulls circled overhead. In the distance she heard the sound of childish laughter.

She looked around for a place to leave the bike and decided on a large boulder just off the lane. Propping it up, Kate returned to the path and stopped. Directly ahead of her stood a small girl with red hair, a dress that was much too long and an expression on her face that could only be indignation.

"Hello," Kate began tentatively. "Who are—"

The child interrupted her. "You've been a very long time. I waited and waited and still you didn't come. Where is my father?"

Kate's eyes widened. "I beg your pardon?"

The girl frowned and backed away. "Whatever is the matter with you, Cat? You sound most strange."

"Cat? But I'm not—" Kate's protest was silenced by a small, well-aimed pebble. First she felt pain, followed by a numbing dizziness and the sensation of falling. Then she felt nothing at all.

* * *

Her face hidden in the shadows, Cat watched her cousin pace back and force across the wooden floor. Janet's stride was like a man's, angry and impatient.

"Holy God," Janet cursed, kicking aside the material of her full gown as it twisted between her legs.

Mary leaned back in her chair and rubbed her temple. Her sister's temper frequently brought on the dreaded headache. "You are as restless as a tigress, Janet," she complained. "Cat will wonder if you are touched in the head."

"Cat isn't such a fool," observed Janet, tilting her head to look at her cousin. "What say you to this, Cat? Are we to attend Jamie's coronation as if all is well in Scotland?"

Rising to her feet, Cat walked to the window of the small bedchamber and pulled aside the draperies. The sun bathed her face in a golden glow, throwing her features into bold relief against the dark velvet.

Mary gasped, amazed all over again at the resemblance between Cat and her sister. They could have been opposite sides of the same coin, with their striking features and green-gold eyes. Only their hair was different. All the Stewart offspring were alike, reflected Mary. Even their temperaments were similar. Without exception, they were bold to the point of arrogance, charming, intelligent and incredibly attractive. It was only she who was different, the changeling in the family. If she and her cousin had been the same age, Mary would have suspected her parents of exchanging children. Curious, she waited to see if Cat's response would match Janet's rebellious one.

"Jamie is the king," Cat replied slowly, turning to face Janet. "His father is dead."

"Are you saying we should countenance this outrage?" Janet's angry voice cracked with emotion. "By the blood of Christ, Cat! Our king was murdered!"

"Not by his son. Jamie has issued a reward to find his father's murderer." Cat's calm voice was soothing, bringing a measure of sanity to the tension-filled room. "Who would you put in his place, Janet? We cannot bring the dead back to life."

Janet's hands clenched at her sides. "Is there nothing to be done then? Am I to wed Glenkirk without a fight?" Her eyes narrowed to slits of molten gold. "Will you go meekly to Patrick MacKendrick's bed when he asks for you as a spoil of war?"

Cat fingered the brilliant red girdle that drew the fabric of her gown tight around her hips. "That will never happen," she said firmly, without further explanation. Even though she was bound by blood to the Gordon women, she would not confide in them. They would never betray her but confidences were extremely dangerous and the stakes were too high. Surely she would be safe in England before long.

Janet sat down on the edge of the canopied bed and unplaited her hair. It was the same honey color as her eyes. "Never disregard the MacKendrick," she warned Cat. "He is like no other man in Scotland. Without promising land or gold he rallied ten thousand troops for Jamie at Sauchieburn. Men follow him without thought of danger. After the king, he is all that matters in Scotland. Mark my words, Catriona: If he wants you he will have you."

Cat shivered and crossed her arms against her chest. The Scots autumn was much colder than in England. "Have I nothing to say in the matter?" she asked bitterly. "Sweet Jesu, I am no serving girl to be given away at the whim of her lord. I am cousin to the king of Scotland!"

In her chair by the fire, Mary stared at Cat. The combination of black hair and green eyes against her red satin gown was magnificent. No wonder the border lord wanted her. She experienced a flash of envy. Perhaps someday a man would look at her the way Patrick MacKendrick looked at Catriona.

Janet stood up and walked to the window. Laying her hands on Cat's shoulders, she looked into her eyes. "I know how you feel, Cat. Glenkirk is not my choice."

Whirling around to face the window, Cat cried out in a choked voice, "You, at least, have been offered the dignity of marriage."

"Is it marriage you desire, cousin?"

Cat sighed. Rage was a wasted emotion. "What is it you want of me, Janet?"

Smiling triumphantly, Janet turned to Mary. "Leave us."

"No, Janet," Mary protested. "This concerns me too."

"God's love, I warrant it does. But it is too dangerous for you to know anything, Mary."

"I shan't tell a soul."

Janet smiled indulgently. "You always say that. See that you do not." She motioned toward the bed and the small chair by the hearth. "We shall sit," she said in the tones of an empress.

Stifling a smile, Cat took the chair and waited for Janet to speak.

"I have been to see Jamie," she said, smiling with importance.

Cat's lip curled. "'Tis late and I'm tired. Is that all you have to report?"

"Listen and don't interrupt," Janet ordered.

Mary smiled. It was good to see the two of them sparring again.

"There will be an uprising north of Stirling on the very day of the coronation," Janet confided, her face flushed with excitement. "The rebels must be warned that Jamie knows. After the coronation he intends to subdue them."

"How do you know this?" Cat demanded.

"Glenkirk is a fool. He keeps nothing from me," she replied scornfully. "After Jamie met with the Pretender, the three of them discussed the rebellion."

"The Pretender?" Cat's voice was unnaturally calm. "I've heard nothing of this."

"No one knows yet," Janet continued. "One Perkin Warbeck, claiming to be Richard, duke of York, has asked for Jamie's aid to invade England."

Cat's heart pounded so loudly she could barely think. *If the duke of York were still alive he was the rightful king of England.* What Henry wouldn't give to know of this. She would be back in England before another se'enight passed.

"Does Jamie believe him?" she asked.

Janet shrugged. "He has the look of the Yorks. Who knows what Jamie believes? Glenkirk says Scotland's policy will be to support him."

"It will mean war," Cat warned. "Henry will not allow his throne to be challenged."

Contempt shone from the golden eyes. "Have you become English to the core, Catriona? What does a Scot care for the threats of an English king?"

"Don't be an idiot, Janie," Cat said impatiently. "Henry is England's king. He proved himself a worthy fighter at Bosworth. Just because he would rather negotiate than wage war doesn't mean he isn't capable of it."

Too agitated to remain seated, she rose and walked to the fire, holding her numbed fingers to the comforting flame. The warmth restored her. She turned back to Janet. Her voice, when she spoke, was terrifying in its intensity.

"Henry Tudor of England is a dangerous man. No one knows better than he that his claim to the throne is through the bastard line of John of Gaunt. Have you never wondered why everyone with even the smallest drop of royal blood in his veins has been killed or imprisoned?" She took a deep breath. "Mark my words, this Perkin Warbeck, whoever he is, will not live to give voice to his claim. Nor will anyone who supports him."

Mary shivered. Cat, in her red gown with her green eyes narrow and menacing, reminded her of a story her brother had once told her of the queen of Hades coming through a crack in the earth to claim the souls of the dead.

"Is that why you left England?" Janet's voice interrupted her thoughts.

"No." Cat's answer did not encourage further probing.

"Your father was first cousin to Richard III," Janet persisted.

"My father is dead."

"But your brother is not."

Mary's eyes widened. Her eyes flew to her sister and then to her cousin.

The two women stared at each other for a long moment. Janet was the first to look away.

"Whatever your trouble is, we are with you, Cat," she whispered. "Blood holds true, at least among the women of our family."

Throwing back her shoulders, Cat walked to the door. She

reached for the knob and paused. "Have nothing to do with Perkin Warbeck, Janie. Trust me in this." Without looking back, she opened the door and left the room.

From far away, Kate heard a woman's voice. She tried to open her eyes and felt a sharp pain against her temple. Groaning, she managed only the slightest flutter of her eyelashes.

"Don't move, lass," the voice said. Something cool was pressed against her forehead and a spoon held to her lips. Cautiously, she opened her mouth. A sharp, minty liquid trickled down her throat. She coughed, turned her head into the pillow and slept.

Hours later, she woke to velvety darkness. Shadows of a flickering fire leapt against stone walls. Tentatively, she explored the blanket covering her body, the rough fabric of the couch where she lay and, finally, the bandage taped to her temple. She tried to turn her head and winced.

A voice, husky and low, came out of the darkness: "I wouldn't do that just yet. You've a nasty cut on your forehead."

Slowly, Kate turned toward the voice. A woman, framed by firelight, sat in a wooden chair. Her hair was red as flame with wings of gray at the temples, and her eyes were clear and oddly slanted above her high-boned, elegant face.

"Are you Maura Sutherland?" Kate whispered.

"Perhaps. Who are you?"

"Kate. Kate Sutherland."

"Why are you here?"

Kate moistened her lips. "I need help. Celia Ward sent me to you."

"What ails you?"

"I don't know." Suddenly Kate felt sick to her stomach. Bile rose in her throat. She turned over and pressed her hand to her lips.

Maura slipped an arm behind her back and elevated her head. "You've a concussion," she explained, holding a bowl under Kate's chin. "I don't think you'll need this, but better safe than sorry."

Already the nausea had subsided. Sagging back into the

pillow, Kate smiled weakly. "I haven't eaten since breakfast."

"As soon as you feel like sitting up, I'll dish up some soup. Before I do that, I would like to know how you came by that cut."

Again, Kate touched the bandage. "I'm not sure, really. I was talking to a little girl. She seemed to think she knew me. The next thing I remember is waking up in your house."

"There are no children anywhere near here."

Kate stared at her, the pain in her head forgotten. "Of course there are. There's one at least, a little girl about seven years old with long red hair."

"You're mistaken."

There could be no response to such a final, definitive denial. Still, Kate knew what she'd seen and heard. "Do you think I imagined her?"

Maura shrugged. "People come here all the time claiming they've seen visions, asking me to help them find their way. Why they seek me out is a mystery no one seems to be able to explain."

"Probably because you're a witch," Kate volunteered.

Maura laughed and Kate caught her breath. Once, years ago, Maura Sutherland had been very lovely.

"Magic is highly overrated. Everyone on the islands is touched with it, nearly everyone in the Highlands as well. Some have the Sight. Others have a way with the land. There's nothing more to it than an understanding of herbs and a reverence for nature. It's our Celtic blood. That's all the mystery there is to it. Our ways are ours alone. We've no need for recruits."

"What about me?"

"I know nothing about you, Kate Sutherland. Are you a person who conjures up visions out of thin air?"

"Yes," Kate whispered. "I wish I weren't, but I've been seeing things that only I can see for as long as I can remember."

With fluid grace, the woman moved out of her chair and knelt beside the couch. Her face was very close to Kate's. "Look at me, Kate Sutherland, and tell me what you see."

It was impossible to deny her. There was something in the

low, smoky tones of her voice that demanded obedience. But first, Kate needed the answer to her original question. "Are you Maura Sutherland?"

"Yes."

Her eyes were clear, colorless, framed by dark brows and ink-black lashes. The pupils were strange, not round but slightly elongated and very large. Kate concentrated on the bright points of light directly in the center. Moments passed. She ached with weariness. Maura's eyes appeared larger now. The grayness was all around her like ocean mist. The walls receded and the fire disappeared. Images appeared before her, dark shapes carrying garlands and baskets, an enormous bonfire, a tall man with green eyes and a much younger Maura dressed in a white gown with her hair hanging down her back. There was music and laughter, drinking and dancing. Around and around, the dancers moved, faster and faster, the colors and bodies a swirling blur. Kate's stomach churned. The sensations were too rich, too real. "Stop!" she cried out, twisting away, dropping her head into her arms. "Please, stop."

The music and color disappeared. Kate lifted her head. She was here, in a firelit room covered with a soft blanket. Maura was seated once again in her chair.

"Are you all right?" she asked when it appeared that Kate was once more in control of herself.

"Yes."

She stood up. "In that case, I'll bring the soup."

She returned carrying a tray with brown bread, a glass of dark ale and a bowl of thick meaty broth with vegetables. "There's more, if you like. Eat slowly and your stomach will settle." She set the tray down on a low stool beside the couch.

"Thank you," said Kate. "Will you eat with me?"

The corners of Maura's mouth turned up slightly. For an American, Kate Sutherland was exceptionally well mannered. "I'll eat later," she replied. "First, I must ask how long you've had the Gift?"

Kate swallowed her mouthful of hot soup, savoring the trail of heat that warmed a path from her chest to her stomach. "The Gift?" she asked when she could speak again. "What do you mean?"

"Your ability to read the thoughts of others."

Kate looked stricken. She swallowed and her hands shook. Carefully, she placed her spoon in the soup and returned the bowl to the stool. "How did you know about that?"

"My memory was reflected in your eyes."

"Is that all it was, a memory?"

Maura's face was very grave. "Memories and how we use them are everything."

Kate hesitated. "Do you see what I do?"

Like shutters, Maura's eyes went blank. "No."

"Then how can you help me?"

Again, Maura smiled. "You're quite presumptuous, you know. I haven't said I would."

"But you're interested. I can tell you are."

"I admit, you've piqued my curiosity."

"Then you'll do it?" Kate held her breath. Maura Sutherland was most likely the closest she would come to her past.

The woman stood up and walked to the fire. Picking up a poker, she pushed the black lump of peat farther back into the hearth. "I'll try to help you, but I've limitations. It is you who will determine how far we go." Replacing the poker, she turned to look at Kate. Her darkened shape framed by flickering firelight was tall and slim and formidable. "You have a powerful gift, but you must also have imagination and a mind that is free. Only a very few from the outside are able to touch other dimensions."

Despite the fire and the warm coziness of the room, a chill worked its way up Kate's spine. "You mean the dimension of time, don't you?"

Maura looked surprised. "Very good. I didn't expect that."

"I've seen faces and heard voices that have no place in the present. It wasn't a hard conclusion to reach."

Maura's smile was tinged with sympathy. "Well then, Kate Sutherland, rest for tonight, and tomorrow we'll begin."

❧ 8 ❧

Kate finished the rest of her ale and leaned back on the pillow, savoring the warm glow of the peat fire and the slightly tipsy feeling brought on by the amber liquid. Not only was Maura Sutherland reticent about her abilities, she discounted most of them. Still, she had agreed to help, whatever that meant.

Tenderly, Kate touched the bandage on her head. Her lids felt unusually heavy. Who was the little girl on the path and why had she called her Cat? Maura had denied that any children lived in the area, yet the girl was too young to be far from home. It was so confusing. She wondered what Niall was doing tonight and if he had gone back to see the portrait of Catriona Wells at Holyrood Palace. Images were coming quickly, too quickly to sort them into a semblance of order.

Kate fought to stay awake, to focus her mind on a single thought. A draft blew into the room and, with it, the clean, salty smell of the ocean. Pulling the blanket over her shoulders, she buried her head in the soft wool. She didn't want to dream, not until she had the answers she'd come for. But the message from her brain to her eyelids didn't compute. She was so very tired. Colors swirled in a myriad of patterns and merged into a single bright light, clear as day.

Cat stamped her foot impatiently. The tingling feeling in her soles and arches was not unpleasant, but it reminded her of how long she had waited. Her entire body felt cramped. The next time, she thought resentfully, Janet could plead her own cause. What could possibly be taking so long? She strained her ears. Through the curtained doorway, Patrick MacKendrick's voice was too low to be heard.

Finally she was allowed to enter. Patrick was alone, seated behind a large desk. Her heart pounded. It was one thing to hatch a scheme in the privacy of her bedchamber. It was quite another to carry it out under the merciless gray eyes of this legend of the borders.

"Greetings m'lord."

"Greetings," the MacKendrick replied courteously. His face was serious, his eyes fixed on the sketch in his hands.

Cat looked at the ground. For some inexplicable reason she found it difficult to make her request. If only she could represent herself as she truly was, without the shadow of Henry of England hanging over her head.

"Lady Janet sends her regards, sir," she began.

Patrick MacKendrick looked up and grinned. His face was relaxed. He wore a white shirt with full sleeves. The brown hands were long, well shaped, and battle-scarred. Once again, Cat noticed the missing third finger on his left hand.

"So, you come for Janet. What of yourself, Catriona?" he teased. "Do you also bring regards, or do you still seek to sharpen your claws on my throat?" When he smiled he looked years younger.

Cat flushed, recalling Janet's tirade when she learned she must ask permission of this man to attend the crowning. "My lady would like to attend the coronation of His Majesty at Scone on the twenty-fourth of the month," she said.

"An innocent enough request," Patrick replied thoughtfully. "Is there anything else the Lady Janet asks?" The courteous appeal did not sound at all like Janet.

"No, my lord." Cat lifted her head and looked directly into his eyes. "Mary and I also wish to attend the coronation." She wet her lips. "Janet wishes to proceed to Methven after the ceremony."

The MacKendrick lifted curious eyes to Cat's face. He was silent for a long time. "Do you and Mary Gordon wish to travel with her?"

"No," Cat whispered.

She felt a presence behind her. Someone had stepped into the room. It was the king. She dropped to her knees.

The MacKendrick started to rise, but Jamie shook his head. "Be seated," he ordered.

"Your cousins wish to attend the coronation, Your Grace," Patrick explained. "After the ceremony, Lady Janet wishes to proceed to Methven."

Jamie's eyes held a mocking glitter as they raked the slender figure kneeling before him. "What of yourself, my lady? Do you also wish to proceed to Methven after the ceremony? Speak, Catriona."

Cat's throat was very dry. "No, Your Grace. Only Janet."

With a measured stare, James surveyed his cousin. Cat worked to control the trembling of her hands.

Unexpectedly, the king nodded. "Tell my cousin she has my permission to go where she wishes. Tell her also that she is a fool."

Cat's hands were cold as ice. She remained on her knees. "I thank you, Your Grace, for myself and for Lady Janet."

"Rise, lass. She awaits your answer with bated breath." The king grinned. "She will live to regret it, but Janet was always difficult."

With a sigh of relief, Cat rose to her feet. Patrick MacKendrick watched as she turned her back on the king and walked out of the room. He wondered if she had ever turned her back in Henry Tudor's presence.

James waited until Cat had left the room. He walked to a chair by the window and sat down. "Why would Janet send Cat to speak for her?" he mused. "And where is the man who claims to be her secretary?" He looked at Patrick. "Have you met the lad?"

Patrick's eyes narrowed. He had his own suspicions about Catriona's lackey. "His name is Andrew," he explained briefly. "They traveled together from Henry's court."

"Perhaps," Jamie said, "and perhaps not. What is not clear is why Catriona Wells needs a secretary."

The MacKendrick tightened his hand around his glass of ale. "Does she read?" he asked casually.

"Aye," Jamie replied. "She reads and writes with a passion that puts even the monks to shame. I would keep my eye on her, Patrick."

Smiling grimly, Patrick nodded. He drained his glass in one long draught. God's bones! Why should the fact that he had no learning bother him so? Reading and writing were a gentleman's luxuries he could ill afford. During his childhood there had been no time for such indulgences. Staying alive had taken every ounce of his concentration.

While Catriona Wells learned her letters in the safety of her English manor, he had crawled through peat bogs, slippery with the blood of his parents, keeping himself from starvation on the raw flesh of small animals skewered with his sword. He had seen his castle burned, his mother disemboweled and his father's head adorn the pike of an English castle. The tortured grimace of Ian MacKendrick's twisted features had forever after haunted his dreams.

Early on Patrick had come to terms with his life. He expected nothing but what he earned for himself. Childhood was short on the borders. By the age of fourteen his battle cry, "To me, a MacKendrick," had rallied thousands of men, leading them on countless victorious raids, burning and pillaging, avenging the atrocities committed by the hated English. The third finger of his left hand had been paid in forfeit for a single moment of negligence.

His persistence had been well rewarded. Next to the king, no other man in all of Scotland held more power than Patrick MacKendrick. His lands stretched from Edinburgh to Glasgow. The security of the nation was in his hands and, just recently, Jamie had sweetened the pot once again by awarding Patrick the wardenship of the border.

Why then did the gap between himself and the bewitching green-eyed English lass seem to loom wider than ever?

Patrick looked up when he felt the king's hand on his shoulder. It was late afternoon and the room was hazy with shadows.

"There are those who rebel against me, Patrick," Jamie said bluntly. "After the coronation there will be no merry-making. We will seek them out and destroy the leaders."

"Where is this rebellion to take place?" the MacKendrick asked casually.

"To the north," answered the king. "At Methven."

Patrick smiled, but his eyes were cold. Now he understood Cat's nervousness. But why had she not asked to accompany Janet Kennedy on her journey to the north? What did she seek to accomplish while all the king's men were putting down this ill-timed rebellion?

A pearl-like dawn lay over the land, but already there was the promise of unseasonable heat. The MacKendrick left Edinburgh at first light. With an escort of thirty men, he rode through the town of Perth on his way to the coronation site at Scone. People stared as he rode by on a large black stallion, his eyes fixed on the road before him. Ignoring the looks and occasional cheers, he rode swiftly, his mind on the events that would follow the crowning.

A thousand men with weapons and cannon had been sent ahead to camp in the hills above Scone, a small force but enough to defeat the traitors. After the ceremony the king would ride north. Later, Patrick would follow. First he must attend to the small matter of Catriona Wells.

Unwittingly, she had given him the opportunity he waited for. He would have something to hold over her head, something that would change the arrogant disdain in those feline green eyes to fear and, in time, to something else entirely. He had never before wanted a woman he couldn't have, but he had never wanted a woman of the likes of Lady Catriona Wells.

The MacKendrick was not born to wealth and he held no hereditary title. Ten years before he had ridden out of Hailes to foster with the earl of Dumferline. Everything he now had, he had earned. His wealth and influence were as secure as the royal standard that soared above the heights of Scone Castle.

Patrick knew he reached high, higher than he had a right to expect. In normal times, no king would countenance a match between a border lord of Hailes and the Royal House of Stewart. But these were not normal times. Jamie had made him an earl. He had given him Hermitage Castle.

Patrick envisioned his servants grading the fields and setting in place the diamond panes of glass ordered from France. It was a home worthy of a countess. He had made a dreadful mistake in his first marriage. He would not make another.

Patrick felt unusually lighthearted. Soon he would see her

CATRIONA

and then he would go into battle. The idea energized him.
He must keep his mind clear. It would be a private battle
between the two of them that could have only one outcome.
He would win. He always won. But first, there was the
coronation.

Jamie would no longer be an uncrowned king, and then
the rest of Scotland would be conquered. As it stood, only
the Lowlands and the borders could be counted as loyal.
The Highlanders, notorious for their haughty disregard for
royal edicts, remained stubbornly aloof.

Before him lay the Tay, still as glass in the sunlight.
Patrick caught his breath, awed by the sheer beauty of his
country. Brilliant flowers covered the hills. Through the
trees he could make out the rooftops of the town of Perth. It
should not be this way at all. The unnatural quiet disturbed
him. There should be dancing and drinking this day. Wine
and ale should run free in the streets and the sounds of
laughter and celebration abound. Candles should be lit and
Masses said for a glorious beginning to a new reign. Instead,
in the north, there would be death. The bards would sing of
a reign that began in bloodshed. Patrick tightened his lips.
No matter. He was accustomed to the sight of blood.

He reached Scone an hour later. After washing away his
dirt in a small retiring room in the castle, he took his
position on the battlements. Jamie would arrive soon. But it
was not the king for whom he waited.

At last she came, with her cousins and the Highland
Gordons. Her head was up and her shoulders back. He
thought only of Cat, immediately dismissing Janet Kennedy
from his mind. She was Glenkirk's problem, and from the
looks of it, the Hepburn would have no easy time taming his
rebellious filly.

Twelve men carrying royal standards, the silver pelican of
the Stewarts glittering on the backs of their cloaks, galloped
on either side of Catriona. Patrick felt a deep, overwhelming surge of pride as his eyes drank in the sight of her. She
was beautiful, and she rode as if the horse were a part of her.

His fingers tightened on his sword hilt as he saw the man
called Andrew riding beside her. Turning abruptly, he
strode down the stairs.

Cat reined in at the same moment he reached her side. Ignoring him, she looked to Andrew to help her dismount.

The lad hesitated, saw the blazing anger in the MacKendrick's eyes and backed away.

Patrick's hands encircled Catriona's slim waist. Cat, furious at the presumption, lifted her whip. Amazed, she saw the gray eyes light with amusement.

"Don't do it, lass," he warned.

Reluctantly, she lowered her arm. "I've no intention of giving you an excuse to complain of my behavior to Jamie," she replied smugly.

Still smiling, he lifted her from the saddle and set her on the ground, keeping his hands at her waist. For a long moment, he stared down at her, saying nothing.

Her hair, blue-black in the sunlight and plaited with gold ribbons, hung past her knees. She wore green velvet trimmed with ermine, and under the winged brows her eyes glowed like a Highland glen in summer.

Cat met his gaze fearlessly. She could smell the soapy scent of his skin. He was always so clean, she thought irrelevantly, her senses sharpened by his nearness. She noticed the hint of black under the clean shaven jaw and the beat of his pulse in the brown line of his throat. His hair was neither brown nor red, but a shade somewhere in between. It shone like streaked mahogany in the summer sunlight.

Under the heavy velvet of her gown, her skin felt hot where he touched her. Her eyes strayed to his mouth. His lips were thin and chiseled. She knew he wanted her. It was a heady feeling. What would it feel like to press her mouth against those lips? She trembled and his hands tightened. He grinned and color stained her cheeks.

She pulled away irritably. Sweet Mary, she thought, fanning herself with her hand. It was almost as if he could read her thoughts.

"Shall we find a place?" He held out his arm and nodded toward Moot Hill.

Cat nodded. The air was still and hot. A crowd of silent nobles had gathered. She moved quickly to the front. Because her mother was sister to a king, her place was near Janet and Mary. She looked warningly at the man by her side, but he kept her hand in a firm grip.

The coronation site was filled with border nobility. Lord Home was there and the Lords Grey and Douglass. Behind her were Fleming and Drummond, their faces serious as befitted the occasion. Before the coronation they had traveled back to their lands for a boot full of dirt to pour on Moot Hill, a traditional gesture proclaiming their loyalty to the newly crowned king.

The Highland clans were absent, hidden in their mountain strongholds, protesting the injustice of this outrage against their rightful monarch. Argyll of Inveraray was the only man present born north of the Grampians.

All thoughts fled from Cat's mind as James exited the castle. He strode purposefully to the top of the hill where the archbishop and the laird of the Ancient House of Fife waited. Dressed in velvet and fur, he walked to the rise and knelt. The bishop, looking like a peacock in his colored robes, chanted the litany. Jamie's replies were firm and clear.

Tears gathered in Cat's eyes. She blinked them away. The lad she had known was now a king, and honesty forced her to admit that he looked the part. The priest handed him the scepter. Sunlight glinted off the metal and settled on the jewels in his golden crown.

Cat closed her eyes and swayed slightly. She had eaten nothing all day. The MacKendrick slipped his arm around her waist and she leaned against him.

The ceremony was over. Well-wishers surged forward to pay their respects as Patrick led her through a side door to the chapel garden. "Why are we here?" she asked.

Patrick's hand rested on the crown of her hair. When he spoke his voice was low and reassuring. "You were faint and needed air."

"Jamie is the king of Scotland?"

"Aye, lass. Scotland has a new king."

She lifted her head and stepped back. Immediately he dropped his arms and regarded her with a thoughtful look. He was relieved to see that the color was back in her cheeks.

"Where do you go now?" she asked suddenly.

His eyes narrowed. "I go with Jamie to Methven. There is rumor of an uprising there."

She nodded, surprising him with her next statement. "Janet goes there also, to warn them."

"The Lady Kennedy is a fool," he replied. "She will be punished."

Cat's eyes widened until he felt he could drown in the warmth of their golden lights. "I would risk a favor of you, sir."

"Ask it."

"Let no harm come to my cousin." She caught her bottom lip between her teeth. Pleading did not come easily to her.

Patrick stared at her for a long moment. At last he spoke. "'Tis Glenkirk you should ask. He is the one she endangers by her misplaced loyalty."

Her hand clutched his sleeve. She smelled of roses. "He will not help her," Cat persisted. "He cares only for what she can bring him. Please, sir. Janet is not part of this. She goes merely to warn them."

She was very close, her mouth inches from his own. Blood pounded through his veins but still he held back, denying himself. He wondered why. She thought him an uncouth Scot, a barbarian, a commoner with no learning and few manners. He would prove her right.

Reaching out, he drew her, unresisting, into his arms. Twisting her hair through his fingers, he forced her head back and looked down into her face. It was a haughty face, saved from coldness by her lush mouth and small, firm chin. Tiny blue veins shone faintly beneath the clear ivory of her skin.

He traced the thin, high-bridged nose and carven cheeks with gentle fingers. Her eyes, a cool clear green, held nothing but curiosity.

They were so close they shared the same breath and still he waited, holding himself back, wondering what it was about her that drew him beyond all rational thought. She was exquisite, with the kind of beauty that came from generations of inbred aristocracy. But it was more than her face that held him captive. It was her courage and the graceful confidence of her body when she moved that first attracted him.

He had never known a woman to have such pride. His

eyes lingered on her mouth. It was the mouth of a courtesan, full and wide, its throat-tightening seduction made for a man. He cursed fluently. He, Patrick MacKendrick, known for his silver-tongued charm, wanted this far more than she did. Bending his head, he succumbed to temptation and set his mouth against the promise of her lips.

Something deep within her sensed his desperation. Her lips parted and she relaxed against the uncompromising strength of his body.

Patrick deepened his kiss, his hands moving over her in the instinctive manner of a ritual more dangerous, more satisfying, and older than time.

Cat froze. His touch, exciting at first, changed to something long repressed and hauntingly familiar. It was dark and ugly and had no place in this peaceful sanctuary a mere stone's throw from the house of God. Fear began in the pit of her stomach, sending tremors of clammy coldness through the pathways of her body. Pushing against him, she broke his kiss and twisted her head away, breathing deeply. She felt his mouth move from the curve of her throat to where her breast swelled over the costly velvet.

Panic drowned out the last of her pleasure. "M'lord," she cried, pushing at him blindly.

Mistaking her fear for passion, Patrick lifted her into the cradle of his hips.

"Please!" she cried.

"I have a name, Cat," he murmured against the side of her neck.

"Stop," she gasped, fighting his strength and her terror.

"Say my name."

Cat stiffened and pulled back, but the persistent pressure of his hand in her hair held her securely against him.

"Say it," he demanded.

"Patrick!" she sobbed, clutching at his hair. The silky straightness slid through her fingers. "Have mercy!"

Patrick frowned. She sounded hysterical. He lifted his head, his breathing ragged. Her eyes were wild with terror. Cursing in Gaelic, he tucked her head against his shoulder and held her still until her tremors subsided.

Long moments passed. She shifted in his arms. He

brushed her cheek with his hand and felt the heat of her skin. Her shame angered him. Deliberately, he set out to spark her temper. "'Tis hardly the place for lovemaking."

Her fear evaporated. Pulling out of his embrace, Cat turned her back, embarrassed to face him. "What we shared can hardly be called love," she snapped.

Turning her around, he lifted her chin, forcing her to look at him. "What would you call it, lass?"

"'Tis plain enough," she muttered. "You want me the way Glenkirk wants Janet. The only difference is that he is willing to wed her for it."

He frowned, wishing he could read her thoughts. "If marriage is what you want," he said gravely, "I can arrange it."

Her eyes were shuttered. "Your conceit knows no bounds, sir. A marriage between us is impossible. My husband will be an earl, at least."

He considered telling her of his newly acquired title and then decided against it. She would know soon enough, and he had a perverse wish to make her forget her pride and admit she wanted him for himself.

Suddenly he grinned, and Cat felt the familiar weakness in her knees. The man had the smile of a sorcerer. It was a heady feeling to watch the lean planes of his face soften into gentleness. For a brief moment she wished she were someone other than Lady Catriona Wells and free to give her hand where she pleased.

"Stranger things have happened," he said gently. "There is no shame in following your heart."

She took a deep breath, holding back the words struggling to escape her lips. It would do no good to antagonize him. His promise was still not secured.

"Will you see that Janet is safe?" she persisted.

Patrick looked up at the sky and frowned. Already he had wasted too much time.

"Glenkirk will see to her," he replied. "Are you blind, lass? No harm will come to Janet Kennedy. The man loves her to distraction." The gray eyes glinted with laughter. "Why else would he ask to wed a she-cat from hell?"

Her eyes darkened dangerously. Before she could reply, Patrick lifted her hand and removed the velvet glove.

Pressing his lips to her palm, he kept his eyes on her face. Her expression revealed nothing, but at the touch of his mouth, she trembled. Satisfied, he released her and walked out of the garden into the street. If his instincts were correct, he had not seen the last of Catriona Wells this day. He would wager everything he owned that she would take advantage of the king's absence.

In his mind, Patrick could see the paneled room that served as the royal study at Stirling Castle. He knew every inch of the massive desk piled high with personal correspondence addressed to the king of Scotland. His mouth hardened. Catriona would not find it as empty as she had expected.

Stirling Castle, the home of Scottish kings since the twelfth century, was a sprawling fortress of round Norman towers, gatehouses and musty turrets. Patrick MacKendrick, climbing the narrow steps to the study where the king conducted the business of state, cursed under his breath. The mismatched jumble of rooms had already caused him to twice miss his turn. It grew late. The guards would soon follow, and he was needed at Methven. Suddenly he stopped, his ears tuned to the sound of human voices.

Flattening himself against the wall, he moved silently to the door and peered inside. Two figures, one obviously a woman, were rifling through the papers on the massive oak desk. The man walked behind the table, his boyish features illuminated by candlelight.

Patrick recognized Andrew Percy immediately. His jaw clenched. Although he would have staked his life that Cat's reasons for leaving England were not what she claimed, it was daunting to have her deception proven beyond all doubt.

Nudging the door open with his toe, he slipped inside, completely hidden by the shadows. Crossing his arms, he leaned against the wall and watched.

"We must find something, Andrew." Cat's whisper held traces of desperation. "Sweet Mary, I'll not be stuck in this accursed country forever."

"Don't lose hope, Cat," the boy replied, leafing through piles of parchment. "Henry can't fault you for what isn't here."

Patrick's eyes blazed at the familiar address. His instincts had been correct: Andrew was no servant.

"Henry can do anything he pleases," Cat snapped, turning to face her companion. "News of Perkin Warbeck's existence isn't enough. I must learn what Jamie plans to do with him."

"What makes you think you'll find it here?" Andrew waved his arm to include the entire desk.

Cat bit her lip, conscious of the time that would be wasted in explanation. "Margaret of Burgundy believes in Warbeck's claim. She must have proof we are unaware of. Somewhere on this desk lies her letter. If I could bring that to Henry, surely he would find favor with me and allow Richard's claim to Ravenswood."

Andrew clasped her shoulders. "Think of it, Cat. This miserable waiting will be over and we can return to England." His face glowed. She didn't answer and he placed his hand under her chin, forcing her to look at him. "You do want to go home, don't you, Cat?"

"Of course, Andrew," she said lightly, kissing his cheek. "There is nothing else I would rather do. Surely you know that."

He hesitated. "Sometimes I wonder. You've been different lately."

She thought of the lean, harsh face of Patrick MacKendrick. Guilt consumed her. In an effort to reassure Andrew, she slipped her arm in his. "Don't be silly. Nothing has changed. All I want is to be done with this and return to England." She rested her head against his shoulder.

Andrew pulled her into the circle of his embrace.

The MacKendrick had seen enough. He stepped out of the shadows. "A moving scene," he said, his voice laced with sarcasm. "A reasonable man might wonder why you chose the king's study for your tryst, but no doubt you'll have an explanation."

With a sense of doom, Cat pulled out of Andrew's embrace and turned to face her accuser. Wetting her lips, she lifted her chin, determined to brazen it out.

"Good day, sir," she said, greeting him as if nothing were unusual. "I had thought you would be halfway to Methven by now. Surely the king is in need of your services."

"It appears the greater need was here." The icy voice chilled her blood.

Patrick noticed Andrew's hand inching toward the dirk at his belt and thought better of him for it. The boy was no coward. "I'd not attempt it, lad," he warned. " 'Twould be difficult to explain were Jamie to return and find a man beheaded in his private study."

Andrew flushed and dropped his arm. His hands shook. "What will you do with us?" he demanded.

"That remains to be seen." Patrick kept his eyes on Cat's face. "If you cooperate, perhaps you'll remain in the tolbooth for the next twenty years. Otherwise"—there was a long pause before the deceptively soft voice continued— "you will be executed."

Andrew's face whitened.

The MacKendrick's gaze never left the pale cheeks of the woman before him. He knew she must be terrified, but she showed no fear. He wondered, not for the first time, how a lady born of royal blood and raised in abundant wealth had become so skilled at hiding her emotions.

Footsteps sounded at the door. Cat's eyes widened as the guards materialized before her. "Are we under arrest?" she asked in disbelief.

"You are," replied the MacKendrick.

"I?" She threw him a contemptuous glance and laughed.

Patrick fought the quick surge of admiration that burned in his chest. She was magnificent. She was also a spy. Her actions had proven it beyond all doubt, and yet she stood before him as arrogant and unafraid as if *he* were the accused.

"Take him," he ordered the guards, gesturing toward Andrew.

They hastened to do his bidding. When the room was cleared of all but the two of them, Patrick turned back to Cat.

"He did little to protect you," he said at last.

"I need no protection," she replied. "Andrew and I knew the stakes from the beginning."

Patrick banished from his thoughts the man who had dared lay hands on the woman he wanted for his own. He looked at her now. She stood very still, waiting for his next move. The only indication of her feelings was the tightly clenched fists pressed against the velvet folds of her gown.

"Come with me," he said at last.

With a brief nod, she moved to the door, assuming she would precede him. In two strides he was beside her, linking her arm through his. Quickly they walked through the corridor and down the narrow stairway.

Two mounts, saddled and ready for travel, their bridles rattling as they snorted and pawed the ground, were surrounded by an escort of twenty men, also on horseback. Cat noticed they were heavily armed. She lifted questioning eyes to the MacKendrick's face.

"Where are you taking me?"

"To Methven," he answered shortly. "The ride will be hard. You'll not be spared."

"I would prefer the tolbooth, m'lord." She pulled her arm out of his grasp.

A light flared in his eyes. For a moment she feared he was angry, but he merely shrugged.

"Your preferences are no longer of any concern, m'lady," he said softly. "You are a prisoner of the crown."

"Then treat me as one," she demanded. "I would rather be imprisoned than spend another hour in your loathsome presence."

He leaned close to her ear, his breath whispering against her cheek. "This is only the beginning, lass," he murmured. "Before another fortnight has passed you will beg for my company." He rested his fingertips on her throat. The sudden leap of her pulse reassured him. He smiled. She was more affected by his touch than she cared to admit. Without another word, he lifted her into his arms and carried her to the waiting horse.

The distance they traveled was not great, but the conditions of the roads made the journey difficult. At pounding speeds, they rode north into the Highlands, making their way through small villages and over twisting, deeply rutted footpaths. It wasn't until late afternoon that the turrets of Lothian Castle appeared in the distance. Cat was exhausted when they finally rode into the courtyard.

The king was astride his horse and the fight was over. Heads, separated from their bodies, lay at his feet and the entire south side of the castle was in ruins. Most of the rebels were dead, and a white flag fluttered from the castle ramparts. Cannon holes had decimated the walls so that Cat could see directly into the great hall. A curving stairway led to what had once been tower bedchambers.

The sun slid behind the hills, leaving the courtyard steeped in shadow. The men on horseback were silent as two figures, one a man the other a woman, made their way down the stone stairway, stepping over the debris into the courtyard.

Cat sat on her horse as if carved from stone. With her heart in her mouth she watched Alexander Hepburn, earl of Glenkirk, place his hand on her cousin's shoulder and force her into a kneeling position before the king.

Janet shrugged off his touch and looked into the dark eyes that continued to haunt her dreams. "Your Majesty," she said.

Cat held her breath as the king appraised his kinswoman from head to toe as if he didn't know what to do with her. She prayed that Janet would hold her tongue.

"Lady Kennedy." His voice was unusually gentle. "You bring no honor to your lord."

Janet was very lovely and Cat remembered that she had been Jamie's first love. She hoped he remembered it as well.

"He is not yet my lord, Your Grace," Janet replied sweetly.

"We can remedy that." James grinned. "What say you,

Glenkirk? Shall I wish you joy of your untamed filly? She can hardly do you more harm than she has already done. Perhaps marriage will calm her. That is, if you still want her."

Glenkirk's dark face became even darker as the red color stained his cheekbones. "Aye," he said gruffly. "I still want her."

"So be it!" James pronounced. "The wedding will be at the end of the week." He looked around at the blood and destruction and then at the ashen faces of his prisoners. "God's wounds," he swore, "we could all use a bit of celebration." Turning his horse, he lifted his hand. "I'm for Stobhall. Is your bonny daughter still unmarried, Murdoch?" he shouted back at the man flanking his left side.

"Which daughter?" Lord Drummond asked.

"The Lady Margaret."

Cat watched Drummond wet his lips. Maggie was betrothed to the laird of MacIain. The wedding would take place in the spring at the MacIain stronghold of Ardnamurchan.

"Maggie is promised, Your Grace," Murdoch Drummond replied. "The settlements have already been agreed upon." His words, carried away by the wind, did not reach the king's ears.

Cat knew it wouldn't matter anyway. For Jamie Stewart, a woman's honor, a betrothal promise, was a trifling inconvenience to be dispensed with at the royal whim. Deliberately, she quelled her thoughts. Maggie Drummond was not her concern. It would go much easier for the lass to acknowledge this honor, an honor that would bring her father land and titles.

Her mouth tightened bitterly. Jamie Stewart had a way with women but he was easily bored. Maggie's red hair and dark eyes were magnificent. Half the men at court were in love with her. Not until young Douglas MacIain, handsome and enormously wealthy, had offered Maggie his love as well as his name, had Murdoch Drummond consented to give away his youngest child. Cat had the sinking sensation that the rebels of Methven would not be the only casualties of Scotland's new regime.

She turned her attention to the earl of Glenkirk and watched as he breathed a sigh of relief before turning to face his betrothed. Janet was staring at him. Defiance shone in her set expression and in the stiff, ramrod straightness of her spine.

Forgetting her own desperate plight, Cat stifled a giggle. Her cousin would drive Glenkirk to distraction. Janet believed her Stewart blood made her invincible. How had it come to pass that a man as steeped in convention as the Hepburn was cursed to love a woman with more arrogance than any knight of the realm? Janet had been a law unto herself since Kennedy's death. She would never again be dominated by a man.

Alexander Hepburn struggled to control his temper. It would hardly help his cause if he embarrassed his betrothed in front of her cousin and the MacKendrick. "That was a close one, lass," he said at last. "Do not expect the king to show such mercy again."

Janet lifted her head. "I'm not afraid of Jamie Stewart."

"Then you are a fool," he said bluntly, moving to stand before her. "If you've no concern for your own life, think of those who would mourn your loss."

"They would survive. My family is familiar with suffering."

He reached out, his large hands clasping her shoulders in a desperate grip. "What of me? Do you care nothing at all for my feelings?"

Her eyes widened, and for the space of a heartbeat Cat thought she recognized something raw and deeply personal in the golden depths. Then it was gone.

"No," Janet said shortly, "I care nothing for you at all."

Stepping nearer, Alexander shook her slightly. "You lie, Janie Gordon. You are not as indifferent as you say." He bent his head, brushing his mouth against hers. Her lips parted and clung to his. Mindful of his audience, the Hepburn reluctantly ended the kiss. Rubbing his thumb along the smooth line of her cheek, he whispered, "Soon this waiting will be over and we'll take our pleasure in more private surroundings."

Janet pulled out of his arms, the color flooding her

cheeks. Shaken by her unexpected response, she had forgotten Cat. The soft nickering of a horse brought her mind back to the present. Her cousin, mounted on an enormous dun-colored stallion, had obviously ridden to Methven with the border lord.

Frowning, Janet pulled her cloak tightly around her and walked to the side of Cat's mount. Laying her hand on the warm flank, she spoke quietly. "Is everything well with you, Cat?"

Cat blinked back tears. The concern in that quiet voice rocked her composure as had nothing else on this ill-fated day. Resting her hand on the golden head beside her, she smiled fondly. Even as a child Janet had been tremendously loyal, refusing to countenance treachery in anyone she loved. Despite the suspicious appearance of her escort, she knew Janet would never believe she had been betrayed by one of her own blood. "I'm under arrest," Cat replied shortly.

"On what charge?" Janet demanded.

Cat looked over at the MacKendrick. His features were hard and very cold, as if immortalized in the timeless perfection of marble. She shrugged. "I know not."

"The charge is treason." Patrick MacKendrick's arctic voice challenged her. "Do you deny it, Lady Wells?"

Green eyes flashing, Cat lifted her head defiantly. "I deny nothing."

He smiled in grim satisfaction. "Bid your cousin farewell. 'Tis past time for us to be on our way."

The words she would have spoken stopped at the lump in her throat. With shining eyes, Cat squeezed Janet's hand and turned her mount to follow her captor.

Janet's clear voice rang out. "Stop, Sir Patrick!"

The borderer did not turn around, but Cat could see the stiffness in his shoulders as he pulled in his mount.

"If my cousin is harmed, I will find you, Border Lord. You will pay dearly for daring to lay hands on a Stewart." The threat floated on the wind and disappeared into the mists rising over the loch.

Spurring his horse, Patrick led his riders across the courtyard and through the trees, instinctively finding the narrow pony path that led to Edinburgh Castle. His thoughts were not on the journey before him. Janet Gordon's curse weighed heavily on his mind. Fortunately he was not a superstitious man or he might have had second thoughts concerning the fate of his lovely prisoner.

The MacKendrick reached up to lift the helmet from his head. After eight long, bone-weary hours, they were here, in the stone courtyard of Edinburgh Castle. Deep in a trench carved out below the portcullis, caged lions paced back and forth, roaring at the smell of fresh meat. Torches burned at the entrance, flooding the weary travelers with welcome light.

Patrick wrinkled his nose against the stench of refuse rising from the moat. Garbage and entrails from the kitchens, waste from the chamberpots and gardyloos, dead animals and even an occasional human body floated in its murky depths. Anyone unlucky enough to fall into the poisonous cesspool would suffer an untimely death.

Turning in his saddle, he looked back at Catriona Wells. Not once during the entire journey had she complained of the pace or demanded food and drink. She expected no deference for her rank although the men, out of consideration for her sex, offered to share their meager rations.

Patrick smiled grimly. Cat's eyes were half closed and she looked ready to faint from exhaustion, but her back was as stiff and unyielding as it had been in the courtyard of Lothian Castle. Dismounting, he strode to her horse and lifted her to the ground. Too tired to protest, she swayed slightly, righted herself and looked up at the tower. There were bars on the small recessed windows.

"Come with me," Patrick ordered.

She nodded. Arguing would avail her nothing. Gathering up her skirts, she followed him past his apartments and up another flight of stairs into a small room in the north turret of the castle. He kicked the door shut with his foot and leaned against it.

Cat looked around. The fire was prepared and the room was unusually comfortable for its size. The floor was completely carpeted and the ten-foot-thick walls were paneled with the finest sandalwood. No drafts would find their way past the fur-lined tapestries. Dropping her cloak on the floor, Cat walked to the hearth and lit the fire. The room was very small. Deep in the pit of her stomach she could feel the familiar nausea take root. Goose bumps erupted on her arms. Whirling around, she faced her captor.

"I would have food and drink," she demanded, "and water for a bath."

He smiled lazily. "You shall have your bath, but first we sup together."

Cat breathed a sigh of relief. He didn't mean to leave her alone after all. She looked around at the furnishings. A massive bed, enclosed in heavy draperies, dominated the room. Her eyes met his.

She threw back her head, contempt lacing her words. "You are as weary as I and in no mood for ravishing."

Patrick laughed. "Your innocence is refreshing. No man is ever too tired for that."

"I will not be forced." Despite her brave words, her voice shook.

His eyes, the color of pewter in the candlelight, boldly appraised her. "I've no liking for rape," he said softly. "When I take you, lady, it will not be by force."

Her mouth fell open. He hadn't touched her or moved one step nearer, but she felt raw and exposed, as if her flesh were thinner somehow and all her nerves on fire. Wetting her lips, she opened her mouth to speak.

A loud knock sounded at the door and she left the words unsaid.

A servant entered bearing ale, a flask of wine, a joint of meat and two loaves of white bread.

"Would you have me stay and serve you, sir?" the maid asked.

"No, lass." The MacKendrick looked first at Catriona and then winked at the maid. "Her ladyship wishes to be alone with me."

Cat flushed with anger. The man's arrogance knew no bounds. She waited until the serving woman left the room. "Was that necessary?" she demanded, her eyes narrow and very green.

"Your temper needs improving." The grin on his face deepened the slashing grooves in his cheeks. "I'd not want the wench to bear the brunt of it."

Cat lifted her chin. "I've no wish to serve you or to sup with you."

"How unfortunate." Patrick made no move toward the food. "If you wish to eat," he said gently, "you will learn to obey me."

Cat stamped her foot, her expression mutinous.

He straightened and took one step forward.

"No!" She held out her hand to stop him. "I'll eat with you as long as you keep your distance."

Patrick nodded. He had won the encounter, and it pleased him to be generous. "I'll not touch you unless you beg me, lass."

Smiling, he pulled out a chair and lowered himself into it. Victory increased his appetite. Cat carved two slices from the meat and poured a glass of ale. She set the plate before him.

"Well done, mistress." His eyes glinted with approval. "You learn quickly."

"All commoners prefer ale," she pronounced, sipping her wine. "I assumed you would as well."

He leaned back in the chair, chewing the tough meat. "Do you delight in insulting everyone or is it me you despise in particular?"

Cat sat down at the table and helped herself to the meat and bread. Jamie's excellent wine was already taking effect. Now that she knew the MacKendrick would not leave her alone she felt relaxed, almost at ease. With her mouth full of food, she considered his question. "I think it is you that brings out the worst in me," she admitted, reaching across the table for his flagon of ale. Draining it completely, she handed it back to him. "I've never met anyone like you."

The gleam in his eyes disturbed her. Hurriedly, she changed the subject. "How did you come to be the king's favorite?"

Patrick poured more ale and drank off the foam from the dripping flagon. "Jamie came to Hermitage almost a full year ago after the English border raid. From Jedburgh to

Castle Douglass there was nothing left but the charred remains of crops and villages." He put his thumb in the butter and smeared it across a piece of bread, offering it to her. She accepted it and their fingers touched. Deliberately, he lifted his hand to his lips and licked away the grease.

Hot color flooded her cheeks. She looked down at her food.

"Jamie knew the raid had taken a greater toll than most," he continued, ignoring her embarrassment. "No family in the borders was spared. I was in Edinburgh for the holidays. My wife stayed at Hermitage."

Startled, Cat looked up again. No one had told her he was married.

"She was near her time and unable to travel," he continued. Only the white line around his lips betrayed his inner turmoil. "The English cut the child from her belly and skewered it with a broadsword."

Cat gasped.

A muscle jumped in his cheek. "I'm told it was a boy."

She pressed her hand to her mouth. "How you must hate us," she whispered, her eyes wide with horror.

He finished his ale and considered her statement. "The English have suffered as well. 'Tis the way of the world when ancient feuds are handed down from one generation to the next. The secret is to be strong. Only when a man fears the strength of another will he allow him to live in peace." He spoke earnestly, as if it was important that she understand. "Jamie Stewart approached me because I alone can hold the borders, while he brings the rest of Scotland to heel." His eyes were brilliant with excitement. " 'Tis a new age, lass, and Jamie is the man to bring us into it. Already he has commissioned the building of ships to compete with Spain's supremacy on the seas. Even Sir Andrew Wood has come around."

Cat bit her lip. Sir Andrew was Scotland's finest seaman. He had been against James but now, with the building of the greatest warships ever to sail the oceans, he would surely pledge his allegiance to Scotland's new king.

"Universities are to be established at Aberdeen and Edinburgh," the MacKendrick continued. "All sons of nobles and freeholders are to receive schooling in mathematics and languages. There is to be judiciary reform and the abolition of the sales taxes. Ambassadors will travel to all the courts of Europe. Have you ever known of such a king?"

His enthusiasm was contagious. Cat was reminded of her brother whenever she brought him an unexpected treat. She imagined the powerful border lord's face were she to tell him he reminded her of a small boy. Her smile widened until she could hold it back no longer and a low, musical laugh burst from her lips.

Patrick stopped in the middle of a sentence, an odd look on his face. It occurred to him that he had never before seen her laugh out loud, and yet he didn't believe she was a woman to brood over her fate. Once again, he wondered how a gently reared lady had acquired such skill in guarding her emotions.

Her parted lips and the soft glow in her eyes reminded him they were alone in the intimacy of her bedchamber. She was very lovely, but seduction was not part of his plan.

"I know now why Jamie trusts you," she said unexpectedly. "If we had met under different circumstances, I too would have liked you very much indeed." She pushed back her chair as if to rise.

His hand shot out, covering hers. "Now, m'lady." He smiled engagingly, but his eyes were hard as flint. "The tables are turned. Tell me why you came to England with a young lord claiming to be your secretary."

"I told you once before—"

"Nay, mistress," he interrupted her. "I know of Henry's queen. Elizabeth of York has a heart like warm butter and would never turn away a relative, no matter how distant."

"Elizabeth does not rule England," Cat snapped. "Her husband does, and his heart does not melt easily."

"There is more to your story, Catriona Wells." Patrick stood up, pulling her with him. "Until your tongue loosens, you will stay here." He released her hand and walked to the door.

"You mean to leave me alone?" she whispered, her hand at her throat.

"Aye, until you come to your senses." He opened the door. "A guard will stay by your chamber and bring you food. You cannot escape. There is no use trying."

"Please"—her voice cracked—"don't leave me."

He frowned. "You are in no danger. The most you will suffer is boredom."

"You don't understand." Tears welled up in her eyes and spilled down her cheeks. "I cannot stay here."

He hadn't expected tears. Nothing in his prior knowledge of Catriona Wells had prepared him for this. Torn by her twisting hands and the unnatural paleness of her cheeks, he hesitated.

"The tolbooth would have been much worse," he said, hardening his heart against her. She was not the innocent she appeared. "The sheets are clean and the food plentiful. Perhaps in time, you'll find the truth is not so difficult after all."

Cat watched him close the door. The lock clicked. For a brief moment, numbness claimed her. And then the walls moved closer. The familiar panic began in her stomach and rose to her throat. Perspiration beaded her forehead. She gagged on the bile coating her tongue. Forcing the terror from her mind, she began to count, willing herself to concentrate, seeking the empty, relieving blackness. Keeping her eyes on the blue tip of the candle flame, she fought her fear, deliberately working to empty her mind of the private demons that allowed no peace.

The shadows deepened and for Cat, alive in a private nightmare, the walls moved nearer. Her cadence wasn't working. Perhaps she had grown lax since arriving in Scotland. For a long time now she had been so careful never to sleep without her maid. Perhaps it was the size of the room that brought on her fear. It was so much smaller than her usual sleeping quarters.

Struggling for air, her senses cried out for escape. She was suffocating in a world of pain and fear and nausea. The terror moved in, reaching for her throat with cloying fingers, blotting out all sight and sound. Shaking with fright, she screamed, again and again, over and over, a primitive unnatural sound that pierced the silent, thick walls of the ancient castle.

❧ 10 ❧

Kate jackknifed into a sitting position and pressed her palms against her pounding chest. Her mouth was painfully dry and her heart thudded against her ribcage in a frightening irregular pattern. Disoriented, she looked around, unable to dredge up the memory of this low-ceilinged room, these walls, the narrow couch that served as her bed, all steeped in the black shadows of predawn, the only light a thin line of glowing peat illuminating the hearth. Dear God, where was she?

On the edge of panic, she fumbled for the end of the blanket. It was twisted around her legs. Frantic to be free of the confining wool, she yanked it out from under her and stood up, breathing heavily, searching the darkness for escape.

A voice, low and soothing, breached the shadows. "You are perfectly safe here, Kate. Nothing can harm you."

Kate turned in the direction of the voice. A figure all in white, with hip-length hair, stood in the doorway.

"Janet?" Kate's lips shaped the name in a sibilant whisper.

"No, child. It isn't Janet." The woman stepped forward into the feeble light of the peat fire.

"Maura? Is that you?"

"Yes."

Dizzy with relief, Kate stumbled to the door and, as naturally as if she'd done it every day of her life, wound her arms around Maura's neck, buried her face against her shoulder and sobbed.

Maura, inexperienced at nurturing, stiffened, waiting for Kate to gather herself. Long minutes passed. Slowly, as if

121

unsure of her welcome, Maura lifted her arms and enfolded the weepy young woman in a tentative embrace. "There, there, child," she murmured against her hair. "It won't be nearly as hard next time. We'll take care of it first thing tomorrow. You'll have your answers soon enough."

"How did you know to come?" Kate's words were muffled and thick with tears.

Maura sighed and stepped back out of Kate's arms. "Magick had nothing to do with it, if that's what you're thinking. It doesn't take a wizard to know that someone with a lump on her head might have a difficult night."

Kate was unconvinced. "Why did you say I'd have my answers soon? How can you possibly know that if there isn't anything supernatural going on?"

Leading Kate back to the couch, Maura fluffed up the pillows and tucked the blanket around her legs. "I didn't rule out the supernatural," she explained quietly. "I merely said it had nothing to do with me."

"I don't understand."

Maura's eyes flashed with the fire of polished diamonds. "I am not a wizard, Kate. I have no power over the past and future. Most of us who follow the earth religions are the same. We can only work with what we are given."

The old familiar hopelessness rose up in Kate's throat. "Then you can't help me after all."

Maura smiled. "Oh, but I can. More than you realize. Everything we need is already here."

"What are you saying?"

"You're very special, Kate Sutherland." Maura spoke slowly, as if explaining an abstract concept to a very young child. "It is you who has the Sight. What you need is someone to show you the way."

"You?"

Maura nodded. "Most definitely, me."

"Then Celia was right. You are powerful."

"No, Kate. You have the power. I have the knowledge. Knowledge can be acquired, power cannot, no matter how much one wants it."

Kate's eyes were haunted and colorless in the semidarkness. "I can't control my dreams," she whispered.

"You will," Maura promised, "if not tomorrow, then very soon after."

"Who is she, the woman who comes to me, the one who has my face?"

Maura's expression was clearly skeptical, as if two halves of her mind were arguing over the answer to Kate's question. Then, without speaking, she leaned over and lifted Kate's feet to make room at the end of the couch. Settling against the cushions, she pulled them back into her lap, stroking the plaid-colored wool absentmindedly. "Have you heard of the twice-born, Kate?"

"No."

Maura sighed. How had a woman like Kate Sutherland, with the magick so strong within her, reached maturity in such ignorance? What kind of parents sheltered a child to the point of danger? Somehow, she had expected more of people with Sutherland blood, even diluted as it was from years spent in America.

"The twice-born are men and women from another time who are unsettled within themselves," Maura explained. "Sometimes it takes more than one lifetime to resolve their conflicts. Sometimes the windows of time open for a later self to step inside and provide help."

A suspicion, terrifying in its absurdity, took shape in Kate's mind. "Are you implying that Catriona Wells and I are the same person?"

"I never imply anything," Maura replied softly. "The truth will come out without my revealing it. More than likely you are no one but yourself. For reasons unknown, Catriona Wells calls to you from the past. There is little you or anyone can do to stop fate."

"In other words, everything is inevitable, our fate sealed at birth no matter what path we choose to take? Isn't that philosophy more suited to a follower of John Knox than Wicca?"

Maura stared at her in surprise. "My goodness. I hope not. He was a dour, dreadful man. Do you know a great deal about John Knox, Kate?"

"Not really. I've read about him, that's all."

"If John Knox is among your choices of reading material, you must read a great deal."

With surprising directness, Kate sliced through the tangent Maura's conversation had taken. "You haven't answered my question. Are you suggesting that I'm at loose ends on this earth because something wasn't settled for someone long ago, in another life?"

"Yes."

The simple statement, unembellished and without disclaimer, somehow made it all the more plausible.

Desperately seeking reassurance, Kate attempted a lightness she didn't feel. "Whatever the problem was, it must have been very important."

Maura's hand, resting on her blanket-covered ankle, tightened. "Make no mistake, Kate. Only something very serious would stalk you across the centuries."

"What if I refused to allow it? What if I just went home and did nothing?"

Maura's answer came quickly, too quickly for Kate to doubt her sincerity. "Your life would be miserable."

"But it would end," Kate persisted. "I can't live forever."

"Silly child." Maura's laugh was soft, indulgent. "Is this how you wish to live your life, afraid of shadows from the past?"

Kate closed her eyes. Tears of fatigue burned the inside of her lids. Embarrassed at her unexpected show of emotion, she turned her face into the blanket. "I'm exhausted," she said, her words muffled by the wool.

"Go to sleep now," Maura soothed her. "You'll be up early. By eight o'clock in the morning the light this far north is too strong for sleep."

A fresh wave of tears rose, pushing the first salty tide over the rims of Kate's eyes and down her cheeks. Should she confess and tell the truth or remain silent? Truth won out. She had nothing to lose. "I'm afraid to sleep," she admitted.

"You poor child, I wouldn't think of leaving you." Maura massaged Kate's feet. "Rest now. You'll have no more dreams tonight."

For reasons she did not attempt to understand, Kate believed her. Gratefully, she pulled the blanket up to her chin and slept.

* * *

Dawn spilled over the Shetlands in waves of charcoal and shadowy blue, streaking the pearly mists like an artist's blended palette. Next came the sun, its white light catching moisture like a prism, fragmenting the colors into a dazzling display of lavender, purple and gold, fading to pink and peach and silver, and finally the cerulean blue of a sky marked by nothing more momentous than a middle-aged sun continuing its timeless orbit across the universe.

Kate woke with a raging headache, the kind that comes with blurred vision and flashing lights and white-lipped, agonizing pain.

"How long have you had migraines?" Maura asked, purposely pitching her voice at a low, soothing level.

Kate moaned and rubbed her temples. "All my life, but lately more than usual."

"Do they follow your visions?"

Kate was beyond reasoning. "I don't think so. I'm not sure." She sensed Maura leave the room. Pressing her palms against her temples, she pushed against the pain. Her Imitrex prescription was in her purse, wherever that was. Where was Maura?

The instant her mind formed the question, she felt the couch give. Maura was back. Cool hands lifted her head from the pillow and held a mug to her lips. The herbal-tasting liquid was barely warm until she swallowed it. Then, searing a path down her throat, it settled in her stomach, producing a healing glow that spread throughout her body. When the warmth reached her head, the pain disappeared.

She sat up warily, unconvinced that it was really gone. "What did you give me?"

Maura smiled. "Nothing serious. Just lady-slipper root and water. It's an herb for headaches."

"Nothing has ever taken effect that quickly before. Why don't doctors know about it?"

"They've known about lady-slipper for hundreds of years. Now they use chemicals that are more profitable." Maura changed the subject. "Would you like something to eat? We've a busy day ahead and you'll need energy. I can't offer you an American breakfast, but how does oatmeal, toast and tea sound?"

"Wonderful." Kate was surprised to find that she really meant it. Oatmeal, bread toasted over a hearth fire and milky tea was exactly what she would have ordered.

Maura watched as Kate sprinkled salt over the cooked oats and ate them without milk, telltale evidence that her parents were natives of Scotland.

"Where do you come from?" Maura asked suddenly.

Kate looked up, surprised. "I thought I told you. I live in California."

"No." Maura shook her head. "I mean before that. From where do your people hail?" She searched for the right words. "What is your nationality?"

Swallowing the last of her oatmeal, Kate placed her spoon back in the bowl. "I don't know," she admitted. "I suppose I'm of Scottish descent. My mother wasn't able to have children and returned to Cait Ness with my father to adopt me."

"I've lived here all my life," Maura said slowly. "No one has been adopted off the island in fifty years."

Kate shrugged. "It really isn't all that important, is it?"

"Perhaps not." Maura felt strange. Her body tingled and all her nerves were on edge. There was something else, something that Kate was deliberately holding back. She pushed it aside. The woman's secrets were her own. "We've a great deal of work to do if we are to begin tonight."

"Tonight?"

Maura raised her eyebrows. "I was under the impression that you were in a hurry. Was I wrong?"

"I never was able to be hypnotized." She tilted her head and asked, "Is that a prerequisite?"

"Not at all," Maura replied, resolving that she would expend her greatest effort to make sure that Kate fell into that semiconscious state of uninhibited release. "Neither the staff nor the keek stane are prerequisites either, although they are convenient. A good bonfire works just as well."

"A keek stane? What is it?"

"An eye to the past and future, much like a crystal ball."

"Celia said—"

Maura held up her hand. "Celia Ward sent you to me. I'll decide which mediums to use, and I can guarantee you that

Celia's dramatic flair won't be in evidence at all." A thought occurred to her. "You don't have a taste for the histrionic, do you, Kate?"

Kate recoiled in horror. "Good gracious, no."

Relieved, Maura's mouth softened. "I didn't think so, but sometimes my instincts fail me."

"Not this time," Kate assured her.

"Good. Now, why don't you use my bathroom while I straighten up. Meet me in the garden when you're ready. I've laid out fresh clothing for you. I think they'll do. We're nearly the same size."

In the face of such generosity, Kate could think of nothing to say beyond a stammering "Thank you."

The water, wonderfully soft and steaming hot, trickled from the showerhead in a steady, inadequate spray. Kate rinsed the lather from her skin. Somewhere, there must be an underground spring. Wrapping a towel around her hair, she reached for another and rubbed her body dry. The clothes were a perfect fit—not what she would have chosen but certainly practical. A calf-length gray wool skirt, black tights, a gray turtleneck and black sweater completed the outfit. Her tennis shoes looked ludicrous beneath the hemline of the skirt, but it was either wear them or go barefoot.

After brushing out her hair and pulling it back from her face in a French braid, she walked outside into the spring sunlight to find her hostess kneeling in the dirt.

Maura beckoned her nearer. "Look." She pointed to a tiny plant pushing its way through the soil in search of sunlight. "My foxglove came through after all. I had my doubts after the last freeze. It's for the heart." She turned a delicate leaf toward the light. "This one is safflower. I use it for fevers, along with red clover for coughs." She brushed a tendril of hair away from her mouth. "Do you enjoy gardening, Kate?"

Kate brushed her fingers against the tiny seedlings. "I don't know. I like plants, but I'm not familiar with anything but the hothouse variety." She thought of her mother's backyard with its cement and brick masonry, its kidney-shaped pool and the garishly bright impatiens imprisoned in Mexican pots, strategically positioned to reflect their

brilliance in the pool's aqua-blue depths. Bonnie Sutherland had filled the inside of her home with greenery but left
the maintenance of it to a service who arrived once a week
to water, prune and replace those plants that had the
temerity to shed brown leaves or grow drooping, unsightly
branches.

Her parents had grown up on Cait Ness, surrounded by
marshland and white-capped water, the drone of insects,
the screeching of curlews and an isolation that went deeper
than anything they could possibly experience walking the
beaches of Southern California. Why had they done it, left
family and friends, everything they knew, for the polished
sophistication of a life so different it may as well have been
on another planet?

Maura pulled a weed out of the soft earth and threw it
into her burlap sack. She approved of the way the younger
woman sat without moving or speaking, her hands still in
her lap, her face bathed in sunlight, allowing the mood to
take her.

"You're very quiet," Maura remarked.

"I was thinking how different it is here and yet I don't feel
at all out of place." She smiled her first genuine smile since
arriving on the island.

Maura's breath caught. "You're uncommonly lovely when
you smile, but I suppose you know that."

"Thank you," Kate replied gravely. For the first time the
compliment didn't make her uncomfortable.

Maura stood up and drew the strings of the burlap
together. "I'll turn these back into the compost heap and
then I'm off to look for something to burn tonight, prefera-
bly sweet flag or juniper. Would you care to come with me?"

Kate nodded and Maura reached down to pull her up.

"I've decided that you should have a keek stane," Maura
continued conversationally as the two women walked
toward the cottage, "but you'll have to make it yourself."

"Does it take long?"

Maura dropped the bag near the door and wiped her
hands on her apron. "Making it doesn't take long at all, but
choosing your materials can. It must be consecrated tonight
by the light of the full moon." She held the door open for

Kate. "I've several clock glasses. I'm sure you'll find one that will do."

Kate watched as Maura washed her hands meticulously, scrubbing each nail with a soapy brush and then drying between her fingers carefully.

Later, after washing and carefully rinsing her clock glass, Kate took it outside and walked down a twisted path until she came to a flattened, sun-baked boulder. She sat down and placed the glass beside her, clasping her hands around her knees and settling in to watch it dry. The solitude made her drowsy. Strange, how acute her senses had become. The sky was bluer and sounds came clearer. Food tasted better. Even her sense of smell had improved. Maybe this was the place for her mother's ashes. She would wait until tomorrow and then ask Maura.

Later, when Maura bent to pick the sweet flag for incense, Kate stopped her. For some reason, the smell of sandalwood was strong in her nostrils. It was sandalwood she preferred, sandalwood she wanted for the consecration of her keek stane.

Maura humored her. After gathering branches of juniper, cedar and sandalwood, she took a small knife from her belt and handed it to Kate, instructing her to cut the branches into uniform chips. They would be used as incense for what Maura called the original fire.

Kate stared into the concave side of the glass and laughed at her distorted image. Here, away from the concrete and plastic of civilization, she could almost believe in magick and second sight. Maura's incredible theory regarding Catriona Wells and the twice-born didn't seem at all ludicrous in this fog-touched world of low-hanging clouds, endless skies and enchanted mists. Kate thought of her mother and wondered how Bonnie Sutherland had managed the transition from this land forgotten by time to crowded freeways, smog alerts and smoke-filled restaurants where the wait on weekends was often longer than two hours. Could she possibly prefer her life as it was now, or did she ache with homesickness?

Kate was utterly content, as if she had waited all her life for lungfuls of salt-laced air, for wind on her face, the drugging warmth of sun on her shoulders soothing her eyelids, the crown of her head and the backs of her hands, for the absolute peace of having nowhere else to go and nothing imminent to do.

This is what it must have been like for the early Christian monks or the Druids, she thought. Every day of their lives the same, devoted to worship, to consistency, to solitude, their only purpose the purification of immortal souls.

The clock glass was completely dry. Kate slid off the rock and walked back up the path toward the cottage. The solitude weighed on her. Where was the child she'd seen the day before on the path? Was she real or just another vision that had rooted deep in her unconscious?

She found Maura in the kitchen, gathering together what looked like art supplies and setting them on a long oak table. Kate recognized black enamel, wood shavings, pieces of smoothly sanded wood and bonding glue. "What are you doing?" she asked.

Maura looked up, shook herself out of her preoccupation and explained. "You'll need these to make your keek stane. I think I found everything." She pulled a large apron from a drawer in the pantry. "Put this on," she ordered. "We'll work on the box after you've painted the convex side of the glass. Two coats should do it. While the first one dries, you can glue together the box and stain the inside. Make it very dark. When you're finished, call me."

Humming softly to herself, Kate picked up the brush and dipped it into the enamel. There was something soothing and tremendously satisfying in construction, even if it was only a box. Very soon, Kate had a perfect cube, large enough to hold her glass, dark on the inside, light on the outside. She set it aside to dry and poked her head into the living room. Maura was sitting by the fire, reading a book with gilt-edged pages.

She looked up. "Are you finished already?"

Kate nodded.

"Good girl. Now pack the shavings in the box so that the glass will rest on them without slipping. Then glue the flat top with the circular cut over the glass. The idea is not to obstruct the glass but to keep it from moving."

Again, Kate did as she was told. It was surprisingly easy.

She lifted the finished box and examined it critically. Engraving the outside with some type of Celtic symbol would improve its appearance, but there wasn't time. Tonight was the beginning of the new moon.

Maura's voice interrupted her thoughts. "It's nearly time for tea. I thought you might like to walk down to the village and have a bite at the Alms. It's lovely, very quiet and private."

Kate thought of Mrs. MacLean and wondered if the fear in her eyes when she'd asked about Maura Sutherland extended to the villagers of Foula. "Can't we eat here? It's just as lovely and every bit as quiet."

There was understanding in Maura's clear eyes, understanding and amusement. "Of course, dear," she said quietly. "I merely thought you might be tired of my company and just the slightest bit curious about the young man at Mrs. Stuart's inn who appears to know you. He made the ferry and should be in town right now."

"How would you know all that?" Kate whispered.

Maura laughed. "Don't start in with that witchcraft nonsense again. Like everyone else, I have a telephone. The call came while you were out."

Kate felt the humiliating red tide sweep across her face. "I don't know a soul in Scotland," she began and stopped, embarrassment forgotten. Her forehead wrinkled. Could it possibly be Niall MacCormack? She was so filled with purpose and anticipation for this place, this moment, and the night to come, that her tryst at the border manor house seemed as if it had happened in another lifetime. Kate concentrated on visualizing Niall's face. She remembered dark hair, gray eyes and lean, capable hands, but his features swam before her, refusing to materialize. She shook her head and spoke aloud. "It can't be Niall. We said goodbye. I was quite definite about it."

Again, amusement flickered at the corners of Maura's mouth. "We don't all see things as unequivocally as you do, Kate. Perhaps he wasn't willing to give up so easily."

"I'm sure it's someone else," Kate said firmly. "It wasn't like that between us. We hardly knew each other."

"We'll see soon enough. That is"—Maura's eyebrows

lifted in a questioning arc—"if you've changed your mind and feel like walking down the hill."

Kate untied her apron and laid it across the chair. "I think you're so anxious to eat out because you're ashamed of your cooking," she teased.

"You found me out. Now, be a good girl and put on a jacket. The weather can change in an instant here and the nights are always cold."

Kate kept a sharp eye out, but there was no sign of the mysterious redheaded girl. The air was clean and sharp and the scent of the ocean grew stronger as they neared the village. She looked around at the jagged rock cliffs cutting into the brilliant blue of the sky, at the bracken covering the low hills, the small boats moored in narrow inlets surrounded by long marsh grass, the black-faced sheep standing unafraid in the meadows, unfettered by fences. There was something about the light here on the northern isles. It was crystal sharp, pure as glass, coloring the russets, greens and browns of the hills and valleys with an ethereal brilliance unknown in regions farther south.

The restaurant was small, with wooden floors and tables, red-checked curtains and mismatched china. A small round woman with wrinkled skin and snow-white hair brought a pot of tea, cups and saucers and linen napkins. "I haven't seen you for nearly a week, Maura. Are you well?"

"Very well, thank you. I'm fortunate to have a guest. This is Kate Sutherland from America." She turned to Kate. "This is my aunt, Kerry Sutherland. Usually I take my tea with her once or twice a week."

So she wasn't an outcast after all. Relieved, Kate smiled brilliantly. The old woman's eyes widened and she glanced at her niece.

Maura's head inclined in the briefest of nods and the old woman lowered her eyes. "What will you be having today?" she asked politely.

"Something that Kate isn't likely to get in California." Maura snapped her fingers. "I know. Salmon on toast and two of your delicious cream cakes. I'm sure there's nothing like them in all of America."

She was right. "That was delicious," Kate announced after the last rich forkful. "I don't understand how you all stay so thin."

Maura sipped her tea, considering her answer. "Here on the northern isles, life is difficult. Much of the work is physical. Few of us have automobiles, which means we walk or bicycle everywhere. Young people find it especially hard. Many of them leave for Edinburgh and London."

"Why did you stay?"

Maura was quiet for a long time. Kate was about to repeat her question when she spoke.

"I was always waiting," she said at last. "Waiting to grow up, to find my way, to learn what I thought would make the difference. I found happiness here, more than I ever dreamed was possible for me. The price was dear, but still worth it, I think. At least that's what I tell myself." Her eyes met Kate's and her mouth turned up in a rueful smile. "Don't even try to understand any of that. I can't imagine why I told you, except that you have the kind of face that invites confidences. It means nothing at all now." She folded her napkin. "If you're finished we'll find Anne Stuart and ask about the young man I told you about."

It was a typical Scots village, one main street with houses backed up to the road. The inn was the same one in which Kate had asked directions the day before.

"His name is Niall MacCormack and he's upstairs in his room," Mrs. Stuart announced after ushering Kate and Maura into a cozy sitting room. "I'll tell him you're here."

"Shall I leave?" Maura asked.

"Of course not," Kate protested. "I told you it wasn't like that. We're barely acquaintances. There must be some other reason that he's here."

Maura watched as the young man with the anxious guarded look on his face opened the door and walked across the room to stand before Kate. She knew exactly what that look meant and wondered if the girl knew the enormity of her influence. Whatever reasons Niall MacCormack had for coming to Foula, it was no coincidence, and he most certainly had no intention of being relegated to the status of a mere acquaintance.

❧ 11 ❧

Kate stared at him in disbelief. He was here in the flesh on the remote island of Foula. She hadn't really believed it until she actually saw him. "Why are you here?" she stammered.

Niall looked surprised. "When you didn't return to Cait Ness last night, Mrs. MacLean called here to be sure you were all right. She was told you arrived yesterday and asked about a room before you went to Maura Sutherland's cottage. That was the last she heard of you. Apparently the phone lines were down when she tried to call Maura."

"That doesn't explain why *you're* here."

Maura noticed the balled fists in Niall's pockets and the tight formality in his voice as he explained.

"After learning that no one knew where you were, Mrs. MacLean phoned the George to find out if anyone was traveling with you. They traced your car to me and asked if I knew of your plans. That's how I found out you were missing."

"I'm not missing and that still doesn't tell me why you came."

"Dammit, Kate. I was worried."

Her words were controlled, her voice careful. "You have no right to be worried about me, Niall. I told you there was no point in continuing our acquaintance."

Maura wondered when he would notice her. Up until now his whole being was focused on the woman before him. Perhaps it was time to interfere before the circumstances became embarrassing. She cleared her throat.

Startled, Niall turned around. Gray eyes met hers and narrowed before going completely blank. "I'm terribly sorry. I didn't realize you were here," he said politely, crossing the room to shake her hand. "You must be Maura Sutherland."

"Yes."

"I'm Niall MacCormack. Kate and I met a few days ago. We visited Hermitage Castle together after she had a road accident."

Maura smiled and withdrew her hand. "It was very kind of you to come all this way to see her, Mr. MacCormack. I'm sure she appreciates it." Maura looked at Kate. "You do appreciate it, don't you, Kate?"

"Of course," Kate stammered.

Niall frowned, his gaze moving between the two women. Something was happening that he didn't understand. Why was Maura speaking for Kate and, more important, why did she allow it? From his brief experience with Kate Sutherland, it was obvious that she made her own decisions. How, in the space of two days, had her personality changed so and why did these two women resemble each other so dramatically?

He shook his head and passed his hand across his eyes in an effort to clear his thoughts. "I came to Foula because of my concern for Kate, Miss Sutherland, but I'm staying at Cait Ness because a discovery of some importance was unearthed only a few days ago. Several ancient Celtic talismans were excavated there and I'm in the process of writing a book. You see, I'm a history professor on leave from the university."

"What is the subject of your book, Mr. MacCormack?"

His eyes met hers and held. "Celtic mythology."

"I see."

Her glance was long and probing, and when at last her eyes released him, Niall was very sure that she had seen much more than he intended.

Maura stood up and walked toward the door. "I shall visit with Anne for a bit. When you're ready to leave, Kate, I'll be in the kitchen."

Kate was embarrassed. He hadn't come solely because of her after all. She looked down at her hands. "I owe you an apology," she said, her voice low.

Niall remained silent, cursing himself for playing the fool. The primary reason for his visit to this remote corner of

Scotland was to see Kate again. She had been on his mind every waking hour since their goodbye. He even made a special trip to the gallery at Holyrood Palace to view the portrait of Catriona Wells. The likeness was remarkable, too remarkable. There was something different about Kate, a timeless quality that he couldn't quite put his finger on.

At first he thought her refusal to see him again had to do with a man, but the more he considered it, her questions about Patrick MacKendrick and Catriona Wells began to unsettle him. They weren't the usual questions people asked when researching family trees. They were more personal, almost intimate, as if she were reliving the relationships of her youth. Niall knew something about the practices of the ancient Celts and even more about the Pectiwita religion still practiced by much of the population in the northern isles, particularly the Shetlands and most particularly Cait Ness, land of the Sutherlands.

"Aren't you going to say anything?" Kate asked.

"I'm afraid to," replied Niall.

"You could accept my apology."

"Is that what it was?"

Heat rose in Kate's cheeks. "What will you do now?"

"Stay the night and take the ferry back to Cait Ness." He studied the red in her cheeks and the slender hands clasped in her lap. "And you?"

She gestured vaguely. "Go back with Maura. We have something to do this evening. Then I suppose I'll go home, unless—" She stopped.

"Unless?" he prodded her.

Kate shrugged. "Nothing, really. There was something I thought Maura could help me with. I'm not sure now."

"You mean because she's a priestess of the Pectiwita?"

Startled, Kate turned the full force of her gaze on him, forgetting to exercise her usual caution. "What do you know about the Pectiwita?"

Niall leaned against the mantel, hands in his pockets. "A great deal. I'm a Scots historian. We arrived at Christianity later than most. The old ways are still practiced in the more remote parts of this country. I would be a poor sort of historian if I didn't intimately know the history of my own ancestors."

"What do you know about the Pectiwita?" she repeated.

He looked at her steadily. "You won't like this, but I'll say it anyway. Maura is very strong. You may not be. Don't do this, Kate."

"She says her power comes from outside herself, from the other person," Kate argued.

Niall shook his head. "Maura's power comes from who she is, from the memories and practices of her ancestors. She was raised from birth to take her place among her followers, as her mother was before her, and hers before that. You have nothing to do with all this. You're an American, raised on television and French fries. How can you possibly know what trafficking with Maura Sutherland will do to your mind?"

Pushing away from the mantel, he crossed the room and sat on the coffee table across from her, settling his hands on her shoulders. "Leave it, Kate. Come back to Edinburgh with me."

She looked at him with haunted cat's eyes. "I can't. Don't you see? I have no choice. She's my last hope."

Involuntarily, his hands tightened and he frowned. "What are you talking about?"

"I need to know why I see what I do."

"What do you see?"

She shook her head. "You'll think I'm crazy."

"Try me."

Kate twisted out of his grasp and stood up. "No, Niall. I don't want to. I can do this myself. When it's over, I'll call you. I promise I will."

He hadn't moved from the coffee table. She turned and met his skeptical gaze with her own defiant one. "Don't look at me like that. If I say I will, then you should believe me."

He rose slowly, his eyes never leaving her face. "I hope you do, Kate. Because you have no idea what you're getting into. When this is over, you may need me more than you realize."

She watched him leave the room. He passed through the entry and climbed the stairs. Kate walked down the hall into the kitchen. Maura and the woman who had given her directions the day before were drinking tea at one end of a long table. Kate cleared her throat. "Maybe we should be going back," she suggested.

Maura pushed her chair away from the table and carried her cup and saucer to the sink. "I'm ready if you are." She glanced sideways at Kate. "Is your friend still here?"

Kate shrugged. "I imagine he'll stay the night. After that, I'm not sure what his plans are. We didn't discuss them."

Anne Stuart laughed. "He'll stay the night unless he wants to swim to Cait Ness. The ferry has gone for the last time today."

Kate's forehead wrinkled. "What if there's an emergency?"

Maura laid her arm across Kate's shoulders. "There are boats for chartering and we've a doctor on the island. In a real medical emergency, a helicopter comes. There's no need to worry, Kate. It's highly unlikely anything will happen again during your visit."

Kate was not convinced. She couldn't leave even if she wanted to. The old familiar claustrophobia began closing in.

"Look at me, Kate." Maura's voice compelled her.

She turned and her gaze was caught and held by Maura's clear, knowing one. "We are going back to the cottage now. Your keek stane is there. Tonight you will make it your own. You will see things you've always wished to see. The time will go quickly, and before you realize it, the days will pass."

Kate swallowed and nodded. The crushing weight on her head receded. She smiled shakily. "You're right, of course. I'm sorry."

The sun was just setting over the western cliffs and the temperature had dropped considerably when the two women started back up the hill. Kate dug her gloved hands into her jacket pockets and tucked her chin into the wool of her muffler. The island seemed lonely and very remote as it hung on the edge of night, the Scottish mist muting the sharp edges of rock and thistle. Kate suddenly felt very far from home. She broke the silence. "Were you born here?" she asked.

Maura nodded. "We were all born here, generations of my family, as far back as anyone can remember."

"Why didn't you ever marry?"

The older woman's mouth twitched. "I was never asked."

"I don't believe you."

This time Maura laughed. "It's true."

"But you're beautiful," Kate protested.

"So are you," Maura returned, "and you're not married either."

"I'm only thirty," Kate stammered. "There's time yet."

"Not really. By your age most women have found their mates. Many times they've found more than one." She glanced at Kate from the corner of her eye. "I think that if you haven't married by thirty, your chances of doing so are very remote."

"Why?"

Maura warmed to her subject. "You see, most people who haven't married by that time have a very good reason. Usually it's because they're quite happy being single. Marriage means changing one's ways, compromising. Not everyone wants to do that as they approach middle age."

Kate thought of her mother. "People don't want to grow old alone either."

"Most women do that anyway," Maura remarked thoughtfully. "There are a great many widows on Foula. We don't come into this world together and we don't go out together. I'm one of the lucky ones. Solitude suits me. *Ciunas gan uaigneas.*"

"What does that mean?"

"Quietness without loneliness."

"I think you've very cleverly evaded my question," Kate observed. "There's a reason you didn't marry, and whatever it is has nothing to do with what you've told me."

Maura linked her arm through Kate's. "You're very observant, you know. Are all Americans like you?"

"Good lord, no." Kate nearly laughed out loud. "I'm not nearly as aggressive as most of them. Anyone else would have found you out long ago."

"You're the first American I've ever known," Maura volunteered. "There was a couple who emigrated, but they were born on the island."

Night was full upon them when they reached the cottage. The door had been left ajar and the main room smelled like the sea. Maura lit the candles on the mantel and gathered the herbs she had collected earlier in the day. "You'll need your keek stane," she said, turning around. "Are you ready?"

Kate swallowed. "I'm ready."

"Good." Maura smiled. "Higher up on the bluff is a good place for the fire. It isn't too windy, but the air is very clear and there are no trees to obstruct your view of the moon."

Kate left the room and returned shortly with the box she had constructed that afternoon. Maura led the way, carrying the firewood, and Kate followed with a woolen blanket and her keek stane. There was no need for a flashlight. The moonlight, unfiltered and pure, without competition from streetlights and neon signs, was startlingly bright. Within minutes after reaching their destination, Maura had kindled a promising blaze. Reaching into the pouch at her waist, she threw something that looked like powder into the flames, then she added the sprigs of sandalwood she'd collected.

Kate spread the blanket on the ground, upwind of the fire, and sniffed appreciatively. The scent was wonderful.

"Sit down in a comfortable position," Maura ordered, seating herself on the blanket, "and close your eyes." Kate obeyed.

"Now visualize Catriona Wells. Don't try to place her in a scene," Maura warned, "just imagine looking at her."

Kate forced herself to concentrate. Almost immediately the image of a slim, black-haired figure with astonishing green eyes appeared in her mind.

Maura clasped her hand. "Now," she said quietly, "clear your mind of everything. If thoughts come into your head, dismiss them. Try not to think of anything in particular. It isn't always easy to do it, but try."

Catriona's image faded. Deliberately, Kate forced her mind to go blank.

"Very good." Maura's voice purred with approval. "Now open your eyes and look into the dark glass of the keek stane."

Slowly, Kate opened her eyes and looked into the eye of the box. It looked different than it had before, murky and discolored. A cool mist settled on her cheeks, and despite the meal she'd just eaten, her stomach felt hollow, as if something deep inside of her was missing. She was here on the bluff with Maura, a spectator waiting for events to unfold. Suddenly the colors separated and a scene, as tiny and perfect as the picture on a television screen, came into focus. She was here and yet not completely so, both spectator and participant. A part of her was in that other place, separated from the world by a mist-shrouded bridge that only a very few would cross.

Patrick had rid himself of his metal breastplate, washed his hands and face and slipped on a clean shirt when he heard her scream. At first he couldn't place it. Then his blood turned to ice.

Reaching for the key to Cat's bedchamber, he flung open the door and nearly collided with the guard he had posted at her room. Clearly the man was terrified.

"Please, sir," the guard stammered, fearful of the border lord's anger, "I did nothing. Moments after you left, her screams began." He crossed himself and whispered, "Could the lass be possessed?"

Patrick thrust the man aside. "Stay here," he commanded. "Tell no one what you've heard this night."

The screams had stopped by the time he reached her chamber. Fumbling with the key, every second seemed an eternity. Cursing his own clumsiness, Patrick fought with the lock. Finally the tooth caught and the metal gave way. He pushed the door open. The room was dark. With shaking hands he lit the candle and looked around.

Curled into a ball, she lay on the floor clothed only in her shift. Her body was completely motionless. For a terrible moment Patrick thought she was dead. Fear quickened his steps. He saw the slight rise and fall of her breasts. He was beside her in an instant, kneeling to lift her into his arms. A harsh intake of breath escaped him. Blood covered her arm, staining the entire left side of her bodice.

For the first time Patrick noticed the gash in her wrist and the carving knife on the floor. His jaw clenched. Carrying her to the bed, he placed her gently on the feather mattress and pressed the back of his palm to her seeping wound.

She moaned and tossed against his hand. He held her down until she was still again. Brushing back her hair, he stared at her face. She looked like a child lying there on the great bed, her forehead wrinkled against an unknown pain. Black lashes lay like half moons on her cheeks, and the purple shadows under her eyes were giant bruises against the porcelain skin. Her unconsciousness disturbed him. Patrick knew her blood loss wasn't enough to cause her harm, yet still she slept, as if by the sheer strength of her will she could wrest the lifeforce from her body.

Patrick frowned. He knew he was strangely vulnerable when it came to this woman. The heart-racing fear that consumed him when he saw her on the floor was like nothing he had ever experienced. He felt responsible, as if in some way he had betrayed her. He was terrified at the power she held over him. She had pleaded with him to stay and he had refused her.

"Please, Cat," he murmured, stroking her cheek with gentle fingers. "Come back to me, lass. Would you leave before ever having tasted that bit of life I promised you?" Bending over her, he breathed against her lips. "Wake up, my darling."

She stirred and opened her eyes. Afraid to move, he waited for her reaction. Her eyes were cloudy with confusion. Then she remembered. With a cry, she wrapped her arms around his neck and buried her face in his shoulder.

"It's all right, lass," he said, "you're safe now."

It was too much. Her tears were harsh and difficult at first, as if she had little experience with crying. Soon they flowed more easily. She wept for a long time, flooding his shirt and his skin, her tears working themselves into his heart.

Patrick held her, his heart aching with pity and pain and something else he refused to acknowledge. Her hair was like black velvet beneath his hand. Gradually her tears stopped and she lay against him. Her bones felt light and small under his hands.

"I'm sorry." She pulled out of his arms.

Not trusting himself to speak, Patrick lifted her wrist and examined the wound. The bleeding had stopped. Without leaving her side, he poured more water into the basin. Wetting the linen towel, he cleaned out the gash and then moved up her arm, wiping away all traces of blood. Tearing a fresh towel in half, he tied it around her wrist and then pulled back the bed covering.

"Your shift is soiled," he said quietly, holding up the blanket to shield her from his eyes.

Cat sat up, pulling the bloodied garment over her head, and dropped it to the floor. Wrapping the sheet around her breasts, she lay back against the pillows.

Patrick counted the seconds in his head. When he deemed enough time had passed, he lowered the covering and tucked it around her. He was completely silent, his face unreadable except for the grim set of his mouth. Her eyes met his and he lowered his head. Never had surrender seemed so sweet. She tasted of salt and tears and innocence. His hands framed the delicate bones of her face and his mouth moved against hers.

Cat couldn't remember when it changed. All at once the sweetness of his touch turned into something else. This wild leaping of her blood was something new. Her lips parted and she knew once again the smooth seduction of his tongue and the sharp, shivery sensation of his mouth against her throat.

All too soon he pulled away, his chest pounding with the effort of his discipline. She reached out to stroke his cheek. Tiny flames came alive in his eyes. Kissing her hard on the lips, he stood up. "I'll send a woman to stay with you," he promised.

"Don't go," she whispered.

He tensed. "Lass." His voice sounded strangled. "I cannot."

A terrifying numbness, like the ache of frost-bitten hands, hovered on the edge of her consciousness. She hesitated, looking up to meet the silver ash of his gaze. The cold fear disappeared, receding to the shadows of her mind. This was Patrick MacKendrick, a man known the length of England and Scotland for the honor of his word. Warmth surged through her.

"Please?" she asked huskily, the golden lights in her eyes beckoning him.

Patrick felt himself weaken. Ever since their first meeting he had dreamed of this. Catriona Wells, graceful and proud, her eyes filled with passion, her lips trembling, willing and naked beneath him. Why then did he hesitate? The answer came to him immediately. He now knew what it was to hold her against him while she sobbed her heart out. He had witnessed her courage in the face of danger and her uncomplaining stamina on a draining journey. He had heard the screams that turned his blood to ice and felt the loyalty she carried deep in her soul.

It was that very loyalty that touched his heart. It was a loyalty deeper and more uncompromising than any he had known. Patrick had searched a lifetime for a woman with the courage to love like that. He had finally found it in the soul of a green-eyed Englishwoman he had no right to claim. It occurred to him that she might be protecting someone. Whoever he was, Patrick intended to make sure that the knave was no longer part of Catriona's life.

"Patrick." Her voice seduced him. "When will you come to terms with your conscience?"

"I want more from you than this."

The words came from deep in his heart. They demanded an answer, the right answer, from her. Under the linen shirt, his shoulders were tense and straight. Her eyes rested on his straight mouth and the thick, black lashes surrounding the remarkable gray of his eyes.

"Somehow I thought that the first time I asked a man to my bed he would be willing," she said softly.

"Don't speak lightly, Catriona," he said tersely. "You know what it is that I want."

She sat up, her face strong with purpose. "I can give you no more than this, Patrick MacKendrick. My life is not my own, to do with as I please. Isn't it enough to know that you were right? You told me one day that you would take me and that I would find pleasure in it."

She was so lovely sitting there amidst the tousled sheets. Patrick's mouth was no longer hard and his voice, when he spoke, was everything Cat had imagined a lover's would be. "You once told me you would not go spoiled to your marriage bed." He moved toward her, keeping his eyes on her face. "I will stay with you, lady, but remember it was you who invited me." Unlacing his shirt, he pulled it over his head. "Tonight you will know what it is to burn."

He came toward her and Cat sucked in her breath. His body, lean, scarred and tight with muscle, was beautifully made. The pounding of her heart was so loud she couldn't think. When at last he reached the bed and his mouth came down on hers, there was no more need for thought.

As naturally as if she did it every day of her life, Cat parted her lips and reached up to encircle his neck with her arms. Her tongue searched tentatively for his and Patrick was lost. He pulled away the bedsheet and pressed his body against hers, sliding his hands from her thigh to the curve of her hip and finally to the exquisite perfection of her breast. Cat trembled at the intimate caress, but instead of pulling away she arched her body in an effort to bring herself even closer to his exploring hands.

"Cat," he whispered, sliding his lips down her throat, "holy God, Cat," he repeated hoarsely, his chest swelling with the breath of pleasure and disbelief. He was eager but controlled, as generous and competent as if he had a lifetime to spend, caressing the smooth surface of her lips, the line of her jaw and the curve of her cheek. With the back of his hand he tested the life in her throat, bending to press his warm lips to the erratic beat. His hand moved still lower, to brush against her breast and the sharp indentation of her waist.

Her startled gasp inflamed him. With his tongue he traced the chiseled line where her lips came together and then the polished edges of her teeth. Blind to everything but the desperate need below his waist, Patrick slid his lips down the slope of her breast and closed his mouth over the peak.

Cat felt no fear, only a dizzy, aching tension that grew with each stroke of his hand. The feel of his body against hers, hard and powerful and strangely protective, gave her courage. He moved against her. The tension within her threatened to explode. She knew nothing but the feel of warm hands and seeking lips, his face dark and alive with need and the cordlike veins in his arms straining to control his passion.

She wanted more. She could feel his restraint and experienced a perverse desire to make him abandon it. He was very close but not close enough. Shifting her body, she pressed against him, inviting him to take what she had never before offered to any man.

He shuddered against her neck and lay still. She moved her hips, but he stopped her with his hands. "Easy, lass," he whispered raggedly, "I need a moment."

Patrick was very near to losing control. Taking deep, calming breaths of air, he waged a battle with himself. Tonight Cat was more than willing, but she had come through a frightening ordeal and her emotions were raw. Would she want him tomorrow or in a week's time? A woman's first loving was often painful. Not until the second or third time would she know pleasure. What if she refused to allow him near her after this night?

Raising himself on his elbows, he looked down at her. Her eyes were very wide and green under the winged brows, and a sheen of moisture highlighted the down on her cheekbones. He had never wanted a woman the way he wanted Catriona Wells. His gaze rested on her mouth. Her lips were parted and swollen from his kisses and her eyes met his, direct and unashamed. Every nerve in his body screamed for possession. He ached with the effort of denying his release. Slowly, he moved against her, holding her gaze.

"Why do you do this, Catriona?" he whispered.

Cat could no longer speak. The pleasure was agonizing. She wrapped her legs around his waist.

Lowering his head, Patrick covered her mouth with his. Moving his tongue and the lower half of his body in the same rhythmic cadence, he teased her, holding back, leaving her longing for a greater unknown pleasure.

"Could it be that you have some small measure of feeling for me?" His mouth was everywhere, on her lips and the sensitive back of her ear, the edge of his tongue tormenting her throat and the round, softer flesh below. "Tell me you do, even if it isn't true."

Her chest rose and fell as she drew in sharp, shallow breaths of air. If only he would finish this and take her.

"Say it," he demanded.

"I—" Her voice caught in her throat. Somewhere, in the recesses of her mind, she knew something was happening, as if her body was gathering itself for one last explosive sensation. The tempo of his movement increased. She lifted her hips, reaching for that elusive pleasure she knew would surely come if he would only enter her completely.

It all happened at once: Patrick's harsh cry as he pulled away, the rush of warmth against her thighs and the shattering spasms that wracked her body again and again until she lay sated and spent, her face pressed against his throat.

Drawing a long and shaking breath, Patrick pulled the covers over them and closed his eyes.

He woke to find her leaning on her elbow, staring at him. Her bandage had come loose and the gash in her wrist was an angry red against the whiteness of her skin. Patrick stroked it gently, a question in his eyes. Before he could ask it, Cat spoke.

"I know you wanted me, Patrick. Why didn't you take me?"

He frowned. "'Twould hardly be a fair thing to ravish a maid who is terrified enough to sleep with the devil himself." His voice lowered seductively. "'Tis an insult to a man's skill."

Her eyes were cool and narrow. "You've thrown away your only opportunity, m'lord. I won't offer myself again."

"That is a promise you will soon break." He closed his hand around her wrist. "Now you will answer my questions. Do you care so little for life that you would take your own before you've even sampled the best of it?"

"The best of it?" She laughed bitterly and pulled her arm from his grasp, twisting her body away from him until she lay on the other side of the bed. "A noblewoman's lot in life rarely improves with marriage. 'Tis only the man who has a say in who he weds."

"What else is there but marriage?" Patrick asked. "Women are helpless. They need the protection of their lords." The moment the words escaped his lips he wished he could take them back. It occurred to him that except for the weakness she had shown hours before, he had never met a woman more capable of caring for herself.

Her voice was laced with contempt and something else he would give a great deal to know more about. "It might surprise you to learn there are times when a woman must deal with dangers every bit as deadly as those you face on a battlefield."

He stared at her, his brow furrowed with indecision.

Finally, he threw back the bedcovers and stood up, stretching with lazy muscular grace. This conversation would keep. The long ride back to Stirling awaited him. He had an audience with James.

Cat's eyes widened in appreciation as she watched him pull on his clothes. The massive shoulders and broad back tapered to a narrow vee at his waist. His legs were tightly muscled, and there wasn't a spare ounce of flesh around his middle. She experienced a flash of disappointment. Someday soon she would wed at the discretion of the king. It was too much to hope that the man who would initiate her into the act of love would be as attractive as Patrick MacKendrick. Who would have imagined that a man, legendary for his reputation with women, would have scruples over bedding a virgin?

The color rose in her cheeks. Who would have thought that Catriona Wells, granddaughter and cousin of kings, would tremble like a mare in heat over the powerful shoulders and handsome face of a common border lord?

❧ 12 ❧

The audience took more than an hour. The MacKendrick was tired and more than a little impatient with the discussion at hand. Before dawn he had ridden out of Edinburgh after procuring the services of a scribe. The precious document he carried was tucked safely inside his velvet jacket.

Patrick did not approve of Jamie's new policy toward England. He knew it was unwise to tease Henry with a rival to his throne. A man so determined to rule that he would stoop to murdering all of his wife's relatives was more dangerous than a rabid wolf.

"Your Grace will take up the support of this Pretender, this so-called Richard of York?" he asked.

"Aye," replied James, pacing back and forth across the room.

"Surely you can't believe the man speaks the truth?"

James closed his dark eyes for a moment. Rest was a luxury denied him since Sauchieburn. When he spoke his voice was weary. "It doesn't matter whether 'tis true or not. Warbeck is a thorn in Henry's side that will fester and burn. We will have a weapon to bargain with."

"There is another way," Patrick reminded him quietly.

James's face hardened. "I'll have none of it!"

"As your loyal subject and your friend, give me leave to speak."

"Very well then. Speak!"

"Henry is old. The heir to the throne suffers from ill health. His younger son may have no heirs of his own."

James shook his head. "Young Henry Tudor is not sickly. There is no reason to believe he will leave no heirs."

"It has happened before," Patrick insisted. "If you rule with your head instead of your heart, a Stewart may have both kingdoms. The Tudor princess is unwed."

"I'll handle England in my own way!"

Patrick knew from the steely quality of his king's voice that it would be foolish to argue further. His jaw tightened but he remained silent.

"God's blood, Patrick!" James stopped his pacing to stand before the window. The opening was small and the walls, ten feet thick, obstructed most of his view, but somewhere in the courtyard, in the gardens or in the jumbled maze of palace rooms, he knew Maggie Drummond visited with her ladies. In the distance the River Tay reflected the deep blue of the cloudless sky. "Would you deny me the pleasures of an ordinary man?"

"It is you who wished to be king, Sire." Patrick repeated Cat's words. "Those who seek to rule keep their thrones through political alliances." His voice gentled. "The choice is yours, my friend: the kingdom or the bonny Drummond lass."

"Be damned to you and this talk of marriage!" James threw himself into his chair and motioned for Patrick to be seated. "'Tis not the reason I requested this audience." He pointed to a piece of parchment on the side table. "The missive is from the duchess of Burgundy. She believes this Pretender is her nephew." He grinned. "Who are we to question the word of a beloved aunt?"

"The duchess is a Yorkist," replied Patrick slowly. "She hates Henry. A monkey could claim to be Richard of York and she would take up his standard."

"She also believes that Richard the Third had nothing to do with the murder of her nephews," James continued. "During his reign England was content with her king. For what reason would he murder his brother's children? 'Tis Henry, whose only claim to the throne is through the bastard blood of John of Gaunt, who had reason to kill them. He stilled all protests by marrying Elizabeth of York and murdering everyone else with the slightest taint of York blood."

"A gruesome tale," said Patrick.

James laughed. The spilling of English blood brought him pleasure. "There is mystery here. All trace of the princes, the true heirs to the English throne, has been lost. Their bodies were never found." He drummed his fingers on the arm of his chair. "Tell me, Patrick: If you were Henry, would it disturb you to know that a man calling himself Richard of York was alive and well in Scotland and that the duchess of Burgundy supported his tale?"

"If I were Henry, it would be worth a great deal to silence him."

"Exactly." The king smiled with satisfaction. "There are still Yorkists in England, sir. Men who would be more than happy to take up the young prince's cause." The dark eyes held a disturbing light. "My sources report that after this man who claims to be Richard, there is only one person with more hereditary right to rule England than Henry."

Patrick's eyes narrowed. He knew James had finally arrived at the purpose for this audience. "Who might that be?" he asked softly.

"He is a mere child," James answered, "by name of Richard Wells. He is Catriona's brother. Currently he resides at Ravenswood, a virtual prisoner, in the care of the earl of Neville, his stepfather."

Patrick's face could have been carved from stone, so still and guarded was his expression. He did not want to reveal what he knew about the woman who moved him more deeply than any other had before her. If Jamie suspected anything was amiss and Cat knew of it, she would have no reason to even consider Patrick's offer.

"Your instincts regarding my fair cousin appear to be correct," the king continued. "Catriona would not leave her brother in England unless she had a purpose. Perhaps she did not run away after all. Perhaps she was sent as an informer." James pressed his hands together into a pyramid and leaned forward in his chair. They were large hands with blunt, strong fingers. Hands capable of seizing and holding a kingdom in their grasp.

Patrick felt a swift and desperate fear for Catriona Wells. Despite her arrogance and fierce pride, she was only a woman and no match for the might and greed of James IV of Scotland. He took the offensive.

"I would ask a favor, Your Grace."

The king's chin tightened stubbornly. "I will listen to no more talk of marriage."

Patrick grinned. "'Tis not your marriage I would discuss, Sire."

A look of dawning wonder replaced the suspicion on James's face. "Is it possible that you are flesh and blood after all, my friend?" He threw back his head and laughed loudly.

With the barest hint of a smile on his lips, Patrick waited for the king to contain his mirth.

"God's wounds, Patrick," he said at last, "I never expected to hear such news from your lips. Who is the fortunate lass?"

Slowly, Patrick reached inside his jacket and pulled out the parchment. Kneeling at James's feet, he held it out to him.

The king unrolled it and began to read. The silence became painful as it extended beyond one minute and then two. Beads of perspiration gathered on Patrick's upper lip. He knew that in normal times his request would be considered a sacrilege. His very life would have been forfeit. Even now, after the victories of Sauchieburn and Selkirk and Jedburgh, after he had proven his loyalty and been given an earldom, he risked much. For such a presumption he could be stripped of his holdings and title, even banished if the king was particularly outraged. Yet life in the borders left little room for caution, and he had not risen to his place in the world without risk.

Like the instincts of a panther when the scent of fresh meat floats on the wind, the border lord knew when to strike. Never had Jamie needed him more. It was time to test the strength of the royal gratitude.

After a long moment James looked up. The dark gaze rested thoughtfully on the warrior kneeling before him. Without speaking, he rose and walked to his desk. Picking up a quill, he dipped it and scrawled his signature. Still without speaking, he sprinkled sand over his name and handed it back to Patrick.

"Rise, m'lord," he said at last. "When shall we celebrate the joyous occasion?"

Patrick slipped the document into a hidden inner pocket and stood up. His eyes warmed with amusement. "First I must tell the lady she is betrothed. It may take some time yet to reconcile her to a wedding date."

Jamie's eyes widened. "You are a brilliant soldier, Patrick, but now I find you've other talents as well. Perhaps I should send you as my ambassador to a foreign court. You've outmaneuvered two Stewarts this day."

"'Twas not my intent to trick you, Sire," Patrick explained. "This marriage assures that Catriona will remain in Scotland. If Henry planned to use her, it will never come to pass."

"How noble of you to sacrifice yourself for my benefit." The dark eyes were alight with laughter. "And how fortunate that the lass is bonny as well."

Patrick grinned. "My thoughts exactly."

"She is part Stewart, Patrick. We are not an easy bunch to tame." James stared at the lean, hard-eyed man standing by the fire, his boot propped against the fender. "I had no idea your thoughts lay in that direction. You must want her very much."

Smiling slightly, Patrick bowed his head, revealing nothing.

Jamie laughed. "By God, you and Glenkirk have much in

common. I wish you happiness, my friend, for you'll surely have little peace."

The MacKendrick's long legs quickly dispensed with the narrow stone steps leading down to the courtyard of Stirling Castle. Exultant with relief at the unexpected ease with which he'd secured his request, he was anxious to return to Edinburgh and Catriona.

Calling for his men, who had passed the time drinking and dicing behind the stables, he mounted his stallion saddled near the portcullis. The men who rode with the MacKendrick did not complain at having their entertainment cut short. Only a fool questioned their laird's instructions. With good-natured curses, they obeyed his command.

"Raise the gate," Patrick shouted, expertly controlling the impatience of his mount.

The guard hastily complied and the men rode out of the courtyard and down the steep incline to the main ford of the Firth of Forth. Reining in his horse, Patrick turned and waited for the last stragglers of his entourage to catch up and fall in line.

He looked up in appreciation at the commanding heights of Stirling, appropriately called the key to Scotland. Located on the main ford of the firth, the giant waterway strategically linked the northern and southern halves of the kingdom. Its possession had been the focus of contention for centuries. After the Battle of Bannockburn was fought in its shadow, Robert the Bruce had dismantled the castle to prevent it from falling into English hands. Only the beautiful chapel, a memorial to Isabella of Mar, remained of the original structure.

His spirits lighter than they had been in a long time, Patrick set his pace, keeping to the firth where the scrub and grasses grew short. Eight hours later he reached Edinburgh. Taking a detour, he led his company past the old Magdalene chapel, now a meeting place for the corporation of the Hammermen, and turned into Candlemaker Row, a narrow street that led to the Grassmarket. It was almost midnight, and the city marketplace was quiet.

Paying careful attention to the dark wynds and twisted

closes where brigands lurked, the riders passed Greyfriar's and turned down Lawnmarket to proceed up steep, cobbled High Street to the castle. Keeping well to the center of the thoroughfare, the men avoided the refuse overflowing in the gutters. The tall Market Cross, gathering place of the clans, loomed ahead and the towers of St. Giles Cathedral were silhouetted against a velvet sky. Dark and brooding, hovering over the city at the top of High Street, was Edinburgh Castle.

Patrick never set eyes on the enormous grandeur of Castle Rock without feeling a sense of awe for those men of vision, those ancient Celtic and Pictish kings, their names no longer remembered over the misty passage of time, who had labored to build a fortress on that slab of granite, hewn and shaped by the gigantic forces of an ancient volcano. What their cowering subjects must have thought, how they must have doubted and mumbled among themselves as they dragged gigantic tree trunks and stone blocks up the steep incline, raising the walls with the primitive adhesive of wattle and mortar. In his mind he could imagine those ancient people looking nervously at the shining black surface of their castle foundation, wondering if the god of fire would take offense and send the shooting flames, the ash and molten lava, to destroy their fields and crops once again.

What had once been a stronghold built for defense was now a palace of grace and beauty. James had constructed a fine great hall along the south side of the castle, and the luxury and comfort of the living quarters was second to none in all of Scotland. Patrick stretched his aching muscles and thought longingly of the well-appointed chamber he called his own.

His mind moved on to Catriona Wells, and he smiled grimly. His orders to the woman he had sent to serve her were to confine the Lady Cat to the room she now occupied with an occasional walk on the battlements for fresh air. He imagined her frustration as she paced back and forth across the wooden floor, her graceful walk with its controlled fury reminding him of the prowling saunter of an angry tigress. He thought of the recessed window from which she could see across the Forth to the Highlands. His blood heated at the memory of the night they spent together in the great bed, with its velvet hangings closing out everything but the two of them.

Under his mail he could feel the reassuring scratch of parchment. Cat was his, by royal decree. He knew—nay, he expected—that she would fight him. But it would avail her nothing. In the end she would succumb, and if she wasn't completely blinded by her stubborn pride, she would come to admit they were well matched. As the gate to the esplanade rose to allow them entrance, Patrick squared his shoulders, unconsciously preparing himself for the upcoming encounter.

Cat lay on her stomach on top of the enormous bed, rolling two gold pieces in her hand. She had won the last round and Crispin, the guard, owed her a considerable amount of money. The day before she had dismissed her female servant, only allowing her to pull a sleeping pallet into the room when night descended. The woman, talking of nothing but remedies for her various ailments, bored her. Catriona preferred dicing with her captor.

It was well after midnight, but lack of exercise and her unaccustomed confinement prevented all thoughts of sleep. Cat listened appreciatively as Crispin strummed his lute and sang ballads of the border. His voice was particularly clear, and the tragic story of Sir Patrick Spens was one of her favorites.

Crispin was enjoying himself. It was a sad lament, ending with the lady of the manor being told of her husband's death. Never had he sung for such an attentive audience. The girl hung on his words as if her very life depended on it.

When he finally rested his lute, Cat sat up. "When will you pay me?" she asked.

He reddened. "Dinna' doubt that I'll find a way? A borderer's word is sacred, m'lady."

Cat hurried to reassure him. "I meant you no dishonor, Crispin." She flipped the coins expertly in her hand. After a moment she said, "I wonder if we could bargain."

Crispin was curious. "How so?"

Her voice lowered to a seductive whisper. "I'll forgive the entire debt if you show me where Andrew Percy is imprisoned."

Sweat beaded on his forehead as he weighed the temptation of such an offer. Finally he shook his head. Regret reflected on his homely face. "I canna' do that, lass."

Cat flushed. "Please don't refuse me, Crispin. 'Tis enough to make one sicken and die locked up this way."

He grinned. "I merely follow orders, m'lady."

"Whose orders?" she scoffed. "Does your lord know everything, or is it that you can no longer think for yourself?"

A voice spoke from behind her. "Whichever it is, is unimportant. The end result is the same."

Cat paled. Slowly, she turned around to see Patrick MacKendrick lounging in the doorway. "How long have you been there?" she whispered.

His eyes were hard. "Long enough. May I inquire as to why you are in such a hurry to leave Crispin's company, m'lady?"

Crispin's frightened voice answered: "She wanted to see Percy, m'lord." He left out all mention of how she tried to bribe him. The lass was in enough trouble already.

"Leave us," the MacKendrick ordered.

Cat's heart pounded. She didn't dare look at him.

Patrick crossed the room and lifted her chin with his hand. Disappointed that she hadn't welcomed him more warmly and feeling the long miles of his journey in every aching limb, he spoke more sharply than he intended. "Why are you wrapped in wool?"

"I didn't want to be recognized when I made my escape." Her muffled voice reached him through the cloth.

"You would have drawn less attention had you paraded stark naked through the halls. In Scotland women don't shroud themselves in the midst of a blistering summer."

Cat recalled the drafts that penetrated the thick walls of Edinburgh Castle and the huge peat fires kindled in every room. Shivering, she stepped away from him and clutched the shawl tightly around her shoulders.

"Where did you wish to go?" he demanded.

She met his hard gaze with defiance. "I told you. To find Andrew Percy."

A jealous rage kindled to life in Patrick's chest. He looked down at her mouth, at the defiant, pouting lips. Those lips had whispered words of love to another man. "What did you hope to gain?" he asked softly.

She flung back her head. "Are you witless, sir? I seek to release Andrew."

His fingers closed over her arm in a painful grip. "Come with me," he ordered, dragging her behind him. When they reached his room he flung her away from him and slammed the door. Breathing deeply, he fought to control his fury.

Cat leaned against the bed and frowned, searching her memory, trying to gauge what made him angrier: Andrew's escape or her own. She watched while he removed his helmet and breastplate, dropping them to the floor. He walked to the door, opened it and shouted for ale before sinking into a nearby chair.

Crispin appeared at the door, followed by a woman carrying fresh linen and ale. Expertly she bathed her lord's hands and face and divested him of his shirt. Cat gazed with interest at the deeply bronzed, heavily scarred chest, no less magnificent than she remembered. The woman pulled a clean shirt from the press and drew it over Patrick's head. Without speaking, she left the room with Crispin.

Patrick's silent stare unnerved Cat. Suddenly she felt a desperate desire for his approval. Moving to stand behind his chair, she ran a tentative finger through the thick hair at the back of his neck. She felt his muscles tighten. He reached up to stroke her cheek. Cat's heart beat more quickly. His head was back, his eyes almost shut. The look of amusement on his coppery hawk's face annoyed her. She dropped her hands and moved away.

Patrick sat up and reached for his flagon of ale. Drinking the head off the dark brew, he watched Catriona. His anger had cooled, leaving a clear cold sense of purpose.

"You are in great danger," he said at last. "Treason, in Scotland, is punishable by death."

"It is so in England as well," she whispered.

"What will you tell Jamie when Andrew Percy is brought to trial as an English spy?"

She wet her lips. "Must he be brought to trial?"

Patrick pretended to study his drink. "Do you have a plan?" he asked.

Her eyes glowed with light and hope. He almost hated to deceive her.

"You could let him go, m'lord," she said. "He knows nothing. Surely you can't think we found anything of value to take back to Henry."

"Why should I do this for you?"

She moved close to him again. "I could make it worthwhile for you, Patrick." His name was a seductive whisper on her lips.

"What are you offering?" He smelled the scent of roses in her hair.

Tilting her head to one side, she considered the matter. "Two gold crowns?"

He nearly laughed out loud. "I've enough gold," he answered.

Her hands clenched. Humiliation turned the color of her eyes to bright gold. "Tell me what you want," she demanded. "Ask and be done with it."

He stood up and reached out, pulling her toward him. His fingers stroked her hair. "I do not bribe easily, Cat. Know that, at least. As it happens, I already have everything I want."

Patrick turned and walked to the chest, picking up the parchment Crispin had removed from his jacket. Holding it out to her, he watched while she brought it close to the light and read.

As her eyes followed the letters across the page, Patrick experienced a surge of envy. He pledged to himself that when Scotland was tamed and the borders subdued, if it took him the rest of his life, he would learn the secrets of the written word.

She read quickly, but her mind refused to accept the unmistakable words. At the bottom of the scroll was the signature, *James, Rex.* It was irrevocable. The edict of a king.

Crumpling the parchment in her hand, she held it out to him. Her eyes were on his face. "So, you have officially acquired an earldom. This is what you hoped for all along, isn't it?" She spat out the words. "A noble marriage to wipe the peasant taint from your heirs."

His jaw tightened at the contempt in her voice. He shook his head. "I could have wed before this. Your cousin Mary is free."

"George would have killed you. Besides, Mary is a child. She would bore you within a week." Cat stepped very close to him, fighting the rush of heat that started deep in the pit of her stomach. "I'll not mingle my blood with yours, Patrick MacKendrick. You'll have no heirs of my body. Try as you might, I'll not bear a son for you. I swear it!"

He grinned and rubbed his finger along the satin skin of her cheek. "As long as we try, Lady Catriona, you'll hear no complaints from me. 'Tis a cold man who would marry a woman only for the heirs she would give him."

"I'll never forgive you for this." Anger choked the words in her throat. "I hate and despise you, I—"

"Enough!" the MacKendrick ordered, gripping her shoulders. "I grow weary of your insults!" He tipped her head back. Her expression was sulky and defiant, her eyes filled with furious tears. Cursing under his breath, he pulled her against him and brought his mouth down hard on hers.

Rational thought left him, leaving room for nothing but the incredible sensations of warm lips and slender curves and butter-soft skin. Desire consumed him with a sudden, raging heat. The overpowering need he felt for this woman was stronger than anything he had ever felt before, and the knowledge terrified him. Long ago, he had learned to guard his emotions, to betray nothing to his friends and enemies other than an implacable, steely resolve to protect what was his. Emotions were a dangerous luxury in the borders.

With a sense of desperation, he tightened his embrace. Molding her tightly against him, he deepened his kiss, achingly aware of the delicious, boneless feel of her pressed against his chest and the perfumed scent of flowers in her hair. She was hot-tempered and arrogant and unbelievably beautiful. Her shrewish tongue and the stubborn pride she held before her like a targe drove him to distraction, and yet there was something innocent and vulnerable about her as well. Something that awakened the protective instincts in him. Faith, he had even lied to Jamie without the smallest thanks from her.

After a long moment he lifted his head. When he spoke, his words were thick and unsteady, as if coming out of a deep, drugging sleep. "Tomorrow we leave for Hermitage and in less than a month you will be a bride. Accept it, Catriona. Resistance is pointless."

"I'll not resist." She trembled. "Please, m'lord, I must request one favor."

"What is it?" At that moment he would have beggared himself to make her happy.

"Allow Andrew Percy to go free."

His eyes were light and hard as flint. Even now, when her own future was most desperate, her thoughts were all for the Englishman.

"Impossible!" he replied harshly. "Percy will stand trial for treason."

"I am as guilty as he," she whispered. "He only came to help me."

The candles, their wells heavy with wax, flickered. A single flame wavered and died out, deepening the shadows in the room. To Cat, staring at the MacKendrick's handsome, high-boned face, it seemed as if he were a graven image come to life, his sole purpose to torment her into losing control.

She stiffened and lifted her chin. She was Catriona Wells and no stranger to suffering. This Scot, this low-born commoner, would never again witness her pain. Her face was very pale and the pupils of her eyes large and luminous.

With shaking hands and more resolve than he realized he had, Patrick put her away from him. Leading her back to her room, he summoned her woman and locked the door. He wasn't foolish enough to believe she had been so taken with his charms that she was now reconciled to her fate.

Returning to his own bedchamber, he threw himself on the bed, fully clothed. He dreamed of Catriona's slim body locked in the embrace of a light-haired youth. The boy was Andrew Percy.

❧ 13 ❧

Kate winced as the feeling came back into her legs. She was stiff with cold. A few glowing embers were all that was left of the fire. Pulling the blanket around her shoulders, she stood up and looked around. Moonlight flooded the cliff in a pearl-like glow, illuminating a slender, solitary figure high on a bluff overlooking the sea. Maura.

Tying the blanket around her shoulders, Kate found the toeholds Maura had used to climb the steep incline. She reached her side, gasping for breath. "How on earth did you manage that hill?" she asked, when her heart beat normally again.

"Practice." Maura faced the sea and the lighthouse on the jutting rocks of Muckle Flugga far to the north. She did not want to discuss the hill or the cold or the meaning of the unsettling vision Kate had experienced. She wanted nothing more than to turn back time to the day she found this unusual young woman lying on the ground near her croft, a bruise purpling her temple. It all made sense now. No wonder she had been drawn to her, sucked in by the pain of her obvious vulnerability. Blood called to blood. Maura had always known that. It was the female of the species that fought to the death for her young. She was foolish to have believed that it would go otherwise with her. Maura did not believe in coincidence. It was fate that had brought Kate Sutherland to Foula. Fate would take her back to Cait Ness and her destiny. She wet her lips and asked the question, even though she knew the answer well enough. "When were you born?"

Kate frowned. "On the fifth of February 1966."

Maura's heart twisted and she smiled bitterly, remembering the day well. "The water sign," she said softly. "Who are your parents?"

"I don't know my real parents," Kate began slowly. "My adoptive parents were Kenneth and Bonnie Sutherland." Her voice lowered. "They're both dead now."

"I'm sorry." Maura had known, of course. Bonnie's lawyer had notified her weeks before. But he hadn't told her about Kate and she hadn't asked.

"I never really thought much about it before, but I must have some family here in the Shetlands. It shouldn't be that difficult to trace them."

"Thirty years is a long time, Kate. You might have a harder time than you think." Bonnie Sutherland was the kindest woman Maura had ever known, the kind of woman who refused to forget those she had left behind. It was only right that Maura should look to Bonnie to mother the child she couldn't keep. Whatever trouble Kate was in had nothing to do with her adoptive mother. Maura was sure of it. "You may have trouble finding someone who will admit to having had a child and no husband."

Kate shrugged. She didn't want to talk about her family's history, at least not her immediate family history. She wanted to talk about her dream. Why was Maura so distant? And why this sudden interest in her family?

"I think you should go back to Cait Ness."

"But I just got here," Kate protested.

"Foula has nothing for you."

"How do you know?"

Maura remained silent.

"Please," Kate whispered. "Tell me what you know."

Maura sighed and pressed her fingers against her temples, berating herself for her foolishness, her pride, and the strange maternal yearning that begged her to hold this fragile young woman tightly in her arms and never let her go. How could she not have seen it? Kate was so very like him. No, it was the other way around: He was so very like her. Maura hadn't begun to realize what it would do to her. Her hands dropped to her sides and she turned to look directly at Kate. "You have your stane," she said softly. "It will tell you what you need to know." She hesitated and then continued: "There will come a time when you think harshly of me. It will go easier for you if you try and understand that choices are not always what they seem."

"I don't understand."

"You will, and very soon."

Kate drew a deep, quivering breath. "Shall I leave tomorrow?"

"It would be best." Maura turned and pointed toward a winding path leading down the bluff. "If you follow the clearing, you'll reach my croft."

"Aren't you coming with me?"

Maura shook her head. "Not yet. I can't begin to think of sleep."

"You saw what I did, didn't you?"

"Yes." The single word was clearly, irrevocably stated.

"He's incredible, isn't he?"

Maura didn't pretend to misunderstand. "Yes," she said again.

"Do you still think Catriona Wells and I are the same person?"

Maura looked into the light, eager eyes of the daughter she had given away. "Does it make a difference what I think?"

Kate nodded. For some reason it did.

Laying her hands on Kate's shoulders, Maura wet her lips. Where were the right words? She needed the right words. "He's dead, Kate. Make no mistake about that. No matter what you see, no matter how tempting it is to believe differently, Patrick MacKendrick, fifteenth-century border lord, is not one of the twice-born. You will not bring him back to life by wishing it."

"You once told me you didn't have the Sight."

Maura corrected her: "I said I didn't have it as you do."

"Then how can you be sure he isn't what I'm looking for?" Her words tumbled over each other. "Maybe he's looking for me, and that's why nothing ever seemed right before this. Maybe we're destined to find each other in this life."

"No, Kate." Maura shook her slightly. "It doesn't work like that. This isn't a movie. There is no spirit or weaver of destinies who likes happy endings. You are here because of a trauma, because something very dreadful occurred and a window in time wasn't able to close. Someone inside that window has waited five hundred years for you and your American upbringing, with your twentieth-century experience, to correct a terrible wrong. Even if you managed to go back in time, you couldn't stay there, nor could you bring anyone forward with you, unless . . ." Maura's hands were shaking. "My God, the generations of people you would affect. Can you really be that naive?"

Kate shook herself free. "I'm not stupid. I do understand everything you've said. And I don't believe for one minute that anyone can transcend time, much less bring anyone back. I merely suggested that it's possible there may be a reason for the way things have worked out in my life. Maybe there is someone I'm supposed to meet, someone who lives here on the islands. Is that so impossible?"

Maura sighed and dropped her hands. "No, it's not impossible. Go now. It's late. You'll need to be up early to catch the ferry." She hesitated. "If you ever need anything—"

"I don't understand. I thought you were sending me away."

Maura shook her head. "I meant if you need someone to talk to, as a friend. You're a long way from home."

Kate stared at her for a long moment, then turned and walked back toward the croft.

Clean and unfettered, the first rays of morning light streamed into the window of Maura's croft and woke Kate. She dressed, dropped her keek stane into her bag and started down the path without any sign of her hostess. Ferris's bicycle was still where she'd left it. She stopped for a minute to listen. The stillness was absolute, with no sign of the child she had seen two days before. Wheeling the bike onto the path, she pushed off and pedaled toward the village.

At the bakery she ordered scones and sipped tea until ten o'clock, time to begin the trek down the bluff to the ferry dock. There was no sign of Niall MacCormack. Ferris was on time to the minute, and the sight of his homely, sympathetic face brought tears of relief to Kate's eyes.

Again the mists shrouded them like a coffin, and again

Kate felt the merciful warmth of a thick woolen blanket draped around her shoulders. She pressed her face into the comforting plaid, and before long the steady lapping of the current, the absolute silence and her late hours of the night before took their toll and she slept.

Dawn lit the sky with a blaze of color. Bound and tied to the saddle of his horse, Andrew Percy waited in the courtyard while the men around him prepared for their journey to Hermitage Castle.

Cat was surprised to see him. Although he was helpless to aid her, his very presence was comforting. Somehow during the long ride she would manage to speak with him. After the MacKendrick returned to Edinburgh, she would find a way to set him free. Andrew would explain to King Henry that she had not betrayed his trust and that this hateful marriage was not of her choosing.

Cat knew her time was running short. Once the news that she was wed to the border lord reached England, her brother's life would no longer hold any value for Lord Neville or his king. Shivering, she drew her cloak tightly about her.

The companionable laughter of the men as they checked their horses while sharing curses and ribald jokes lifted her spirits. She stared at their lean, sun-bronzed faces and the brawny arms and legs shockingly bare below the brilliant plaids they wore wrapped around their bodies. She was conscious of a strong desire to confide in Patrick MacKendrick. Perhaps he would send his men into England to guard Richard. With men such as these to protect her brother, surely no harm would come to him. She immediately shrugged off the idea as impossible. Patrick was angry with her. And even if he were not, the fate of twelve-year-old Richard Wells was no concern of his.

Patrick's eyes were hard and his face lined with weariness when he lifted her to the saddle. Morning had obviously come too soon for him. Cat remembered the familiar way his hand had settled on the beautiful Lady Douglass's shoulder and felt a sudden stabbing jealousy at the thought of how he had most likely spent his last night in Edinburgh. She was oddly disappointed when he did not linger near her side but rode directly to the gate, taking his position at the head of the company. Her spirits brightened. If he did not intend to keep a close watch on her, she would have more opportunity to speak with Andrew. Cat resolved to delay their journey as much as possible.

It was almost noon and already the day promised unusual heat. Catriona looked around appreciatively at the country-side. She had never before seen the borders. Journeying to Scotland by ship, she had sailed through the Firth of Clyde and disembarked at Greenock. From there, Andrew had hired a barge, which had taken them to Glasgow. Only the last fifty miles to Edinburgh had been covered on horse-back.

The MacKendrick, his dark head bare, a concession to the heat, materialized at her side. "Is it as you expected?"

Cat smiled and shook her head. "It is even more beautiful than Ravenswood."

Surprised and pleased by her generous answer, Patrick grinned and waved his hand to include the land before them. "When we reach the far edge of this moor, we will be on MacKendrick land."

"So soon?" Her eyes widened. She had thought to have more time. The breathtaking beauty of the country held her spellbound, seducing her senses, distracting her mind from its original purpose. Before she was even aware time had passed the pale, dawn-streaked sky had warmed to the brilliant blue of late morning. Golden grass and clusters of dark green pines lined the banks of slow-moving burns, their icy depths as clear and deeply blue as the sky they reflected.

Patrick, his skin burned to a deep brown, smiled boyishly. The day was turning out better than he had expected. The clean wind and bright sunshine energized him, and he no longer felt traces of fatigue, remnants of his nearly sleepless night. It was good to be home. "We won't reach Hermitage until nightfall," he answered. "Are you tired, lass? Would you prefer to rest for a time?"

Cat opened her mouth to reply she could ride forever. Before the damning words left her lips, she recalled her plan. "I am rather tired," she said, hoping he would blame the sun for the telltale color rising in her cheeks.

An hour later they stopped again. This time the men chafed impatiently at the delay while Cat unplaited her hair near a trickling burn and splashed water over her face.

The third time she asked to stop, the MacKendrick refused her.

"Nay, lass. We've wasted too much time already."

"I must, Patrick," she insisted, desperation evident in her voice. She had been unable to communicate with Andrew. "Would you deny me a moment of privacy?"

He hesitated. There was no doubt in his mind that Cat was deliberately attempting to delay them. Was there a reason she wanted them outside in the open country when night fell? His instincts, well honed and razor sharp, were instantly alerted. The air was still. He looked around. Not a movement, other than the gentle swaying of the grass, interrupted the serenity of the landscape.

His gaze, moving carefully across the hilly grassland, rested at last on Catriona. Like a curtain of midnight silk, her unbound hair hung over her shoulders, black and shining, absorbing the drugging heat of late afternoon. Beads of perspiration wet her brow, and the shadows of fatigue under her eyes looked like bruises. Patrick's expression softened. She was only a woman. Lifting his hand, he shouted the order to halt.

"Hurry," he ordered, clenching his jaw. Gone was the brief interval of sympathy he had felt for her.

She was gone for much longer than he expected. "You've delayed us enough, m'lady," he growled. "There will be no more stops."

Frustrated at her inability to catch even a moment with Andrew, Cat's voice was unusually sharp. "Have some consideration for my sex. You have no skirts to hinder you."

Silenced by her rebuke, Patrick waited until she was mounted again. Urging his stallion forward, he set the pace, watching the setting sun with a sinking heart. They would not reach the safety of Hermitage for several hours. After sunset, riding the borders was risky enough for a party of men. For a woman it was unthinkable.

Night descended quickly in the Lowlands. Without warning darkness fell, extinguishing the golden glow of dusk with ruthless expediency. The velvety blackness brought with it a light wind, cool and soothing against the burning fire of Cat's cheeks. Riding at the back of the company of men, she heard the sound before anyone else. Precious seconds passed before the MacKendrick gave the signal to rein in the horses. Straining her ears, she listened again.

Patrick had known for over an hour that they were being followed. Hoping to outrun his pursuers, he had refused all requests for food and drink, forcing Cat and his men to ride at a merciless pace. The unmistakable sound of hooves, sharp against the rocky paths, the jingle of harness and stirrup, the clang of targes knocking against sword hilts, could no longer be ignored. He thought quickly. His only hope was to reach the narrow pass through the hills.

With a resounding yell, he shouted at his men to head for the pass. The passageway narrowed dangerously, which would force the men to ride single file for agonizing minutes until it opened out into a clearing surrounded by granite boulders. Patrick searched out Cat immediately. He spoke to the man closest to him. "Take the lass and wait at the other side of the clearing. If I give the word, ride for Hermitage. The rest of you lads gather around. We'll meet them on our terms."

They waited just inside the entrance to the pass. Patrick could hear breathing and a muffled whisper from the men behind them. Then there was silence. His own nerves were as steady and sharp as the blade of the dirk resting against his thigh. Many a lad, consumed by fright on the eve of his first battle, had mustered his courage simply by glancing at the controlled, confident visage of the border lord. Surely no man facing death could appear so calm, so completely without fear.

What no one knew was that Patrick MacKendrick had come to terms with death. He had cheated it so often, and seen it claim its victims in such varied, unspeakable acts of atrocity, that it no longer had the power to move him. The very fact that he still lived and walked the face of the earth was in itself against all the odds of God and man. The MacKendrick was not a religious man, but he believed very strongly in fate. When his time came, he would be ready. Fear was a wasted emotion.

Even Catriona, inexperienced at warfare and hidden from view behind a large rock, gained a measure of calm by recalling the lean, chiseled face and fierce, unswerving eyes of the man she knew would protect her with his life.

"We can take them, sir," whispered the man next to the MacKendrick.

Patrick nodded. Even though it was too dark to see, his ears had not failed him. They were few in number.

"Show yourselves, knaves," a rough voice commanded.

Patrick raised his eyebrows in surprise. It was a border accent he heard, but from the wrong side. Were the men lost or had they planned this foray? Their leader was obviously angry. Something had gone wrong with his plans.

"This is MacKendrick land," said Patrick. "We've no need to answer to you."

There was silence again. Then the voice spoke: "I know who you are. 'Tis you, MacKendrick, who are at a disadvantage. If you refuse to show yourself, we'll cut you down."

"I'm not witless, lad," Patrick replied lazily. "There are no more than a dozen of you."

"Cowards," the man taunted. "Are you afraid to meet us like men?"

Patrick laughed out loud. "If you wish to taste our metal, come closer, Sassenach."

The Englishman cursed fluently. A torch flared in the darkness and he stared into the faces of his enemies. Their numbers were equal, but he could see that the Scots were better armed. "Shall we settle this in single combat?" he asked.

This was usual on the border. Still, the MacKendrick considered it before he answered. If Catriona Wells had not been waiting in the darkness, he would have agreed readily. As it was, every action he took jeopardized her safety. Seconds passed, and he nodded his head. Patrick never took long to make his decision.

"Fair enough. Shall we say the victor is the first to draw blood?"

"Aye," the man agreed, sliding from his horse. "First blood is acceptable."

Patrick dismounted and stretched his legs. He wore a light mesh-covered mail that covered his arms and chest. The sharp edge of his sword glinted wickedly in the torch-light.

The Englishman moved toward Patrick. He was short and overly heavy. Men from both sides formed a circle with their horses and faced each other, eager for the sport to begin. Patrick stared at his opponent, his eyes narrowed. The first lunge would set the pace.

The clansman ordered to guard Catriona moved to where he had a clear vantage point. There wasn't a man on either side of the borders that could best the MacKendrick. He grinned with anticipation.

Cat wasn't so sure. Her hands were icy cold and a sick, aching fear clutched at her heart. She couldn't bear to look, and at the same time she couldn't turn away.

Patrick studied his opponent with seeming indifference. The man was too heavy to be a swordsman. Most likely he would strike quickly to avoid a prolonged fight. The border lord was prepared for his first swift thrust. He sidestepped it easily and followed up with a sudden feint to the Englishman's exposed side. The two blades locked together and then disengaged. The Englishman was already breathing hard.

Again and again, Patrick parried the flashing sword, using the dirk in his left hand with a grace and skill that only experience could bring. The Englishman's wrath grew when he realized the MacKendrick's intent. He attempted to draw back but already he had overly extended himself. His breath came in deep, laboring gasps. Helpless before his opponent's unhurried skill, he panicked and lunged forward.

Patrick stepped aside just in time to avoid the deadly edge of the man's blade. The time had come to finish it. Quickening his pace, he maneuvered the Englishman back against the rocks, sliding his sword along the man's ribs. Positioning himself carefully, he lifted his sword and with a final, powerful thrust disarmed his opponent. The blade slipped from the man's hand to lie in the dirt at his feet. Patrick stepped back, resting the point of his sword on the ground.

Quick as a fox, the Englishman reached for a knife concealed in his boot. Before he could rise and take aim, Patrick was on top of him, his sword pressed with deadly intent against his throat. The Englishman gagged but he dared not choke. His numb fingers dropped the knife.

"You are a coward, Sassenach," the MacKendrick taunted as he stood up. "The word of an Englishman is worth even less than I thought." His eyes glowed silver in the torchlight. "Hold out your hand."

The man's face was a ghastly white. He climbed to his knees. "Please, sir," he begged, "have mercy."

"What happened?" Cat asked the silent clansman.

"The bastard tried to kill the MacKendrick after the fight was fairly won."

"What will he do?"

"When a man is found to be without honor, it is the usual custom to lose a hand."

"Oh, God, no!" Cat pressed the material of her cloak tightly against her mouth.

"The MacKendrick would never cut off a man's sword hand," he reassured her. "He plays a game to teach the Englishman a lesson. There is no one in all of Scotland as merciful as the border lord."

In fascinated horror, Cat watched the drama played out in the wooded clearing. Patrick's lean features and narrowed eyes had never looked more like the devil's spawn. It was an Englishman whose life he played with. One of her own. Why then did she feel no kinship with her own countryman?

Patrick lifted his dirk. The man cried out and closed his eyes. He opened them in surprise when he felt the cold steel against his cheek and then the fiery pain. The MacKendrick had run the point of his blade across the man's face, opening his skin in a scar he would wear for life.

"Mount and get hence," Patrick ordered, never taking his eyes off the enemy before him. "The next time I find you on MacKendrick land, I'll cut off your sword arm."

The Englishman rose and stumbled toward his horse. Cat breathed a sigh of relief as the sound of hoofbeats died out in the darkness. She had learned an invaluable piece of information: Patrick MacKendrick was not deliberately cruel. He was capable of showing mercy to an enemy. She smiled. Somehow she would find a way to work this character flaw to her advantage.

❧ 14 ❧

Her room at Mrs. MacLean's bed and breakfast was exactly as she'd left it. With a grateful sigh Kate turned on the bath tap, shed her clothes, twisted an elastic ponytail holder around her hair and stepped into the steaming water. Just like home. No, better than home—tasteful furniture, modern amenities, excellent food and complete privacy. She sank back, rested her head against the old-fashioned porcelain tub and closed her eyes.

Maura's words had disturbed her. Her power was strong. The woman was hiding something. She knew when to look away and when to bring down the shutters that so effectively prevented anyone from reading the message in her eyes. Even though Kate had used all her concentration, she couldn't see it.

Kate pulled the elastic from her hair and sank down into the tub, completely submerging her head. She opened her eyes, watching as her hair took on a life of its own, the dark strands floating to the sides of the tub. What could Maura be keeping from her? Out of breath, she arched her back and sat up, taking in deep lungfuls of air. Her thick curtain of hair touched the middle of her back.

Reaching for the shampoo, Kate poured a liberal amount into her palm and massaged it through her scalp. Her ears popped and she heard voices downstairs. Someone else, most likely a woman, was visiting Mrs. MacLean. She turned on the tap, rinsed her hair and reached for a towel.

The feminine voice sounded high and young, like a school-girl's. Kate pulled the plug and stood up, wrapping the towel around her hair before reaching for another one. She didn't feel like making conversation with a stranger, but she was hungry and Mrs. MacLean had promised scones with tea.

Thirty minutes later she stared into the mirror, critically assessing her appearance. The water in Scotland was different. It did wonders for her hair. Thick and full, it fell past her shoulders in soft waves, a style impossible to achieve in California. She had taken time with her makeup. A soft rose blush sculpted out dramatic cheekbones and a new eye shadow called Heather emphasized the startling green of her eyes. She was pleased with her calf-length skirt and brown leather boots, but they needed a splash of color. Opening the armoire, she found a cherry-red cashmere sweater and pulled it over her head. She frowned at the mirror. Something was still missing. Rummaging through her bag of cosmetics, Kate found her lipstick, the exact shade of her sweater, and applied it carefully. Flushed with confidence, she walked down the stairs into the parlor.

A girl, somewhere between eighteen and twenty, very blond and tastefully dressed, sat across from Mrs. MacLean. She was lovely, with the Scandinavian good looks Kate had begun to associate with many of the islanders.

"Here you are at last, Miss Sutherland," said Glennis MacLean. "Just in time for tea. I know I should introduce you, but it is so confusing. Do you mind if I use your first names?"

"Not at all," said Kate and the girl in unison.

"Very well." Mrs. MacLean nodded at Kate. "Miss Kate Sutherland, this is Lady Victoria Sutherland. Lady Victoria, Kate Sutherland from America."

"I'm very pleased to meet you, Kate," said the girl politely. "I've never been to America. My father said he would send me when I've finished my studies at university. Do you have family on Cait Ness?"

"I'm not sure," Kate replied slowly. "Other than my parents, I don't know very much about my family."

Victoria's eyes widened. "How odd. Perhaps we're re-lated. All the Sutherlands are. You do look very familiar."

She turned glowing eyes first on Mrs. MacLean and then back to Kate. "Wouldn't it be exciting to find a long-lost relative from America? We could keep in touch and I could visit you when I come."

Kate laughed. The girl was refreshingly straightforward. "You're welcome to visit and stay with me even if we're not related."

"How lovely." Victoria clapped her hands. "Then you must visit my home as well. Come tomorrow, with Mr. MacCormack. My father will be here by then. He'll be so pleased."

Kate's eyebrow lifted. "Mr. Niall MacCormack?"

The girl nodded. "He was my professor in Edinburgh. Now he's here on Cait Ness researching his book. I've come to invite him to dinner."

"I don't want to intrude," Kate began hastily. "We can arrange another time for my visit."

The girl's eyes were huge and very unusual, their color a pale celestial blue with chips of white flecked throughout the irises. Kate couldn't remember seeing anyone so fair.

"You must come," she pleaded. "I never know what to say to the professor when I'm alone with him. He's really quite wonderful, you know."

Kate exchanged an amused glance with Mrs. MacLean. "I'm sure he is. If two strangers at the same time won't be too much for your family, I'd be delighted to accept your invitation."

Victoria laughed out loud. "I'm so glad. You can entertain my father while I show Niall—" She blushed. "I mean, Mr. MacCormack, the castle."

Kate's eyebrows lifted. "You live in a castle?"

"Oh dear, didn't I tell you?" Mrs. MacLean interrupted. "Victoria is the daughter of the laird and his late wife."

"I see." Kate's mouth curved. This absurd child saw her as a suitable companion for her father, probably a stuffy balding man the image of Winston Churchill.

Glennis MacLean rose from her chair. "It's past time for tea. I'll bring the tray in."

Victoria jumped up. She was taller than Mrs. MacLean, nearly Kate's height. "I'll help you," she said. "I love setting out the pastries. Cook won't allow me in the kitchen at home. You don't mind if I leave you for a moment, do you, Kate?"

"Not when it's for such a good cause."

Victoria nodded and followed Mrs. MacLean into the kitchen.

Kate reached for the newspaper lying on the end table and settled back into the comfortable couch cushions. A cozy fire blazed in the hearth, and the afternoon sun flooded the room with golden light. The sounds of china and silver and companionable voices drifted in from the kitchen. Long moments passed. Kate basked in thorough, satisfying contentment.

"Hello, Kate." A voice, low and masculine, came from the foot of the stairs.

Startled, she turned, catching her elbow on the edge of a lamp and reaching out to steady it before it fell. When she turned back to Niall, she was completely composed. "I didn't realize you were staying here. I didn't see you on the ferry." Kate had forgotten how attractive he was. Framed in the doorway, he looked very tall and approachable in faded jeans and a cable-knit sweater. His hair was streaked from the sun, and the high bones of his face and his hands resting easily at his sides were burned a deep bronze.

"I took the afternoon boat. There aren't many places to stay on Cait Ness. I hope it doesn't make you uncomfortable."

"No," she lied. "Not at all. In fact, thanks to you, I have a dinner invitation tomorrow."

Niall frowned. "I don't understand."

"Victoria Sutherland came to ask you to dinner. We met and she invited me as well." Kate's eyes danced. "She seems to have a particular interest in you."

Niall's brow cleared. He didn't look the slightest bit embarrassed. "Victoria Sutherland is a charming child. One day she'll be a lovely woman, but not for quite some time. Her home, however, is very worth seeing, and her father has a collection of heirlooms that is the envy of every historian in Scotland." He looked thoughtful. "If I remember the family history correctly, it may interest you as well."

"Why?"

He shook his head. "I'd like to be sure of my facts first."

Kate sighed. "Everyone seems to be very concerned about my welfare."

Niall stared at her profile. No wonder, he thought. She exuded a curious innocence, every emotion exposed and vulnerable, her fragility evident in her sensitive mouth, the shadowy circles under her leaf-green eyes and the coiled tension in the length of her too-thin body. Deliberately, he stopped himself. Kate Sutherland had made it all too clear that she did not appreciate his interest. "I'll take a minute to go upstairs and clean up," he said. "Tell Mrs. MacLean that I've arrived, but you needn't wait for me."

Kate watched him walk away. Niall was so sensible. There wasn't the slightest awkwardness in his manner. She was silly to have worried about seeing him again.

Victoria was ecstatic that he'd arrived and even more so when he graciously accepted her dinner invitation. "Father will be so pleased. He's wanted to meet you ever since he read your book."

"I'm flattered," replied Niall. "It will be an honor to meet him as well."

"My father is fascinated with history," Victoria explained to Kate.

"Really? All aspects of history, or a specific area?"

"Mostly the history of the isles. We've an interesting past, you know."

"I've done some research," Kate said slowly, "mostly to prepare for this trip, but I'd like to know more."

"Between Mr. MacCormack and my father, you'll know everything there is to know," Victoria promised.

Kate laughed. "I can hardly wait."

When Victoria's father rose from the upholstered wing-back chair and took Kate's hand in his own, she was completely tongue-tied. Hunter Sutherland, laird of his clan, duke of Dornach, *Dinc Chat,* was a complete surprise. Tall and fit, with a full head of gray-black hair and light-filled hazel eyes, he looked much younger than his fifty-three years. No wonder Victoria had no qualms about matching him up with women two decades his junior.

"Welcome to Dornach Castle, Miss Sutherland," he said in a voice that held the barest hint of a Scots brogue.

"My pleasure." She hesitated. "I'm sorry, but British titles escape me. Mrs. MacLean said the proper address was 'Your Grace,' but I really don't think I can say it with a straight face."

The duke's eyes warmed with laughter. "Spoken like a true republican. What would you like to call me?"

Kate thought for a minute. "I don't really know. May I tell you later?"

"Of course, my dear. Until then, why don't we use first names. Mine is 'Hunter.'"

She knew she would never be able to call him that either. There was something about this Scottish duke that shook her to the core. He was handsome and courtly in an old-fashioned British way, but Kate was no stranger to handsome men, and this one was fifteen years beyond her reference point for sexual attractiveness. There was something in his eyes when they rested on her. Shock perhaps, or disbelief, maybe even suspicion, followed by dawning awareness. He turned away to greet Niall before she could put her finger on it.

Dinner was wonderful, or it would have been if Kate had known the reason for the duke's intense scrutiny. Every time she looked up from her plate, his eyes were on her face. Finally the ordeal was over, dessert cleared, coffee and brandy drunk, cigars declined.

"Would you care to see the picture gallery, Kate?" asked the duke. "We have the largest collection in the country outside of Edinburgh."

"Thank you." Kate laid her napkin on the table. "I'd like that very much."

He rose and came down the long expanse of table to hold out his arm. "Shall we?"

Kate stood up and slipped her arm through his. She looked expectantly at Niall. "Will you join us?"

"Yes."

Victoria pouted. "I wanted to show you the archives. We have some wonderful old Celtic and Scandinavian artifacts."

Niall hesitated, looked briefly at her downcast face and summoned his most charming smile. "As much as the gallery tempts me, I believe I'll pass this time. Victoria, I would be delighted to have you guide me through the archives."

Victoria beamed.

"Another crisis averted," Hunter said dryly. "Victoria, my darling, you're really much too old for this. It isn't at all attractive and serves no purpose other than to emphasize your extreme youth."

Blood rose in the girl's fair cheeks but she said nothing. Kate ached for her. She was no longer interested in the gallery, nor did she wish to be alone with Hunter Sutherland. Mrs. MacLean's flower-studded guest room seemed very far away. If only she could get through this night.

The hallway was very long and dimly lit, with wall lamps that looked like candles. The carpet runner was Persian wool, rich, plush and jewel-colored. Oak floorboards gleamed with lemon oil, and hunting scenes framed in dark mahogany lined the walls. The duke maintained a light, even flow of conversation, seemingly unconcerned that Kate did nothing more than nod her head or answer in the briefest of monosyllables.

The portrait gallery was on the second floor. Anticipation traveled from her spine up through her fingers and down to her toes. Her hand tightened on his arm. She felt his muscles tense, but the even flow of his words continued as he stopped at each portrait, explaining its history. This wasn't what he wanted her to see. Kate knew it, and she knew Hunter Sutherland knew it. Why were they playing this game, as if this were just another night and the time they had together would last forever?

Suddenly he stopped, and Kate looked up at the portrait before her. Her eyes widened and she gasped. The girl was small-boned and black-haired, with clear, pale green eyes. She was very young and the clothing was different, but there could be no mistake. The face that stared back at Kate was so like her own that she could have been the artist's model. "Catriona Wells," she whispered. "I can't believe it. She looks exactly like me."

Hunter Sutherland frowned. "You know who she is? What else do you know?"

"Only that in the gallery at Holyrood Palace is a painting of Catriona Wells and that she resembles me. Niall told me."

"I think we can safely say that 'resembles' is an understatement," the duke said dryly.

Kate turned her head to study the profile of his maturely handsome face. When he felt her gaze and their eyes met, she spoke: "Why is this painting in your family gallery? I thought Catriona's mother was a Stewart and her father an Englishman."

Hunter nodded. "Catriona's mother married an Englishman named Wells while her sister, Anne, married Adam Gordon, second earl of Huntly, in 1479. After the death of her uncle, the ninth earl of Sutherland, Anne succeeded to the title. Her first son became the earl of Huntly and her second became the earl of Sutherland. Catriona MacKendrick, countess of Bothwell, is my ancestor."

"Can you tell me why she looks like me?"

His eyes narrowed. "I have an idea. You are a Sutherland, aren't you?"

Kate shook her head. "Not really. I was adopted by the Sutherlands but I don't believe there is a biological tie. Of course it's possible. My parents found me on this very island, so it's likely I do have some Sutherland blood."

"How old are you, Kate?"

"Thirty."

Hunter frowned. "There have been no adoptions on this island in my lifetime."

"That's what Maura said. But it *was* thirty years ago. Maybe an unmarried woman wouldn't want her pregnancy to be known. At least that's what Maura told me."

Hunter's jaw was tight, and a thin white line rimmed his lips. "How do you know Maura Sutherland?"

For some reason that she couldn't identify, Kate was reluctant to tell him. "I was exploring the cliffs of Foula and I hit my head," she improvised. "When I woke up, I was in Maura's cottage."

"I see." His eyes were distant, his expression thoughtful, as if Kate and the portrait gallery had disappeared and he was far away. Suddenly he smiled, and his vacant look vanished. "Have you seen enough, Miss Sutherland? Shall we join my daughter and the latest recipient of her admiration?"

Kate's temper hovered on the edge of civility. "Is it Niall you object to, my lord, or your daughter's very natural inclination toward an attractive man?"

"I thought we'd agreed on first names."

Kate shrugged her shoulders. "You called me 'Miss Sutherland.' My mother taught me to be polite to my elders."

Hunter looked amused. "Touché! Point well taken, my dear. Allow me to explain. Victoria is forever falling in love. Discerning who among her very inappropriate suitors is actually in love with her and who merely desires her fortune can be quite expensive."

"Niall doesn't need money."

"Everyone needs money."

She hesitated.

"Out with it," ordered the duke. "This evening has become more amusing than I could have imagined."

"I don't think Niall sees your daughter as anything more than a child. There must be fifteen years between them."

He bit back a smile. "Possibly," he conceded, "but a fifteen-year age difference is not uncommon in Scotland."

"I'm sure Niall sees it the way I do," Kate replied firmly. "In fact, I know he does."

"Really?" The duke studied her face. "In that case, I stand corrected and we shall say nothing more on the subject."

Relieved, Kate walked beside him down the stairs into the well-lit parlor. A rolling cart with a pot of tea and delicate pastries stood near the fire. Niall and Victoria sat across the table from each other on separate couches. Niall stood up when Kate and the duke entered the room.

Hunter Sutherland raised his eyebrows. "Finished already? Victoria couldn't possibly have shown you the entire collection."

Niall smiled politely. "Perhaps some other time. It's very late. I think Kate and I should be on our way."

"Please stay for tea," Victoria begged.

Kate interjected. "Niall's right. It is late and I couldn't eat another bite after that wonderful dinner. Thank you very much for your hospitality." She turned toward the sulky girl. "I'm looking forward to our next visit, Victoria. Please come as soon as you can."

Victoria's face brightened. "I'll do that, if you really want me."

Kate smiled warmly. "It's settled then."

Later, in the car, Niall broached the question that had bothered him ever since Kate had disappeared up the stairs on the duke's arm. "Did he have anything interesting to show you in the gallery?"

Kate stared out the window at the night-dark cliffs hovering menacingly close to the road. Finally she spoke. "I saw a portrait of Catriona Wells. I wonder if it's the same as the one in Holyrood Palace." She turned to Niall. "Do you know?"

He shook his head. "No. But it shouldn't be difficult to find out. When you go back to Edinburgh, visit the palace gallery."

Kate thought out loud. "He said the Sutherlands married into the Gordon clan. Catriona is his ancestor."

"More likely Janet and Mary Gordon are in the direct line. Catriona Wells was a first cousin."

"Do you think that's why Catriona and I resemble each other?"

"I don't know," Niall said slowly. "But I'm sure you're on the right track."

She looked at him helplessly. "Where do I go from here?"

Niall grinned. "To the Feast of Beltane, with me."

"What's that?"

"A pagan celebration of spring."

"When?"

"Tomorrow night, right here on Cait Ness. Families from all over the islands attend. You won't be disappointed."

"What is it like?"

Niall stared straight ahead while he spoke, concentrating on the dark road ahead. "The men of the islands start a huge bonfire while the women prepare traditional food for the feast. Everyone gathers around the fire to chant and sing while they wait for the young woman chosen to represent the Celtic Goddess of Spring. She leads them in local dances, circling the fire. A man, playing the role of the great horned stag, makes his way to the woman and leads her away from the dancing to consummate the ritual of fertility. Meanwhile the people left behind drink and dance and feast for the rest of the night."

Kate was amused. "What an interesting way to justify illicit sex!"

Niall laughed. "I would never have imagined anyone from California describing sex as 'illicit.' Besides, it really isn't all that shocking. Usually the couple is already partial to one another."

"You have a very odd idea of the typical Californian, and it sounds like an orgy to me."

"Not really." Niall ignored the first part of her statement. "An 'orgy' implies something entirely different. The couples who choose to practice the ritual are often married or nearly so. It's merely a loosening of inhibitions."

Unconvinced, Kate remained silent until Niall pulled into a space in front of Mrs. MacLean's establishment and turned off the motor.

He moved so that his back rested against the door and looked at her. "Is something bothering you, Kate?"

She felt the slow burn make its way to her cheeks and was grateful for the concealing darkness. "Not really. It's just that Hunter Sutherland believes everyone interested in his daughter is a potential fortune hunter."

He frowned. "He doesn't give her much credit, does he?"

Kate shook her head.

"He's wrong, you know. Victoria is a slightly spoiled but very charming girl who is perfectly capable of finding a man interested in her for the right reasons."

"I know that."

His mouth tightened. "Did you tell him?"

Kate refused to look at him. Her voice was so soft that he leaned closer to hear her words. "In a manner of speaking. I told him you weren't a fortune hunter."

Niall was silent for a long time. "It's quite flattering to

have you champion my cause," he said softly, "but you can't possibly know whether I am or not."

Astonished, she looked up and their eyes met. "Of course I can. I've seen where you live. You're obviously well respected in your profession. You don't need money, and Victoria is a child. You said it yourself. That doesn't sound like a man bent on making a girl fall in love with him."

His pupils were large, the gray irises mere rings around the black circles. He stared at her, his eyes lingering on her lips, her chin, the carven bones sculpting her cheeks. Kate forgot to breathe. Slowly he reached out and pulled her against his chest. She closed her eyes and his mouth came down on hers in a hard, possessive kiss.

Instinctively, her lips parted against his tongue and her arms slipped around his neck. After a long time his mouth gentled, his hands moved from her waist, above her ribs and the sides of her breasts to support the back of her head. Leaning over her, his tongue filled her mouth, again and again. Drugged into a mindless haze of sensual pleasure, Kate did not protest when his hand slipped beneath her sweater and the lacy cup of her bra to stroke the sensitive skin beneath. His mouth left hers to trail kisses down her neck. She arched her back to give him better access to the tiny row of pearl buttons down the front of her sweater. Concentrating on the slow, sure movement of his hands baring her breasts, she ignored the slide of his lips until they closed, hot and seeking, over her right nipple.

Gasping, Kate pulled away. Sensations too deep, too intensely piercing, washed over her. She didn't want to feel this way, not now, not yet, when everything was still so unsettled. Niall knew that. She'd told him often enough. The air between the two of them sizzled with tension.

Suddenly she was angry, and the words, intentionally wounding, left her lips. "You're very good," she said, after her breathing normalized. "But I would have believed it without a demonstration."

Deliberately, Niall reached across the seat to button her sweater. "You're either incredibly naive or a complete fool," he said softly. "I can't decide which. Shall we go in? Mrs. MacLean is probably worrying as we speak."

"Of course." Kate scrambled out of the car. "I didn't mean to keep you."

His lips twitched. "The pleasure was mine."

She was very conscious of his hand resting against the small of her back, guiding her up the steps and through the unlocked door. Glennis MacLean sat on the couch, knitting.

"Oh, my dears, you're finally back." She chuckled. "How did your evening turn out?"

Kate answered immediately. "It was very nice, thank you, but all that food made me tired. I think I'll go straight to bed."

Mrs. MacLean nodded. "Do that, dear. I've warmed your sheets with bricks. They hold heat so well, you know." She smiled at Niall. "Are you deserting me as well, young man?"

"Not yet," replied Niall. "I'll have a cup of tea first and then read awhile. There is something I'd like to ask you about."

"Very well. Good night, Kate. I hope you've no plans for tomorrow. It's the Feast of Beltane, and preparing the food is part of the pleasure."

"Niall's already told me about it. I'd love to help with the food, Mrs. MacLean."

"Wonderful. Run up to bed now, dear, and have a good rest."

The night was cold, but the hot bricks had warmed the sheets to a toasty temperature. Kate snuggled beneath the thick quilt and mentally thanked Mrs. MacLean for her thoughtfulness. She closed her eyes, expecting to fall asleep immediately.

It was a gradual transition. At first she didn't notice that much more than her vision was involved. This time she smelled peat smoking from the chimneys, tasted clean rain on the wind and felt every aching bone in her exhausted body. Catriona's portrait danced before her, changing the darkness behind her eyelids to the rich, jewel-bright colors of the European Renaissance.

❧ 15 ❧

Cat was surprised when she saw the turrets of Hermitage Castle looming against the night sky. It wasn't at all impressive in size. Constructed in the shape of an H, it sat upon a small hillock with a clear, unobstructed view of the borders. Until James had gifted it to Patrick MacKendrick the impregnable fortress, gateway to Scotland, had belonged to the earls of Douglass. Because of its vulnerable location so close to England, the castle could only be entrusted to one whose loyalty had been proven without question.

Cat knew that Jamie was not overly fond of Lord Douglass and his beautiful lady. She experienced a brief surge of satisfaction at the thought of Patrick's mistress in disgrace and then had the remorse to feel ashamed of such an uncharitable sentiment. As her horse's hooves clattered across the wooden drawbridge, she recalled the rumors whispering that no woman, except those born within the walls, had ever before entered the castle gates. She frowned. If not at Hermitage, where had Patrick MacKendrick lived with his late wife?

The clansmen set up an ear-splitting clamor to announce their arrival. Cat watched wearily from her horse as the iron portcullis was lifted slowly above the curved arch of the gatehouse. With the back of her hand she wiped her forehead, grimacing at the dirt on her fingers. She needed a bath and food.

Patrick made his way to her side. Leaning across the space that separated their horses, he pulled a twig from her hair. "There is no one of importance inside," he said quietly, "but you'll feel better if you arrive looking presentable."

"Thank you," she muttered, suddenly uncomfortable with the intimacy of the moment. It was almost as if they were already master and mistress of the castle, newly arrived home from a tiring journey. Cat wasn't ready for such familiarity from the MacKendrick.

With an inscrutable look on his face, Patrick watched her wipe the worst of the day's grime from her cheeks and forehead with a handkerchief. Tucking the soiled linen into her sleeve, she followed him into the courtyard. When he lifted Cat to the ground, his hands stayed at her waist. "Can you manage the walk up?" he asked.

About to reply that she could manage as well as he, she looked up at his face. Flickering silver lights warmed his eyes and his face showed the strain of the past several hours. He grinned ruefully. "I don't know if I've the strength to carry you upstairs, but I'll give it my best."

Cat looked up at the narrow twisting stairwell, its steps shallow and treacherously steep. "We can lean on each other," she teased, offering him the brilliance of her candid smile.

Patrick forgot to breathe. Even with her tangled hair and dirt-streaked face, the still beauty of Catriona's face had the power to rob him of speech. Cupping her cheek gently with his hands, he drew her into the circle of his arms.

Her head was tucked under his chin, her forehead against his throat. She could feel the steady beat of his pulse. All thoughts of resisting melted under the tenderness of his embrace. Remembering his fatigue, she spoke softly. "We should go up. You must be nigh to swooning after such a fight."

"Hush, lass," he said. "Don't say anything."

His voice was deep and warm. His hand gently caressed the shining crown of her head. For a long time he didn't move. Cat couldn't remember ever feeling so content. She could have stayed there forever, enjoying the touch of his hand on her hair. Never would she have believed the legendary border lord, so hard and ruthless, could be tender and gentle, wooing her into submission with the magic of his charm.

Suddenly, without warning, in the torchlit courtyard

before twenty grinning clansmen, he lifted her chin and kissed her.

Cat was drowsy no longer. The need for sleep disappeared, the firm lips possessing hers demanding a response. Her fingers clung to his shoulders and her mouth parted.

He was the first to pull away. His eyes glittered, and Cat could hear his shallow breathing. Leaning against him briefly to catch her breath, she wondered if the pounding she heard was her own heart or his.

"Will you forget your pride and admit there is fire between us?" he asked, his voice pitched low, for her ears alone.

"There is fire between many a man and maid," she answered, pulling out of his arms and turning toward the stairs. "Marriage is another matter entirely."

Patrick pulled her back against him. She could feel the rigid muscles of his thighs through her gown.

"Explain your words, m'lady."

"Not now, Patrick," she demurred. "I'm tired."

His grip tightened on her wrist, twisting it slightly. "Now!" he ordered.

"Unhand me," she hissed through clenched teeth. "I'll not be mauled like a tavern wench."

"Speak!" The dangerous softness of his voice frightened her.

"Very well." Twisting out of his grasp, Cat turned to face him. "Only a fool looks for passion in the marriage bed." Her eyes were pale and filled with light. "You know that yourself, m'lord."

"Aye." Patrick nodded. " 'Tis so for many nobles. But I am not noble born, and coming from the lips of a maid, the sentiment sounds cold."

"I am noble born," she spoke deliberately, "and I won't always be a maid."

His eyes veiled, he waited silently for her to explain.

For reasons that were unclear even to herself, Cat was angry. She hurled the damning words at him. "Lady Douglass finds favor in your eyes, does she not?"

With a lightning-swift movement she was wrenched off her feet and into his arms. Patrick swore, murmuring words that Cat had never heard before. Listening in fascinated horror, she knew that this time she had provoked him too far. Tentatively she reached up to touch him. Her fingers found the tight muscle along his jaw, the hollow in his cheek, the firm, cool lips and the rough stubble of a new growth of beard.

"I'm sorry," she whispered.

He lifted her hand to his mouth. They were beautiful hands, long-fingered and slender, the nails raised and perfectly oval. He pressed his lips to her palm.

"You are not Lady Douglass." Despite the softness of his touch, his words were clipped and hard. "God help you if I ever find that you played me false. Do you understand me, Catriona?"

Her eyes were wide and gold on his face. She shook her head slowly. "Nay, Patrick. I don't understand you at all. But I do believe you."

He nodded, satisfied with her answer. Anger had given him new reserves of energy. Lifting her into his arms, he climbed the stairs. Around and around they went until it seemed to Cat they would climb forever. The stairwell was very narrow. She closed her eyes against the dizziness that always came when she was confined to closed-in quarters and prayed that soon they would stop.

Patrick had planned well. Her chambers were high in the south tower. At its foot would be Cat's morning room. On the next landing were her servant's sleeping quarters. High above, reached by a richly carpeted stair, was her bedchamber. Until her wedding, he had assured her that she would never sleep without one of her women. After that, thought Patrick, smiling in anticipation, she would never sleep without him.

Once again on her feet, Cat looked around her with pleasure. The rooms had obviously been prepared with care. They were paneled against the drafts, and there was a fireplace in every one. Fragrant sandalwood burned in the grate in her bedchamber. The window measured ten feet from the floor to the ceiling, and its tiny panes of glass had been scrubbed so clean they sparkled like diamonds. Long curtains fell to the floor, and on a fine day she would be able to see clear to Edinburgh and the Firth of Forth.

"My thanks, sir," she said shyly. "You have gone to a great deal of trouble to ready this room for me."

Lifting her chin, he pressed a hard, brief kiss upon her lips. "The room is not intended for you alone, lass. Soon you'll learn to share it." His eyes were bright with laughter as he nodded toward the bed. "I've come to appreciate the comforts of a well-appointed bedchamber, both inside and out of the sheets."

Cat waited until the door closed behind him before stretching out on the feather bed. The comforting sound of women's voices floated up from the room below. Promising herself that she would remove her clothing after a brief rest, she closed her eyes and immediately fell asleep.

Even before she awoke, Cat knew that someone else was in the room. Feigning sleep, she lifted her eyelids a fraction and peeked at the intruder through her lashes. Shocked beyond measure, her eyes flew open and she sat up. A girl of no more than six or seven years stood by the side of the bed, staring solemnly down at her.

Cat smiled. "Good morning."

The child's serious look vanished and she smiled back. "Good morning to you," she replied.

Cat was enchanted. She liked children, and this one was particularly attractive. Thick red-gold curls were caught in a ribbon at the nape of her neck and her eyes were a lovely, clear gray. Those eyes reminded her of someone, but she was still hazy from sleep and couldn't recall who it was. The child was richly dressed, and the locket around her neck was of the finest gold.

"What is your name, lass?"

"Isobel," answered the child.

"Do you live near here, Isobel?"

She laughed. "I live here, m'lady, at Hermitage."

Cat's curiosity was piqued. Patrick hadn't mentioned there was anyone besides servants living at Hermitage. "Where are your parents?" she asked, flinging the covers away and sliding her legs over the side of the bed. "They must think me terribly lazy to sleep away the morning. Did they send you to wake me?"

Isobel shook her head. "My maid told me about you. I waited as long as I could for you to wake, but I couldn't wait any longer. No one knows I'm here," she confided. "My mother is making perfume in the kitchen and my father rode in last night from Edinburgh."

That explained it, thought Cat, as she sat on the low stool before the vanity and reached for her brush. The child was related to one of the men who had accompanied them from the castle. Cat frowned. Her clothing was unusually fine for one so young. The MacKendrick must pay his men well.

Isobel slid off the bed and took the brush from Cat's hand. "May I brush it?" she begged. "I promise not to pull. My mother often has me brush her hair at night."

Cat was no match for the pleading look in the gray eyes. "It would please me very much to have you brush my hair," she said gently. "I'm fortunate to have such a willing handmaiden."

"'Tis so black," said the child admiringly as she pulled the brush through the shining strands. "If it were plaited, the braid would be as thick as my hand."

"Aye," said Cat, staring at the girl's reflection in the glass. She looked so very familiar. Awareness danced at the edge of her memory, hovering just out of reach. Where could she have seen the child before this?

Tugging at a difficult tangle, the pink tip of her tongue visible at the corner of her mouth, Isobel asked the question that her burning curiosity could no longer keep contained: "Morag said you are betrothed to my father. Is it true?"

The impact of her artless words was not lost on Isobel. The beautiful lady had suddenly gone quite still. The child knew instinctively that behind the frozen peace of her expression, Catriona Wells was enraged. Isobel shrank back against the bed.

"What is your father's name, lass?" The ominous tone of Cat's voice did not match her controlled features and veiled eyes.

"Patrick MacKendrick," the child whispered.

Cat turned away from the mirror and searched Isobel

MacKendrick's face. The cobwebs faded from her brain. She had been a fool not to see it. Those eyes, like water over sun-whitened stones, the thin-lipped, mobile mouth and determined chin, the high-boned face with its promise of beauty, could belong to no one else but the bairn of Patrick MacKendrick.

Her hands clenched. He had tricked her, forced her to come to Hermitage where she was friendless, made her believe it was marriage he offered, even kissed her in front of his men. Cat flushed with rage and humiliation. She had allowed him to do unspeakable things to her body, to arouse emotions she had never believed herself capable of feeling, when all the time he had a wife.

Catriona lowered her eyes, remembering a night of cold and stars and firelight when they had shared a simple meal. Patrick had told her of his wife and the child within her, killed by English borderers. Cat burned from the memory of her own sympathy. She had played the fool. How he must have laughed behind her back.

Rising from the stool, she turned toward the child. The MacKendrick would pay for his deception. Cat forced herself to smile. The lass was blameless. Still, she was old enough to learn that a man could only have one wife at a time, even a man as powerful as her father.

"You are mistaken, Isobel. Your father and I are not betrothed. He is already married."

Isobel opened her mouth and then closed it without speaking, afraid to risk the frozen rage again. Intelligent enough to know that her innocent words had upset her father's guest, she still didn't understand why.

She inched toward the door, pausing for a moment on the threshold. "I'll be leaving now, m'lady. Fiona will be up shortly with food."

Closing the door behind her, Isobel sighed. Catriona Wells looked like an angel when she slept, and at first her smile had been lovely. Why had she behaved so strangely? Shrugging her shoulders, Isobel ran down the stairs to the kitchens to seek out her mother.

❧ 16 ❧

Patrick waved his hand impatiently. "Tell Lady Wells I cannot see her now."

It was already too late. Cat passed through the massive wooden door, beautifully carved and flanked with guards, to stand before him. The expression on her face did not bode well for peaceful conversation.

Patrick rose politely, acknowledging her presence, and then sat down again. Two men compiled lists beside him. The large rectangular table was covered with papers, ledgers and a brass container to keep the sealing wax hot and sticky.

"I would speak with you privately," Cat said through clenched teeth.

Patrick sighed. Her temper was fast becoming a burden. "I'm occupied at the moment," he replied. "Can it wait?"

"No!" The single word burst indignantly from her lips.

He frowned as his eyes rested on her shaking hands. She was very near to losing control. Pushing his chair back, he stood up and gestured toward the scribes. "Leave us," he ordered. The men were quick to do his bidding. A guard looked up and Patrick nodded. In seconds the room was completely cleared.

"What is it, lass? Weren't the sheets clean enough?" He smiled, hoping to coax the strained expression from her face.

" 'Tis not the sheets I object to, sir."

"Tell me what troubles you."

"How long were you going to keep up this pretense?"

Patrick frowned and walked over to the fireplace. Propping his boot on the fender, he hooked his thumbs through his belt. "What pretense?"

She spat out the words: "When Jamie agreed to our marriage, did he know you already had a wife?"

"Of course." Patrick's eyebrows drew together. "'Tis no secret."

"And you still intend to wed with me?" Her outraged voice quivered.

"Aye." He nodded. "'Tis what I intended all along."

"Holy God, Patrick. Would you condemn your immortal soul to the fires of hell and mine with it?"

"Enough!"

The cold rage in his voice silenced her. Refusing to show her fear, Cat watched him cross the room to stand before her. She winced as his hands gripped her shoulders.

"There will be no more talk of your noble Stewart lineage. You may be well versed in the arts of reading and writing, mistress, but you are woefully ignorant of Scottish history. The Stewarts are descended from cattle reivers and horse thieves, much like the rest of us born north of the borders. If your noble English blood recoils from the touch of a Scot, so be it. You'll soon learn to live with it." His eyes glittered as he pulled her closer, his mouth no more than an inch from hers. "I'll warrant I can even make you like it."

She was struck speechless. Tiny blue veins throbbed at her temples. Under the black winged brows her eyes, huge and pale, showed no fear, only a strange unguarded look of horror.

His anger faded. "Before the month is out, we will exchange wedding vows and you'll share my bed, however much the thought disgusts you."

Cat found her voice at last. "Where will Isobel's mother sleep?"

"Where she's slept for the last seven years; with her husband." His words were louder than before, his patience stretched to the breaking point.

Cat gasped. "Do you deny that Isobel is yours?"

"Of course not!" Patrick struggled to control his temper. The woman was truly exasperating. "Even if I wished to, I could not. The child is the image of me."

"But her mother is alive," Cat whispered. "You told me she died during a raid, and her child with her."

At last he understood. "Can a woman who has reached the age of twenty truly be such an innocent?" he asked, amusement coloring his voice.

She pulled out of his arms and turned away, a picture of injured dignity. "Spare me your mockery, Cat."

"I never married Isobel's mother, Cat." He stood behind her, his mouth close to the shining hair. She smelled faintly of roses. Calling upon a lifetime of discipline, he kept his hands at his sides, making no move to touch her.

"Why not?" The words were out before she could call them back. Embarrassment stained her cheeks. Now he would think she was jealous.

Patrick smiled. For a woman who loudly protested her disinterest, she was unusually curious about his past.

"Brenna Sinclair was a bonny wench," he explained. "Once, long ago, we came together for a night. But that is all in the past. She's wed now and her choice was a wise one."

Cat turned to face him, her eyes wide and steady. "Did her husband know of the child before he wed her?"

Patrick nodded. "You give a man no credit, Catriona. He loved her."

"Do you know him?"

"Aye."

"And Isobel's mother?" Cat persisted, her cheeks flaming. "Was she disappointed that you wouldn't marry her?"

"It wasn't like that, Catriona," he replied. "There was nothing between us."

Somehow Cat knew, were she to seek out Brenna Sinclair, that the woman would tell a different story. Never in her life had she known anyone remotely like Patrick MacKendrick. With a careless grace he stood before her, the laughter turning his stern mouth into a thing of beauty. His eyes were silver in the morning light, and his high cheekbones and the strong line of his chin were thrown into bold relief against the tapestries lining the walls. Cat measured the powerful thighs and shoulders against her own proportions and felt very small. No woman on earth, especially one who had shared this man's bed and borne him a child, would be satisfied with less than marriage vows. She felt a sudden, stabbing pity for Isobel's mother.

"If there is nothing between you, why do you keep her here?"

Patrick's face hardened. "Isobel is my daughter. I'll not ask her mother to give her up. Are you so small that you cannot accept a child born out of wedlock?"

"Of course not." Cat waved the notion aside impatiently. "It seems strange that the two of you can behave as if nothing ever happened between you."

Smiling at her naiveté, his hands closed again on her shoulders. "I told you once before that I am no monk. There were others, before and after Brenna. For five years I was married. The past is over." He could feel the tension in her shoulders. Massaging the delicate bones at the nape of her neck, he bent close to her ear. "Have no fear, lass. You'll not share me with anyone."

"Your conceit knows no bounds, sir."

He grinned lazily. "Do you want me, mistress?"

"No!" she blurted out. His hand, tangled in her hair, prevented her from backing away. "Loose my hair."

"I like the feel of it in my hand, and you shall want me." He twisted a heavy strand around his fingers and pulled her closer, his lips a whisper away from the full, courtesan's mouth. "By God," he muttered, "I'll make you want me." Crushing her slim body against his, Patrick's only thought was to tame her, to quench the wrath in those blazing green eyes, to replace it with desire for him alone.

The kiss was ruthless and passionate, demanding and lustful. There was nothing of giving in the hot, insistent mouth and probing tongue. Cat knew she had provoked it. From the very first, when she had called him a traitor in the great hall in Edinburgh, her fate was sealed. Every instinct told her to submit, to placate him. Sliding her arms around her neck, she parted her lips, moving against him, accepting and responding to the sensual assault of his hands and lips, his teeth and tongue.

His lips moved down her throat to the covered swell of her breast. The heat of his mouth seared through the cloth, his breathing harsh and difficult. Finally he raised his head.

She lay back in his arms, one hand fastened in his collar. Her breasts rose and fell. Slowly, her eyes opened. She looked up at him and straightened.

He released her and crossed the room to stand by the mantel, willing his shaking hands to their customary steadiness. "I leave for Edinburgh today," he announced, when his voice could be trusted again. "Until now, I questioned the wisdom of leaving you alone, but perhaps 'tis better this way."

"Are you afraid I'll run away?"

Patrick considered the question. "No, lass," he said at last. "You won't run away. 'Tis myself I don't trust. These are bitter times. If I do not survive to stand beside you on our wedding day you'll have nothing to be ashamed of."

"You would do this for me?" Disbelief reflected itself in her voice.

His face was grave in the shadowed room. "And for myself. I want no more bastard children to call me father."

"Do you have more?" His answer was surprisingly important to her. Because her eyes were on his face, she saw the exact moment his expression changed. A mocking smile replaced his previous concern.

"Surely the women at court must have regaled you with gossip?"

Cat wished she had left the matter alone. "I believe Janet mentioned you occasionally," she replied.

He threw back his head and laughed. "God's blood," he swore. "Your cousin shared Jamie Stewart's bed for more than a year. Yet 'tis my virility she speaks of with such certainty."

Cat repeated her question: "Do you have more children?" Her eyes, like shards of clear glass, pinned him to the wall.

His mouth twitched. "Janet has been misinformed. I've only Isobel. There may be others I know nothing about, but since no one has come forward, I hold myself blameless. 'Tis no easy life for a man without a wife."

"Nor is it for a woman, wed or not," Cat retorted. "I would willingly change places with you."

Patrick grinned. "That would be a shame. But your sentiment brings us back to the beginning of our conversation. 'Tis fortunate that Jamie has requested my presence in Edinburgh." Pushing himself away from the wall, he walked toward her.

Cat took one step backward and then another, until she felt the damp coolness of stone against her back. His hands rested on both sides of her, palms against the stone, imprisoning her against the wall. She looked up at the handsome, chiseled face moving ever closer, and her stomach dropped. His lips brushed her forehead.

"When I return, Janet and Mary will be with me," he said, stepping away. "They will help you prepare for the wedding. Don't spend all my gold, lass." He grinned. "I'm not a poor man, but even I have my limits."

With that he was gone. Below, in the courtyard, she heard the jingle of spurs and the clatter of hooves on the cobblestones. The portcullis strained and creaked. Cat's heartbeat quickened. He was leaving. She ran to the narrow window, high in the wall, and stood on her toes.

A brisk wind blew north from the sea. The MacKendrick standard shone brightly against a brilliant sky. Pipes skirled and the men laughed, their spirits lifted by the wind and the sun and the clear sky of morning. Cat's heart pounded and her blood sang. For a moment she forgot she was English and had no business wishing them well on their journey.

When the last man disappeared through the gates, Patrick reined in his horse and turned. His head was bare, and from her place at the tower window, Cat could see the sun blazing like a halo around the dark fire of his hair. He grinned and raised his arm. Cat, watching him control his mount, felt a hot flash of pride.

Turning the stallion away from the castle, Patrick rode ahead to lead his men. She watched the wide, leather-clad shoulders disappear beyond the rise of the hill. The portcullis dropped with a heavy thud. She shivered and closed her eyes, chiding herself for her weakness. It did no good to rage against the ways of the world. A woman's lot was to remain safely at home while her lord roamed the countryside in service to his king.

Cat tucked a tendril of hair behind her ear and straightened. Andrew Percy was imprisoned somewhere inside the dungeons of the castle, and the sooner she found him the better. Her preoccupation with the gray-eyed laird of Hermitage was foolhardy. Patrick MacKendrick had enough broken hearts to his name. She would not add hers to the list.

Cat wiped the perspiration from her forehead and leaned against the hewed-stone wall. She had been unable to find even one clue as to Andrew's whereabouts. Normally her sense of direction was excellent, but the narrow corridors and twisted passages of Hermitage would confuse even a master mapmaker. It seemed as if the original architect had consigned practicality to the devil when he'd designed the castle. More than a dozen stairwells led to nowhere, and she'd soon lost count of the number of cold, musty hallways and even colder and mustier bedchambers. She felt sorry for the servants who lugged heavy buckets of water up the damp, steep stairs and even sorrier for Patrick and his guests who, no doubt, were forced to eat cold food and congealed gravies due to the great distance between the dining hall and the kitchen.

Frustrated by her lack of progress, Cat walked across the courtyard to the kitchen. The scent of flowers perfumed the air. She stepped inside and sniffed appreciatively. Several women, obviously servants, stood around a large, rectangular table pounding flowers with stone pestles. Another was removing wilted rose petals from a glass plate smeared with animal fat.

Cat recognized their purpose immediately. They were making perfume. Before her mother died, Cat had often helped her scrape the flower-scented fat into large pans. It was then heated and poured into dainty jars for the ladies of the household. Larger amounts were saved to make scented candles and incense for the holy chapel.

The women acknowledged her presence with curtsies and shy smiles before again concentrating on their tasks. A wave of nostalgia, so real it was almost painful, swept over her. How long had it been since she had worked side by side with another woman, sharing the simple rituals of domestic life?

As naturally as if she had done it every day of her life, Cat walked over to a woman who stood alone. Working on the opposite side of the plate, she began picking out the wilted petals. The woman smiled and her face turned into a thing of beauty. Cat relaxed. Until now she hadn't realized how nervous she was. The tenants of a Scots border castle had every right to treat an Englishwoman with hostility. Apparently she needn't have worried. Patrick MacKendrick's servants were either very well-mannered or they held no grudges.

Cat and the woman worked across from each other in companionable silence for almost an hour, disposing of the wilted flowers, heavy with fat, and then pressing the freshly pounded petals against the sticky plates. The day was unusually warm and the kitchen, with its constantly burning fires, even warmer. Cat raised her arm and, with the back of her hand, pushed a strand of hair off her forehead. Her gown was stained and her back wet with perspiration, but when she looked at the neatly stacked plates she felt a surge of satisfaction. For the first time since she'd arrived in Scotland, she had done something useful.

She smiled at the woman beside her, noticing that she wasn't dressed in servant's garb. The color of her gown was muted and very plain, bearing little resemblance to the richly dyed clothing of the nobility, but her bodice was trimmed with lace and the wedding ring on her finger was gold.

Cat broke the silence. "I am Catriona Wells," she said, extending her hand.

The woman smiled, showing even white teeth, and took the proffered hand in her own. "'Tis a pleasure to meet you, m'lady." Her lilting brogue was warm with welcome. Cat was surprised to see that she was much younger than she first appeared.

"What shall I call you?" Cat persisted.

The woman hesitated. Her eyes were a rich dark amber, the color of Scots whiskey. At last she spoke. "I am Brenna Sinclair."

For almost a full minute, the name meant nothing to Cat. Then she remembered where she had first heard it and her smile froze. This woman with her auburn hair and gold-dark eyes, whose smile transformed her face into breathtaking loveliness, was Isobel's mother. She flushed with anger. Patrick MacKendrick had bested her once again. With honeyed words, he had convinced her that he kept Brenna at Hermitage because of Isobel. Her gaze moved over the lushly curved bodice and slim waist of the woman who had given the border lord his only child. Anyone with eyes could see that a man, married or not, did not discard a woman who looked like Brenna Sinclair.

Cat was too overcome to hide her feelings behind her usual mask of calm. Shock and betrayal revealed itself in the too bright eyes and frozen smile. She was furious with Patrick for his silver-tongued deception and more furious with herself for feeling anything at all. When would she learn to trust her own instincts?

The MacKendrick's reputation with women stretched as far away as London. Men took one look at his lean, muscular height, at the mocking laughter on his dark face, and the lazy, almost feline grace with which he moved and kept their wives close, fearing that even the most chaste woman would be tempted to stray. Before Cat had witnessed his power, she scoffed at their lack of faith. Her opinion had changed. Now she knew they were wise to take care.

Lowering her eyelids, Cat burned with shame. She too felt the pull of that incredible charm he exuded without effort. Faith, on the strength of his flashing smile, the man could bewitch the kelpies into coming out from the shadows of their watery hiding places. It was good that she and Brenna had met. Knowing that Patrick kept a beautiful mistress would prevent her from making a fool of herself.

Taking a deep breath, she raised her head. Brenna looked miserable. Cat's eyes softened. Brenna Sinclair was blameless. To her misfortune, she had loved and borne a child to a man she could not wed. She was as much a victim of the MacKendrick's greed as Cat herself.

"Can we still be friends, Mistress Sinclair?"

Brenna's smile widened with relief. She had been terrified that Patrick's betrothed would convince him to send her away. "Indeed we can, m'lady. I would be honored if you would share a meal with me."

Cat nodded and watched as the woman filled a basket with bread and oatcakes. With a sharp knife, she sliced off several thick hunks of cheese and added it to the contents of the basket. Finally she poured a healthy portion of ale into a sheepskin pouch and drew the strings together. Slipping it over her shoulder, she beckoned Cat to follow her.

The two women walked across the cobbled courtyard to the portcullis gate. "Angus," Brenna shouted at the guard, "raise the gates. We're going to the loch."

The man grinned and lifted the gate, allowing them to pass. Within moments, Cat found herself seated on the grassy bank of a secluded glen. At her feet a slow-moving burn danced over mossy rocks on its way to the sea. The sky was a deep blue, and two towering oaks completely concealed the castle turrets. It was as if she were completely free from the confines of Hermitage, her only gaoler a red-haired lass with eyes the color of a frightened doe.

"This is my favorite spot," confided Brenna as she spread the food out before them. "I come here often with Isobel when my husband is away."

Cat looked up, startled. Brenna Sinclair had spoken of her husband with affection. She broke an oatcake in two and bit into it. "How long have you been wed?"

"Seven years," replied Brenna. "We married after I learned that I carried Isobel."

Cat waited for her to continue. A thousand questions hovered on the edge of her tongue, but until Brenna revealed her daughter's sire, common courtesy kept her silent.

Brenna's cheeks were tinged with color, but she met the green-eyed gaze without shame. "Isobel told me how she went to your room this morning. Patrick should have told you about her. I'm sorry, m'lady."

"There is no need for apologies." Cat's lips were stiff from holding her smile. "'Tis not the usual thing for a man to tell his betrothed about his mistress or their children."

"No, you don't understand." Brenna knew she must make her see. "I was never Patrick's mistress." The color of her cheeks deepened to a rich apricot. "We were together only once, when I was very young." The lie came easily to her lips. She had rehearsed it many times, ever since that first night in the courtyard when Patrick had returned with the Englishwoman and Brenna had seen, with her own eyes, this time the laird of Hermitage married for love.

"I wanted to wed John Sinclair from the first," confessed Brenna, "but we quarreled. I was very angry that night and Patrick was very drunk." Her voice lowered to an embarrassed whisper. "I seduced him to punish John. Patrick would have married me even though he was laird and there was no love between us, but when John asked for my hand, such a sacrifice was no longer necessary." She looked down at her hands. "I have been very happy with my husband and he is a wonderful father to Isobel, even though Patrick acknowledges her as his own."

"Why do you tell me this?" Cat asked, regarding her steadily.

Brenna Sinclair forced herself to meet Catriona's direct gaze. This woman would be Patrick's wife. There was something about her, something regal and poised, of a quality that Brenna had never seen before. There was pride and courage etched in the fine bones and haughty, beautiful features, but there was generosity as well. An ordinary woman would never have offered friendship to one who was little more than a servant. It would be difficult to tell Catriona Wells anything less than the truth.

"I don't want you to hate Isobel, and Patrick has known enough unhappiness," she admitted at last.

Catriona cut through the subterfuge. "Do you care so much for him, then?"

"Yes." Brenna hung her head. It was a relief to finally admit the truth. She closed her eyes, expecting to hear the voice of Patrick's betrothed telling her, in clear, frigid tones, that under the circumstances it would be better if she and her daughter left Hermitage. Instead, she felt cool fingers clasp her hand. She opened her eyes to find the English-woman's face, warm with sympathy, close to her own.

"Poor lass," murmured Cat unbelievably. "Won't you trust me? Surely such pain is unnecessary."

Brenna burst into tears. "I've loved him all my life, but he never noticed me."

Cat pulled a linen handkerchief from her bodice and handed it to the distraught woman. She accepted it gratefully and wiped her nose.

"I never blamed him," Brenna continued. "Why should

he notice a simple clansman's daughter when rich, beautiful women like yourself throw themselves at his feet."

Cat stiffened. The woman was impossible. As if she, Catriona Wells, would ever humble herself for any man. Opening her mouth to deliver a sharp rebuke, she looked at Brenna's tear-stained face and remained silent. The poor creature's suffering more than made up for her unconscious slight.

Brenna's tears flowed more slowly. "Most of what I told you is true, m'lady. John did want to marry me and we had quarreled. Patrick was drunk when I came to his bed that night. I'll never forget his face when I told him I was with child." She shivered. "His eyes were cold as ice, but he told me he would marry me. That's when I went to John. He loved me, you see, and was happy to take the child as well." She sniffed and scrubbed the tear tracks from her face. "I've never seen Patrick so relieved. Two years later he married Mary Ferguson."

"And then?" Cat prompted. She was fascinated by the tale and hadn't noticed that the afternoon sunlight had almost disappeared.

Brenna's mouth thinned. She stood up quickly and began gathering the remains of their food into the basket. "I've said enough. The rest is for Patrick to tell you."

Cat sat on the ground, a thoughtful expression on her face. "You've told me everything else, why not this?"

"She deserved the end that came to her!" The words were out of Brenna's mouth before she could stop them. "Mary Ferguson was selfish and cruel. Despite what she did to Patrick, he was good to her. You must believe that, no matter what you hear."

Cat's answer was cut off by a voice calling through the trees. "Mother," the childish voice shouted, "'tis Isobel. Where are you?"

"Here, love," Brenna Sinclair reassured her child. "Lady Catriona and I are here, by the loch."

Seconds later a small figure, dressed in a blue skirt and jacket, ran down the grassy bank to stand before them.

"You're very late," Isobel admonished her mother.

Brenna smiled. "Did you miss me?"

Isobel shook her head. "I went to the stables. Angus and I groomed the horses. He said I may ride tomorrow." She tilted her head to one side. "May I, Mother?"

"Not tomorrow, love." Brenna sighed regretfully. "I'll not be able to get away until later in the week, and you cannot ride alone."

Isobel's lip quivered. Cat, familiar with her younger brother's temper, expected her to argue. Instead, the child merely nodded and slipped her hand inside her mother's. Moved by the drooping shoulders and unusual discipline exhibited by so small a girl, Cat spoke. "I'll take you riding tomorrow, if your mother agrees."

Isobel's mouth opened in a circle of surprise. The black-haired woman was speaking to her, and she was smiling. She looked up at her mother, a question in her eyes.

Brenna considered the offer and nodded her head slowly. "If it wouldn't be too much of a burden, m'lady, I think it would be a good thing for Isobel to know you better. After all," she added, "you will be her stepmother."

Without comment, Cat took Isobel's other hand in her own. Brenna need never know that if all went according to plan, the marriage between Catriona Wells and the border lord would never take place.

❧ 17 ❧

Kate woke to the sound of boat horns, their rich, deep bellows muffled by thick mists shrouding the island like a blanket of smoke. Looking at her watch, she shivered and pulled the quilt over her shoulders. Five o'clock in the morning was much too early to wake up. She had three hours before Mrs. MacLean started cooking, enough time to sort out the meaning of her incredibly lifelike visions. It wasn't until she had looked into the eye of her own keek stane that she realized the recurring dreams were the progression of a complicated plot, the details of a story unfolding before her while she slept.

She had recognized the little girl immediately. Isobel MacKendrick was the child who had mistaken her for Catriona Wells. Some strange aberration had pulled her out of the past and into Kate's consciousness. Now, after seeing the portrait in the Sutherland gallery, Isobel's assumption made sense. It all fit: the too long dress, her odd accent, the imperious tone of her voice. Maura Sutherland had told the truth. There were no children living near her croft. The girl was an illusion, springing from the same part of Kate's memory as her vivid dreams.

It was not Isobel whose image haunted her waking hours, nor was it the child's mother, the lovely Brenna Sinclair. It was Patrick MacKendrick, a man who walked the earth five hundred years before.

In her entire experience, Kate had never met anyone who came close to Catriona's border lord. The icy gray of his eyes warming to liquid silver, the strong planes of his face stretched across remarkable cheekbones, the firm, thin-lipped mouth, the powerful strength of his arms and the battle-scarred, muscled body that no amount of time spent in an air-conditioned gym could achieve was as different from a contemporary businessman as a gelded quarterhorse hired for pony rides was from a stallion running free in the wild. He possessed her thoughts, the way he stood, tall and lean as a deer rifle, his air of capable command, the quick narrowing of his eyes when he sensed a threat and the way his grim mouth changed to a thing of beauty when his eyes lit on Catriona Wells.

There was something else as well, something she'd refused to admit until yesterday. The dreams were becoming more real. At first they were two-dimensional, as if she were viewing a movie screen from a safely distant seat in a crowded theater. But now they were much more than that. Kate could smell moisture in the air, the sweetness of new grass, the mustiness of rooms left untouched for decades, the rose petals Catriona had worked on with Brenna to make perfume. She was no longer a spectator. She saw and smelled and touched and tasted as if she had stepped into the distant past and crawled inside the mind and flesh of Catriona Wells.

A thought occurred to her: Why had her adoption been kept such a secret? Her breath caught and a look of horror froze the expression on her face. Had she really been *legally* adopted, or had the couple she called her parents wanted a child so desperately they had stooped to kidnapping? Could the reason for Hunter Sutherland's intense regard be that he had known her real family? She dozed off with the questions crowding her brain, then woke to the insistent ring of her portable travel alarm.

Kate threw back the covers and swung her legs over the side of the bed. Shivering, she made her way to the bathroom and turned on the shower. Misty warmth drove the chill from her bones, and the stiffness in her arms and legs immediately disappeared. Fifteen minutes later, her skin rosy from vigorous rubbing, she wrapped a towel around her hair and stepped out of the tub. Working quickly, before the heat left her body, she pulled on thick argyll socks, gray leggings, a red sweatshirt and tennis shoes. It was nearly time to help with the cooking for the feast. Brushing her hair back into a French braid, she walked down the stairs into the kitchen. Glennis was up to her elbows in flour and currants.

She smiled. "My goodness, you look cheerful. Sit down and I'll do your breakfast."

"Don't bother," Kate protested. "I'm still not hungry after last night's dinner, but coffee would be wonderful."

The older woman wiped her hands on her apron and reached for an old-fashioned, cast-iron percolator. Measuring out the coffee with a tablespoon, she filled the pot with water and turned on the peat-burning stove.

Kate couldn't remember ever seeing a real coffee pot. At home coffees with names like Vanilla Nut and Swiss Chocolate were topped with foaming milk, sprinkled with chocolate, nutmeg or cinnamon and brewed in drip-style coffee makers or French presses. Percolators were from another era, the Folger's era, when coffee was drunk black and no one worried about caffeine or elevated blood pressure.

"What shall I do first?" Kate asked, lifting the delicate cup to her lips. "I'm not terribly creative when it comes to cooking, but I can follow a recipe." How odd. Her voice sounded strange. Was it her imagination, or had it acquired a slightly British flavor?

Obviously Mrs. MacLean hadn't noticed. Her forefinger rested against her mouth and her head was slightly tilted, a pose she assumed when deep in thought. "Why don't you start with poacher's stew," she said. "Yes. That's the way to begin. You won't need a recipe. It's simple enough. Take the rabbit and cut it into chunks." She nodded at the counter by the window where a headless, gutted carcass with a gaping cavity for a middle sat in a bowl. "Fry it up with some onions, salt and pepper, a little fat, a bit of water, and simmer it for a few hours. Chop turnips, some carrots and parsnips and whatever else you find in the garden that survived the winter. That should take up the next hour or so."

Kate swallowed, picked up a kitchen knife and walked to the counter where she stared at the pale flesh of the skinned rabbit. "I've never eaten rabbit before."

"It's quite good. Rather like chicken, with less meat on the bones. You won't want any bones in the stew, though."

"Where shall I start?"

"By cutting it apart, of course. Just cut through the joints, the same as you would with a chicken."

Embarrassed by her ignorance, Kate forced herself to stare at the rabbit. She cleared her throat. "When I lived with my mother, her housekeeper did most of the cooking," she confessed. "On her nights off my mother would cook. But the only chicken she made was boneless breasts, with the skin cut off."

"Only the breasts?" Mrs. MacLean sounded confused. "What does she do with the rest of it?"

"It comes that way from the store." Kate turned around. "Even when I was living on my own, I never cooked much. I mostly just ate the frozen microwave dinners."

Glennis MacLean laughed. "Never mind. Just boil the whole thing. The meat comes off the bones quite easily that way."

Relieved, Kate did as she was told, adding water, onions and spices. The potatoes and parsnips she brought in from the garden were familiar and much more manageable. Soon a healthy mound of vegetables was ready for the pot. "Now what?" she asked, drying her hands on her borrowed apron.

"The meat pasties need assembling," decided Glennis. "There should be two balls of dough in the refrigerator. Divide each into four smaller balls and roll them out to the size of a pie plate, thin enough to bake easily but thick enough to hold the meat inside. When you've finished that we'll move on. After that there's criachan and pirr, a true Shetland drink."

Kate was overwhelmed. "Does everyone bring this much food?"

Glennis nodded. "Sometimes a great deal more if your family is large or if you bring guests. Two dishes for everyone attending, that's my measuring stick. Three of us will be attending and we've six dishes."

"The three of us?"

Glennis counted on her fingers. "Mr. MacCormack, you and me. I don't believe anyone will be checking in tonight. I've no reservations, and Ferris will be busy ferrying people from the small islands."

"Do the other islands have their own celebrations?"

"They do. But this one is the largest and most traditional. It's a wonderful excuse to see old friends and families who have moved away." She smiled approvingly at Kate's neatly rolled out circles. "Well done. Now fill half the crusts with the meat mixture in the refrigerator and seal them with a fork. Brush some egg across the tops, prick them with tines and put them in the oven. Everything cooks at the same temperature in my kitchen."

Kate's stomach growled. She glanced guiltily at Mrs. MacLean. "I should have had something more than a cup of coffee for breakfast."

"Never mind." Glennis washed her hands in the sink. "It's almost lunchtime. I hope I haven't worked you too long, my dear."

The sound of the door opening, then closing, and the tramp of rubber-soled work shoes on wood floors stopped Kate from answering.

Niall's tall figure appeared in the kitchen doorway. "Am I in time for lunch, or shall I grab something in town?" Kate kept her eyes on her task, but he could see the telltale flush staining her cheeks. She wasn't as immune to him as she would like to believe. Her sophisticated comment last night threw him until he remembered the eagerness of her hands and her sweet passionate mouth opening for him. A woman who responded like that couldn't be involved with anyone else. Why was she resisting?

Glennis MacLean, looking from Niall to Kate, pretended to frown but her twinkling blue eyes gave her away. "There is always food in my kitchen, Mr. MacCormack. Go up and wash and I'll have a hot meal on the table by the time you finish. Maybe Kate will keep you company."

Kate opened the cupboard in which she knew Glennis kept the plates. "I'll set the table before I change," she announced over her shoulder.

Glennis stirred the contents of a pot on her enormous stove. "Don't fret it, love. You've worked enough today. What you need is a bit of lunch and a nap. On the night of Beltane, no one sleeps."

Kate was tired. Maybe if she rested awhile before lunch she would have more energy. A late lunch would keep her out of the kitchen while Niall ate. Niall MacCormack's presence had a way of blurring the clear-cut lines of her objectives. The appetizing smell of Glennis's cooking followed her up the stairs, permeating the feather pillow she tucked behind her head.

Her last thought, before her eyelids felt too heavy to lift, was of her mother's ashes. Soon she would have to find a place to scatter them. But where? Finding the right location was turning out to be far more complicated than she had imagined. A final resting place should be special, meaningful. Why hadn't her will been more specific? A thought occurred to her: Maybe Maura would know of a place. Kate's eyes closed. What role would Maura play at the Feast of Beltane?

"I canna' do it, lass," the guard said regretfully. "Your da would have my head if anything happened to you."

"My mother gave me permission, Angus," Isobel insisted, "and Lady Wells is here to see that I come to no harm."

The guard hesitated. How could he tell a child of tender years that it was her caretaker who might do her harm? Still, if Brenna had agreed . . . Unaware that his thoughts were reflected in his uncertain expression, he stared down at Catriona, trying to read her intentions.

Cat's eyes narrowed in amusement. The guard was a fool. Anyone who knew Patrick MacKendrick would never seek vengeance through his child.

"I value my life, Angus," she called out. "Your fears are groundless."

Still he waited, consumed with doubt.

Isobel thrust out her lower lip. "Open this gate at once, knave, else I'll tell my father you refused to obey me."

The gate creaked open. Cat laughed out loud. It appeared that Hermitage Castle was under the thumb of a tiny red-haired termagant with a healthy temper.

Side by side, the woman and child rode in silence, following the narrow pony path between the trees, until the castle disappeared from view. A small burn trickled downward from the hills and disappeared in a clump of bracken. Isobel crossed the stream, laughing with delight, as her pony's hooves sprayed water over her boots, wetting the hem of her skirt.

A surge of well-being warmed Cat's chilled flesh. The child's spontaneous laughter, the sun-washed moors and the melodic droning of the bees brought back memories of earlier, happier times. What would it be like to let down her guard, to allow herself to love the fascinating man whose presence was stamped on every inch of land, on every stone and wall and door of the lonely, mysterious fortress that faced the English moors? She had forgotten what it was like to sleep without nightmares, to feel protected, to awake refreshed, her days marked by nothing more significant than an occasional visit from the clergy or a banquet held in celebration of a successful hunt.

Patrick MacKendrick offered her the peace she craved. His only condition was that she accept his hand. It occurred to her that he had never mentioned his heart. Was the lord of Hermitage never lonely? If it wasn't Brenna Sinclair, was there another woman who held his affections? The image of

Alison Douglass's mocking smile flashed through her mind as clearly as if she stood before her. Cat flushed with shame. It was almost as if the woman could read her thoughts and had reached across the miles to chide her. What would a man who could have any woman he wanted know of loneliness? If it were not for a boy's life, Cat would consign Ravenswood to the devil and accept Patrick's offer without reservation.

"You're a fortunate lass," she remarked when the child rode by her side again.

"Why?" Isobel tilted her head to look up at the figure beside her. She hadn't expected to like Catriona Wells, but the woman surprised her. She treated her as she would another adult, not a troublesome child who must be humored because she was the laird's daughter.

"My mother was not so understanding as yours," Cat explained. "When I was your age I spent most of the day inside, learning my lessons."

Isobel looked at her curiously. "Can you read and write?"

"Of course." Cat looked surprised. "My father was an earl."

"Is an earl better than a laird?" Isobel asked after a moment.

"Not better, lass." Cat spoke gently, careful not to wound the child's pride. "Of higher rank, perhaps, but not everyone considers that important."

They rode in silence to the slope of a hill. The only sound was the haunting cry of a solitary curlew as it circled overhead. The pine scent was very strong. Deep in thought, Isobel allowed her sure-footed pony to pick his way between the boulders, finding the easiest way down. At the base of the hill she stopped beside a huge rock and, using it as a ledge, slid from her saddle to the ground.

Cat was close behind her. "You've done this before," she observed, watching Isobel stretch out on a grassy mound.

The child nodded and held open her arms as if to encompass the entire valley. "You can see all of the borders from here. Isn't it lovely?"

Cat, who had grown to womanhood in the lush green of an English countryside, had to admit it was lovely indeed.

Shading her eyes with one hand, she looked across the valley. Blue-green pines slashed a bolt of color against a turquoise sky, and wild grains waved in the wind like an ocean of gold. The land had a wild, uncivilized sort of beauty, different from the ordered farmlands of her home, much as an English gentleman was different from a rebel Scottish laird.

She looked at Patrick's daughter seated on the grass. She was very young to be so self-assured. Perhaps it wasn't surprising, considering who she was. She wasn't dimpled and white like an English child, but something about her demanded a second look. Her hair, more red than gold, was pulled back in a plait and her eyes, steady on Cat's face, showed no sign of impatience. A cluster of freckles covered her nose and cheeks, and the tanned skin of her arms was evidence of long days spent in the sunlight.

"Well?" Isobel asked.

"Well what?"

"You're staring at me," she said reprovingly. "Why do you do that?"

For the space of a heartbeat, Cat was shocked into silence. Then she laughed. Not the dainty, restrained laugh of an English lady but a loud, clear sound like the pealing of chapel bells.

Isobel was entranced. She had expected a lecture on proper deportment, not an explosion of mirth so loud that it chased the birds from the trees and brought tears to the eyes. Cat was nothing like the prim and proper woman she had imagined. Perhaps she would revise her opinion of English ladies. "Will you teach me to read?" she asked abruptly.

Cat wiped her eyes with her sleeve. She sat down near Isobel. "I'm sure your father will teach you when he feels the time is right."

"No." The red head shook vehemently. "He won't."

"Come now, Isobel," Cat reasoned with her. "No man in your father's position wants his child to remain ignorant."

Isobel refused to look up.

"All right." Cat sighed. "I'll teach you. But tell me one thing: Why do you want to learn?"

Isobel's voice was very low. "After I learn, I shall teach my father."

Cat stared at the little girl, a curious expression on her face. Suddenly she smiled with such brilliance that it took Isobel's breath away. With a brisk, graceful flick of her wrist, she picked up a twig and broke off the stem, leaving a sharp point at the end. "Shall we begin?" she asked in a brisk, no-nonsense voice.

"Now?" Isobel's eyes were very wide.

"Is there a better time?" Cat traced the letter *A* in the dirt.

The child stared at the symbol. In her excitement, she forgot that the woman beside her was little more than a stranger. Moving closer for a better view, she leaned her head against Cat's shoulder. "What does it say?" she whispered.

"Nothing yet. This is a letter," Cat began. "'Tis part of a word. After you learn the sounds of different letters, we shall put them together to make words. Then we'll go on to sentences and pages." Her voice was low and serious, as if what she said was of great importance. "It is sentences that give meaning to thoughts, Isobel. When you read, you learn to understand the way others think."

The bright head nodded, in perfect agreement at the wisdom of such a statement. "That is what my father says."

"Why did he never learn?"

Isobel traced the letter with her finger. Her tongue rested at the corner of her mouth as she concentrated. "There was no one to teach him."

Cat was confused. "If no one at Hermitage reads, why are there so many books in the library?"

"My father orders them," the child announced. "Brother Rupert brings them from the abbey."

Mystified at the incongruity of such a situation, Cat remained silent. If the man wanted to spend enormous amounts of gold for something utterly useless to him, so be it. Bending close to Isobel, she drew another figure in the dust. "This is the letter *B. A* has two sounds, *B* has only one."

The morning passed quickly. Cat was pleased with her pupil's progress. Isobel was intelligent and very determined. In no time at all, she would master reading and writing.

" 'Tis time to go, lass." Cat stretched and looked up at the sky. "Angus will be thinking I've kidnapped you."

Isobel's lip curled. "Angus is a fearful old woman." Her eyes followed Catriona's to gauge the position of the sun. "It grows late," she admitted, "and I am hungry. Learning is hard work."

Cat laughed. "You've done well. I've never had so adept a pupil."

Isobel's eyes sparkled. "I wish to surprise my father. You won't tell him, will you, m'lady?"

"No," Cat promised. "I'll leave that to you."

The sun was beginning its descent when the two reached the portcullis gate. Old Angus breathed a sigh of relief. The lass looked a mite sunburned, but other than that, none the worse for her morning ride in the country. Not ten minutes before their return, the MacKendrick and his guests had ridden in from Edinburgh.

Bustling activity transformed the once peaceful courtyard. Servants ran from the kitchens to the main hall, rolling barrels of ale and carrying huge trenchers of food. Others disappeared up the stairs to the guest chambers, dragging steaming pails of water up the dangerous steps. Men guzzled drams of usquebaugh or flagons of ale while they groomed their horses and shouted good-natured curses across the yard. Everywhere she looked, Cat could see the bold, blatant red of the MacKendrick plaid.

She recognized the stallion immediately. There was only one man who could tame such an enormous, frightening beast and still walk the earth in one piece. Cat was sure the two mares were not from MacKendrick stables. Excitement brought a wave of fresh color to her cheeks when she saw the saddles strapped to their backs. They were women's mounts. Perhaps Patrick really had worked a miracle and persuaded the earl of Glenkirk to part with his new wife. If so, Janet and Mary Gordon were somewhere inside the walls of Hermitage Castle. Her eyes warmed with pleasure at the thought of her cousins.

Cat grasped the pommel of her saddle and slid to the ground, turning toward Isobel. Before she could take a step toward the child, a handsome clansman blocked her way. Cat recognized him as one of the men who had shared his bread and wine with her on their ride from Edinburgh. She watched as he strode to the side of the shaggy pony and lifted Isobel into his arms. "Here you are at last, missy." He nuzzled her neck affectionately. "Your mother was beginning to wonder if you were ever coming home."

Isobel slipped her arms around the giant's neck. "Did you bring me anything?" she asked, returning the man's bone-crushing hug.

"Just like a lass," he teased. "Always wanting a pretty bauble. Come with me and I'll show you what I have for you."

Isobel and the tall man disappeared through the door of the castle. All at once Cat understood. The handsome, blond giant with the teasing grin was John Sinclair. She laughed out loud and walked through the arched doorway and into the entrance hall. Any doubts she may have harbored regarding Brenna's story vanished completely. The tall, blond Viking who had married Isobel's mother wasn't the kind to tolerate another man in his wife's bed or even in her thoughts.

At the foot of the stairs, Cat hesitated. She wanted very much to look for Janet and Mary, but she was filthy. For some reason the idea of facing them covered in dust was distasteful to her. The fact that Patrick would be with them and might find her lacking in comparison to her cousins had nothing to do with it. She merely wanted to be clean. She placed her foot on the first step. A loud shriek stopped her.

"Cat!" Janet's voice was like a clap of thunder as she crossed the room to the stairs and threw her arms around her cousin. "Where have you been? The guard said you left hours ago."

Cat pulled out of her embrace and her eyes widened. Marriage obviously agreed with Janet. She had never looked more beautiful. The thin face with its high cheekbones glowed with health, and she was richly dressed, as befitted the countess of Glenkirk. Her blue brocaded gown with its low neck and tightly molded waist had been cleverly woven with gold threads to complement Janet's thick tawny hair and amber eyes.

"I've been riding with Isobel," Cat answered. "Come

with me while I bathe and I'll tell you everything." She lifted her skirts with one hand and, resting the other on the wall, began to climb the narrow stairs. "You look wonderful, Janie. Where's Mary?"

"In her chamber. She's not well," Janet answered shortly.

Cat stopped and turned around. "She is ill, yet you allowed her to make the journey from Edinburgh?"

Janet shrugged. "Mary is not a child. She wanted to see you. Perhaps you can help her."

"I am no healer," Cat protested.

Janet shook her head impatiently. "Mary needs no healer, Cousin. What she needs is someone with influence—No!" She held up her hand to stop the words forming on Cat's lips. "I'll say no more. We'll talk while you change."

After the servants had filled the tub and collected her soiled clothing, Cat dismissed them and sank down to her chin in the scented bathwater.

Janet sat on the bed, watching her cousin's black hair float on the soapy surface, and hesitated. Her plan had seemed so simple at Glenkirk. Cat was Patrick MacKendrick's betrothed. If anyone could reach him, she could. Everyone knew of the border lord's influence with the king. Now, for some reason, the words stuck to her tongue.

"Out with it, Janie," said Cat, wincing as she touched a blister on her heel. "You were anxious enough to make the journey from Edinburgh."

"I came for your wedding," Janet protested. "Do you think my purpose is merely to use you?"

Cat sighed. "No, of course not."

Janet slipped off her kirtle and drew her gown over her head, laying it on the bed. Clad only in her shift and slippers, she knelt by the tub and, taking the soap in her hand, began to lather Cat's hair.

"When Mary rode to Glenkirk to tell me her news, I thought of you," she said. "You are to wed the MacKendrick, and if anyone can stop this, 'tis he." Her hands moved rhythmically, soothingly, over Cat's head. "Two men rule Scotland," Janet continued, "Jamie Stewart and Patrick MacKendrick. When one seeks a favor from Jamie, the person to approach is Maggie Drummond. I've already asked her for help. She doesn't think Jamie will change his mind. You are Mary's only hope."

Cat waited impatiently for Janet to explain just what it was she was supposed to ask Patrick.

"Mary is to wed Perkin Warbeck, the Pretender." Janet's hands had stopped their movement. Cat could feel them tremble as they rested against her scalp. "They are to carry the York standard into England and declare war against Henry."

"Dear God," breathed Cat.

"Is it possible that Jamie is right?" Janet crawled to the front of the tub to face her cousin. "Could the Pretender win the English to his cause?"

Cat wet her lips. Her eyes were the icy green of a frozen loch. "No, Janie," she said gently. "If Mary goes to England as the wife of a man pretending to be Richard of York, she will die."

Janet's face whitened. "We must stop the marriage, Cat. My sister does not deserve this."

Cat nodded, even though her heart sank. Janet was naive. Her year with Jamie Stewart had taught her little. A king did not consider the desires of a woman when his kingdom was at stake.

❧ 18 ❧

Kate tied the sash of her wraparound wool skirt tightly around her waist and flipped up the turtleneck of her white sweater. Glennis had predicted that the night would be "a mite cold," which, when accurately translated, meant frost-bitten toes and numb fingers. Over thick argyll socks, she pulled on black boots, brushed the sides of her hair up into a barrette behind her head, stuffed the entire shining mass into a white woolen tam, grabbed her coat and hurried downstairs. Glennis and Niall were waiting for her. To her delight, Niall wore a kilt.

"I'm sorry that I missed lunch," she apologized to her landlady. "I was more tired than I thought."

"Never mind." Glennis nodded at the wrapped platter in her arms. "You won't go hungry tonight. We've plenty of food."

Kate laughed and rescued a bowl balanced precariously on Niall's arm. "Let me help," she offered.

Niall relinquished the bowl, glancing appreciatively at Kate's green eyes and dark hair against the snowy wool of her tam. "Be my guest."

The cliffs of Lerwick were ablaze with lights from a hundred smoldering campfires. Kate stared wide eyed, her cheeks red and tingling from the cold. She hadn't seen so many people together since leaving Edinburgh. Where had they all come from?

An arm slipped through hers and a light, high voice spoke into her ear. "I'm so glad we found you in this crush. Beltane is much more exciting when you watch someone experience it for the first time." The voice belonged to Victoria Sutherland.

Kate turned her head to see the duke deep in conversation with Niall and Glennis MacLean. "I'm very glad you came, Victoria," she murmured. "You can explain everything to me." The girl nodded and released Kate's arm to exchange places with her father.

Hunter Sutherland removed the bowl from Kate's grasp and tucked her arm through his. "This is the first Beltane I've seen in thirty years," he said quietly.

Kate looked up at the symmetry of his profile. "Why?"

He laughed. "Are all Americans so blunt?"

She considered his question. "Much more so, I think. My parents are Scottish, born and bred right here in the Shetlands. With American parents I would probably have no reserve at all."

"Tell me about your family."

"There isn't much to tell. My parents found me here on Cait Ness and arranged for an adoption. My father was educated in America and did well in investment banking. Later, my sister was born. We were very comfortable. It was a good life."

Hunter probed further. "And now?"

"My sister married and has a son. Both of my parents are dead," Kate answered stoically. "I moved back in with Mother to help her through things but she never seemed very happy after my father's death."

Hunter saw the unshed tears in her eyes and wisely offered no sympathy. "Why have you come to this part of Scotland, Kate?" he asked instead.

She hesitated. Why was the truth so difficult to admit? "I came to find out about my family," she said at last, "and to bring back my mother's ashes." It was a partial truth, the only one she could speak without everyone believing she was insane.

"Have you had any luck?"

Thoughts that had no business becoming words sprang to her lips. "I don't think luck has anything do with it. Do you?"

Hunter stopped, the strength of his arm forcing her to stop with him. "Look at me, Kate Sutherland," he ordered. "Look at me and don't turn away."

Slowly, Kate pulled out of his grasp and raised her eyes to his face, knowing she was powerless to hide what he would surely see.

He stared first at the cool perfection of her features, the clean, sharp bones and perfect symmetry of nose, mouth and teeth. It was all there in her face, just as he knew it would be: the slant to her eyes, the thin, haughty nose, her wide sensual mouth. The others were far ahead now, disappearing into the mists that surrounded the ceremonial site.

Hunter drew a deep breath, gathered himself and looked into her eyes. The green depths drew him in, farther and farther, back to another time, another Beltane, when a red-haired girl showed him the narrow precipice between passion and heartbreak. He would give anything for it to have turned out differently. Dynastic instincts, ancient and primitive, pulled at him. He was laird of Clan Sutherland, protector of his people, defender of the shield. Maura had no right to do what she had done that long-ago, magic-filled night. She had no right to tell him nothing, to forever remove his choice. Looking into the grass-green eyes of the woman before him, he had an overwhelming desire to weep.

"Have you seen enough, Your Grace?" Kate asked.

He smiled. "I could look at you forever, lass. Surely you know how lovely you are."

Again the compliment didn't bring the usual tide of humiliating color sweeping across her face. "Thank you," she said simply. "Shall we go on?"

"By all means. There is someone I especially want to see."

"Do I know the person?" Kate asked.

His jaw tightened and he stared straight ahead. "No one knows her. But you've met. Maura Sutherland never misses a Beltane."

Kate's forehead wrinkled. Surely the acquaintance of a duke was of some significance. Maura had never mentioned Hunter Sutherland. "Will she be pleased to see you?"

"I doubt it."

She knew she had passed the boundaries of courtesy, but something deep inside her refused to let it rest. "Why?"

"I've a question to ask her." He tucked her arm back under his. "That is all I will say on the matter, for Maura's sake."

"Have you known her long?"

"Forever." Hunter's face was grim again. "It looks as if someone has come back for us."

Kate looked ahead, straining to recognize the tall, lean figure walking purposefully toward them through the mist. He moved like an athlete, head down against the wind, hands loose at his sides, his plaid kilt swinging around bare knees and muscled calves. Kate's heart pounded and her hand crept to her throat. Dear God, it couldn't be, not here, not now. This time she wasn't asleep in some netherworld place where visions flourished.

Suddenly the man looked up and grinned, a straight line of white in the darkness. Kate breathed a sigh of relief. It was Niall, and she was genuinely pleased to see him.

"We thought you were lost," he said when he reached

them, his smile not quite reaching his eyes. "Glennis was worried."

"I imagine she wasn't the only one," Hunter commented dryly.

Niall's smooth voice had an edge to it. "As a matter of fact, your daughter was also concerned."

"Then I must reassure her immediately." Hunter returned Kate's bowl, nodded his head and walked on.

She watched him disappear into the darkness. "I can't figure him out."

"What do you mean?" Niall's voice was carefully neutral.

"Yesterday I had the feeling he was flirting with me."

"And today?"

Kate shrugged. "He acted more like an uncle or an older brother."

"But not a father?"

She looked up to find his eyes, cold as ice, narrowed on her face. "Not a father," she said mechanically. "He's not old enough to be my father."

"The duke of Sutherland is fifty-three years old."

"He's not the least bit fatherly."

"No," said Niall. "I don't imagine most women would think he was."

Kate looked pointedly at Niall's bare legs beneath the plaid wool and changed the subject. "I never knew modern-day Scotsmen wore kilts."

"It's traditional when we're celebrating." He glanced at her profile. "What do you think of our custom?"

"I think it's very attractive," she said, surprising him. "You've got great legs. They're dark, like a lifeguard after a summer on the beach. I always thought Scots were fair-skinned people."

"Some are. Most are descended from a mixture of Celtic and Pictish tribes, with some Irish and Scandinavian thrown in." He took her gloved hand and lifted it to his lips before guiding it into his jacket pocket.

For some reason the brief caress unnerved her. She wanted nothing more than to throw herself into his arms and feel his mouth on hers again.

"Thank you for the compliment," he said formally,

interrupting her thoughts. "I don't believe anyone has remarked on my legs before."

Quick color warmed Kate's cheeks. Grateful for the concealing darkness, she remained silent until they reached the crowd gathering around the fire site. They found Glennis and Victoria immediately. Hunter was nowhere in sight.

"There you are," Glennis greeted them. "The torch will soon be lit."

"Where is Sutherland?" Niall asked.

Victoria answered, "He'll be back soon. We're not to worry about him." Her words were loud against the sudden hushed silence.

Kate strained to look over the shoulders of a couple standing directly in front of her. A woman in a white gown, her long fair hair streaming about her shoulders, walked toward the summit carrying a fiery torch. Six women in blue followed her. She moved slowly, rhythmically, murmuring words in a language that sounded familiar yet hovered on the outside edge of Kate's understanding.

A tall tree trunk, stripped of its branches and decorated with ribbons, had been erected in the center of the fire site. The fair-haired woman lifted the torch, waited for the high-pitched wail of the pipes, then hurled it into the dry kindling. Immediately the wood caught. Except for the crackling of dry hardwood, the eerie lament of a lonely piper and the crash of silver-touched waves against sun-bleached cliffs, the silence was ominous. No one spoke. Flames licked the wood and grew. Kate could see the blue crescent, the ancient Druid symbol, painted on the forehead of the woman chosen to represent the Goddess.

Making no sound, the gathering waited for the last bit of kindling to catch. The pole was surrounded by a circle of fire. A murmur rose from the spectators. The trio of pipers lifted the bagpipes to their lips. The sweetly haunting melody drew a sigh from the crowd. Food was unwrapped and passed around. Following the piled-high platters were jugs of liquid, disarmingly cool on the lips, warm to the tongue, hot and choking on its way to the stomach.

Kate's head swam and she clutched Niall's arm for support. She blinked. Her eyes watered and the swaying shapes around her blurred. People laughed and drank. Couples positioned themselves around the fire and danced with pointed toes and complicated steps that looked like something between a ballet and a square dance.

The woman with the crescent on her forehead moved through the crowd toward the spot where Niall and Kate stood. Occasionally a man stepped out and stood before her. She smiled, drank from the horn at her waist and shook her head. Kate watched as the woman acted out the role of the Goddess, stopping to speak to the islanders, touching their shoulders, leading them to the circle of dancers surrounding the fire. The woman had turned to move in the opposite direction when she hesitated. Removing something square from the pocket of her gown, she flipped open the lid and stared at it.

Kate's eyes widened. Of their own volition, her fingers slipped inside her pocket to touch her keek stane. She had an overwhelming desire to use it. Before she could act, the woman lifted her head. Across the sea of people her eyes met Kate's and locked.

Even if she'd wanted to, Kate could no more look away from that pointed green gaze than she could will the moon to fall into the sea. For endless seconds the woman's eyes claimed her. Kate's heart slammed inside her chest. She felt exposed, drained, as if she'd walked for a long time through tall grass and dry sand. She knew that the woman understood her as intimately as a mother knows the face of her child.

A cool mist rose from the sea, muffling the noise of the pipes and the gay, swirling figures. There was no fire, no Niall, no Glennis, only two women alone on a fog-shrouded bluff, two women who shared a dark heritage and a haunting secret.

Kate watched the woman come closer, the cold wind urging her forward, the white gown billowing around her body. When she stood directly before her, the woman reached out, her hand settling lightly on Kate's wool-covered shoulder. The music was suddenly louder, and the shape of the mist had changed. It circled the cliff in a half moon, leaving the foaming sea alive and bathed in white light. Around the ceremonial site and the swirling dancers, the sky cleared. Torches glowed against the darkness. The bonfire, now a comforting orange and gold, warmed the air.

The golden-haired Goddess beckoned and Kate followed, pulled by strong arms and persistent hands, into the ring of dancers. Someone pressed a cup into her hand. She drank, and the liquid burned a fiery path to her stomach. Again her vision blurred and she was warm, warm with the euphoric glow of fermented alcohol untainted by water and ice.

Of their own volition, her feet moved to the music. She dropped the cup and large hands folded over hers. The tempo of the pipes increased. Her feet moved faster. Faces new and familiar flashed before her. Hunter Sutherland was there, fists balled, staring at Maura, his eyes filled with pain and rage and hunger. Victoria passed by, her cheeks pale and wet with tears. Catriona Wells and Isobel MacKendrick looked at her solemnly, their faces blurred by the mists of time. Kate closed her eyes, her senses reeling. The music, the fire, the hot pungent odor of cooked game, the weightless, giddy laughter rising in her throat. Round and round the fire she danced, tireless, her feet moving, eyes closed, relying on the two who held her between them. She felt a kinship with these people, this land, the leaping fire and the blond Goddess who shared her sight.

Once again the music changed, darkened and slowed into a single haunting blend of notes and melody. Strong arms circled her waist, matching her steps. Blunt hands discarded her hat, pulling her close. Fingers sifted through her hair. She opened her eyes, her lashes grazing a hard masculine cheek. His scent was familiar. She tried to pull away, to see his face, but the hand on her hair anchored her to his shoulder. She sighed against his neck. He lowered his head, their eyes met and the blood froze in her veins.

Gray eyes looked down at her and narrowed. Sun-darkened skin stretched across sharp high bones, and hair the color of dark mahogany fell across his forehead.

She lifted her hand to trace his lips and hesitated. The tension within her coiled and tightened like an overly wound spring. "This can't be, it just can't be," her mind screamed before his mouth silenced her and his hands pressed her back and down against the softness of damp earth.

Her breathless protest was lost in the heat of firm lips closing over hers, of warm skin that smelled of woodsmoke, of searching hands evoking banked fires and the pounding of dark blood as it left her heart. Through closed eyelids, she saw swirling color, exploding light and shadows, hazy and dark, against the blinding brightness.

His words, murmured low and soft, were muffled against the soft wool of her sweater. She felt his mouth on her chin, her throat, the slope of her breast. Again she looked at his face. His eyes were closed and his hair was streaked with reddish lights, but his features had changed. They were still lean and angular, the hollows shadowed beneath high bones, the mouth firm but kind, the nose thin. But it was no longer the face of the border lord that she saw. It was Niall MacCormack who held her beneath him, and she was deeply, profoundly grateful. His eyes opened and she felt the sudden instant blaze of passion spring to life within her. "Don't leave me," she whispered. "Please, don't leave me again."

"My darling," he murmured against her bare skin, "I'll never leave you."

Beneath her, the moss was cool and soft. Above her, wide shoulders blocked out the sky. She wound her arms around his neck, pulling him down to her seeking lips. He tasted of whiskey, sage and spiced wine. Her breasts filled his hands, and when she shifted to meet his growing need, he was already swollen and hard against her thighs. Heat surged through her. She lifted her hips and pressed against him. He thrust once, filling her completely.

Her heart beat a steady cadence. He met and matched its pounding rhythm. Over and over he moved inside her, waiting until she cried out beneath him. Only then did his control break, and the warm, lifegiving tide flooded through her. Spent and relaxed, she slept with her cheek pressed against his chest.

He knew she was close by. Something inside of him, an instinct perhaps, never failed to warn him when she was near. Through the moonlit darkness he walked, feeling her presence as strongly as he had when he was a boy in love with a copper-haired beauty who loved him back. He found her on the cliffs, a slender white-clothed figure outlined against the darkness.

The spongy earth muffled his footsteps. From ten feet away he called her name, but she didn't turn. Neither did she show surprise. Why would she? he thought bitterly. Her Sight, or whatever she called it, would have warned her of his intent long before he began his descent to the cliffs.

He moved closer. "Thirty years have passed us, Maura. Won't you speak to me, even now?"

She turned and her eyes widened. Without the slightest trace of self-consciousness, her gaze moved over him, noting the changes of the last three decades. Maura had forgotten how tall he was, the tallest man in Cait Ness, and how beautiful the still, dark planes of his face. He was still dreadfully handsome, although age had not forgotten him. She saw it in the silver spray lightening his hair, in the crow's feet marking the corners of his olive-green eyes, at the bitterness twisting the once-laughing lips. But he was lean and narrow-waisted, and his arms were strong. Hunter Sutherland was fifty-three years old, and he still took the eye the same as when he was a young man, more so perhaps, because there are more eye-taking men when one is young and not so many after the years take their toll.

He knew about Kate. Maura saw that he knew and that he was not pleased with the decision she had made so long ago. Still, there was no point in postponing the inevitable. She touched her tongue to her lips and came right to the point. "Do we have anything to speak of?"

"Aye," he said grimly, "we do."

She sighed. "Speak then, and be done with it."

He took a step toward her. "How could you do it, Maura? How could you give our daughter away and not even tell me? What of her birthright? What of who she is?"

"And who is she, my lord?" She stood before him, the wind pulling her hair back from her face. The widow's peak dividing her forehead stood out against the whiteness of her skin.

"She is my daughter," he shouted, "the daughter of the duke of Sutherland."

Maura corrected him: "The *bastard* daughter of the duke of Sutherland."

His face whitened as if she'd struck him. "That was your choice," he said bitterly. "I wanted to marry you. I asked you even before Beltane."

"It wasn't possible."

"I loved you. Through all the years between, I never stopped loving you."

She shook her head and looked away. "You had a wife and a child."

He took her hands in his. "I still love you."

Tears flooded her eyes. She looked directly at him. "Don't, Hunter. What if I told you that Katherine Sutherland isn't your daughter?"

"I don't believe you. I've seen her. She is the image of my ancestor's portrait in the gallery." He tightened his hold on her. "She is also very like you."

"We are all Sutherlands. All of us resemble one another."

"Are you saying another man gave you a child?" A tiny smile hovered at the corners of his mouth. "I'll not believe that one either. You were never faithless."

She shook her head and tried to explain. Why was she always so tongue-tied with this man? "We gave her life, nothing more."

The groove in his forehead deepened. "I don't understand."

"She grew up in America with Bonnie and Kenneth Sutherland. She knows nothing of this life, of you and me, of the differences that separated us. Americans believe they can do anything, marry anyone, and it makes no difference. Here, it still matters who your parents are. Would you tie her here by telling her who you are? Would you make her less than your legitimate daughter?"

His mouth tightened stubbornly. "I would never allow her to be less than Victoria."

Maura continued, determined that he should hear the truth, no matter what he believed. "Kate is here for a reason, Hunter. Something happened, something terrible enough, unsettling enough, for her to return over and over again to the same nightmares, the same emptiness, until she rights the wrong that was done in the past to a woman named Catriona Wells." Her voice was anguished. "Please accept this. Don't harm the daughter who *is* yours and the memory of her mother. To reveal that you are Kate's father would bring nothing but heartache to those you love."

Hunter had stopped listening the moment he heard the name *Catriona Wells*. Maura knew nothing of the portrait in his gallery. Why should she? She had always refused the invitations to his home, and he had never spoken of his distant ancestor. How would she know of his link to the Stewarts?

"Please, Hunter."

Her plea brought him back to the moment and to the proud, ageless perfection of her face. She was not as beautiful as her daughter. Her features were too strong, her cheeks too sculpted, her nose too sharp; but for Hunter, all women seemed insignificant when compared to her striking elegance. Wings of silver touched her temples, and the bones of her face were more defined than when she was young. But her body was thin as a girl's, her skin unlined, and her hair, thick, fine and straight, fell unbound to her waist.

"Please what?" he whispered, his hand moving to the richness of her hair.

"Don't tell Kate what you know."

His hand stilled. "She wants to know. She came all the way from America to find her family."

"She'll find it soon enough without anyone telling her. You don't have to give it to her all at once."

"Why not?"

Maura stepped closer. She was desperate, and she knew what he wanted. She had seen that look in his eyes often enough. "Kate is very confused. She's seen things she can't yet accept. She needs time." She reached up to touch his cheek. "You both need time to realize the truth."

His skin flamed beneath her caressing fingers. "Perhaps I already know the truth."

Maura smiled tenderly and shook her head.

She was so very close. Her skin smelled like lavender. He breathed in deeply.

Her voice was rich, husky, intimate. "You know nothing of truth, Hunter Sutherland. I can feel it."

His hand cupped her cheek. "Show me," he said softly. "Show me your truth."

Maura was a girl again, the past thirty years forgotten, her mind full of another time, another Beltane. She shook her head. "I'm too old," she protested, but his mouth silenced her words. After a long moment, when she could breathe again, she felt his lips against her throat. Pushing her protests to the back of her mind, she called forth her youth, molded herself against him and wound her arms around his neck.

❧ 19 ❦

It was late before Cat saw the MacKendrick. Dinner had come and gone with no sign of him. She knew that if she didn't make her request soon, her nerve would disappear.

Opening the press, she pulled out three gowns and examined them critically. Only the last would do. Holding the soft folds against her body, she looked into the glass and smiled. It was by far the most flattering dress she owned. The expensive satin, green as spring grass, reflected the color of her eyes. Cut low at the bodice and tight across the hips, it was sinfully revealing. Cat would never have dared wear it at King Henry's conservative court. Now it was just what she needed. Humming a ballad of the borders, she slipped it over her head and turned to look back over her shoulder.

Reflected in the mirror she could see the pale skin of her back, completely exposed, where the material was cut away.

She flushed and bit her lip. The gown was designed for one purpose only. Patrick, wise in the ways of women, would know that purpose. She only hoped it would serve her without compromising her virtue. Taking a deep breath, she left the room in search of the border lord.

Patrick's dark head was bent over the accounts. Numbers, unlike letters, held no mystery for him. Dinner had been marvelous. Unable to leave his room until the accounts were complete, his servant brought him a platter piled high with crab and oysters. When he had commented on the unexpected treat, the man had replied that Lady Catriona, after a thorough inspection of the kitchens, found them wanting. At her insistence the menu had been changed. Patrick grinned. She was taking an interest in the estate. It was a beginning.

A knock sounded at the door. He looked up. "Come in," he said expectantly. When he saw the figure framed in the doorway, his mouth dropped and he forgot to rise. Cat closed the door and stood before him, saying nothing.

Hooded and unreadable, his gaze moved over her figure, noting the tight cloth molding her slim hips, the glimpse of a shapely ankle behind the slit in her skirt, the daring cut of her bust. He lingered, pointedly staring at the indecent expanse of creamy flesh spilling from her bodice. He stood up and casually walked over to the fire, leaning against the mantel, one leg crossed over the other, his fingers resting on the buckle of his belt.

The color rose in Cat's cheeks but she held her head high, refusing to look away. Patrick's eyes glinted with amusement and something else that threatened to steal the air from her lungs.

"Please." She gestured nervously toward the chair he'd deserted. "Sit down."

"After you, mistress."

"I prefer to stand." She straightened her shoulders and walked over to him, offering the material she carried in her arms. "I've brought you something. That is, I've made you something. Please accept it."

He looked down at the bundle she held out. It was a cloak of finest wool, sewn with dainty stitches and embroidered with the seal of the MacKendricks. Patrick was startled. For the first time in his life he was at a loss for words.

Their eyes met and held. "Thank you, Catriona," he said, his voice not entirely steady.

In the clear gray depths of his gaze, his heart was there for her to see. She looked down quickly, afraid she would disgrace herself. If only it could have begun differently for the two of them.

"I regret to say that I've nothing for you," she heard him apologize. "I came home as quickly as I could. Will you forgive me?"

Cat shrugged. "It doesn't matter. I didn't come for gifts. I came to ask a favor."

"What is it?"

She turned away. It was difficult to concentrate while looking at him. "I want two things."

Patrick laughed. "You haven't the look of a greedy lass. If you want something, I'm sure the reason is sound."

"You must stop Mary's wedding to Perkin Warbeck." She hadn't intended to blurt it out, but there it was.

The silence lengthened until Cat could stand it no longer. She forced herself to turn back to the MacKendrick.

There was an odd expression on his face. "I cannot help you, Catriona," he said at last. "God knows I've tried to talk Jamie out of his foolishness, but he will have none of it."

"Because of Maggie Drummond?"

He nodded. "James fancies himself in love with the lass."

"Perhaps he is," answered Cat slowly.

"You told me once before that there is no place for sentiment in a royal marriage."

She was looking at him strangely. "Perhaps I was wrong."

He took a step forward and would have reached for her, but she put out her hand. "There is something else I would ask of you, m'lord."

"Say it," he ordered curtly.

"Release Lord Percy. Allow him to go home. He has done nothing."

He held his temper and drew a long breath. "It seems as if I can be of no help to you at all. Percy's fate is sealed."

Cat was done with pride. "Please," she begged.

Patrick's jaw tightened. "Is he so important to you?"

"I've known him all my life."

When he didn't reply, she spoke again. "What of my cousin? Mary will die if she leaves Scotland with the Pretender. Have you no compassion in your heart? Is a woman's life worth so little?"

Patrick sighed and ran his hand through his hair. "There is more involved than Mary," he said wearily. "Our whole policy toward England would be questioned if Jamie backed out of the marriage now."

"Is there no other wench in all of Scotland suitable to marry this so-called duke of York?"

She was so very lovely standing there before him. Patrick found it hard to concentrate. If it were possible, he would have granted her anything in his power and damned Jamie and English foreign policy to hell. The scent of roses clung to her hair, and her skin, milk-white against the green of her gown, gleamed like Chinese porcelain. He would give years of his life to have the right to carry her up the stairs, strip that absurd gown from her body and bury himself in the promise of her sweetness.

Instead he answered, "Jamie has no sisters and there is no other woman who is cousin to the king of Scotland."

Cat drew herself up proudly. "I am cousin to the king of Scotland."

The only sign that Patrick fought to keep his anger in check was the whitened knuckles of his clenched hands. "You are spoken for."

"You have the power to change that."

His hands reached out to grip her shoulders. "Neither I nor anyone else can stop the marriage." He did not specify to which marriage he referred. "I will do what I can to protect Mary. That is all I can promise." He shook her slightly. "You will not interfere, Catriona. Do you understand me?"

"I despise you," she whispered, pulling out of his grasp. "If Mary dies, I'll never forgive you." She opened the door and walked out without a backward glance.

For a long moment Patrick stared at the spot where she had stood. Then with lightning swiftness, he picked up a stool and hurled it against the diamond-paned windows. Shards of glass fell to the floor.

Several hours later, Brenna Sinclair held the candle high above her head so as not to wake her sleeping daughter. She would have preferred that Isobel sleep in the quarters she shared with John, but Patrick insisted the child have her own room in the castle. Each evening before she retired, Brenna walked down the clammy halls of Hermitage and tucked her daughter in for the night.

She frowned and held the candle closer to the bed. Her gasp at the empty sheets gave way to a thankful sigh as she saw the two figures in the chair. Holding her hand over the flame, she smiled at the sight of Isobel and the haughty English lass sound asleep in each other's arms. A piece of parchment and a quill lay on the floor at their feet.

Isobel was similar enough to Catriona to be her own child, Brenna thought to herself as she gazed at the sleeping figures. It was less a similarity of coloring than of bearing. Stamped on their clear, chiseled features was the same uncompromising look of pride that even unconsciousness could not erase. They seized the moment, these two, ready for whatever excitement life could bring them.

Brenna sighed. She did not crave the adventurous spirit so evident in her child and Patrick's future bride. Difficult as it was to admit, the woman suited him. Brenna understood the appeal a woman such as Catriona Wells had for the chief of Clan MacKendrick. They would found a dynasty unlike any other. She only hoped the two of them would not kill each other first.

Closing the door behind her, Brenna left the room in search of Patrick. He would put Isobel to bed without waking her.

The stairway, almost completely hidden in the night shadows, led directly to the great hall. The smell of roasting meat and unwashed bodies was strong. Smoke from the peat fires at opposite ends of the room clouded the air like a thin mist. At first it was difficult for Brenna to see. A tall man pushed himself away from the wall, placing himself in her path.

"May I serve you, madam?"

Startled, Brenna dropped the candle she carried. A booted foot crushed the flame and she recognized the white-blond head of her husband.

"My goodness, John!" Brenna placed her hand on her breast. "You startled me."

His cool blue eyes moved over her slowly, taking in the flushed cheeks and shaking hands. "You haven't answered me, Brenna."

"I'm looking for Patrick," she stammered, despising herself for her reaction. Why did he always make her feel as if she had done something wrong? "Isobel wishes to see him," she lied.

He considered her answer. "'Tis late for the lass to be awake."

"Lady Wells is teaching her to read. They forgot the time."

John nodded. "Patrick is there." He pointed to the large group of men in the center of the room.

Brenna's eyes adjusted to the light and she saw him. He was in the midst of a large group watching two brawny clansmen dice good-naturedly on the floor. The jeering crowd was laying wagers on the final outcome.

"I'll be back in a moment," Brenna assured her husband and crossed the room. As soon as the men saw her, their boisterous ribaldry stopped.

Patrick stood up, masking his concern. Brenna Sinclair did not usually seek him out. "Is the bairn all tucked in for the night?" he asked.

She hurried to reassure him. "All is well, Patrick. There is a small matter for which I need your help." Conscious of the jealous eyes of her husband, Brenna did not take Patrick's arm. She led him out of the room, warm with body heat, into the chilled hallway and up the narrow flight of stairs.

"You will see why I couldn't wake her," she said as they made their way to Isobel's bedchamber. "The two of them are sleeping so contentedly. 'Tis odd for Isobel to take to a stranger so quickly. Don't you agree?"

He remained silent.

Brenna despised the mindless prattle of her conversation. She bit her lip and looked away. Patrick's presence always had the same effect on her. His light, mocking gaze reduced her to blushing confusion, almost as if he knew of her secret longings. Once, long ago, on a night of moonlight and magic, he had wanted her. In a rush of blinding passion, they had come together, heedless of consequences. And then Isobel was born. She looked up at him from under her lashes. Did he ever remember what it had been like between the two of them? She frowned. More than likely Patrick MacKendrick had bedded a hundred willing serving wenches in the days and months that followed. She was no more or less to him than any other.

Patrick opened the door to Isobel's bedchamber, allowing Brenna to precede him. The two figures in the chair were undisturbed. Brenna moved to disengage Isobel's arm from around Cat's neck. A hand on her shoulder restrained her. She turned to look at Patrick and was shocked at the naked emotion on his face.

"I'll see Isobel to bed. You have no need to further concern yourself."

Brenna opened her mouth to protest and then closed it without speaking. It would be futile to argue. Wordlessly, she left the room, leaving the door slightly ajar. She was not happy with the turn of events. Catriona was a lady under the protection of the king. If she were compromised, it would dishonor the MacKendricks. Brenna's feet moved reluctantly away from the room. Her laird had ordered her away and she had not the courage to disobey.

The night was clear. Patrick registered the fact subconsciously as he watched the silvery moonlight play over the features of the woman before him. Like crescent moons, dark lashes rested against her cheeks. Her hair was very black against the bright flame of his daughter's. Isobel's chest rose and fell as she slept contentedly in Cat's arms. Did all women know the manner of motherhood instinctively? he wondered. Or was there a special bond between these two?

A surge of possessiveness swept through him. He wanted to give this proud, difficult woman a child of her own, to watch her belly swell with his seed, to see his son suckle at her breast. Dynastic instincts were new to Patrick. For the first time he looked at a woman in terms of children and permanence, fidelity and growing old together. He wanted Catriona Wells to look at him through eyes of love.

He placed the sleeping child on the bed and pulled the blankets around her. Cat stirred when her burden was lifted from her, but she did not awaken. Her head fell back, exposing the purity of her smooth white throat. Patrick cursed silently as he lifted her into his arms, damning his vulnerability for green-eyed women with shrewish tongues. Shifting the length of her body more fully against his, he opened the door with his boot.

Cat burrowed against him, twining her arms around his neck. Blood pounded in his head. He gritted his teeth and began the endless journey to her room.

"Damn Brenna," he swore under his breath. Why hadn't she just left Catriona asleep in the chair? She would have come to no harm and he wouldn't be tortured by the sweetness of her breasts pressed against his chest.

"Where are you taking me?" Cat's voice was low and clear, surprising Patrick from his thoughts. She hadn't removed her arms from around his neck.

Tense with need, he avoided the wide eyes looking up at him. His reply was curt. "To your room."

"Is there something wrong with my legs?" she teased.

Startled, Patrick looked down. Her eyes sparkled with laughter. He grinned. A sense of humor was more than he'd bargained for. At the door of her bedchamber, Cat leaned over to lift the latch. Patrick stepped inside but did not immediately release her. He looked down at her face. What would it be like to throw caution to the winds and forget that she was the cousin of Jamie Stewart? In a heady moment of madness, he hovered between sanity and behaving as an ordinary man, alone in a sweetly scented room with a beautiful woman in his arms. He could feel her eyes on his face watching, waiting. His glance rested briefly on her mouth. Sanity won.

"What are you thinking, m'lord?" The breathless quality of her voice surprised him.

His eyes narrowed. When he spoke, his words were light and bantering. "I'm thinking that some promises are better broken."

"What promises are those?"

Holy God! Catriona Wells was flirting with him. "If I told you, sweetheart, you would brave the wild moors at midnight to run from me."

He could see the reddening of her cheeks in the dim, candlelit room.

"If you mean to frighten me into thinking you would seduce me, I'd not believe it," she said firmly. "I've been here with you for many a night and have managed to keep my reputation and my virtue."

"You persist in believing me honorable, lass." Amusement colored his speech. "And yet, look at what I've accomplished in only three nights under the same roof with you." His grin deepened. "I'm sure Elizabeth of York would call the holy fathers to pray for your soul were she to see you now." His smile faded. "I may yet grow tired of waiting."

Cat was no longer amused. "You delight in mocking me."

Patrick dumped her unceremoniously on the bed. He leaned against the wardrobe in no hurry to depart.

"'Twas not mockery, Catriona." He spoke slowly, firelight etching the prominent lines of his cheekbones with golden light. He was once again the proud laird of Hermitage, careful and remote. "There is no shame in bedding a man. Some women have found it enough for a lifetime even when there are no wedding vows."

Who was the woman he spoke of? Was it Alison Douglass or Isobel's lovely, sad mother?

"I will never be one of your women, Patrick." Her expression was very serious as she sat there, cross-legged among the bedclothes, looking absurdly lovely. "When I wed, it will be for life. There will be no other lovers for my husband or myself."

Patrick recognized the words for what they were: a thinly veiled warning not to take her for granted. He felt unusually gay for so somber a moment. Cat did not wish to share him.

He took a step toward the bed.

She pulled back in alarm, her eyes wide with something dark and forbidden that caught at his heartstrings.

"Don't," she commanded him. "I can't think when you are near me."

Patrick grinned. "There is that, at least," he murmured. Lifting her chin in his hand, he forced her to look at him. "Do you think you can bring yourself to use my name on a regular basis?" he asked, surprising her.

For a long moment, their eyes locked. At last she nodded.

Satisfied, Patrick bent his head and briefly touched her lips with his. "Your virtue shall remain intact until you choose otherwise, lass," he murmured. "I'll not force what will come in time."

Cat sighed as she watched the door close behind him. The man had a curious effect on her. She felt weak and vulnerable, as if she had no resistance at all. Lying back in the comfortable bed, she prayed for the strength to withstand his devastating charm. He was the MacKendrick, England's enemy and hers.

❧ 20 ❧

Catriona's wedding day dawned clear and cold. Two weeks before the weather had changed, and the heat of summer was gone for another year. The dank smell of early winter rose from the harvested fields, and gusts of biting wind moaned against the windowpanes of Hermitage. In the meadow, on the banks of the trickling burn, wild mustard, once a golden spray of color against the orange gorse and purple heather, shriveled and browned and dropped their petals in preparation for the dormant season to come.

Catriona stood on her balcony and looked north toward Edinburgh and the shining blue water of the Firth of Forth. For three weeks she had searched for Andrew. Desperate for information, she had finally confided in Janet. Her cousin had bribed the guards and scoured every dungeon below the castle to no avail. Andrew was nowhere to be found. Now it was too late. Jamie Stewart had arrived the night before and no power on earth could stop the wedding of Patrick MacKendrick and Catriona Wells.

A breathless sense of anticipation fluttered in the pit of her stomach. In less than two hours she would be wed to the MacKendrick. Cat thought of the night to come. Oddly enough, she was not afraid. Ever since he'd shared her bed in Edinburgh Castle, she had ceased to fear him. There was something about the clear, rain-colored eyes and severe, uncompromising mouth that told her he would take his pleasure in the usual way of men.

Cat smiled. Not many women of her rank were as fortunate as she. Lady Douglass had not been invited to the ceremony. She, along with a hundred others, would wear ashes this day. Patrick MacKendrick, laird of Hermitage, earl of Bothwell and Jedburgh, advisor to the king and legendary warrior of the borders, would no longer be a matrimonial prize. A hated Englishwoman would be the new countess of Bothwell.

She tensed as the door opened quietly. Someone threw logs on the fire and then left the room. Footsteps crossed the floor to her side, and once again Cat relaxed. She would recognize Janet's step anywhere.

"Cat"—Janet's urgent voice sounded in her ear— "you've less than two hours."

Cat turned and frowned. "Where are the servants? I wanted to bathe first."

As if on cue, four women entered the room carrying a large wooden tub. They placed it before the hearth. Six more followed with steaming buckets of water. Janet dragged an ornamented screen to shield her cousin from the maids' prying eyes and sat down on a stool.

Cat stepped behind the screen and, dropping her robe on the floor, sank gratefully into the hot water. "Is everything ready?" she asked, as Janet filled a pitcher with bathwater and poured it over her head.

"I should hope so," Janet retorted. "I've never seen anything so lavish in my life. What were you thinking of, Cat? 'Tis almost as if you wish to marry the MacKendrick."

Cat closed her eyes and leaned back in the tub. Janet's fingers against her scalp were soothing. In her mind, she calculated the cost of the provisions. Patrick had told her to be frugal, but she had spent nearly a thousand pounds of his gold. For a moment she quailed at the thought of his eyes, angry and cold like chips of splintered ice. Then she dismissed her fears. She was the cousin of Jamie Stewart. No one attending her wedding would remember it as a paltry affair.

"The wedding will take place whether I wish it or not," Cat replied. "I'll not have Jamie's court say Patrick is miserly with his gold."

Janet's eyes widened. She was no coward, but at that moment she was glad it was Catriona and not herself who would stand before the border lord when he demanded a reckoning. Cat had ordered the courtyard fountains to flow with wine and candles of the purest wax for every hall and bedchamber. New plate and linen, platters and table knives were delivered daily to the castle, and the wine goblets she'd ordered directly from Edinburgh were embossed in gold with the MacKendrick crest. Janet shuddered when she looked at her cousin's wedding dress. The diamonds winking from the heavy white folds were worth a king's ransom. Patrick MacKendrick had paid dearly for his wife. Janet wondered if Cat appreciated quite how much.

Her hair rinsed, Cat climbed from the tub and wrapped herself in a towel. She frowned, lost in thoughts of her own. Had she forgotten anything? Two hundred quarters of wheat, three hundred tons of ale and wine, one hundred oxen, five hundred sheep and swine, two thousand quails and ducks. There would be hot pasties of venison, fish and oysters, dishes of jelly, hot and cold baked tarts and custards. Sugared sweetmeats would grace the tables, and each night of the celebration, huge frozen tankards of usquebaugh would be rolled into the great hall. Hot pokers would be thrust into the frozen mass and a white liquid that lay like a burning heat in the stomach would be drained off and drunk.

"Your dress is beautiful," Janet whispered as she helped Cat into a low-cut shift and silky petticoat.

Cat nodded and sat down on a stool to have her hair brushed dry.

"I've never seen such hair," Janet said admiringly, ignoring her cousin's silence. "'Tis as glossy and black as a crow's wing and it curls at the ends."

Cat's eyes in the glass were sharp and green. She said nothing.

"He loves you, you know," Janet whispered. "Jamie told Glenkirk that Patrick was strung tight as the strings of a lyre when he requested your hand." She leaned forward to dip her finger into the rouge pot and then gently dabbed the crimson paste over Cat's lips. "'Tis rumored that he tricked Jamie into it."

"Nay." Cat broke her silence. "There was no need for trickery. Jamie would be a fool to deny Patrick. He holds the borders against England." Patrick would be her husband. She would allow no ugly rumors regarding their marriage to circulate through the court.

Janet brushed powder across Cat's cheeks. "What happens now, Catriona?" she asked. "What of Richard?"

Cat reached for the jar of perfumed oil on the table and dabbed it on her throat and wrists. "I know not," she admitted. "My only hope is to find Andrew and send him back to Henry. If Neville believes I was forced against my will and that my intention is to return to England, he will not harm the boy."

Janet's eyes met her cousin's in the glass. "There is another way."

"I'll not hear it," Cat said firmly.

"I'll say it anyway," Janet blurted out. "Confide in Patrick."

"No!" Cat stood up quickly and reached for her gown.

"Trust your husband, Cat," Janet pleaded. "If any man can bargain with Henry Tudor, 'tis Patrick. I'd stake my life on it."

"'Tis not your life that is in danger," Cat reminded her. "It grows late." She slipped the dress over her head. "Help me with this."

The dress was white velvet with deep, wide bands of ermine. Janet laced up the back and stepped in front of her cousin to settle her skirt. She gasped. Cat was as lovely as a princess. Her face glowed with such radiance that Janet could hardly bear to look at her. Instead, she looked at the dress, tight at the bodice and waist, falling in soft swirls to the floor. The sloping shoulders rising from the deep square neck were as smooth and pale as fine porcelain. Cat's only jewelry was a huge diamond that hung between her breasts. Her hair, blue-black and shining, swung like a cloud around her face and waved down to her knees.

Janet's eyes burned with tears. The Stewarts were well represented. In all of Scotland there would be no woman to equal Catriona Wells this day. Perhaps the border lord would not mind spending a fortune to win such a wife after all.

Once again the door opened. Mary slipped into the room and stood before her cousin's slender, white-clad figure. Her cheeks were pale and she was very thin, but she smiled as she looked at Cat. "You are the loveliest bride I've ever seen," she said softly.

Cat bit her lip. "Mary," she began, "I couldn't manage your request. I'm sorry."

Mary shook her head. "Think no more of it. It was a hopeless gesture from the beginning." She reached out and folded Cat in her arms. "Take care, love, and be happy." Her voice dropped to a whisper. "Patrick MacKendrick can be a formidable enemy, but I don't believe he would harm a woman."

Cat nodded and stepped back. She lifted her chin. "Shall we go?"

Janet and Mary went down the stairs first. Cat waited several moments, took a deep breath, and followed.

The chapel was hushed, and pale sunlight filtered in through the diamond-paned windows. The features of the guests blurred together. Cat saw only the MacKendrick. His dark face was still and quiet, his lips unsmiling. Under the high bones, the hollows of his cheeks were very pronounced. Everything about him—his stance, the dark velvet of his tunic, the sculpted mouth and square jawline, the stabbing force of his direct clear-eyed gaze—gave the impression of ruthless strength. Cat panicked. She couldn't go through with it. Swaying slightly, she hesitated at the entrance of the chapel.

Patrick's eyes narrowed. He knew exactly what she was

thinking. He moved toward her quickly and held out his hand.

Catriona allowed him to take her arm. With his other hand he lifted her chin and looked into her eyes. His smile instantly warmed her.

"'Tis always difficult the first time," he murmured close to her ear. "Come. Bad luck follows those who keep an archbishop waiting."

They knelt before the altar. Surprisingly, Cat's voice was clear and strong. Patrick's hand was warm. She heard his replies, confident and low, as he repeated the timeless vows. And then it was over. She was married to the border lord.

Before they left the chapel, he took her in his arms and briefly kissed her. Cat looked up. His face was serious and worried. This time it was her turn to reassure him. "It can't be all that bad, m'lord. People do this every day and manage very well."

He grinned and put his arm around her and they left the chapel.

Back in the castle the feasting had begun. The banquet table stood slightly raised on a dais, with dining tables all around. The tablecloths were of finest linen and reached to the floor. Crystal sparkled and silver gleamed. Catriona and Patrick greeted the tenants and servants outside the chapel before proceeding to the great hall. On the second floor, hidden from the guests, minstrels played.

The royal cup was filled and presented to James. Then the goblets of the guests were filled, signaling the beginning of the procession of food. In between courses, there was entertainment, dancing girls, musicians, muses and jugglers. Cat saw and heard none of it. Her mind was completely filled with the lean, dark man by her side.

She had eaten and drunk very little. Night had fallen. The food was exquisite, the entertainment better than any she'd ever seen. Patrick looked pleased despite the cost. The hall glowed with candlelight. It was almost time.

"Is there anything else you desire, m'lord?" Cat's voice was hoarse.

The MacKendrick looked at her steadily. "I think not."

She nodded and looked around, acutely conscious of his presence. The hall was elegant, the guests satisfied. All of Edinburgh would speak of this wedding for years to come. Her hand looked small and white on the table beside his. For months she had vowed she would never have him. Today she had broken that vow. Gathering her courage, she wet her lips. " 'Tis time to retire."

"I'll give you until half past the hour."

"Aye." With a brilliant smile, she stood up. All conversation ceased and a loud cheering rang out in the room. Patrick stood beside her, his arm around her waist. Cat curtsied to James. He raised his glass and smiled.

Then she ran, out the big doors and up the stairs, Janet and Mary at her heels.

"Hurry, they come!" a voice from behind cried out.

Lifting her skirts, Cat reached the top of the third landing and looked down at the pursuing crowd. Her heart pounded. She felt vibrantly alive. With a laugh, she ran the rest of the way to her chamber.

Safely behind the closed door of her room, Cat looked at her cousins and began to shake.

Quickly, Mary poured out a dram of usquebaugh and held it to Cat's lips. "Drink it," she ordered. "It will calm you."

"She'll need more than that," replied Janet, who had accurately assessed the look on Patrick's face as he watched his wife leave the dining hall.

"Hush." Mary shook her head in warning. "Turn around, love," she said to Cat. "I'll unlace you."

Cat felt much as she had as a child when her mother had come to bid her good night. The drugging liquid soothed her, and she did not protest as Mary lifted the dress over her head and looked around for her nightgown.

"Dear God," whispered Janet as she held the flimsy silk to the light.

" 'Tis from France," said Cat, stepping into the gown and adjusting it over her shoulders. It was white but not the least bit virginal. Gathered under the waist and slit to a deep vee between her breasts, it spoke of perfumed bedsheets, softly lit candles and intimately entwined bodies.

"Why bother?" asked Janet.

Mary giggled. "Does it have a wrapper?"

Cat nodded and pointed to the bed where a sheer mantle lay. Even with the robe on, her skin gleamed indecently through the fabric.

The huge feather bed was turned down. Cat could see that the linen was fresh. Two more embroidered pillows had been placed on the left side and a long-handled warming pan was tucked between the sheets.

She looked at herself in the glass. Her eyes were wide and golden in the candlelight and her skin unnaturally pale. She pinched her cheeks and watched a tinge of color appear.

There were footsteps in the hallway and then the door burst open. Jamie Stewart, aided by Glenkirk and several other men, escorted Patrick into the room. His shirt was unlaced and he smelled of spirits. The men were laughing. One of them held Patrick's tunic.

"We've come too soon, it seems," said James, staring at Cat's revealing gown.

"Not at all," she answered coolly. "You are always welcome, Your Grace."

Patrick moved to her side and put his arm around her. "But not tonight." He grinned. "And not ever in my bedchamber."

The king laughed. "His lordship grows anxious for his lovely bride. Let us leave, lads. The merrymaking has just begun."

When the last man had disappeared down the stairs, Janet squeezed Cat's hand and followed them out of the room. Mary kissed her cousin's cheek and would have gone the way of her sister, but Patrick's hand on her arm stayed her.

"If you are ever in danger, lass, call on me."

Mary looked up. What she saw in the strong, confident face reassured her. "Thank you, m'lord." She smiled. "Take care of my cousin."

The MacKendrick grinned. "I intend to do so as soon as you leave the room."

Cat watched the bantering interplay in detached silence. It was as if she took part in a dream and none of the events that had occurred this day had any place in reality. Then Patrick turned toward her, and all at once everything became very real indeed.

His eyes moved deliberately over her body and then back to her face. "You are white as a glaistig," he said gently. "Surely you know there is nothing to be afraid of."

She looked at him helplessly. How could he understand? There was no way to describe this feeling inside her, no way at all to reveal the confusing emotions pulling her apart. She hadn't the words to explain to a man who lived by his sword and the power of his name how it was that the world was not a safe haven for women and children.

Something of her desperation must have showed in her face. His voice, when he spoke, was very low. "Catriona, look at me." Green eyes met gray. "You are my wife, but I'll not force you. I'd have it go differently for us."

Cat was afraid. Not for what he would do to her body but for the hold he would have on her heart. She did not want to love him, but perhaps it was already too late for that. After everything she had done, after all he knew and kept to himself, after the thousands of pounds she had squandered and the risk he had taken to win her, this night, at least, she could give him. Cat knew, if the truth were told, it was something she wanted very much for herself. In the long, lonely months and years ahead she would have this memory. She took off her robe and dropped it on the floor, her hands moving to the tie at her waist.

Patrick sucked in his breath as the nightgown slid from her body to join the robe on the floor. Accustomed to full-figured women, he was enchanted anew with the slim, perfect proportions of the woman before him. She was exquisitely formed, her body slender and toned by days spent on horseback. High-breasted and long-legged, her small waist flared out to gently rounded hips and slim thighs. Like a curtain of ebony her black hair flowed down her back. Her smile welcomed him.

The heat rose in his limbs. Never in his wildest dreams had he believed she would come to him so willingly. He reached out and drew her into his arms. He looked down at her face and smoothed back her hair. She wound her arms around his neck. Slowly, he bent his head to her mouth and kissed her. The kiss was gentle and searching, his only thought to win her trust.

Her lips clung to his. Without breaking the kiss, Patrick slid his arm beneath her knees and carried her to the bed. His mouth moved to her throat and then across her shoulder and down the slope of her breast. He pulled away abruptly to stare at the ceiling. His breathing was labored, and he was very close to losing control. Patrick had been without a woman for a long time, ever since the day Jamie had agreed to give him Catriona's hand in marriage. The emotions flooding through his body were new. He needed time to sort them out.

Cat's skin burned where his lips had been. The hard-muscled body lying against hers felt very right, as if he belonged here beside her. She pressed against him, her senses clamoring to re-create the unexpected rush of pleasure that his hands and mouth evoked. Her fingers walked down his hair-roughened chest, resting on his stomach. She heard his harsh intake of breath and felt the muscles under her hand clench. Experimentally, she rotated her palm around the indentation of his navel.

He reached out and caught her wrist. "Enough, lass," he gasped hoarsely. "Hold still for a moment."

Delighted with her power, Cat sat up and stared at him. His eyes glittered silver in the moonlight.

"Twice now I've offered myself to you," she teased, "and always you tell me to wait. I'm beginning to believe the rumors of your prowess with women are false."

He grinned. "In truth I've never had so eager a bed partner."

"Are you complaining?"

"Nay, lass. But we've all night and I'd not have it over before 'tis even begun."

Fascinated, she watched him divest himself of his remaining clothes. The color rose in her cheeks and she was grateful for the concealing darkness.

He held out his arms. "I'm ready if you are."

With a sigh that was almost a sob, Cat lowered herself into his arms and found once again the blissful pleasure of his mouth on hers. His kiss deepened and her lips parted. Time stopped, and Cat knew nothing but the pulsing of her blood and the aching tension produced by his mouth on her skin. It was hard to breathe, impossible to think. Instinctively she parted her legs and opened to the hard, insistent length of him.

Patrick's need drove him. Nothing mattered but the softness of the woman in his arms. Her lips against his skin were warm and giving, and her fingers stroking his chest were driving him insane. He couldn't get close enough. Sweat beaded his forehead as he moved both his legs between hers. She was ready for him. Slowly, his head pounding with the effort of his control, he entered her. Her arms tightened and her teeth marked his shoulder. Sensitive to her pain, he moved forward slowly. She arched her back and cried out. He waited no longer.

Moments later, an eternity later, he looked down at her. She lay quietly in his arms, her lashes dark against her pale skin. She was beautiful, he thought dispassionately, her face innocent and vulnerable in the light of the dying fire. For the first time he noticed there were shadows under her eyes, and the corners of her mouth were pinched and turned downward.

Patrick had seen enough of life to know that Catriona Wells had suffered greatly. What was the sorrow she kept to herself? When had she assumed that mask of implacable calm she showed the world? According to Jamie Stewart, she had been a mischievous child, beloved by her parents, intelligent, compassionate, filled with laughter. When had the course of her life changed? Where had she learned to lie so convincingly?

He cursed under his breath and gently removed his arm from beneath her body. Tucking the covers around her, he stood up and walked to the window, his arms crossed over his chest. The air was icy cold where the wind seeped through the glass, but he felt none of it. Pain twisted his insides and his mouth was grim. Once again he had played the fool for a woman, and this time he had not even the excuse of youth and inexperience.

Catriona's eyes, spilling with light and yearning, had weakened him. Her outrageous pride and the clear, direct way she had of looking at a man convinced him to lower his guard. He was mistaken. His lovely young wife had already been deflowered. Catriona had given her heart and her body to another man.

It mattered little to Patrick that she had taken a lover before marriage. Rape and handfast were common in the borders, and maidenhood was no measure of a woman's chastity. What he could not forgive was her lie. A woman's loyalty was beyond price because it must be freely given. His jaw clenched. Who was the man? Who had the brazen audacity to take the maidenhood of a Stewart noblewoman and not offer her his name?

A low moan interrupted his reverie. Cat twisted on the bed in the throes of a nightmare. Patrick crossed the room and sat down beside her. Her eyes were open and filled with fear. He knew she couldn't see him.

"Please," she begged in a broken whisper. "The cold—it hurts me—bring them back—don't leave me—I can't bear the dark." Tears streamed down her cheeks. "No, please," she gasped, "not again—I won't—you can't make me—oh, God, no." Her hand snaked out, raking his skin with her nails.

Patrick gripped her arms at the elbow, heedless of the blood running down his shoulder. "Catriona." He shook her gently. "Wake up. 'Tis only a dream."

She tensed and lay still. Closing her eyes, she turned her head away, her breathing shallow and painful. Patrick watched as the unreachable, frozen mask he recognized settled over her features.

When she had once again slipped into sleep, he released her arms. His hands shook and a white-hot, killing rage swept through him. So that was the way of it. Only a fool would mistake the matter. Catriona hadn't lied. She simply refused to accept her rape, pushing her horror to the darkest corners of her brain where it remained hidden, resurrecting itself in her nightmares. He had heard of such a thing before. It happened to green soldiers after their first bloody battle.

He recalled her terror that night in Edinburgh and the tiny scars on her wrists. It was amazing that she could respond at all. A thought occurred to him, and immediately he felt better. Catriona didn't despise his touch. Indeed, she had welcomed him to her bed. Her response was more than he'd ever hoped for. Perhaps, in time, she would come to trust him as well.

Lifting the covers, he climbed into the bed and pulled her into his arms. She stirred but did not wake. Patrick tightened his embrace and kissed her temple. She whimpered and burrowed her head into his shoulder. His eyes watered and burned. Somewhere in England walked a man whose days were numbered.

Struggling through layers and layers of suffocating darkness, Kate fought her way into the restoring daylight. Acutely conscious of her racing pulse, she heard the flap of fluttering curtains and felt the icy wind sting the tip of her nose into numbness. Between the sheets, the heavy woolen blanket and thick quilt, her body was comfortably warm. She breathed in deeply and opened her eyes. The nightmare was over, and a pearl-like dawn pierced the darkness. Her arm ached from lying beneath her. She tried to turn and froze.

An arm, tanned and masculine, heavy with the dead weight of sleep, curled around her ribs possessively. *She was in bed with a man at Glennis MacLean's boardinghouse.* Uninvited memories of Beltane intruded into her mind, and she remembered Niall. Without moving her head, she focused on the flowered wallpaper, the perfume bottle she had brought from home, the alarm clock, her brush and comb, their teeth and bristles fused together in a lover's embrace. This was no dream. She was definitely in the twentieth century.

Her nerves vibrated, edged with a raw vulnerability she couldn't explain. The feelings she'd experienced last night were new and shocking. They belonged to the leaping fire, the shadowed cliffs, the pull of the foam-white sea. This flower-studded guest room was no place for the disturbing sensations swallowing her reason.

Carefully she pulled away, attempting to extricate herself from the arm that held her. First she felt resistance, a slight tightening of pressure around her waist, and then release, callused fingers lingering briefly on the swell of her breasts. *He was awake.*

Kate's cheeks flamed. She had to face him eventually. Gathering her nerve, she held her breath and rolled over. He stared down at her, his eyes veiled, his jaw shadowed with a dark beard. She was very aware of his bare body pressed against hers. Her heartbeat accelerated. Stunned by her reaction, she stammered incoherently, "What are you doing here?"

Amusement colored Niall's voice. "Isn't it obvious?"

Kate chewed the inside of her lip. "That's not what I meant." She shifted to avoid touching him. "How did you get here?"

"I brought you home," he said simply. "You asked me not to leave you."

Her cheeks burned. "I see. Did we . . . ?"

He twisted her hair around his fingers and gently pulled her head back to look into her eyes. What he saw there satisfied him. Deliberately, he set his mouth on hers. "Yes," he said, when he had lifted his head, "and we're going to do it again."

Kate let go of her breath. It came out in a soft, gasping sigh of relief. "If you don't mind, I'd like to do it right now."

His body hardened instantly, and when he moved over her, exploring her breasts with urgent hands and seeking lips, she opened for him as naturally and readily as a flower to the sun. "My God, Kate," he groaned, thrusting deeply. "I can't wait. Come with me. Come with me now."

With every powerful surge of his body, heat and passion climbed within her, side by side, until the molten wave of tension crested and she cried out, pulsing around him. At the same time he stiffened and, with one deep thrust, pushed her flush against the headboard and poured into her.

This time she woke before he did. Beneath her lashes, she studied him. Above the quilt his bare chest and shoulders were wide, not like the bunched artificial body of a weight-lifter, but lean and fit with the smooth natural grace of a man who moves more than he sits. His neck was strong and his head, with the chiseled features relaxed in sleep, was beyond handsome. She'd seen it all before, of course, but not with the awareness of the previous night between them. He was compellingly attractive, even if he wasn't Patrick MacKendrick.

His eyes opened slowly, and his words shocked her. "I love you, Kate. I know it's sudden, but so help me, I've never said that to another woman."

Fear, immediate and consuming, prevented her from speaking coherently. Finally she formed the words: "Don't, Niall. The only response to a declaration like that is to tell you I feel the same way and I can't say it."

"Why not?" She had said she couldn't, not that she didn't.

She pushed the pillow behind her head and sat up, speaking in a whisper. "This really won't work. I told you that in the beginning. I'm so sorry."

Niall was sorry too, sorrier than bloody hell. He knew that she wanted him to tell her it would be all right, but this time he wasn't biting. He was tired of playing the gentleman and even more tired of her mind games. There were names for women who appeared interested one minute and the next gave a man the cold shoulder. Stubbornly, he remained silent.

Kate touched his arm. "You really are angry, aren't you?"

Damn right he was angry and hurt, more than he cared to show. What was it about Kate Sutherland that made her so appealing to him? Even after what was undeniably the most humbling experience of his life, he still refused to accept defeat.

"I'm not angry," he lied, "and I'll prove it to you." Throwing the blankets aside, he stood up and pulled on his clothes, leaving his feet bare. Walking back to the bed, he stood above her. "Come with me to the dig site today. There's something I want to show you."

Kate lay still, wrapped in the bedsheet. "What has the dig site got to do with anything?"

"It has a great deal to do with me. It's my life. After last night and this morning you can't pretend there's nothing between us, even if it is just physical. I'd like to find out if that's all there is on your end or if it's more than that. I'm thirty-four years old, Kate. I'd like to marry and have a family."

She felt the rise of her old panic. "And if it isn't more than that on my end?"

"Heartbreak isn't a game, and it certainly isn't conducive to productivity," he explained reasonably. "If you can't share my feelings, I won't see you again. Spending some time in each other's company should resolve that question rather quickly." He was at the door now. "Think about it. You don't have to decide immediately."

Kate stared at the closed door for several minutes, then lay back down and looked out the window. It was still much too early to get up. She pulled the quilt up to her chin. Niall MacCormack was either incredibly self-confident or he wasn't serious. Odd that she couldn't tell which. It was completely unlike her. She could read most people like a book. Kate closed her eyes.

❧ 21 ❧

Kate smiled and stretched lazily. She was completely relaxed with the loose-limbed, easy contentment that sexual release brings when the sex is very good. Not that she was all that experienced with *good* sex. The pattern she had set in former relationships had been to avoid intimacy for as long as possible, and when it no longer was, pretend that the earth moved with every shattering climax. The truth was it was never shattering, and she probably wouldn't recognize it if it were.

The idea of spending the day with Niall was very appealing. He was attractive, decent and, unlike most of her involvements, completely available. During one of her therapy sessions Kate had been forced to admit that her usual choices for male companions were those encumbered with either ex-wives or unsettled, messy divorces, for a very obvious reason: She didn't want commitment.

Niall MacCormack, on the other hand, was a force to be reckoned with. Not only was he eligible, he was definitely looking for commitment. However, she reminded herself, she had made her position completely clear. If Niall was hurt, he had only himself to blame. Not that she wanted him to be hurt. She closed her eyes and thought back to the way his hands felt on her skin. No, she didn't want him to be hurt at all. What she wanted was impossible. Niall would be much better off with that child who adored him, Victoria.

She sat up, swung her legs over the side of the bed and winced. Like a slow burn deep inside, she felt the soreness between her legs. Nearly a year had passed since she'd walked out on David Crane after his white-lipped profession of love for another woman. When she stopped to analyze her emotions, it wasn't David's defection that bothered her. It was the fact that she'd been held up to scrutiny and found wanting. Not until last night had anyone taken his place in her bed. There had been other chances, of course. There always were. But something inside of her rebelled at the idea of another doomed relationship based on hormonal urges that disappeared when physically satisfied.

Awkwardly she stood up and made her way to the bathroom. Morning light filtered through the window and settled on the mirror. With her forefinger, Kate traced her reflection. She looked different this morning, younger, less harried, more relaxed. The strained look around her eyes was gone. She shrugged, turned on the bath tap and stepped into the shower. Lovemaking was obviously good for her appearance.

A sticky wetness ran down the inside of her thigh. She froze in horrified awareness. For the first time in her life, she'd completely forgotten about protection. Despite her Southern California upbringing, Kate was a traditionalist. She did not believe in abortion, nor did she approve of unwed motherhood. It all hit too close to home. If and when she ever got pregnant, she wanted the news to be welcome both to herself and to the father-to-be who would most definitely be her husband. The very idea that she could have forgotten something as vital as birth control stunned her.

Moist as baby's breath, the shower spray steamed around her. She tilted her head, allowing the warm water to bathe her face and throat. It really wasn't the right time of the month for anything to happen, she reassured herself. Of course, a woman could never be completely sure, but the odds against it were very good. She shook her hair over her face. It smelled of peat and smoke and the wild, spicy scent she recognized as Niall. Automatically she reached for the shampoo. What time, she wondered, was a person supposed to arrive at a dig site?

"What are you saying?" demanded Victoria Sutherland. Her hands were clenched, the knuckles round and white under the tight skin.

Her father sighed and turned toward the window, bolstered by the view. Jagged cliffs stained white with bird droppings stood framed against a gray sky and grayer sea. Terns and curlews circled against each other above the whitecaps and, hidden just behind the first heather-colored rise of distant Foula, was Maura's tiny croft. The thought of her gave him courage. "Kate Sutherland is my daughter, your half-sister," he repeated.

"I don't believe it."

He turned back to face his younger daughter, struck as always by the lack of anything Sutherland in her phenotype. She was all her mother, from the Scandinavian fairness of her hair and eyebrows to the ice-blue color of her eyes, evidence of Viking raids on the western coast of Scotland centuries before. "It doesn't really matter, Victoria," he said gently. "What is fact still stands, whether or not you believe it."

"Who is her mother?"

"Maura Sutherland."

Victoria gasped. "Good God! The witch?"

Hunter's mouth turned up in a smile he couldn't control. "If you like."

"I suppose you knew it all along," the girl raged. "After all, Kate is the image of *your* kind of Sutherland. I suppose everything belongs to her now and she shall give me an allowance to live on. How dreadful for you that she wasn't born a boy. Then you could really disinherit me."

"Don't be absurd."

"Did you love her?"

"As much as anyone can love a child he's never seen for thirty years."

"Are you daft?" The pale eyes snapped with temper. "I meant her mother, Maura Sutherland."

He nodded. "Very much."

"Why didn't you marry her?"

"She wouldn't have me," replied Hunter simply.

Victoria's anger cooled slightly. "Why not?"

He shrugged. "She had the strange idea that a woman like herself wasn't a suitable mate for the duke of Sutherland." He laughed bitterly. "More likely she made the choice of giving up her hereditary position or marrying me. She chose her birthright."

"What happens now?"

Hunter stared at this angry young woman with her folded arms and uncompromising stance and realized that he didn't know her. Had he ever? he wondered, vaguely remembering a toothless smile and wispy, light-touched curls. "I would like it very much if you would welcome her," he said gently. "She's come a very long way to find her family."

Victoria's fair cheeks flamed. "Has it ever occurred to you that your happy reunion doesn't include me?"

Hunter exploded. "Of course it includes you. You are my daughter, my only child born of my legal wife. Every advantage has been given to you from the moment of your birth. Can you be so self-serving that you would deny another, your own flesh and blood, her rightful home?"

Tight-lipped and mutinous, Victoria considered her

father's words. "And if I were?" she asked at last, her voice cold as winter rain.

"That would be a shame, my dear," Hunter explained coolly, "but despite your objections, Kate is as much my daughter as you are, and I've many years to make up for."

"I see." Victoria walked across the room. Without turning, she stood at the door, her face averted. "In that case, why don't you ask her mother here as well?"

"Victoria," Hunter began, "be reasonable."

She held up her hand. "Say nothing more. I've had a long day, and the thought of you and that woman disgusts me."

"It was long before your mother, Victoria. Surely you know that."

She turned her head so that Hunter could see her profile. "Did you ever love Mama?" she whispered.

"Of course I did, every bit as much as she loved me."

"That doesn't answer my question."

Hunter sighed. "I don't want to lie to you, my dear. Your mother and I were very good together. We met, decided we would suit and lived our lives very comfortably."

"So it was a marriage of convenience for both of you?"

"Yes."

She was looking directly at him now, the fair eyebrows drawn together in a frown, trying to see him as a woman would. He was handsome, one of the handsomest men she'd ever seen, and the years had been more than fair to him. Hunter Sutherland looked to be in his middle forties, a decade younger than he really was. His body was strong and fit. He had rich dark hair dusted with gray and his eyes and nose reminded her of an eagle, watchful, ready and proud. Victoria was willing to wager that, for her mother, the marriage was more than a union of convenience.

"I was desolate when she died," Hunter said softly. "You must remember that."

Victoria nodded. "I remember that you sent me to school soon after."

"It was what she wanted. Cait Ness is no place to raise a lady."

"Did Maura ever marry?"

"No."

"If you loved her so much, why didn't you go back to her?"

"It wasn't like that, Victoria. She wouldn't have me when I was young and unencumbered. Why would she want a widower with a small daughter to raise?"

"You are the duke of Sutherland. Everyone wants you."

Hunter laughed. "Thank you for that, but I doubt it. Maura is very discriminating. She refused me once. I had no reason to believe she had changed her mind."

"And now?"

The duke's face was dark with color. "Now I intend to welcome my daughter into our home. Maura is welcome to do as she pleases."

"What if she wants you again? Would you have her?"

The question was deeply personal and quite improper, but Hunter knew that if he didn't answer there wasn't a prayer of a chance that Victoria would accept the situation. He thought of the night before and felt the sweet pull of blood to blood and the intoxicating magic of Beltane. "God help me, but I believe I would," he said honestly.

Without another word, Victoria left the room.

Cat awakened to weak fingers of sunlight weaving through the bedclothes. Her arm, on top of the blankets, was cold, but everywhere else she was quite warm. Something heavy lay across her waist. All at once she remembered where she was. Color flamed in her cheeks. What must Patrick be thinking? She turned over to find him staring at her. Her color deepened and she pulled the covers up around her neck.

Patrick grinned. "'Tis too late for that, lass," he teased. "I've seen every last inch of you."

"Not in the daylight, you haven't," she replied tartly and buried her head so that only the crown showed above the blankets.

Surprisingly, he did not protest. First the heat of his breath and then his lips brushed the top of her head. "You've nothing to be ashamed of, Catriona," he said huskily. "You're the bonniest woman I've ever seen."

Her voice was muffled. "I'm not ashamed."

"What is it then?"

She hesitated and then spoke. "I've never slept beside a man before. 'Tis an awkward feeling, and I don't know what to do."

The bed shook with his silent laughter.

She lifted her head and sat up, holding the sheet against her breasts, ready to take him to task for laughing at her. His eyes were very bright but there wasn't a hint of a smile on his lips. He lay back against the pillows, his arms behind his head, and considered her words.

"I know what you mean," he said reasonably. "I've often felt that way myself."

"You have?" Cat was skeptical.

"Of course. The first time a man makes love to a woman and wakes up beside her, he doesn't know what she wants." He was speaking conversationally, as if the matter was of little importance. "Should he make love to her once more or should he leave? Should he ask to see her again or wait until they meet at a later time? Was she disappointed with his skill as a lover? Did she compare him with other men?" He turned on his side, resting on one elbow, to look at her. "'Tis a difficult moment."

Cat was speechless. She stared at him, her mouth open. Suddenly he grinned, and it was then that she saw the teasing glint in his eyes. Collapsing against his chest, she laughed with relief, more grateful to him than words could describe for easing the tension of the moment.

"Shall I tell you how to make the morning after less awkward?" he murmured much later when her laughter had died and she lay dozing in his arms.

"How?" Cat stretched lazily against him.

"Like this." His hand swept across her hips and up to her breast, cupping it possessively. "I want you, Cat," he muttered, pressing his lips against her throat. "I don't think I've ever wanted anything more in my life." He kissed her open mouth. "Tell me that you want me."

Awkwardly, her hands moved down his back to the tight line of his buttocks and legs. "Yes, Patrick," she murmured, "I want you as well."

He stiffened as her hands moved between their heated

bodies. When her fingers tentatively closed over him, he waited no longer. The intensity was deeper this time, the pleasure more satisfying, as he knew it would be. A second loving was always better than the first when the way is known but not yet familiar.

Bracing himself on his elbows, he stared down at her. She was breathing more deeply than usual. Her eyes were closed, and a sheen of perspiration dampened her forehead. Exercising all his control, he waited until she opened her eyes. He moved against her, smiling tenderly. "Come with me, *mo chridhe,*" he whispered. "Let me show you the way of it."

Catriona nodded. The aching tension produced by his slow, sensual movement was turning into something more, and she wanted it to continue. Instinctively, she arched her hips.

"My God, Cat," he gasped.

Her mouth formed a small, perfect circle of pleasure. The tempo of their rhythm ebbed and flowed until Cat could hold no more. Her low, guttural cry of pleasure matched the peaked tension in the corded muscles of his back, and once again she felt the sudden surging warmth spreading throughout her belly.

Cat stared at her husband as he slept. Despite the growth of new beard, his face looked younger, less dangerous. His cheekbones gave him a gaunt, forbidding look, but his mouth was relaxed and his lashes were beautifully long and thick. Obeying an irrepressible urge, she pressed her mouth to his lips.

Almost immediately, his eyes flew open and he smiled. Gray lights danced in their depths. "No more awkwardness, I hope."

She laughed and shook her head. "No, m'lord. Your cure was quite effective." Her voice lowered teasingly. "You needn't have worried, Patrick."

His brow creased. "Explain yourself."

"Your reputation is well earned. No woman would ever find you wanting."

Cat was delighted to see the red of embarrassment darken his cheeks.

"An orchard needs planting," she read from the book of accounts, "and all the old stumps must be pulled out. Angus MacKendrick bids you remember that the roof of his croft must be repaired before the winter snows." Cat's fingers moved swiftly down the page and Patrick felt the familiar stir of envy at her facility with words. They were in his study working their way through the massive stacks of parchment on the desk.

It was a mere two weeks after their wedding and already he had noticed a difference in her. The vast lands of Hermitage needed constant supervision, and she had both the energy and ability to see to whatever needed to be done. Never had the business of running an estate gone so smoothly. More often than not, her quick intelligence made short work of a normally time-consuming task, and Patrick admitted with rueful chagrin that her experience concerning domestic matters was far superior to his own.

To his surprise, he found that he preferred her company to anyone else's. She was lovely and arrogant and swift to anger. But underneath her stubborn facade, she had a direct honesty and sense of fairness that weakened his resolve and caused him to question his uncompromising view of life. Her vivid beauty stirred his blood. Every night he came to her bed resolved to keep his heart detached and instead gave himself up, a willing victim to the hot, melting magic of tangled hair and trembling lips, of silken skin and straining limbs reaching up to hold him close. Patrick knew, with a sense of inevitability, that he was in danger of losing his very soul to a woman who refused to trust him.

Reaching for the flagon of ale at his elbow, Patrick looked at his wife. The memory of their coupling the night before caused his throat to go dry. She looked as pure and wide-eyed as the Virgin Mary. Anyone seeing her dressed in her pristine blue velvet gown and white collar, her hair pulled back in a single plait, the thick braid resting on one shoulder, would never have believed her capable of such unbridled passion.

She smiled, and Patrick cleared his throat. "Will you accompany me to Angus's croft?" he asked. "His roof has been postponed long enough, and Mairi is anxious to meet you."

"Why?" Catriona asked bluntly.

" 'Tis only natural for a tenant to wish to meet her new mistress," replied the MacKendrick. "Besides, Mairi was my wetnurse." He grinned. "She still thinks of herself as my mother. In her mind, no one on earth is worthy enough to be my bride. It is her inspection you must pass to be truly accepted at Hermitage."

"I can hardly refuse such a challenge." Cat laughed. "Give me ten minutes and I'll meet you downstairs."

True to her word, ten minutes later, Patrick lifted her to the saddle of her horse and strode to his own mount. Just as the portcullis gate rose, allowing them to pass, a childish voice stopped them.

"Dada," Isobel called out, lifting her skirts to run toward her father. Panting with her exertions, she lifted accusing eyes to his face. "You promised to ride with me today, and it is already almost noon."

The MacKendrick looked at his small daughter and frowned. Reaching down, he pulled her up, seating her before him on the saddle.

"So I did, lass," he admitted. "When I made the promise I had no idea today would be such a busy one. Will you forgive me?"

Isobel pouted. "I've been waiting a very long time."

Patrick's eyes twinkled. "Surely since you've been so patient already, you can wait one more day."

"But I don't want to wait another day."

He sighed. "I've been too lenient with you, lass. 'Tis not for you to decide."

Cat interrupted them. "How far is it to the croft?"

"An hour or so," Patrick replied.

"An hour isn't too long a ride for the lass," said Cat. "Why not take her with us?"

Isobel turned glowing eyes on her father. "Oh, may I, Dada?" she begged.

Patrick was no match for the hopeful eyes of his daughter.

Nodding his head, he lifted Isobel to the ground. "Tell your mother and hurry back."

He turned toward Cat. "I had hoped to spend the day alone with you," he said, his voice low and caressing.

The color rose in her cheeks, but she met his look steadily. "Isobel is a child. Until now she's had you all to herself. Imagine how she must feel to see you spend every waking moment with another. 'Tis amazing she has any affection for me at all."

Patrick's look was thoughtful. "I'd not considered that," he admitted. "You are wise beyond your years, Catriona. How is it that you know so much about children?"

Her smile faded and her face resumed its expression of frozen quiet that meant he was probing into deeply personal areas.

"I have a brother who is not so very much older than your daughter."

"Your brother," Patrick continued, ignoring her icy look, "is he happy living in England with his stepfather?"

"Why?" Cat was wary.

"Perhaps he would like to make his home in Scotland with you."

A wild, surging hope flared in her chest. Her heart hammered. Was it really possible to defy Neville and King Henry and bring Richard to Hermitage? She looked at the quiet strength of the man beside her, at the slashing grooves in his cheeks and the firm, thin-lipped mouth. His eyes, steady on her face, were the gray of hammered steel, hard and ruthless and capable. If anyone could make the impossible come to pass, it was Patrick MacKendrick.

Isobel's delighted laugh floated across the courtyard. "I'm coming, Dada, and I want to ride with Cat."

The mood was broken and Cat was relieved. She needed time, time to decide her course of action. By now Henry must know of her marriage to the MacKendrick. Richard's life was already in grave danger, and Andrew was nowhere to be found. Patrick was her only hope. Her thoughts were in turmoil. For a long time she had relied only on herself. It was a hard habit to break. Trust did not come easily.

* * *

The croft was a typical border bothy with a thatched roof and walls of rock and wattle and mortar. Cat had to bend her head to enter the low-hung doorway. She looked around curiously. Never in her life had she thought to cross the threshold of a peasant family. In England such a thing was unheard of. She was surprised to find it quite welcoming.

A large table filled most of the room, and a peat fire, smoking slightly and sweetly aromatic, kept the temperature quite warm. Along one wall, cribs with plaid blankets were stacked against each other, waiting to be pulled out when the family was ready for bed. Two haunches of venison, dried and salted, hung from the ceiling, and a loaf of sliced brown bread sat on the table, ready to be eaten.

A young woman sat on a stool, an infant at her breast, and Mairi MacKendrick, excited at the prospect of visitors, rushed around offering refreshments to her guests.

Patrick declined both. After introducing Cat to the older couple, he stepped outside with Angus. Despite the chill in the air, he took off his shirt and jack. Bare-chested, clad only in his breeks and boots, he climbed up on the roof to repair the damage. Later, when Cat walked outside to see what was keeping him, her mouth dropped open. In England gentlemen did not stoop to menial labor, especially on behalf of a tenant.

She watched the play of muscles across his back and the sheen of sweat glisten on the bronze skin. The wind lifted his hair. Angus said something in Gaelic and Patrick threw back his head and laughed. She swallowed and stepped back into the bothy. Never had a man appeared more appealing than her husband at that moment.

"Will you have a bit of oatcakes with us, lass?" Mairi's soft voice broke into her thoughts.

Cat's mouth watered. She looked at the meager supply of food on the table and politely declined. "Perhaps Isobel would care for one," she suggested, looking over at her stepdaughter.

The child appeared enchanted with the bairn. He wasn't more than a few weeks old. The wrinkled redness of birth had disappeared, but the small head, still too heavy to be supported by his neck, rested against the young woman's shoulder.

"Isn't he beautiful?" Isobel breathed, looking down at the infant.

Cat smiled and walked over to the baby. The dark fuzz on his head reminded her of Richard. A lump gathered in her throat. "May I take him?" she asked, holding out her arms.

The young mother hesitated. Cat smiled reassuringly. The woman nodded and held out her child.

Taking him gently in her arms, Cat folded back the blanket and buried her face in his neck. She breathed in the baby scent of him and a surge of desire, so strong it weakened her knees, swept through her. What would it be like to have this sweetness for her own? Even now she could be carrying a child. A child with her black hair and Patrick's gray eyes. She looked at Isobel and blinked back tears. Isobel would welcome a tiny brother or sister. It must be lonely for her, the only child of the border lord, behind the walls of Hermitage.

She felt a cold draft. Instinctively, Cat held the baby closer to her breast and turned toward the door. Patrick, fully clothed, stood on the threshold, staring at her. A look passed between them and a sharp, sweet ache pierced her heart. If she bore him a child, Cat knew she would never leave this man. She wasn't sure she had the courage to leave him even if she didn't.

Halfway to Hermitage, they stopped under a shelter of trees. Patrick reached into his pack and brought out bread and salted meat. Isobel pouted until he produced a pouch of sweet criachan. The mixture of honeyed oats and whiskey was delicious and satisfying. Cat was completely content.

Leaning against a boulder, she watched Isobel drawing in the dirt with a sharp stick. Cat closed her eyes for a moment, breathing in the clean scent of the autumn wind. She was jerked out of her reverie by Patrick's sharp voice.

"Where did you learn this?" he demanded.

Cat's eyes flew open and she straightened nervously.

"I wanted to surprise you." Isobel's reply floated back on the wind. "Are you angry, Dada?"

"Of course not." He brushed her question aside. Kneeling in the dirt, he took her hand in his and spoke more gently. "What does it say?"

"'Tis my name," the child replied proudly. "Isobel MacKendrick. I wanted to surprise you. Cat promised not to tell."

"Did she teach you?" he asked as Cat came up behind them.

Isobel nodded her head. "Are you pleased?"

Patrick's voice was rough with emotion. "Very pleased, lass. I knew you were clever. Can you read as well?"

"Aye." She nodded again. "I tried to read some of your books, but I couldn't manage the words. Lady Janet brought some from Edinburgh and Cat changes the words on paper to make it easier for me."

"Does she now?" He turned his piercing gaze on Cat.

"I didn't think you'd mind," she stammered, determined to defend Isobel. "We can stop if you insist, although I think the lessons mean a great deal to the child."

Patrick's face held none of its usual mockery. "I thank you from the bottom of my heart, Catriona. I'm deeply moved that you care so much for my daughter."

Cat moved her hand in a motion of protest. "It was nothing, really. I enjoy it. I would do it for anyone."

"Well then"—the gray eyes bore into her very soul—"will you do it for me?"

She stood still as stone. It was not such an unusual request under the circumstances, but it was something she had not expected. For the entirety of their relationship, Patrick had been in control, using his strength to bend her will, demanding that she submit to his wishes. This would change the balance of power and put them on a more equal footing. She would be the one with the power of her knowledge, and he would allow it. For Cat, this level of sharing, this sense of intimacy, was something she wasn't quite sure of.

"Would it be so very difficult?" he asked, his voice low.

"Nay." Cat shook her head. "I'll teach you, m'lord. 'Tis the least I can do."

Patrick noticed the formal address. She had retreated once again behind her mask of calm. He frowned. Someday Catriona would forget her past and admit she hungered for the love of a man much like any other woman.

❧ 22 ❧

Kate sat down and pulled on the high rubber boots Niall had tossed to her from across the bank. The excavation site was pure marshland, and her canvas tennis shoes were nearly ruined before she'd noticed the dark mud oozing up to her ankles.

Annoyed at first, she soon realized that the incident had its positive side. She'd forgotten to feel embarrassed about the night before and this morning. The last remnants of self-consciousness disappeared entirely when Niall sat down beside her and grinned. It lit up his face, revealing, far more than words, his pleasure in the morning, the moment, and her presence beside him.

"You came," he said, his eyes registering approval of the slender, black-haired figure seated knee-deep in marsh grass and sunlight. "I'm pleased."

Kate narrowed her eyes against the glare. "Did you think I wouldn't?"

He considered her question. "There were moments. You're not entirely predictable, you know."

His words were right but that was all. Something had changed in their three-second discourse. Kate could feel it. Niall was searching her face as if he didn't quite believe what he saw.

"Is anything wrong?" she asked.

He hesitated. "No, of course not—it's just that . . ."

"Go on."

Again he shook his head. "Never mind. Pardon me. I'm not entirely recovered from yesterday."

Kate's cheeks flamed and she turned away, waving her arm to encompass the enormous hole staked out and geometrically divided into gridlike sections. Half a dozen mud-covered figures wielding shovels looked like small lumps clinging to the sides of the basin. "I've never seen anything like this." She looked directly at him. "What made you decide to invite me?"

"Beltane," he said simply, holding her glance, knowing that further explanation was unnecessary.

Despite the color staining her cheeks, Kate nodded. This time she did not look away.

Niall stood up and held out his hand. "May I show it to you?"

She allowed him to pull her to a standing position, very conscious of his hand holding hers. "Is there more?" she asked.

"Much more. Some of it should especially interest you."

"Why is that?"

"You're a Sutherland and you were born here. This is your heritage, as far back as the ancient Picts, the original inhabitants of the isles. There are theories, of course, but no one knows where they came from before they settled here."

Kate stepped carefully through the marsh grass, her boot prints filling immediately with sludge as if the soil and grass had conspired to erase all evidence of her crossing. "I've read a little about them," she said, recalling the few facts from her memory. "They were believed to have mystical powers and a strong communion with nature."

Niall nodded. "There are some who say they've passed the white magick down through their descendants. Scotland is filled with those who practice the ancient rites of the Druids."

Her heart drummed erratically. "Witches?"

He shrugged. "Perhaps, although a different sort than the kind that terrify children and ride broomsticks."

Kate recalled her experience with Celia Ward. It no longer seemed real. Her stomach churned. "What kind of witch is a Druid?" she asked, anxious to know if his answer would be the same as Maura's.

"The kind that have the Sight." His eyes were on her, measuring, questioning. "The kind who celebrate Beltane."

Kate withdrew her hand. "You mean Maura Sutherland?"

"And others, although none so powerful as Maura."

She stopped, disregarding the sucking pull of the bog beneath her boots. "You don't like her, do you?"

"On the contrary, I like her very much. Who wouldn't? She's quite pleasant. But I don't disregard her powers, as some do."

Kate changed the subject: "Tell me more about the Picts."

Niall led her toward the north side of the dig, talking as he walked. "We know that they occupied the country north of the Firths of Forth and Clyde. They spoke a language that is no longer in existence. They rode and fought from chariots, completely naked and deeply tattooed. Their weapons included a small round shield called a targe, a short spear or staff and a dirk, which is a knife. They lived in huts sunk deep into the ground, and when pursued by an enemy they could live for days hidden in the bogs with only their heads exposed. They ruled the Orkneys and the Shetlands for hundreds of years, and their kings were very powerful. Rights of succession were matrilineal, through the mother."

Kate interrupted: "How can you possibly know that?"

"Most everything we know comes from studying their art. Quite a few well-preserved examples have been found. Come along. I'll show you."

She followed him into a large tent, where a long, rectangular table displayed several stone objects.

Niall pointed to the first one. "This is a rather crude specimen. The carvings are hewn out of undressed stone. But we can tell from the symbols that the artist was religious, that he worshiped the sun and the seasons."

Kate ran her fingers over the rough markings. They looked like nothing more than natural erosion from the rain and wind.

Niall moved to the stone on the end. "This one is far more sophisticated. Notice the geometric shapes and the realistic quality of the animals. This stone reveals that the artist believed the sun disappears into a lower world at night, symbolizing light and dark, or life and death, a concept that is the basis of all mysteries."

This time Kate could see it: the sun dropping below the

horizon, animals frolicking in a bountiful glen, shadowy shapes occupying a world below the ground. She touched it reverently. "It must be fascinating to do this kind of work."

His eyes lit up at her obvious interest. "I think so."

"How do you know the people on these islands are descended from the Picts? Maybe they were conquered and killed by the Celtic or Viking tribes who came later."

"They were conquered by Celts as well as Norsemen, but the Picts weren't driven away. They influenced the invaders with their own practices. Druidism appears to be the aboriginal faith of all Britain. The invaders grafted the native customs onto their own mythology. Names remain, celebrations, even positions at court. The Lord Lyon, King of Arms, incorporates the pre-heraldic Celtic office of Sennachie of the royal line of Scotland. We can thank chivalry for that. The chief duty of the King of Arms was to proclaim, in Gaelic, at the coronation of a king his genealogy as far back as seven generations."

He leaned against the table and drew her, unresisting, into the vee of his outstretched legs. "The Lord Lyon's two special courts are held in May and November and retain their ancient names, Beltane and Samhain. So you see, Kate, pagan festivals are still celebrated all over Scotland. Call it witchcraft if you like. I prefer to think of it as a cultural celebration."

Lifting her chin, he slowly, very slowly, bent his head to her mouth.

"I thought we were going to see if there was more than just a physical attraction between us," she murmured huskily.

He stopped a hair's breadth from her lips. "Kate. I want to kiss you. Don't stop me."

Their eyes held for a long moment. Then she lifted her head.

Kate knew, the moment his lips touched hers, that she had waited the entire morning for this. At breakfast when she forced down tea and picked at her scone until it was nothing more than crumbs beneath Glennis MacLean's knowing gaze, she hadn't yet realized what it meant. On the ride over, the rusty chain of her rental bike protesting the rocky path and twisting roads, the mounting tension in her chest, the dryness of her mouth and the frequency of her stops to swig spring water and suck on peppermints was nothing more than nervous anticipation. Wondering how he would behave, whether he would touch her, not admitting that the tremendous attraction she felt toward him had kept her remote and cool.

Now, even more than last night, that part was over, and the moment he looked at her he would know how she felt, if he didn't already. But it wasn't enough, and she didn't know why. There was something between them, a barrier she couldn't explain or breach.

Niall raised his head. Kate's eyes were closed. He watched as they opened, slowly, reluctantly, as if from a deep and comfortable sleep. Twin seams of black lashes trembled, separating into crescents of brilliant green. The lids fell back until she stared at him, her pupils wide and dark, obliterating all but a thin ring of color.

For the space of a heartbeat he'd felt it, the same breath-stealing response, the call of blood to blood, the heat rising within them just as it had last night and the first time he'd kissed her in his study. But too quickly she ended it, as cleanly and completely as if there had never been anything at all between the two of them. What was it about her that made him feel more than he'd ever imagined he could? It was almost as if she were two people, one loving and vulnerable, the other resistant, cool. The muscles of his jaw tightened. Psychology did not appeal to him. It had no absolutes, a deficiency that aligned it more closely with art than with science.

He concentrated, forcing himself to see what it was that he couldn't place in his mind. She looked the same, and yet her expression was different, as were the hollows of her face. Her mouth turned down at the corners, something he hadn't noticed before, and the timeless quality in the depths of her eyes was no longer there.

Niall was a scientist, trained to use his senses, not only to find evidence but to exhaust the endless possibilities along the road to discovery. The slightest turn of a handle, the design of an urn, the twist of a torque could mean the difference of a thousand years. He was rarely wrong. After ten years in the field he had made only one significant error. Something told him his instincts hadn't failed this time either. Kate Sutherland was somewhere else, and whomever she saw behind those blank eyes had nothing to do with him.

Cat lifted the candle and peered into the dimly lit library. Stretched out in a chair, a bound volume in his hand, sat her husband. Books were piled on the table before him and several more lay at his feet. She sighed. It was almost as if he intended to make up for a lifetime of lost learning in only a few short weeks. It was really quite remarkable that he had mastered the skill so quickly. Cat couldn't help but feel ashamed when she compared the eagerness with which he absorbed his lessons to her own childhood reluctance to learn her letters so many years before.

The weeks had passed quickly. There was nothing more she could teach him. Already Patrick was more proficient than most men. He read quickly and accurately, and his script was meticulously neat. Now it was late and she had waited long enough. Cat cleared her throat.

Absorbed in his task, Patrick hadn't noticed when she entered the room. Now he looked up. When he saw the slim, white-clad figure silhouetted by candlelight, he smiled.

"Is it time already?" he asked.

"Past time," Cat replied. "I feared you would fall asleep in your chair once again."

"I'll be up in a moment, lass. Tonight you won't sleep alone. I promise." He returned to his book.

Cat stamped her foot. "Patrick."

No answer. Setting the candle on a side table, Cat walked behind her husband's chair and rested her chin on his shoulder. "What are you reading?" she asked.

"Do you believe that the world turns around the sun, Catriona?" he asked abruptly.

"Why, I never considered it." A frown appeared between her brows as she thought out loud. "If you believe in the logic of men of science, it would appear that it cannot be otherwise. But the Church refuses to countenance their beliefs." She sifted her fingers through his thick, dark hair and gently rubbed his temples. "Does it matter?" she asked reasonably.

"It would matter a great deal to know the truth," the MacKendrick replied emphatically.

Cat moved aside the soft linen collar of his shirt and brushed her mouth against his throat.

"What I wouldn't give to sail the ocean and follow the sun to the new worlds." Patrick's voice was filled with longing.

"It wouldn't please me at all," Cat mumbled, her lips making short exploratory forays down the back of his neck.

"I've heard of a sea captain, a Venetian, who believes the journey can be done in three weeks' time."

Cat grew more aggressive. Her hands slid underneath his shirt, massaging his chest. Gently she nipped at the bare skin of his shoulder with her teeth.

"I wonder how he can be so sure," Patrick mused, continuing his conversation with himself. "Perhaps it has something to do with the trade winds."

"Patrick MacKendrick!" Cat's green eyes blazed, her hands on her hips, as she confronted him. "Days have gone by since you've shared my bed, and when I try to seduce you, all you can speak of is trade winds and the Indies. If I knew what it would do to you, I never would have taught you to read."

Patrick looked startled and then amused. He set the book aside and stood up, facing her. In the leaping light of the fire, his face was hidden by shadows. In a voice softer than velvet, he spoke: "Why didn't you say what you wanted?"

"To be neglected because a husband prefers his books to his wife's bed is hardly something a new bride cares to admit," Cat snapped. Why did he not touch her?

"Perhaps a new husband needs an occasional invitation," he replied gently.

Her eyes widened. Was the man really such a fool? "What did you think I was doing a moment ago?"

"Was it an invitation, Cat? Do you want me?" There was nothing of mockery in the steel-like gaze fixed on her face.

Her cheeks colored to a deep rose, but she met his glance steadily. "Aye."

"Why?"

"Why what?" The man was exasperating. He made no sense at all.

"What am I to you, Catriona?" he replied. "All at once I find it necessary to know."

"You are my husband," she replied, striving for patience.

"I'd be more than that."

The intimate, probing note in his voice was new to Cat. She was not at all sure she wanted to continue this line of conversation.

"What do you want of me, m'lord?" she asked breathlessly. Her lungs ached in her chest and she found it difficult to breathe. She knew what he wanted her to say, but suddenly it was very important that he say it first.

He gave no quarter. "I would have your love," he answered simply.

She hesitated, staring into the dark rain-colored eyes, afraid to give him such power.

"Spoken or unspoken, words are just words, Cat. Speaking them aloud does not change what already is."

She swallowed. He was right. It would be a relief to finally admit it. "Aye." Her voice was low. "My feelings for you are like nothing I've ever known. 'Tis doubly hard for me to say, for I know not what you think of me."

He reached for her then and, cradling her in his arms, sat down on the chair. "I have loved you since I first saw you kneeling at the feet of Jamie Stewart."

Cat smiled against his shoulder. "I knew someone else was in the room."

His mouth on hers stopped all further conversation. Later, with his lips on her breast, he lay her on the wolfskin rug and caressed her with such tenderness that tears sprang to her eyes. When he claimed her at last, Cat knew she had come home.

Kate blinked, straightened, and backed out of Niall's arms. Disoriented, she couldn't remember where she was. Her vision slowly sharpened, and Niall's features, at first fuzzy and unfocused, became clear. She smiled uncertainly. "What were you saying?"

He summoned his most charming smile. "It wasn't important. If you would like to see more of the site, I'll be ready shortly. There are a few more artifacts to catalog."

"Do you mind if I walk around for a while myself?"

"Not at all. Just ask someone if you've any questions."

The air was colder than it had been earlier, and the sun had disappeared. Kate stuffed her hands into her down-lined pockets and walked along the edge of the trench. She was very close to something important, something that would make a difference in the puzzle of her relationship with Catriona Wells and Patrick MacKendrick. Her own life had become less important to her, less real and colorful than the intrigue and romance of Jamie Stewart's Scotland. If it were possible, she would linger forever in that hazy world, blurred by time, existing somewhere between waking and sleeping, a world where she walked in another woman's footsteps, sharing the beat of her heart, the weight of her fear and the slow, sweet knowledge of her husband's desire.

The only thing holding her back was Niall MacCormack. Kate found herself thinking about him at the oddest times: the way his mouth separated over straight teeth when he smiled, the strength of his lean, sunburned hands, the loose-limbed, easy grace of his wide-shouldered body. His presence prevented her from immersing herself completely in Catriona's life. If it wasn't for Niall, she would will herself into a trance until the entire mystery of Catriona Wells was solved, no matter how long it took.

Something glittered in the dirt. Kate stooped to pick it up. It was the remnant of a glass bottle, broken and stained but beautifully crafted. Her mouth went dry and her breath came in deep painful gulps. The scent of roses was all around her. Her hand tightened on the bottle. A sharp pain seared her thumb. She winced and stared at the widening red line on her pale skin.

"Perfume," she said out loud, "a perfume bottle." She could see the intricate design of the cut glass, the delicate shape of the stem, the stopper with its blue ribbon. Instinctively she closed her eyes and sniffed. It was every bit as clear as that day at Hermitage when she and Brenna had made perfume in the kitchen. Kate corrected herself: She hadn't been there at all. It was Catriona who had worked side by side with Brenna. Then why could she smell roses and feel the hot room and her sweat-stained gown? Why could she see plates of rose petals pressed against glass and oil, golden and aromatic, stored in jars on the shelves?

Terrified, Kate opened her eyes. Nothing had changed, not the site with its geometric grids, not the workers with their shovels nor the tents constructed on a low bluff facing away from the sea. *It wasn't a dream. She remembered everything, and it wasn't a dream.* "What is happening to me?" she whispered to no one. "Please tell me what is happening to me."

Clutching the glass fragment in her hand, she began to run, her boots heavy with mud, her gait awkward. *I've got to get away from here!* her mind screamed.

Niall stepped out of his tent, his eyes narrowing as they lit on the slim figure in full flight across the grass. "What the—" He cupped his hands over his mouth at the same time his legs registered the command to follow. "Kate, wait!" he shouted.

She reached the tree where she had left the bike. Hands trembling, she swung her leg across the bar and fumbled for the pedal, cursing the clumsy boot that hampered her coordination. Bending down, she pulled off the boot and dropped it.

Niall reached her just as she found her balance. Catching the handlebars, he pulled her to a stop. "What happened?" he asked when he could breathe again.

Her eyes were wild and, despite her flight across the marsh, her skin was very pale. A thin white line circled her lips. She shook her head, unable to speak. Niall searched her face and frowned. Then his gaze dropped to her hand. The blood had dried, staining her hand a dark, rusty red. Wedged tightly in her palm was a piece of jagged glass. Prying it from her fingers, Niall examined it carefully. After a moment he slipped it into his pocket, took another look at Kate's face and made a decision. "You're coming with me," he said firmly. "I'll take you home in the car."

Deep in their own thoughts, neither noticed the silence as they drove back to Glennis MacLean's guest house. Niall, going over the events in his mind, racked his brain, to figure out why a fifteenth-century perfume bottle would send Kate Sutherland into a state of flying panic.

Kate opened the door before the car had come to a complete stop. "Are you coming in?" she asked.

He shook his head. "I've more work to do. I'll bring the bike back later. Make yourself a pot of tea. You look as if you've seen a ghost."

Her mouth turned down at the corners. "It wouldn't be the first time," she said softly. "Goodbye, Niall, and thank you. I don't know what came over me."

"Kate." Glennis waved her in. "There's a message for you from his lordship. He's coming to see you. I've invited him for tea."

Kate hung her jacket on the coat rack and ran her fingers through her hair. "I hadn't really planned to be here," she said, turning to face her hostess. "I think I'm coming down with something."

"Oh dear." Glennis pressed her fingers against her lips. "Say no more. Go lie down immediately and I'll bring you a cup of tea. The duke will have to wait."

Grateful for the reprieve, Kate washed the blood from her hand and pulled off her remaining boot and both her shoes before sinking down into the feather duvet. Her head really did feel strange, and the last person she wanted to see was Hunter Sutherland.

It seemed like moments later when she looked at the clock. She must have dozed off. It was already late afternoon. There were voices in the downstairs parlor. Niall must have returned by now. Her stomach growled and she sat up. Hopefully she hadn't missed tea. Pulling a brush through her hair, she rinsed her mouth, slipped her feet into flats and walked downstairs. Standing near the fire, sipping amber-colored liquid from a brandy glass, was the duke of Sutherland.

A quick surge of anger leapt to life in Kate's chest. Apparently a duke was above social convention. Ignoring him completely, she stepped into the room and spoke to Glennis. "I hope it's not too late for tea. I overslept."

"The very thing." Glennis beamed at the duke. "Miss Sutherland felt unwell this morning. Are you better now, my dear?"

"Much better. I thought Niall would be back by now."

"He should be here in time for dinner. Meanwhile the duke has something he must say to you. I'll leave you alone."

Kate turned reluctantly to face him. It was time he learned that Americans didn't believe in special privileges or titles. "You are very persistent, aren't you?"

Hunter Sutherland appeared amused. "I've been told so."

"What could possibly be so important that couldn't wait until tomorrow?"

He set his glass down on the coffee table and lowered himself into one of the Queen Anne chairs facing the couch. "Please sit down," he said, gesturing toward the chair beside him.

Kate took the couch instead, adjusting the pillow behind her. She did not see his lips twitch.

"For me, what I have to tell you is extremely important," he began, his face completely composed. "Whether it will be for you, I can't say. You did come to the Shetlands to find your family, did you not?"

"Yes, I did."

"Is that still important to you?"

Her annoyance forgotten, she leaned forward, elbows on her knees, eyes shining. "Very important. Have you found something?"

He nodded and reached for his drink, draining the glass. Swallowing had suddenly become difficult. Managing at last, he set down the glass and looked directly at her. What he saw in her face made him reconsider his plan of stating it directly. He would begin at the beginning. Maybe then she would understand.

"I was born here on Cait Ness," he began. "The plan was that I would go away to school at eight years old, just as my father had before me. He died when I was quite young, and my mother hired a tutor and kept me home until I was fourteen. There were hours to spare, and I wandered across the island, drawn to the schoolhouse where the native children were taught. I was welcome there, and most afternoons I sat in the back of the room and learned my lessons along with them. Actually," he remembered, "the teacher was far superior to my tutor and my education improved a great deal. It was there that I met Maura Sutherland."

Kate had been preparing to interrupt, but she kept silent.

"From the beginning she drew me." He smiled ruefully. "She drew everyone. There was something about her, a light-touched, magical, soothing quality. She knew our minds, our fears, our pettiness and far, far more than that. I had lived on Cait Ness all my life, but I had never seen the herons nesting in the aeries, nor the hidden streams, silver with wild salmon. With her I saw it all. At night the tides are high on the islands and the seas are treacherous. But not so for Maura. Somehow she knew where the ocean grass choked and the undercurrents pulled. Her compassion for nature was astounding. Christ, it was 1956. No one had heard the word *conservation*. Maura hadn't heard it either but she lived it, stepping carefully, eating and drinking sparingly, turning back to the earth what she took from it. I remember that she ate very little meat. At first I assumed she was poor. Later I learned it was preference."

Kate shifted nervously. She had an unsettling premonition that was fast becoming an unthinkable fear. "Please go on," she said hoarsely.

"She never showed partiality for any of us, not even I, laird of Sutherland. It bothered me more so, I think, than I realized. I took my revenge in the thousand small ways that schoolboys do. I was insufferably rude, pulling her hair, hiding her books, stealing biscuits from her lunch, teasing her for the red in her hair and her long, immature body. I'm sure she hated me, but at least I was remembered. I made sure of that. You see, my fourteenth birthday came and I left Cait Ness for England. It would be years before I returned—nine, to be exact."

"Why so long?" Kate asked. "What about holidays and vacations?"

He shrugged. "I came back at Christmas, of course, and other times. But the school term was over. Class differences are rigid here. I could never have gone to her home. It would have damaged her reputation beyond repair."

"What happened when you came back?"

Hunter smiled, and the years rolled back to the day he returned to Cait Ness. By making discreet inquiries, he learned where Maura spent her afternoons and climbed the cliffs to where she sat beneath the low-hanging clouds. Her book lay forgotten in her lap and her eyes were closed against the wash of sunlight bathing her face. Few women could stand within a circle of such pure light without showing some disadvantage. Maura was the exception. Her clear, unblemished skin glowed like alabaster, and her hair, thick and fine and very straight, fell across one shoulder. He could see that she was still tall, but no man with eyes would ever call her body immature. When she felt his presence and fixed her cloud-colored eyes on his face, he forgot to breathe. It was then that he knew there was no one like her. There never would be.

Kate interrupted him. "What happened when you came back?"

"I pursued her," he said honestly, "every hour of every day. She refused me until the night of Beltane. You see, she claimed to be the chosen of the Wicca, a high priestess of the ancient Druid religion. There is no possibility of marriage for those who wear the blue crescent."

"You would have married her? I mean—was that possible?" Even Kate, raised in the liberal culture of Southern California, saw the problem.

"Marriage was all that was possible."

"Couldn't you have just—"

"No." His face was set in the rigid, uncompromising lines of northern ice floes. "It wasn't possible. A Druid priestess does not limit herself to one man."

Kate looked down at her hands. "I see."

Hunter's face softened. "No, you don't. But you will. I claimed her at the sacred fire of Beltane when her resistance was low and her need at its peak."

Her face burning, Kate kept her eyes on her hands.

He continued. "When the sun rose, she made her choice. It wasn't me. I left the island. Two years later I married. The feelings between my wife and I did not go beyond respect. I never saw Maura again until yesterday at Beltane."

"Why not?"

"She had moved to Foula. I was bitter and thought it best to leave matters as they were." He leaned across the table and lifted Kate's chin, forcing her to look at him. "Then you came and I knew that Maura had taken with her a great deal more than my heart."

"What do you mean?" Kate stammered.

"You are my daughter, Kate," he explained gently, "the daughter Maura and I conceived the night of Beltane."

❧ 23 ❧

"I don't believe you," Kate whispered. "I stayed in Maura's home. She would have told me."

Hunter's mouth tightened. "Would she?"

"Yes, she—" Kate stopped as the memory of Maura's final words floated through her mind. *There will be a time when you think harshly of me. Try and remember that things are not always as they seem.* Could this have been what she meant? Had she known all the time that Kate was the daughter she had given away? "Why didn't she tell me?" she asked, deliberately sealing off her emotions to numb the rushing pain.

Hunter looked perplexed. "It's absurd, really. She has a notion that you are here for someone else, someone from another time, and that until the situation is resolved, your life will remain unsettled. She also feels greatly indebted to your adoptive mother."

"Why?"

"There was no one else in the world to whom Maura would entrust her child. Bonnie Sutherland did her an enormous service." Hunter frowned. "I believe Maura feels that to claim you as her own would be to deny your adoptive mother the credit that is her due."

Kate pressed her fist against her chest to assuage the painful squeezing of her heart. "Do you agree with her?"

Hunter covered her hand with his. "You are my daughter, Kate. If I had known that you existed thirty years ago, you would never have left Cait Ness. This is your home, the home of your family. You are descended from the noble line of Clan Sutherland. I showed you the portrait in my gallery. How can you doubt it?"

"Catriona Wells." *Catriona . . . Catriona . . .* The cadence sounded again and again in her mind until she thought her head would break open and the name echo off the walls of Mrs. MacLean's flower-printed sitting room. She looked at Hunter. "Maura believes that Catriona Wells needs something from me."

"Perhaps, but *we* don't have to believe it."

Kate shook her head. "Something doesn't feel right. I thought I would know my mother. I can usually see—" She stopped.

The duke's regard was very intent. "You have it, don't you?"

Kate pretended ignorance. "What?"

"I saw it the night of Beltane when I looked into your eyes. You have the Sight, just as Maura has it."

There was no point in denying it. She nodded. "Yes. I have it, but not always, and I can't control it the way Maura does."

"She's been trained from birth, Kate. I don't imagine a normal American upbringing includes immersion in pagan rituals."

Kate couldn't help laughing, a small pathetic sound on this day of confessions. "No, it certainly doesn't."

"You're very like her."

She stood up, stuffed her hands into the pockets of her sweatshirt and began to pace back and forth across the room. Her need to move, to summon her energy, forcing her troubled thoughts into some kind of order, was instinctive. Hunter watched her, recognizing the same frustrated rhythm he had seen in Maura just this morning when he'd backed her to the wall with his determined logic to tell Kate the truth.

"Have you told anyone else?" she asked, still moving.

"Only Victoria."

"Victoria!" Kate stopped to stare at him, her eyes wide with horror. "I can just imagine how she took the news! After all these years, an older sister, born of a woman half the island is afraid of, would be enough to drive anyone over the edge."

Hunter frowned. "You're exaggerating. No one is afraid of Maura. They respect her privacy, but she's harmed no one. There is nothing to be afraid of."

"That isn't what Glennis MacLean believes."

He relaxed. "Glennis is a Lowlander and new to Cait Ness. She came here after Maura had already left for Foula. She's heard stories, that's all. The natives love to spin tales. As for Victoria, she's more concerned about her inheritance than anything else. You needn't concern yourself with her."

"I hope you assured her that I have no need of an inheritance. My father left me a comfortable trust. Money isn't a problem for me."

"Perhaps not," replied Hunter lightly. "However, you are my daughter, just as Victoria is, and the Sutherland name is an old and proud one. I have no sons; therefore everything that is mine will be divided between the two of you."

"I'm sure she was thrilled with that," muttered Kate.

He stood up and faced her. "My estate is mine to do with as I please. Neither your wishes nor Victoria's are important here. You are a grown woman and Victoria is nearly there, although the probability of her mind achieving the adult state as quickly as the rest of her is neglible at best. Your lives are your own. I, however, have another twenty years if I'm fortunate. I do not wish to spend those years alone."

Somehow Kate knew what was coming next. "Maura?" she asked.

The duke laughed. "Maura. I may be presumptuous, but I believe she is not altogether indifferent to me."

Kate took in his unusual height and the lean elegance of his dramatic good looks. "Who could be?" she said under her breath.

"I beg your pardon?"

"Never mind. It doesn't matter. Where is Maura staying? I know she's here on Cait Ness. The ferry doesn't run today."

"In the croft where she grew up. It's near the end of the road."

Kate started for the stairs.

"Where are you going?" he asked.

"To get my jacket. I need to see her."

"Kate." He walked to the stairs and rested his arm on the banister. "That may not be the wisest course at the moment."

"I can't wait anymore," she said. "I've already waited thirty years."

Hunter sighed. Kate was definitely a Sutherland, with a double dose of stubbornness in her genes. He walked back into the sitting room to warm his hands at the fire.

Moments later she ran down the stairs. "Tell Glennis that I won't be staying for tea and probably not for dinner either, unless Maura throws me out."

"Whatever happens, she won't do that," Hunter promised. "Just don't expect too much."

With one incredulous backward glance, she slammed the door behind her and, without looking up, ran into Niall MacCormack's solid chest.

He reached out to steady her. "Where are you going in such a hurry?"

"To Maura Sutherland's." Unexpected tears streaked down her cheeks, and she wiped them away. "She's my mother and he's my father. He told me himself." Kate knew she was babbling but she couldn't stop herself. "I was with her for nearly three days. She knew all the time and never told me."

Niall had recognized the duke's roadster parked on the road. He frowned. "It's late. Do you have a flashlight?"

Kate shook her head. "I won't need one. It doesn't get dark until eleven o'clock, and it's just five now."

He took a minute to think. What if Maura refused to have Kate for the night? "I'm coming with you," he said in a voice that she had never heard before.

Kate did not protest when he retrieved a flashlight from his car, took her hand with his free one, and led her through the tiny village to the foot of the hills. They walked, tensely at first, without speaking, and then more companionably as he coaxed the incredible story from her lips.

Kate had not known Niall MacCormack long enough to know what everyone else did: that the white line around his lips only appeared when he was very angry or very worried. It was there now. He had been silent for a long time, except for an occasional comment to encourage her story. Finally he interrupted: "Are you saying that Maura believes you're here to help Catriona Wells, a woman dead for nearly five hundred years?"

Kate nodded.

"Does he believe it?"

"No."

"What about you, Kate? What do you believe?"

"I'm not sure," she said wearily. "All I know is what I feel and see. I'm not normal, Niall. I know that now. You can laugh if you want, but I was just as skeptical in the beginning as you are. Now I see that there are just too many coincidences to ignore."

"Such as?"

Her hand stiffened in his but she did not pull away. "There are so many things—"

"Tell me, Kate. I want to help you."

Looking up into his capable masculine face, Kate felt a surge of hope. Maybe he really could. "It started when I was a child," she began. "I felt as if I didn't belong in my own family. I never felt the enthusiasm other children felt. Nothing was new or surprising or unusual. Things moved differently for me than for other people. I always felt as if I were waiting for something. Relationships were impossible. I've never had a best friend or even a boyfriend that I wanted permanently and then—" She stopped and bit her lip.

"Please go on."

"This part is the most difficult of all because it's the most unbelievable." She stopped, pulled her hand away and stepped in front of him. "Look at me, Niall. Look at me and don't look away."

At first he was only aware of the color, a deep intense green without the slightest tint of blue or hazel. Then he noticed something else and looked more closely. There was light behind the small black circle, light and movement, drawing him in. He couldn't move away. "What is it?" he demanded. "What are you doing?"

"Shhhh. Don't say anything," she whispered. "You're wondering if I'm crazy. No," she corrected herself, "not crazy, just unbalanced by everything that's happened. You're worried and even a little bit frightened because you know something of the practices of the Pectiwita and you believe them to be dangerous. You think Maura has some type of hold over me and you have reservations about whether the duke told me the truth." She gasped and stepped backward. "You think Maura will try and keep me here. She is nearing her time and no one has been selected to take her place." Kate clutched his arm. "Niall, you think Maura wants me to take her place."

His face was grim. "What am I thinking now, Kate?"

She looked away and the impact was almost physical.

"I don't know. I don't want to know anymore. Are you satisfied? I can see your thoughts. How many people do you know who can do that?"

Niall remained silent.

Kate turned back to the path. "Well, I know someone who can, and she's going to explain everything, tonight. You don't have to come any farther if you don't want to. I can imagine what you must be thinking."

"Why don't you look at me and find out?"

"No, thank you. I've had enough rejection as it is."

Niall stopped and stared thoughtfully at her averted profile. "Is that why you keep me at arm's distance? Because you don't trust me?"

"I don't know," Kate replied honestly.

"It isn't something you ever will know until you give me a chance," he said. "Trust takes time."

"Sometimes people don't have enough time."

"Sometimes they only think they don't."

"Please, Niall. I can't think about this now. My mind is filled with this . . . this"—she waved her arm—"this telepathy thing."

His hands grasped her shoulders. "I'm here, Kate. I'm here in the present and I love you. Don't forget that when you're communing with the past." Pulling her against him, he kissed her until he felt the slow, sweet rise of her response. Reluctantly he lifted his head. "I'll wait here."

Maura's cottage loomed ahead. Kate cleared her throat nervously. "Do you mind? I really should see her alone."

He shook his head. "I'll give you an hour. If you don't give me some sign that you're alive and well, I'm coming in."

She laughed nervously. "Don't be ridiculous."

Cupping her cheeks, he brushed her lips with his. "Take care, Kate, and good luck."

She left him searching for a comfortable boulder to lean against and walked the rest of the way to the cottage. The door was open, and Maura was pulling a loaf of bread from the oven. It smelled delicious. "Come in," she said without turning around. "I had a feeling you'd be coming. Would you like jam or honey with your bread?"

"Jam, please."

Maura smiled. "I thought so."

With new eyes, Kate watched the woman who had given her life slice bread, set the table and pour tea.

Finally Maura looked up. "Sit down," she said, taking the opposite chair. "The sooner you ask the sooner we'll both feel more comfortable."

Kate sat. "Hunter told me."

Maura nodded. "He said he would. I couldn't dissuade him."

"Why would you want to?" Kate burst out. "How could you keep it from me?"

Maura looked astonished. "Because you've something very important to do and because I could see your unhappiness. I wanted to help you, to fix this aimlessness you claim to have. You didn't need the distraction of knowing your parents are alive and living here in Cait Ness. When this is over we can discuss all that. It is enough for you to know that I did what was best for you under the circumstances, despite what Hunter believes."

"He still loves you," Kate said irrelevantly.

"Yes. So he says."

Kate looked startled. "Don't you believe him?"

Maura sighed and absentmindedly lifted the grainy

wheaten bread to her lips. "I want to, but love has different faces." She waved her hand toward the open door. "Up here, alone with nothing but the sky and the sea, it's easy to profess undying love. It's not so easy when family and friends and the practices of a lifetime are involved. I'm not like the villagers. Something happens to people who live alone on a pile of rock, battered season after season by rain and wind and sun. I need space and great amounts of time alone."

"Did you ever wish it had gone differently for the two of you?"

Maura smiled bitterly. "Every day of my life."

"Then why—"

Maura interrupted her. "This isn't America, my dear. Electricity wasn't introduced to the islands until twenty years ago. We still don't have cable television and most of us have never owned an automobile. Change takes a great deal of time. Thirty years ago I hadn't the courage or the will to change."

"And now?"

"Now, it will be up to Hunter, and Victoria."

Kate fought against the tears threatening to surface. "What about me?"

Maura's clear, colorless eyes filled with warmth. "You are a remarkable person, Kate. You will find your way no matter what happens to the rest of us." She leaned closer. "Look at me, *Catriona.*" She pronounced the name strangely, with a roll of the *r,* and for the first time it seemed to Kate that the name belonged to her. "Somewhere in time a woman waits for you," Maura continued, "a woman who gave you the color of your hair and eyes, the shape of your face, the quickness of your mind. Without her you wouldn't exist. Go to her, Kate. Give her what she needs and, in so doing, save yourself."

Kate was drowning in the swirling silver of the witch's gaze. Colors and sounds whirled past, and then came the wind, a terrible rushing wind that pulled at her flesh and tore her hair and pounded her ears. Patrick was there, Patrick and Isobel and Richard, Janet and Mary, Jamie and Maggie, Henry and Elizabeth and Neville—oh, God, no, not Neville! "I don't want to!" she screamed. "Stop this. Stop it now! Please. I can't."

Maura's voice came through the wind. "As you wish, Catriona. You have the power. Will it to stop."

Almost immediately, the roaring diminished and the wind stopped. Like the slowing of a carousel, the room righted itself. The steaming tea, the cozy warmth, the intense regard of the gray-eyed woman were exactly the same as they had been moments before. Kate swallowed and lifted her cup for a sustaining gulp of tea. "What happened?" she asked hoarsely. "Why did it stop?"

"You stopped it," replied Maura.

"Why couldn't I stop it before?"

"Probably because you never tried or else you never wanted to." Under the soaring brows, the gray eyes assessed her keenly. "Come now, my dear. Have you ever really wanted to return before this?"

Kate forced herself to admit the truth. "Why now?"

"I've already told you that I don't see what you do. My guess is that the window is very near."

"What window?"

"The moment where you are able to go back and confront the fear that has followed Catriona Wells across the centuries."

"And if I don't go back?"

Maura shrugged. "The choice has always been yours. If you resist the call, your life will continue as before. You will be Kate Sutherland, the woman who came to Cait Ness searching for her past."

"What if I can't do it?"

Maura's hand shook as she set down her cup. Kate's voice had changed from the flat vowels and casual consonants of an American tourist to the enunciated precision of a Renaissance aristocrat. It was the sign she waited for. "Did you know that the course of history can be completely changed by the absence of only one seemingly insignificant person?"

"I've never thought about it."

"A misplaced presence in the wrong place at the wrong time can create havoc with destiny. If you don't go very soon, you won't be able to."

"I don't believe in destiny." The American accent was back again.

Maura spoke quickly. There was little time left—enough for the going, but the coming back would be very close. "Of course you do. Do you still have your stane?"

Kate nodded.

"Take it out."

Slowly Kate removed it from her pocket.

"Remove everything from your thoughts, everything except for the image of Victoria Sutherland. Then look into the stane."

Almost immediately, the murky darkness cleared and Victoria's slim figure and blond head came into view. She sat at a huge banquet table beside Niall MacCormack, and she wore a wedding gown and veil. There were people everywhere. A waiter passed out thin slivers of white cake. Kate concentrated on Niall's face and on his thin brown hand resting on the table beside Victoria's. The third finger of his left hand was encircled with a gold band. Why didn't he touch her? He was obviously the groom. Why did he look so empty, so completely unlike the man waiting for her outside of Maura's croft? And why did the idea of Niall and Victoria stir up such a raging fury inside of her? The image blurred and blended into darkness.

Maura's hand closed over hers. "Don't you see, Kate? If you wait any longer, the window will close and you will be unable to return. If you don't go at all, you will forever be haunted by images of another place and time. Either way, the images in the keek stane are real. The only way to prevent them is to take Catriona's place."

Much more than an hour had passed. "I have to see Niall," Kate said softly. "He's waiting for me." There was no answer. "It isn't my fault," she cried desperately. Maura's face was wet with tears, and still she didn't speak. "I can't help it. You know I can't. I want to see Niall."

Maura looked down at her hands. "Go," she said. "Go back to Niall, you foolish child."

Slowly, without looking back, Kate stood up and walked through the door.

Maura sat alone in the darkening kitchen. She did not

clear the tea plates nor light the lamp. The cat rubbed against her ankles, the moon rose, and still she did not rise. In loving Hunter Sutherland, in refusing all others, she had committed a terrible sin against the teachings of her faith. A price would be paid for that Beltane so many years ago, a terrible price, and she was powerless to stop it. She would go about her duties and live her life knowing that her own child walked in two worlds, comfortable in neither. Cradling her head in her hands, she watched the tears slip through her fingers, spotting the ivory-linen tablecloth. Eventually her forehead came to rest in the crook of her arm, and she slept.

The smell of fried fish woke her. The room was bright with lamplight, and the fire was stoked and burning briskly. Kate had divided the haddock and fried potatoes and placed them on two plates. The table was set.

"What is this?" asked Maura groggily.

"Food." Kate licked her fingers and dipped a potato slice into brown sauce. "I refuse to watch my life pass by without sustenance."

Maura's brain refused to function. "What do you mean?"

The grass-green gaze held her own. "If I can see the future through the stane, can I also see the past?"

Maura nodded.

"I want to see what I'm going back to before I actually go back. Can I do that?"

Hope gathered in Maura's chest. "I think so." She reached out, broke off a bit of fish and nibbled it. "It won't be pleasant. If it were, you wouldn't be here."

Kate wiped her fingers on a napkin, twisted her hair up behind her head and let it fall again. She sighed. "Can it be any worse than living without purpose, without friendship and love?"

Maura shook her head. "No, child. Believe me. I know."

"Will you help me now?"

Maura reached out and clasped Kate's hand. "Need you ask?"

With her eyes on Maura's face, Kate reached into her pocket and took out the stane.

❧ 24 ❧

Dressed in Hepburn livery, Andrew looked about furtively. No one was in sight. Other than his unshaven face, he looked no more unusual than any other messenger seeking admittance to Hermitage.

"Lift the gates, knave," he shouted to the guard at the portcullis. "I bring a message from Linlithgow."

Amazingly, his credentials weren't questioned. The gates creaked open and he rode into the courtyard. It was late afternoon, and servants were busy with preparations for the evening meal. He forced himself to stroll casually past the maids. No one paid him any attention. With a sigh of relief, he slipped through an open door into a narrow passageway and strode down the hall with long, unhurried steps. Around the next corner and up the stairs was the north turret and, if Mary Gordon's information was correct, Cat's apartments. A step sounded behind him. Andrew turned the corner and did not look back.

Bounding up the stairs, he listened at the nearest door. The room was empty. Continuing up another flight, he heard her voice. Someone answered. It sounded like a child. He turned another corner and flattened himself against the wall, prepared to wait. Within moments he heard a door open, and a small girl passed within inches of his hiding place. He breathed a sigh of relief. Cat was alone. With a quick glance in both directions, he walked quickly to her door and opened it.

Her eyes widened in shock and then filled with tears.

"Don't." Andrew put his arms around her. "I escaped two days ago and came straight here." He rested his cheek on her hair. "How are things with you?"

"Oh, Andrew." She leaned against him. "You must leave immediately. Patrick will kill you if he finds you here."

"I'm afraid that isn't possible. The castle gates have already closed for the night. If you can find a place for me, I'll leave first thing in the morning."

"You must ride for London," Cat insisted. "Find out what the king plans for Richard. Tell Henry this was none of my doing." Her eyes were bright with unshed tears. "Let no harm come to my brother, Andrew. There is no one else to help him."

He pulled her head to his shoulder. "Hush. Fear not. I'll see that the lad is kept safe." He hesitated. "Are you well, Catriona? Does he keep you against your will? If so, nothing on earth will convince me to leave you here."

Cat bit her lip. If she told him the truth, would he keep his promise? She looked into Andrew's face. "The MacKendrick was not the husband of my choice," she said at last. "But we are wed according to the laws of holy Church." Her eyes pleaded with him. "Be happy for me, Andrew. He is a better man than most."

Andrew nodded and stepped back. There was nothing to be done. Cat was lawfully married to the MacKendrick. He would have said more, but the look on her face stopped him. "Have you a place for me tonight?" he asked instead.

"It will not be necessary to wait for morning. There is a passage from this very chamber to the outside gate. Isobel showed it to me."

Andrew grinned. "I should have known you would find a way."

She walked to the end of the room, moved aside the tapestries and pushed lightly on the wood. A door in the wall moved aside, revealing a narrow entrance to a hidden passage. "It leads to a clearing beyond the gate. Go, now. I'll meet you with a fresh mount and food."

"How will you get out?"

"Never mind." Cat's hands urged him on. "Hurry. It will be dusk by the time I reach you."

Andrew looked down at her face, hesitated, then turned into the passage.

* * *

"Open the gates," Cat ordered the guard at the portcullis.

The man stared down at her. " 'Tis nearly dark, m'lady. The MacKendrick has ordered the gates closed for the night."

"How dare you, knave!" Her haughty face was stiff with anger. "Do you forget who is mistress of Hermitage? I want to ride."

Shaking his head, the guard gave the signal and the iron gate creaked open. Cat rode through quickly without looking back, conscious of the man's eyes on her.

Gradually the sound of her horse's hooves faded in the distance. The guard shrugged. His watch was almost finished. If the Lady Catriona was foolish enough to ride the borders in the late afternoon, it was up to her husband to protest.

She rode past the sloping hill to the other side of the burn. Where was Andrew? As if in answer to her silent question, he crawled out from underneath some shrubbery. Her sigh of relief was almost a sob.

He lifted her from her horse. "My thanks, Cat," he said, his hands still at her waist. "I knew you wouldn't fail me." He looked at her searchingly. "Are you sure you won't come?"

Cat shook her head. Her eyes held his. "Remember your promise: Keep Richard safe and send word as soon as you can."

"You may rely on me."

The wind, damp and cold, whistled through the trees. Cat smiled tearfully. "Take care, Andrew," she whispered. "God bless you."

He swung into the saddle and looked down at her. "If you need me, I'll come. Remember that."

She nodded. "Go now."

"What will you tell him?" Andrew's face was creased with worry. It would be difficult to face a man like Patrick MacKendrick with anything less than the truth.

Cat shrugged.

The pain in her eyes smote his heart. "Tell him I forced you," Andrew said desperately. "Mary said he loves you. If so, he'll believe that."

She shook her head before he had finished speaking. "No,

Andrew. I'll not lie to Patrick again. He deserves that, at least. Go now. I'll stay here long enough to give you a start."

"Goodbye, Cat."

She lifted her hand, no longer able to manage words. For a long time she waited, until the horse and rider had disappeared beyond the hills. The sky was patched with clouds and the last remaining rays of light nearly gone before she walked back to the castle gate. The path was uphill. Wind moaned through the long grass. Its cold sharpness burned her eyes, reddened her skin and tangled her hair. She barely felt the cold. All her thoughts were on the man waiting inside the walls of Hermitage Castle.

At last she reached the gates. Cat shouted to the guard, but the wind carried her words across the moors to the sea. In desperation she removed her boot and pounded on the wooden entrance. She could hear the sound of barking dogs and hooves clattering against cobblestones. Slowly the gates swung inward. She saw him immediately. Her eyes moved to the woman at his side. For the first time that long afternoon, she felt the cold.

Cat stood very still, watching as Patrick came toward her. Ignoring him, she addressed the woman who waited quietly by her mount.

"Welcome to Hermitage, Lady Douglass," she said. "What a pleasant surprise. Patrick didn't tell me to expect you."

"I didn't know," Patrick began.

Alison cut him off. "I bring a message from the king. Patrick is to ride for London in the morning. Jamie wishes his presence at Henry's court."

Cat flicked her whip against her skirt, her eyes level on the woman's face. "How convenient."

Alison flushed and dropped her eyes.

"'Tis not what you think," Patrick broke in. "God's wounds! I'll not defend myself for something I had no part in."

Cat smiled mockingly. "Of course not, m'lord."

He frowned. "Where have you been?"

"Riding."

"Where is your mount?"

Her courage failed her. She stared at him mutinously, refusing to speak. He would have to beat it out of her. Alison Douglass would be a witness to her humiliation.

Patrick's eyes moved over her face and then narrowed. "I would speak with you inside, m'lady."

Without a word, Cat preceded him into the castle. "I'm so sorry that I cannot show you to your apartments, Lady Douglass," she called back. "Patrick will be pleased to take you."

Patrick's hand snaked out to grip her arm and pulled her into a fire-lit sitting room. He released her and bolted the door behind them. Cat's heart pounded and she prayed for time.

"Lady Douglass brought another message from Linlithgow."

Cat recognized the silken danger in his voice. She hoped her answer was steady. "Oh?"

"It seems that Andrew Percy has escaped." He was so close to her that she could smell the clean scent of his skin. "You wouldn't know anything about that, would you, Lady MacKendrick?"

She lifted her head and stared at him, saying nothing. He knew. Somehow he knew what she had done.

"This time you've gone too far." The slashing grooves in his face deepened. "You should have heeded my warning, Catriona."

The enormity of what she'd lost swept over her. Blind with rage and despair, she lashed out at him. "I care not for your warnings, MacKendrick. If Alison Douglass is more to your taste, go to her. She was your mistress, was she not? Perhaps she still is." Cat vowed to hold the burning tears inside even if it killed her.

"You have spirit, Catriona," Patrick said softly. "But you lack wisdom. One without the other is worthless."

His thick dark hair was disordered from the wind. She longed to slide her fingers through its springy softness, to have his arms fold comfortably around her, to have his mouth soften and part over hers. A lump formed in her throat.

"Patrick," she whispered, "you know so little about me."

He said nothing. The light she was used to seeing in his eyes when they rested on her was gone.

Cat walked to the door. Without looking back, she said, "My reasons are my own, Patrick. From the beginning I told you how it would be."

His words surprised her: "Leave me, Catriona. Leave before I hurt you."

Throwing the door open, she walked down the hall and up the stairs to her chamber. Her bathwater, strewn with rose petals, awaited her. Later, dressed in a crimson, sable-lined robe, she dismissed her maid and stretched out on the bed. Her eyes watered as she stared at the fire. Not since her mother died had she felt so desperately alone.

The following morning Patrick MacKendrick left for Edinburgh without saying goodbye to his wife. Bitter jealousy left the taste of bile in his mouth. After what they'd shared, she had ridden out of Hermitage to help the Englishman escape. Her past rose up to haunt him. Perhaps he had been wrong and Andrew really was her lover. It would not be the first time he had misjudged a woman.

Alison nudged her mount forward until she rode beside Patrick. "Must you scowl so, Patrick? Jamie will think that marriage does not suit you."

He looked at the pretty, animated face of the woman by his side. Alison Douglass was blatantly obvious. But she was honest. Even her husband knew of her affairs. Patrick knew for a fact there was not a deceptive bone in her body. Although she didn't move him to the bone-weakening desire he felt whenever he looked at his wife, she was bonny enough. There had been a time when he thought her very bonny indeed. It would be a relief to spend time with a woman who had no hidden motives and obviously adored him.

James Stewart, king of Scotland, stood in the doorway and looked at the attractive picture before him. Maggie Drummond, dressed in a gown the color of daffodils, was resting on her couch. Her face looked very young and vulnerable in the throes of sleep, and for a moment James had the grace to feel ashamed.

Maggie was little more than a child. He had taken her away from her home and family, married off the man who loved her to another woman, and kept her here at court for his own pleasure. He had little time for her. Faith, he had little time for any personal desires. Yet she had never once complained.

Maggie stirred and opened her eyes. For a moment she stared at him solemnly. Then she smiled and held out her arms. James crossed the room and kissed her. She sighed and pulled him down to her side. He had been gone for over a week, and Maggie had worried.

"Where have you been, James?"

He frowned. "To France. Charles, His Royal Highness, has offered one hundred thousand pounds for Perkin Warbeck, the person who calls himself Richard, duke of York."

"Did you accept?" Maggie asked.

James shook his head. "Nay, lass. I reminded him that Richard applied to us first."

"Perkin Warbeck must be a very powerful weapon for the king of France to offer so much."

James grinned. She called him "Warbeck," or "The Pretender," never "Richard." Maggie refused to offer up an opinion, but it was clear enough. " 'Tis a weapon I am most grateful to hold over the head of my old adversary, Henry of England," he said.

Maggie hesitated. "Mary Gordon does not wish to wed with this so-called duke of York."

He reached out and pulled the combs from her hair, which tumbled past her shoulders, straight and fine. James wove his fingers through the flame-colored tresses. " 'Tis unlike you to hold Warbeck in such dislike, Maggie," he said. "Has he ever offered you insult?"

"I despise him," Maggie burst out unexpectedly. "He is weak and womanly, and his nose drips." She turned to the man by her side and put her arms around him. "Surely you can see that he lies, Your Grace. Please don't make Mary wed with him."

"Warbeck loves Mary." James brushed her protest aside curtly. The imploring look in her eyes undid him, and he spoke more gently. "I cannot call off the marriage, love. It would be the ruin of our entire policy toward England. We must claim to support the Pretender."

Maggie's shoulders slumped. Mary Gordon's fate was sealed, and she dared say no more on the subject. The wedding would take place in two days' time. She rubbed her head against his shoulder. "Promise me you'll let no harm come to Mary. She is so gentle and shy."

James looked surprised. "Mary Gordon is my cousin. She has the protection of her name and rank. There is nothing to fear, lass. Even Henry would not dare lay a hand to her head."

Maggie nodded, satisfied. James would keep his word.

His voice near her ear was rough with desire. "You are beautiful, Maggie, lovelier even than the first time I saw you."

She blushed and refused to meet his eyes.

Puzzled, he lifted his hand to her chin and turned her face so that she met his eyes. "What is it, lass?"

"I am with child," she said simply.

His face was dark, stoic. "When?" was all he said.

"In July." Maggie knew he couldn't marry her. Still, she wished he would offer.

"Why did you not tell me sooner?"

Maggie's temper flashed. "Does it matter?"

"Aye." The dark eyes narrowed with anger. "This is not the time for a child between us. I cannot wed you now, Maggie. You know that."

She lowered her eyes. "I never even considered it. In your position you can hardly marry every woman you get with child."

"Stop it!" His fingers, hard and hurting on her shoulders, would leave marks. "It isn't like that. You are the woman I love."

She sighed and leaned her forehead against his. "I'm sorry, James. I didn't mean it."

"I'll never hurt you, love," James whispered, pressing his lips to her soft skin.

"Hush." She knew how much it meant to James to honor his word. She knew also that such a promise was impossible to keep. He was king of Scotland. His marriage would be a political alliance. Knowing this, Maggie did not for a moment regret what she had done. Jamie Stewart was her destiny. Long ago she had made her decision to give her heart and soul to this man, whatever the cost.

James looked into the dark, exotic eyes of the woman he loved. Her skin was like porcelain, her cheeks the color of ripe peaches. She looked wise and content and very lovely. His child had filled out the slender curves of her hips and breasts. A surge of possessiveness swept through him. If he couldn't have Maggie as his queen, he would have no other. Scotland would have an heir in his younger brother.

He traced the smooth line of her cheek with his hand. "You are so beautiful."

"Thank you." She smiled.

Sighing, he stretched out beside her and fell asleep against her breast.

The English court was stiff and formal. Patrick felt ill at ease in the cold throne room. Keeping his eyes on Henry VII's lined face, he crossed the room and knelt at his feet.

"Rise, Sir Patrick," the king ordered. "I'm delighted that James could spare you."

"I believe you have a message for him, Your Grace. A message of such importance that it could not be delivered by a courier."

Henry nodded and stood up. "So I do."

Patrick was surprised to see that Henry was small and slight, hardly the fierce warrior who destroyed his enemies without remorse. His lips were a mere slit in his face, and the bony ridge of his forehead was very evident under the light, thinning hair.

Then Patrick looked into the crafty blue eyes and his entire perception of the English monarch changed. Henry was a dangerous man. He had no need of physical prowess. His strength lay in the shrewd intelligence shining from his sharp-eyed gaze. He assessed people with the same accuracy and thoroughness that Jamie displayed when reading his intelligence reports.

Patrick was something of a judge of human nature himself. He carefully wiped all traces of expression from his face. Henry would find the border lord no easy mark.

The king smiled and gestured toward a nearby door. "Shall we retire to a more private setting?"

Patrick bowed. "As you wish."

The room was comfortable and intimate. Low tables and embroidered chairs were clustered together by the fire. Patrick was surprised to see a young girl, richly dressed, seated in one of the chairs. She rose as they entered the room.

She did not bow but walked gracefully to the king's side and kissed his cheek. Henry patted her arm.

"Please, sit." He waved Patrick to a chair. The border lord raised his eyebrows and looked askance at the girl.

"This is my daughter, the Princess Margaret," replied Henry.

Patrick knelt before her and lifted her hand to his lips. "My pleasure, Your Highness."

Margaret smiled and Patrick saw that, unlike her father, she was lovely. Elizabeth Woodville's blond beauty had resurrected itself in the silvery fairness of her granddaughter.

"You may go, Margaret," her father said.

She withdrew her hand from the MacKendrick's. "It was my pleasure as well, m'lord," she said. Her voice was low and clear. Henry watched her leave the room before speaking.

"What think you of my daughter, MacKendrick?"

Patrick was puzzled. "She is most charming, Your Grace."

"Charming enough to tempt Jamie Stewart?"

Patrick's heart sank. "The Princess Margaret is lovely enough to tempt any man," he answered.

Henry had not missed the expression on the border lord's face. "We want peace," he said. "The stakes are high. You hold York. You know Jamie better than anyone, MacKendrick. Would he marry?"

Patrick's jaw tightened. He wet his lips and considered the question.

Henry smiled, satisfied. The border lord wanted peace. He would speak for the marriage.

"I don't know if Jamie will wed at this time," Patrick said at last.

Henry frowned. "Will he give up York?"

"No." Patrick shook his head. "Jamie will never abandon Richard of York."

"Richard of York," Henry spat contemptuously. "More likely the son of a milliner. Does this Pretender truly believe he can take my country?"

Patrick shrugged and remained silent.

"Would it make a difference if he saw Margaret?"

"A year ago, perhaps," Patrick answered, "but not now."

The king's mouth settled into angry lines. He rubbed his chin. "So," he said softly, "England and Scotland sit in stalemate because of the Drummond lass?"

Patrick's eyes narrowed. "News travels quickly to London."

Henry surveyed his nails. "I received another piece of news recently," he said softly. "I must congratulate you on your nuptials, m'lord. 'Tis not often that an Englishwoman finds such succor in Scotland."

Patrick's face was bland. "Catriona Wells came to Scotland seeking Jamie's support. You gave her stepfather control of her fortune. What was the lass to do?"

"Tell her young Richard asks for her." The king smiled thinly. "He is well, for now."

"Is there any reason he should not be?" The MacKendrick pretended ignorance.

"None at all." Henry stood up. "Return to Jamie with my terms. Perhaps he will live up to his reputation as an intelligent ruler and accept my daughter's hand in marriage. I await your answer with anticipation."

Patrick bowed low and backed out of the room. "Damn," he swore under his breath. Cat's brother was in danger and his hands were tied. At this moment, Jamie was arming the Pretender with ships and men to storm the English coast. If he rode through the night, he might be able to relay Henry's message before the first troops landed on English soil. He thought of Hermitage and its close proximity to the English border. Cat would never forgive him for abandoning her brother, but could he ever forgive himself if the castle was besieged and he were not there to protect her?

* * *

"You are mad, Mary." Janet stared in horror at her sister.

"He is my husband. Would you have me abandon him?"

Swearing a vile oath, Janet paced back and forth across the room. "There must be a way," she muttered.

"You'll hurt the child if you don't stop worrying," Mary warned. "Glenkirk will not thank me if you are upset."

"Glenkirk can—" Janet stopped and flushed. The words that were about to pass her lips were not complimentary ones. It was hardly a fair thing to criticize one's husband behind his back.

"I am the princess of York, Janie," Mary continued. "It matters not that it was forced upon me. My husband and I are political figures."

"What if you renounce your claim?"

Mary shook her head regretfully. "James would never allow it."

Janet looked into her sister's shining eyes and wondered, once again, where Mary had acquired that gentle serenity with which she accepted her fate. Her own nature, as turbulent as the storm-tossed Atlantic, was so far removed from Mary's calm it was hard to believe they shared the same blood.

"Are you sure your husband has been completely honest with you?" she asked.

"Please don't interfere." Mary gripped Janet's shoulders tightly. "I'm reconciled to this. When Warbeck disembarks on English soil, I shall be with him."

"My God, Mary." Janet stared at her incredulously. "You cannot love him."

"He needs me."

"Perkin Warbeck isn't a child. He is a contender for the English throne. Cat believes that when Henry finds him, and he will, all those who support him will die."

Mary's composure faltered. "What am I to do, Janet? Don't you see that you make it even worse for me?"

Janet, intent on her thoughts, didn't answer. Her brother George was banished from Scotland for two more years. Cat was determined to return to Ravenswood, and now her devoted little sister was leaving and it was doubtful Janet would ever see her again. The future looked very bleak indeed.

"Please, Brenna." Catriona's voice held a desperate note. "You must get well. If only you would try. Think of the child." Overcome with weariness, her head dropped into her hands and she sobbed uncontrollably.

Heat emanated from the emaciated figure beneath the bedclothes. Brenna Sinclair's gaunt features bore testimony to her struggle of the past week. Within a day her harmless cough had developed into a raging fever that swept through Hermitage, descending upon freemen and tenants, callously disregarding the tear-streaked faces of kin, their hands clasped in prayer, their knees bent and aching from the stone floor of the chapel.

The dead could not be buried quickly enough. Cat ordered every servant who could still stand to burn the rotting corpses. The stench of seared flesh and human hair permeated the thick walls of the castle until it seemed as if the very walls dripped of ash and smoke and death.

The courier she had sent to Patrick in Edinburgh came back empty-handed. "His Lordship remains in England," the man replied. Resentment, sharp as the stabbing pain of a knife wound, shot through her. Patrick was in England, her England, at the sane and healthy court of Henry VII, while she was here at Hermitage nursing his child and burying his tenants.

For most of the victims, death came swiftly. Brenna Sinclair was an exception. She lingered on in a state of delirium, her hair dank, her flesh shriveling on bones that grew more brittle every hour. For nine days she fought for her life. At first, when she didn't immediately succumb, Cat had hope. But now, as the hot fever held the frail woman in its clutches day after exhausting day, she knew the battle was lost.

Her strength spent from nights of sleeplessness, Cat drifted into a fitful doze. When it first became obvious that Brenna was terribly ill, Catriona had been surprised at the extent of her feelings for Isobel's ill-fated mother. The gentle, quiet woman had proven her friendship time and again in the long months since Cat had come to Hermitage.

For the first time in her life, Catriona had a friend her own age to confide in. That the woman was a Scot and not of noble blood had long since become unimportant. With her death, there would be a void at Hermitage for a long time to come.

Someone touched her shoulder, and instantly Cat was awake. The intense heat from the figure on the bed was gone.

"M'lady," a tentative voice spoke, "she is with God. May she rest in peace."

A small man garbed in the identifying robes of Rome made the sign of the cross over Brenna's body. Immediately, Cat stood up for his blessing.

"I'll wait outside until you are finished," Cat said, hurrying to the door. The bitter herbal smell and airless confinement of the sickroom threatened to overpower her. She felt ill. Outside in the corridor, she took a deep cleansing breath. The air still carried the scent of smoke. Inside the room she could hear the priest reciting the familiar, age-old litany for the dead. Her eyes burned and her mind turned back.

She was no longer leaning against a wall in Hermitage Castle. She was home at Ravenswood, and the priest was shaking the vial of holy water over her own mother. Cat fought against the familiar panic. Forcing herself to concentrate, she counted the steps leading from the landing to the great hall and watched shadows creep across the crimson carpet. She listened to the rain trickling down the windowpanes and the wind whispering against the outside walls.

Father Beaton opened the door quietly and cleared his throat. Cat straightened to her full height and met his pitying glance. He nodded. "It is finished."

"Thank you," she said, and she watched as he disappeared down the stairs. The stiff material of his cassock made rustling noises against the floor.

Hours later, after the funeral arrangements were made, Cat climbed the stairs to her chamber. Without removing her clothes, she fell into the soft comfort of her bed and slept. Her dreams were troubled and restless. Unable to find a comfortable position, she turned over on her stomach and threw her arms out on both sides of the feather pillow.

Instantly, her eyes flew open. With one hand, she tentatively explored the dimensions of the warm mound beside her.

She sighed with relief and sat up. The faint moonlight streaming through the window lit the delicate features and tear-stained cheeks of Isobel MacKendrick. She lay curled on her side, much as she must have done in her mother's womb with her thumb in her mouth. Cat's heart softened with pity and she gathered the little girl against her. It was never easy to lose a mother. For a child of seven, it was doubly hard.

Isobel's small hands clutched at Cat and she uttered one deep, shuddering breath, but she did not waken until the first rays of dawn crept through the window and touched her face. Cat watched as the thick lashes separated and gray eyes peered up at her. The child seemed confused. In that first moment between sleep and wakefulness, she had forgotten the events of the preceding day. Cat knew at once when memory returned. Her chin quivered and tears filled her eyes, making them even brighter than before.

"Mama's dead," Isobel whispered.

Cat nodded, a lump in her throat.

"Why did she leave me?"

"Oh, Isobel." Cat sighed. How was it possible to explain the workings of fate to a seven-year-old child? She stroked the flame-red curls. "Your mother didn't want to go, lass. 'Twas the fever."

"Is she in heaven?"

"Yes." Cat's voice broke and she hugged Isobel tightly. "She is watching you this very moment from her place in heaven."

"What will happen to me?"

Cat frowned. "What do you mean?"

"John will leave Hermitage. He only stayed because of Mama. Must I go with him?"

"Of course not!" Cat's voice was firm. "You will stay here with your father and me. You belong to us."

Something in Catriona's pale green eyes and the emphatic set of her mouth convinced Isobel. "When will Da come home?" she asked.

Cat's smile disappeared. "I know not," she replied. The

hurt look on Isobel's face shamed her, and she relented. "When the king no longer needs him, he'll come," she said gently. "And when he does, he'll expect to see a young lady with roses in her cheeks." She threw back the covers and stood up. "Come. We are already late for Mass."

Isobel climbed out of bed and slipped her hand into Cat's. "You won't leave me, will you, Cat?" she asked.

Cat bit her lip. Isobel couldn't know the extent of what she asked. She was a child who had lost her mother and she desperately needed assurance. The shining gray eyes looking up at her so pleadingly had no knowledge of the forces that shaped destinies. Cat couldn't deny her. Neither could she lie. She knelt before the child.

"You will live a long life, Isobel," she promised. "Your father is a powerful man. You will always be well cared for."

With the directness of the man who sired her, Isobel saw through the placating words. "Are you going away?" she asked.

"I don't know," Cat replied. "I don't want to, but perhaps I must."

"Will you come back?"

Cat flushed and lifted her chin. "Aye. If I'm still welcome, I shall come back."

The small chapel was nearly empty. Cat wasn't surprised. Too many were still recovering from their bout with illness. She smiled encouragingly at Isobel before turning her attention to the priest. The sweet smell of incense wafted through the air as the low, moving cadence of the Latin chant resounded from the altar. At last the benediction came. It was finished. Brenna Sinclair would rest in the grounds of the church where she was baptized as a babe and had worshiped all of her life.

Cat's eyes moved over the plain, wooden coffin. There had been no time to have it properly carved. Despite Brenna's lack of rank, Catriona had ordered that the woman's remains be buried in the cemetery at Hermitage, instead of burned. Isobel would not be deprived of visiting her mother's resting place.

The dead woman, pale and motionless against the satin lining, looked strangely peaceful, as if she were merely asleep. Death had released Brenna's expression from the ravaged effects of her illness. She would kneel before her Maker with the serene beauty Cat remembered from their first meeting.

Later, after the mourners had followed the coffin to the burial site, Cat opened the door to her own chambers. The past weeks had taken their toll and she was looking forward to the blissful comfort of uninterrupted sleep. She closed the door behind her and bent to remove her shoes. A hand closed over her mouth.

"Don't be afraid, Cat," a familiar voice warned her before removing his hand. "'Tis only I, Andrew Percy."

Cat whirled around to face the intruder. "Andrew," she gasped. "What has happened? Why are you here? Is Richard in danger?"

"Hush." He laid his finger against her lips. "All in good time. I'm on my way to Edinburgh to warn Mary Gordon away from England. There are spies everywhere. Henry knows all the Pretender's moves. If she follows him, she will be imprisoned."

"Good God!" Cat's face was white. "Go then. Why do you tarry here?"

"There is more."

His words filled her with foreboding. "What is it?" she cried. "Speak."

"Richard has been imprisoned in the Tower."

"Why?"

Cat's anguished question tore at his soul. "Henry offers his daughter to James," he explained. "Unless Scotland's king weds with the English princess or relinquishes the Pretender, Richard will pay with his life."

"Of what charge is Richard accused?" Cat whispered. "He is a mere child."

Andrew snorted. "Since when does Henry Tudor need a charge? He is the king, Catriona. Henry is merely using Richard. Jamie would never allow anyone with a drop of Stewart blood to perish at the end of an English scaffold."

Cat thought of Maggie Drummond's lovely face, remembering, with an inevitable sense of doom, the gamin's smile, the dark mysterious eyes, the elfin grace of her long thin hands and the burnished copper of her hair. She had bewitched Jamie Stewart from the first moment he saw her. Even now, when she was great with child, he remained uncharacteristically faithful.

She shook her head slowly. "Jamie will never give up Perkin Warbeck and he will never abandon Maggie. My brother is less than nothing to him," she said bitterly. "I must return to England."

"What can you do?" Andrew asked.

"I will offer Ravenswood to Neville," Cat replied. "If that fails, I will take Richard's place as Henry's hostage. I am the countess of Bothwell and Patrick MacKendrick's wife. Even if Jamie would consign me to the devil, Patrick will not. He will come for me."

Andrew whistled softly under his breath. "You have great faith in this border lord, Cat. I pray he will not fail you."

The fleeting image of a hard mouth and eyes as cold as shards of ice flashed through her mind. She lifted her head. "He will come for me," she insisted, knotting her hands into fists to still their trembling, "if only to save his pride. I wish I could tell him why I leave. He'll not think kindly of me for running away after the suffering we at Hermitage have endured the past several weeks."

Andrew reached out and drew her into his arms. Cat leaned against him gratefully. After a long moment, he spoke.

"If you care for the MacKendrick so deeply, why did you never tell him of Richard and the reason you were sent here?"

"What good would it have done?" Her voice was muffled against his shoulder. "Why should Patrick risk his life to save a lad he's never seen? If he knew how desperately I needed to return to England, he would never have left me unguarded." She lifted her head and stepped back. "It was right that I kept silent. Go now. Give Mary my love and God speed. I pray you arrive in time."

Wrapped in a foul-smelling blanket, his face smeared with dirt, Andrew waited behind the kitchens of Edinburgh Castle for the second day in a row. Every morning and evening the poor of the city were allowed inside the gates. There they waited for the castle cooks to discard leftover food from the royal banquet tables.

Disguised as a beggar, Andrew hid himself in the crowd and pushed his way into the courtyard. After the feeding frenzy abated and the peasants made their way back to the city, he slipped into the shadows near the back gardens and waited for Mary Gordon to show herself.

He was about to give up hope when a small, bulky figure in the full bloom of her pregnancy slowly made her way to the bench near his hiding place. It was Janet. He grinned under his dirt. It was amazing that he recognized her at all. The enormous young woman walking awkwardly down the path was nothing like the slim, graceful firebrand he remembered. He stepped into her path and held out a dirty hand. "Alms, m'lady?" he croaked. "Alms for the poor?"

Janet sighed and reached into her pocket. "I've only coppers," she said regretfully, "but you may have them all." She reached out to drop the coins, careful to avoid touching him.

His hand closed over hers in a viselike grip. She gasped and lifted her eyes to his face. "How dare you!" she cried. "Release me at once."

"In a moment, Lady Janet." Andrew's voice resumed its clipped tones. "Don't you recognize me?"

Her eyes, the gold of twin moons, narrowed. "Andrew?" she gasped. "What are you doing here?"

"I came to warn Mary. She should avoid England at all costs. Warbeck is a marked man."

"You risked your own life for this?" Janet asked incredulously. "Art daft, man?" Something suddenly occurred to her. "What is my sister to you, Sir Andrew?"

Andrew reddened. "She is a kind and gentle lady," he said. "Nothing more."

Janet stared up at him. He met her gaze steadily. At last she nodded and relaxed her shoulders. "You are too late despite your good intentions. Mary left for England early in the week." Janet rubbed her back. God's bones, she felt like an old woman. Would this child never be born? She gestured toward the seat at the end of the path. "Help me to the bench, Andrew," she ordered, resting her hand on his arm.

His lips twitched. Janet was as autocratic as Jamie Stewart himself, although she would never admit it.

"Have you seen Cat?" she asked.

"Aye." Andrew had almost forgotten his promise. "She bids me give you a message for the MacKendrick. Richard Wells is imprisoned in the Tower. She goes to take his place."

"Holy God!" Janet's lips were the color of bleached bone. "How could you agree to such a thing?"

Andrew's eyes danced. "Catriona is much like yourself, m'lady. Woe is the man who stands in the way of the mighty Stewarts."

"Don't be absurd." Janet's cheeks were very pink. "Go now, m'lord, before someone discovers you. I'll find a way out of this mess. Never fear."

Andrew grinned. "Not for a single moment did I doubt you, Lady Janet." He lifted her hand to his lips. "Farewell."

❧ 25 ❧

Janet looked down at her swollen belly with distaste. Two weeks ago, hoping to intercept her husband, she had summoned the last vestiges of her strength and managed the ride to Edinburgh. How could she possibly make it to Stirling in her condition?

Her lips tightened. She had no choice. Alex was at Stirling and she needed him, more than she cared to admit. He was the only one who could warn the MacKendrick that Catriona would soon be at the mercy of Henry Tudor. With her hand pressed to the small of her back, Janet walked slowly back to her chambers.

Two hours later, the groom stared at her incredulously. "Lady Glenkirk," he gasped, "Stirling is more than a day's ride from here. You'll bring on the babe."

"How dare you question my wishes?" The queen of Scotland herself could not have looked more regal than Janet at that moment. "Saddle my horse," she ordered imperiously. "My guard grows impatient."

Wetting his lips, the groom looked at the men on horse-back waiting patiently in the courtyard and drew a small measure of comfort. Perhaps Lord Glenkirk would not have his head after all.

There was a commotion at the gates and a sudden shout of laughter. Janet grew hot and then cold. She would know that laugh anywhere. Moments later, Alexander of Glen-kirk, his helmet under his arm, strode into the stable leading two horses.

The moment he saw Janet he stopped. His eyes moved from her face to the weight of her stomach and then to the saddled horse at her side. A murderous rage blinded him to all but the red haze blurring his vision. Dropping the reins, he started toward her.

Janet gave an inarticulate cry. Moving faster than she had in a very long time, she crossed the space that separated them and threw herself into her husband's arms. Glenkirk was shocked and more than a little confused. In all his months of marriage to this unpredictable woman, she had never invited his embrace. Slowly his arms closed about her and he bent his lips to her hair.

Janet's heart hammered so loudly she was sure he could hear it. She couldn't explain the feeling that propelled her into the arms of this man she swore would never possess her heart. All she knew was that he was tall and strong and capable and she had never been so glad to see anyone in her entire life. Every instinct clamored for his touch. Tears of relief streamed down her cheeks.

Alex was startled. Janet never cried. "What is it, my love?" he whispered into her ear. "What troubles you so?"

"I've missed you so much," she confessed. "Don't leave me again, Alex. I've been such a bad wife, but I'll make it up to you."

A light glinted in Glenkirk's hazel eyes. He would have

given all he owned to hear those words from the lips of Janet Gordon. He nodded his head toward the door and the groom discretely disappeared, leaving them alone.

"What do you think would be a fitting retribution for all I've endured at your hands?" he teased.

Janet lifted her head. A slight smile hovered at the corners of her husband's mouth. She ran her hand over her stomach. "Isn't this retribution enough? My looks are gone and I can barely walk." She dropped her eyes, unable to meet the brilliant heat of his gaze.

Alex lifted her chin, forcing her to look at him. "You are the bonniest woman I've ever seen," he said huskily. "I've thought of nothing but you for weeks. Night after night your face haunted my dreams. Now I find my imaginings pale in comparison to the flesh-and-blood woman."

Janet drew a deep breath. The question must be asked even if it destroyed the fragile trust between them. "There are rumors that Alison Douglass sought out Patrick only to be spurned."

"The Lady Douglass never held a place in my heart, lass. Not even before I met you."

Janet searched her husband's face carefully. What she saw in the roughly hewn features satisfied her. Suddenly shy, she dropped her eyes. "I would be the only woman in your heart, Alex," she whispered.

He laughed exultantly. Holding her face between his callused hands, he brushed her lips gently with his. "You are there, my love. You always have been."

With a sigh of relief, Janet sagged against him. The barrier she had erected between them melted away. Alexander loved her, and she had nothing more to fear.

"Where were you going?" he muttered, nuzzling the soft skin of her neck. She was so clean, and she smelled of flowers.

"Oh, Alex!" Janet pulled out of his arms. "I'd almost forgotten. You must find the MacKendrick. Catriona rides to England. Her brother has been imprisoned in the Tower."

He smiled and pulled her back into the circle of his arms. "My journey will be a short one. At this moment, Patrick seeks an audience with Jamie. We rode in together."

Janet's mouth dropped open and she stared at him in

wonder. "Don't you know?" she asked. "Jamie sailed with Mary and the Pretender for England. Their destination is Cornwall. Warbeck believes the people there to be friendly to his cause."

Glenkirk stared down at her. "Are you sure of this, Janet?"

Her eyes flashed indignantly. "Would I mistake a matter that concerns my own sister? I tried to dissuade her from going but she would have none of it."

He cursed. Taking her arm, he strode out of the stable into the courtyard, pulling her after him.

"Where are you taking me?" Janet cried.

Abruptly he stopped, noticing for the first time her labored panting. As if she weighed no more than his claymore, he lifted her swollen figure into his arms and continued his pace.

Janet rested her head on his shoulder. "Where are we going?" she repeated.

"To find Patrick. Jamie must be stopped, or we may all be bowing to an English king before the year is out."

"Don't be angry with her, m'lord," Janet pleaded. "She only left because of young Richard."

"Did she now?"

Patrick MacKendrick's words were polite enough, but there was something about the white-lipped mouth and icy eyes that unsettled Janet. She did not envy Catriona her husband. She moved closer to Alexander.

His big hand closed over hers. "What of Jamie and Warbeck?" he asked.

"They can bloody well burn in hell," Patrick replied bitterly. He pulled on his breastplate and helmet.

"Patrick!" Alex reached out and touched his shoulder. "This concerns all of us."

The border lord stood very still, as if struggling for something deep inside himself. Finally he spoke. "It is in the hands of destiny, my friend. I have done everything in my power to persuade our king. He is a stubborn man." Patrick's piercing gray eyes burned through the slit in his helmet. "The irony is, one short year ago our Jamie would have worshiped at the feet of Margaret Tudor even were she not Henry's daughter."

"Poor Maggie," Janet muttered. "She is a dear lass. I'll warrant she knows nothing of this."

Patrick thrust his sword into its scabbard. "Do you have a message for your cousin, Lady Glenkirk?"

She met his glance steadily. "Cat has suffered a great deal, m'lord. Be kind to her. She cares deeply for you."

"Deeply enough to trust me, I presume?" The mocking words rang through the metal.

Janet blushed and her eyes dropped.

"No, he said bitterly. "I thought not. Have no fear. Catriona will return to your loving arms unmarked. I'll not beat her, although she deserves it." With that he left the room.

Janet shivered and hugged herself. It was not fear of the whip that caused her to speak for Cat. Although painful, it was over quickly. It was the ice in the MacKendrick's eyes that worried her. Cat needed tenderness and compassion. Janet did not believe the border lord knew the meaning of either.

The merciless anger that held Patrick in its grip did not dissipate until he had almost reached the English border. Swiftly his stallion carried him past the silent villages of Selkirk and Galashiels and Hawick. Finally, he saw the walls of Hermitage, dark and tall in the distance, a stone's throw from England. His anger rose again.

What he had told Janet was only a small part of his pain. He felt betrayed. Catriona was his wife. He had bared his soul, revealed his secret longings, given his heart into her keeping, and this was how she repaid him. She had helped Andrew Percy escape, and now, when his back was turned and she knew he couldn't stop her, she had run away into a danger so great it would be a miracle if her life was spared. Holy God, didn't she think enough of him to know he would have returned for Richard? Was he such a monster in her eyes that she believed he would allow an innocent child to languish in the Tower of London?

The wind whipped against his helmet as he passed his

home without stopping. Inside the heavy metal, his face felt like a block of ice. A savage oath escaped him. No matter how she lied or what she had done, he loved her still. He, Patrick MacKendrick, womanizer and warrior, lord high admiral of the seas and legend of the borders, was snared fast in a silken web. His captor was a slip of a lass with a waspish tongue and eyes the cool green of a glen in springtime. Somehow he had known from the very beginning that there would be no one else for him in all the world. She had ruined him for other women. The humiliating disaster with Alison Douglass had proven that.

A sudden, numbing fear clutched at his heart. If Cat were imprisoned and left alone in the cold darkness of an empty cell . . .

Patrick no longer felt the cold. He spurred his horse to greater speed.

The kitchen maid smiled her pleasure as she smoothed out the linen cloth and surveyed the table. The poached salmon was perfect. Maggie Drummond, her sister, Sybil, Alison Douglass and the Lady Janet of Glenkirk were to sup together at a very elegant and private breakfast. The maid carefully poured the sauce over the eggs and added a pinch of salt just as the cook had instructed her. The ladies would be pleased.

Inside the intimate dining room, goblets of gold plate inlaid with priceless jewels rested on a damask-covered table. Porcelain plates, so thin they seemed almost transparent, had been carried from Constantinople, across the Himalayas, along the treacherous trade route from Asia, specifically for the purpose of gracing the royal table of James IV of Scotland. Flemish wine cooled on a block of ice. Knives, their blades thin and pointed, rested daintily on linen napkins. Flowers from the palace conservatory were strewn around the food platters, their scent mingling with the smells of baking and cinnamon and sugar.

Maggie Drummond's custom of an informal weekly breakfast had become quite fashionable. Many ladies of noble blood would have sacrificed much to be invited to the table of the king's favorite. But Maggie was insistent that only close personal friends and family were welcome. No one, no matter how influential, was invited for political purposes.

Janet reached the door at the same time as Maggie. The two women were very near the end of their pregnancies, and the entrance wasn't large enough for both. Maggie chuckled and moved aside, allowing Janet to enter first. They took their places at the table and Maggie reached for the wine.

"Have you heard from Mary?" she asked, pouring the clear liquid into Janet's goblet.

"No." Janet frowned.

"I'm sorry I couldn't help, Janie. I tried, but it was too late."

"Say nothing more," Janet warned, nodding toward the two women who entered the room.

Sybil smiled and greeted Maggie and Janet. "I'm very hungry," she announced. "Where is Alison?"

"'Tis early yet," answered Maggie. "Give her a few more minutes." She sipped her wine and poured some for Sybil.

Once again Janet was amazed at the difference in the two sisters. Except for her huge stomach, Maggie was slender and golden, a woman of grace and mystery, with red hair and eyes so brown they seemed just short of black. Sybil's fair skin and pretty, dimpled face bore no resemblance at all to her sister's seductive beauty. Janet toyed with the stem of her goblet and watched as Sybil greedily drank down the expensive bouquet.

"I'm sorry to be late." Alison, flushed and breathless, sank into her chair. "I had a previous engagement."

Janet's lips twitched. Now that she knew Alex was not involved, Alison's preference for married men seemed almost amusing.

"No harm done," Maggie assured her. "The bread has just arrived." She passed white bread and delicious sweet buns around the table.

The women broke the bread, and each took only one small piece for herself. After the meal the leftovers would be distributed to the poor.

Janet was hot and the salmon rich. She reached for her wineglass and raised it to her lips. The cool liquid had barely touched her tongue when Alison raised her glass.

"Shall we drink a toast to freedom?" she said.

Maggie laughed. Her hair, pulled back from her temples with golden combs, reminded Janet of a flaming sunset. "Whose freedom, m'lady?" she asked.

"Why ours, of course." Alison's eyes danced. "We shall drink to the freedom of every woman whose husband is away." She lifted the goblet to her lips and swallowed a long draught. Reaching across the table, she touched her glass to Maggie's. "Let us also drink to every man who manages to escape the clutches of a nagging wife, if only for a little while."

Janet left her wine untouched. Her back ached and she felt sick to her stomach. Maggie and Sybil both drained their glasses. Suddenly Maggie slumped and cried out. Holding her middle, she threw the goblet aside and doubled over. It landed on the floor and rolled to the doorway. Sybil fell to her knees behind the table.

White with fear, Alison's face broke out in a cold sweat as stabbing pains seared through her. "Help me!" she implored Janet. "Please, help me!" Her head hit the table, tearing a deep gash in her temple. Blood flowed down the white cloth and onto the floor.

Somewhere a servant screamed, and the sound spurred Janet into action. Ignoring Alison, she grabbed a bowl, dumped the fruit on the floor and ran around the table to kneel beside Maggie.

"Call a physician," she ordered a servant. "Hurry."

Cradling Maggie's head, she spoke to her softly. "Fear not, love. Help is on the way. You didn't drink enough to hurt you."

Maggie's grip on Janet's wrist was surprisingly strong. "Tell him I love him," she whispered. "Tell him to think of Scotland."

Janet's tears flowed freely. She held the bowl under Maggie's chin, holding the red hair away from her face. Maggie gagged once. Nothing came up. She looked strangely peaceful.

Alex ran into the room, followed by the doctor. "Janet," he cried, "are you—"

She shook her head and lifted her tear-streaked face to her husband's. " 'Tis Maggie. I fear she's dying."

Alex reached for the unconscious woman. Her face looked beautiful, as if she would awaken at any moment. The doctor forced his finger down her throat. It was no use. Maggie Drummond had drawn her last breath.

The physician's face was pale. "Call a priest," he ordered.

Janet stopped him with a hand on his shoulder. Her stomach clenched and a painful cramp held her immobile. "I drank too," she whispered. "Will it harm my babe?"

"It would have happened before now," he reassured her. "'Tis fortunate you are near your time."

Two hours later Janet's labor pains began. The ache in her back accelerated quickly, leaving no time to prepare for the searing agony that threatened the last remnants of her fragile control. Limp and spent after each mounting bout of tension, she took deep gulping breaths, readying herself for another onslaught of pain. Day turned into night and still it continued. Twice she lost consciousness, her mind shutting off the abuse to her tortured body.

A woman entered the room bearing water and clean linen. Another exited, carrying towels stained with blood. Glenkirk, his face haggard and white, clenched his fists. He felt helpless, and the feeling terrified him. Fear, such as he had never known, consumed him. Was he to lose Janet now, after everything that had passed between them?

A cry pierced the walls. He could bear it no longer. Striding to the door of the birthing chamber, he pushed it open and stepped inside.

"You shouldn't be here, m'lord," the midwife warned him. "You'll only upset her."

Alex ignored her and sat down on the bed. Dark circles surrounded Janet's beautiful eyes. Her lips were cracked, her hair damp with sweat. He had never loved her more.

"I didn't know it would be like this," he muttered. "I swear I didn't."

Unbelievably, she smiled. "Would you have done anything differently, m'lord?"

Startled, Alex stared deeply into her eyes. They twinkled back at him. He threw back his head and laughed.

Janet winced and her face contorted with pain. Alex took her hands in his. He was experienced in dealing with pain.

A clean sword thrust into the flesh and quickly withdrawn could not be compared to the endless agony of childbirth, but still it was something.

"Breathe deeply, love," he ordered. "In and out, that's it." He modified his own breathing to match hers. "Go with the pain." He watched her follow his lead. "Good girl."

She lay weak and exhausted, her eyes on his face, waiting. Again it came and again she worked, concentrating on his eyes, his mouth, the firm shape of his lips. The lifeforce, pushing the child from her sweat-soaked body, ebbed and flowed for nearly twelve more hours. At last the midwife crowed triumphantly.

"He comes!" she announced. "You must push, m'lady. The child will be born soon."

With all her strength, Janet bore down. Tears spilled over onto her cheeks. The pain was different, somehow, the pressure more intense. She was so very tired.

The midwife reached between her legs and suddenly there was relief. A piercing cry rent the air. Janet's head fell back and moments passed. Her eyes widened as a swaddled red-faced bundle was placed into her arms.

"'Tis a boy, m'lady," the woman said. "A fine lusty boy."

Janet pushed back the blanket and looked with wonder upon her son. Alex took a deep shuddering breath and turned away. His eyes were moist. For the rest of his life he would remember this moment, his spirited hoyden of a wife looking like the Virgin Mary, her face aglow with love for the child in her arms.

"Oh, Alex," she breathed. "He looks just like George."

Alexander bent over the child. He did indeed resemble Janet's brother. The tiny face was already stamped with the Gordon features. His eyebrows grew in the same soaring line as his mother's. His nose was high-bridged and aquiline, his mouth wide and expressive. Only the bit of hair on the baby's head had nothing of Janet. It was red, as red as Glenkirk's own.

Gently, Alex took the child from his wife. The baby yawned and flailed his arms. No wonder Janet had suffered. The infant was good-sized and heavy for a newborn. Alex slid his finger inside the miniature palm. Instantly, the baby gripped it. Grinning with pleasure, Alex sat down beside his wife.

"Thank you, my love," he whispered reverently. "I know it was a terrible ordeal, but I'm very glad he's here."

Janet's smile held such unguarded happiness, Alex felt as if his very bones would melt.

"I'm glad too," she said.

Despite the fact that Sir William Neville was nearing fifty, he was still tall, lean and flat-bellied. His hair, shorn close to his head and overly fine, had not yet begun to thin. Most women of King Henry's court considered him a fine figure of a man.

To Catriona, he was the embodiment of all things evil. The fear gnawing at her vitals had increased with every mile she rode toward Ravenswood. Now, as she stood in the drawing room facing her stepfather, she was so terrified that all coherent thought escaped her. She merely stared, her eyes wide and empty, waiting for him to speak.

"What a pleasure to see you at last, my dear." Neville's lips pulled away from his teeth in the semblance of a smile. He reminded Cat of a fox.

"I came for my brother," she stammered.

"What a pity." The oily voice was tinged with amusement. "You arrived too late. Richard is on his way to London."

"That's a lie," Cat lashed out. "Henry released him days ago. He told me himself."

"I'm sure Henry's reasons for such a deception are sound," replied Neville. "You served us poorly, Catriona."

Her voice cracked. "I had no choice. Andrew explained everything."

Neville walked to the table and poured himself a goblet of wine. "Ah, yes. The estimable Lord Percy. A man besotted by your charms. Henry and I could scarcely credit his report."

"Andrew spoke the truth," she insisted woodenly. "You know I would never leave Richard here."

"You were prudently named, my dear," the smooth, mocking voice continued. "A cat always manages to land feet first. I believe Henry and I underestimated you. Within a few short months you persuaded the most powerful man in Scotland to marry you." Neville sipped at his drink. "Where is he now, Lady MacKendrick?"

Cat refused to answer. Neville's hand tightened on the stem of his glass, shattering the fine crystal. She stared in horror as blood dripped from his hand, mixing with the dark red wine. It had been foolish to come with such a small guard. The men waiting in the courtyard were no match for Neville's men. A bitter taste rose in her throat. Neville's men! The phrase filled her with contempt. They were Ravenswood's men, Richard's by right. She lifted her chin, her green eyes blazing at the man who had been her mother's husband.

"It is you who have served us poorly, m'lord. By forcing my hand and stealing my brother's inheritance, you have betrayed a sacred trust. I can only be grateful my mother did not live to see such a day."

Almost before she had finished uttering the damning words, Neville was across the room, his hands crushing her shoulders in a painful grip. "Enough!" he shouted, his face dark with anger. "If your mother had lived, none of this would be necessary. I would have heirs of my own. The future would be secure."

"Aren't you forgetting my brother?" Catriona sneered. "He is, after all, the master of Ravenswood."

He brushed her question aside. "What is Ravenswood compared to your mother's estates? She would have provided well for all of her children. As their father, I would have shared in that."

"So you chose to accuse a child of sedition?"

Neville looked down at the face he had dreamed of for more than three long years. During his wife's illness and subsequent death, he had remained the devoted and faithful husband in body if not in spirit. When Catriona returned from her first season at court he had become aware of her as a woman. Her green eyes and slim, lissome body haunted him. At first his desires had shocked him and he fought to suppress such immoral thoughts. But as his wife continued to ail and her beauty disappeared, an incredible idea began to take root in his mind. He would marry Catriona. The Stewart fortune as well as the portion left to her by her father would become his to control. If Richard did not live to produce heirs of his own, Cat's children would inherit Ravenswood.

He had miscalculated when it came to the girl herself. She had always been well bred and extremely polite. He flattered himself that she enjoyed his company. He had not counted on her stubborn refusal or the shrinking horror in her eyes whenever he came near. In the end he threatened her with the convent, and when his threats went unheeded, desperation forced him to commit an unthinkable act. Even now, more than a year later, he regretted the course of events that led to his actions. But Catriona had left him little choice. By flatly refusing to consider his offer of marriage, she had sealed her fate.

Neville considered the haughty, beautiful face so close to his own. She stirred his blood as no woman had before or since. Despite her marriage, Catriona Wells was his. She had belonged to him long before she became Patrick Mac-Kendrick's wife. She would belong to him again. Only he knew how to turn this proud, arrogant woman into a terrified, sobbing shadow of herself, heartbreakingly grateful for his presence and his touch.

He reached out to caress her cheek and she shrank back. What had it taken to bring her back? The bond with Richard must be even stronger than he imagined. It was an act of sheer courage on her part to return with so small a guard. Perhaps she thought her husband's name would protect her. Neville smiled thinly. She was wrong.

"It wasn't difficult to persuade Henry of your brother's guilt," he continued. "Your marriage to the border lord convinced him that you could not be trusted. A small hint, placed at the right time, convinced him that you conspired with Richard to raise support for the Pretender."

Cat's face whitened. Her arm was numb where Neville maintained his brutal grip. "That's a lie," she said.

"Perhaps. However, Warbeck is now on English soil and your cousin is his wife."

"What do you want from me, William?" Cat asked. "You may have Ravenswood. I'll take Richard back to Scotland."

"I think not." His voice lowered to a seductive whisper. "There is a better way."

The warmth in his words chilled her blood. Memories, surpressed and painful, flashed through her mind. Cat took a deep breath and wet her lips. "Tell me."

"Annul your marriage and become my wife."

"An annulment isn't possible," she said, looking at him steadily.

"Anything is possible." Neville stroked her arm. "We will say that you were forced into marriage with the MacKendrick. The dispensation will come by the time our first child is born."

She gasped. "You would make me your whore while I am wed to another?"

He threaded his fingers through her hair. The scent of her perfume made him dizzy. "You've shared my bed before," he said hoarsely. "I'll not wait a year or more to have you share it again."

For the space of a heartbeat, Cat stared blankly at Neville. Then the fog that had taken over her brain lifted and she recalled the shameful horror of the months following her mother's death. Her stomach heaved, a comforting blackness invaded her mind and she slid to the ground.

❧ 26 ❧

Kate closed her eyes, intentionally breaking her concentration. The scene in the stane lost its focus and disappeared. She felt Maura's hand on her arm and opened her eyes, forcing herself to meet the older woman's uncompromising gaze.

"I told you it would be unpleasant," Maura said softly.

Kate shook her head. "'Unpleasant' isn't the word I would have used," she said, mentally chastising herself for her own naiveté. From the beginning the signs were there. Why hadn't she seen it? She'd had enough therapy sessions with Lillian Spencer to recognize that Catriona's repressed memories were the result of a sexual assault. It was ironic really, considering how long Lillian had spent trying to dredge up incidences of Kate's childhood molestation and come up dry. The good doctor's instincts had been right all along. She just had the wrong lifetime and the wrong woman.

Maura interrupted her thoughts. "What are you going to do?"

"I'm not sure." Kate bit her lip and thought out loud. "If only I knew something that she doesn't, something that would keep him away." She looked up. "He doesn't know that Patrick is on his way."

"Patrick believes that Cat went to London to save her brother. He'll go there first."

"I thought you said your Sight wasn't as good as mine."

Maura shrugged. "I see only what you do. The rest is just logic. Maybe . . ."

"Yes?"

"Maybe you do know something that she doesn't."

"What do you mean?"

"When you first came to Foula you mentioned that you had seen a therapist, a woman named Lillian Spencer."

"I still don't understand."

"Maybe you don't want to."

Kate leaned her elbows on the table and rested her forehead in her palms. "Don't do this to me, Maura. I can't play games now. Just say it."

"Very well. What you have that Catriona doesn't is knowledge. Catriona Wells was a frightened virgin not yet out of her teens when Neville first violated her. Unless I am mistaken, you are not that."

Kate looked up, meeting the other woman's eyes steadily. "No," she said, "I'm not."

"Tell me what you've learned. You must know something about men who abuse women."

Still unsure of what Maura wanted, Kate spoke haltingly. "I know that control is the reason for rape, not desire. I know that men who rape women have a poor self-concept. They lack confidence." Her voice grew stronger. "They're usually afraid and contemptuous of other men, and many of them were raised by cold, manipulative mothers. They rape to get even. Many times they can't perform in normal relationships." All of a sudden she understood what she needed to do. "What if I can't stop him?"

Maura stood up and walked to the sink, staring out at the view from the window. After a while, she turned on the faucet and splashed water over her face and throat. Without turning around, she spoke: "Rape is an unspeakable travesty, something that a woman doesn't forget, something that changes her life forever. I can only imagine what a young, inexperienced girl must feel when something like that happens to her. The advantage you have is that you will recover, Kate. Your experience here, in the twentieth century, has given you strengths and strategies not even imagined in Catriona's time. You will not blame yourself."

"Are you saying that I should deliberately go back and endure it?"

Maura turned around. She crossed her arms against her chest to stop her trembling. "Do you have an alternative?"

Drawing a deep breath, Kate held it inside her lungs for a long time before exhaling. She looked around the room, taking mental notice of the pots hanging from the ceiling, the hum of the refrigerator, the glow of the light from the modern bathroom off the kitchen. She thought of her sister, her nephew, the languid pleasure of sipping margaritas on the sun-steeped sand of a California beach, all she had, all she knew. A painful knot formed in her stomach. "Will I remember anything when I return?" she whispered.

"I don't think so. What you will gain is something you've never had before: peace of mind."

"Will I know you?"

Maura's mouth curved. "You have the Sight. We'll grow to know each other very well."

"Then I won't say goodbye."

Wisely, Maura remained silent. She watched as Kate flattened her palm and stared directly into the stane.

When Cat awoke she was in her own bed at Ravenswood and someone had taken her clothes. It was dark and she felt a curious tingling in her blood, as if something inside her vibrated, giving her courage and power. A single candle burned on the side table and a maid sat in a chair by the hearth. When Cat sat up, clutching the sheets around her, the woman left the room without speaking.

Tying the sheet into a knot over her breasts, Cat stood up and searched for more candles. She found three in the drawer of the press and lit them. Then she walked over to the glass. It was still too dim to see clearly, but something was different. She studied her face, molding the planes with her palms. She had grown up during her months in Scotland. The childish roundness was gone, leaving sharp, high-boned cheeks and shadowed hollows. Her lids were heavier and her mouth turned down more than it had before, but it was the look in her eyes that stunned her. Those eyes were not the eyes of the woman who had pleaded for sanctuary at the feet of Jamie Stewart a brief year past.

Neville entered the room. His eyes narrowed when he saw her standing, surrounded by candlelight. Recovering quickly, he began removing his clothing until he was completely naked. "I hope you'll be sensible this time, Catriona," he said, sucking in his stomach. " 'Tis a wearisome thing to always be locking you inside a darkened room before you agree to share your favors."

She waited for the familiar panic to raise its head. When it didn't, she lifted the candle and studied Neville's nude body. "Would you say you are experienced with women, my lord?"

He eyed her cautiously. Catriona did not usually ask questions. "Experienced enough."

"Do you bring them pleasure?"

"Your mother never complained."

The candles flickered, throwing long shadows against the wall. She continued to measure him, her eyes moving from the narrow shoulders and hairless chest to the slight fullness at his middle. That was new. Neville was normally too disciplined to carry extra weight.

"My mother had but two men in her bed, my lord. How would she know to complain?"

"And you know so much?" he scoffed. Neville was beginning to feel uncomfortable.

She nodded at his shrinking manhood. "You are so very small, my lord—in the way of men, I mean."

Furious, he reached for her, moving quickly, grabbing her wrists and dragging her to the bed. "Enough!" he panted, forcing her down. The sheet fell away. Sucking in his breath, he ran his hand down her neck and over one breast and lowered his head to the smooth curve of her throat. "I had forgotten how lovely you are," he murmured.

Instead of cringing, Cat spoke calmly: "Patrick will kill you even though there is little need."

He felt himself go soft. Damn the woman. Neville lifted his mouth from her throat and waited, pretending interest in her words.

"There are men at the Scottish court who know the art of lovemaking, my lord," she said matter-of-factly. "They teach others less adept, men like yourself. Of course, you are older and smaller and have not their . . . advantages," she finished delicately. "But perhaps you might learn enough to keep a woman awake."

His face burned. "What is this perversion you speak of?"

" 'Tis no perversion," Cat assured him, surprising herself with the fluidity of her falsehood. "Nobles send their sons to them, that they will learn to keep their wives satisfied." She smiled coyly. "I'll warrant they could keep a harem satisfied."

He drew back, horrified. "The MacKendrick encouraged you in this?"

She nodded. "At first. Since our marriage, there has been no need. Patrick is an exceptional lover."

Furious at her casual dismissal of his prowess, he pulled her head back and ground his mouth against hers, thrusting deeply with his tongue. His hands, rough and punishing, were everywhere. "Do they teach women as well, Lady Bothwell?" he panted, moving between her legs.

Inner forces gathered together, doubling her strength. Cat forced herself to remain remote. "Of course, m'lord." Deliberately she reached down, cupped him cruelly for an instant and released him. He was still not fully aroused. "You are no longer young, Neville. Patrick has taught me well, but I cannot perform miracles." The incredible words came out as if she'd practiced them over and over for just this occasion.

His breathing came in short, shallow gasps. "Now that you are a whore, Catriona, you have a vicious tongue. Very soon you shall show me what you've learned."

"As you will, my lord." Cat clasped her arms behind her head and stared at the ceiling while William attempted to raise his manhood. Concentrating, she removed herself from the heaving body on top of her. Patrick's image rose in her mind. She could see him as clearly as if he stood before her, tall and dark and leanly muscled. His eyes were amused and the slashing grooves in his cheeks deepened as a look of tenderness turned the corners of his mouth into a smile. There was no one else in all the world with whom he shared that smile, not even Isobel. William Neville, with his bony shanks and grasping mouth, could not touch her. Nothing could mar what had always been there from the very beginning. The strange coupling of the border lord and a green-eyed English lass from King Henry's court was written in destiny.

Cat's heart and mind were far away. What was happening here in her childhood bed had nothing to do with her life. She was Patrick MacKendrick's wife, and he was more of a man than she had ever hoped to find. He knew from their wedding night that she wasn't a maiden, and yet he had never reproached her, never accused her of lying to him, never questioned who her lover had been. He had taken her as he found her, and if he was less than satisfied with their bargain, he had never spoken of it. Not until the day she had betrayed him and helped Andrew Percy escape. Cat didn't notice when Neville rolled off of her.

Breathing heavily, he refused to look at her, his face rigid with rage and shame. Never before had his body failed him in this way.

"Are you finished, my lord?" she asked sweetly. "I couldn't tell."

Slowly, his lungs filled with air and his rage abated. There was something different about her, he thought, something he couldn't quite identify. He sat up and stared at her. "You've changed, Catriona," he said at last.

She returned his look. There was pity in her eyes. Patrick would kill him. William Neville was a despicable man, but she wouldn't rejoice at his death. Her mother had loved him, and in his own way, Neville had been a good husband to her. There was something she had to tell him, and it would give her a good deal of satisfaction.

"I no longer fear you," she said. "I know that whatever you've forced upon me is no longer of consequence. You know little of bringing a woman pleasure, William."

For a moment Cat thought he would strike her. Then he rose from the bed and, without bothering to pull on his clothing, stalked out of the room. She felt curiously spent, as if she had carried a tremendous burden for a great distance and it had finally been lifted from her.

Tomorrow she would learn the truth about Richard. The servants would know where he was. Turning over onto her stomach, she fell asleep.

Patrick was three leagues north of London when he heard the news of Maggie Drummond's death. The courier, sent by Glenkirk, had ridden through the night to catch up with him before he reached the city. The MacKendrick bowed his head, allowing himself a moment of grief for the lovely young woman who had graced Jamie Stewart's life for such a brief period of time.

Maggie had been a child of light and flame and laughter. Her heart was as warm as wild honey. Those she loved, she loved forever. She had had the misfortune to give her heart to the king of Scotland, and in the end it had killed her. Not for a moment did Patrick believe Maggie's death was unintentional. The monarchs of Spain, France and England all had marriageable daughters. Alive, Maggie Drummond was an obstacle in their path.

Perhaps it was better this way, Patrick reflected. Maggie would never grow old. She would never live to see her beauty fade and her lover turn to others, fairer and younger than she. Her child would never know the shame of the bastard brand and she would be spared the anguish of watching Jamie pledge his vows to a woman more suitable to be queen of Scotland. He remembered the regal beauty of Elizabeth Woodville's granddaughter. Now there was a woman fit to be Scotland's queen! She would handle Jamie's women and his temper with one frosty, contemptuous glance.

Patrick urged his mount forward once again, giving a silent thanks to the shrewdness of Alexander Hepburn. Glenkirk had thought quickly and used Maggie's unforeseen death to his advantage. Patrick now had a powerful bargaining tool with which to secure Cat's release and her brother's as well.

Not by the merest flicker of an eyelash did King Henry reveal his surprise when Patrick crossed the throne room and knelt before him.

"Did you ever leave London at all, my friend?" he asked.

"Indeed I did, Your Grace," Patrick replied, taking the offensive. "But when I returned home, I realized something essential to my happiness and peace of mind was left behind in London."

Henry was intrigued. "What could be so important that you would ride from London to Edinburgh and then back again without even a single night's rest?"

"My wife." The words, clear and loud, echoed throughout the chamber.

"'Tis a serious thing to misplace a wife," Henry agreed, surveying a large emerald on his finger. The stone caught the light, throwing long green lines on the polished floor. Its color reminded him of Catriona's eyes. His lips thinned in disapproval. "Do you have reason to believe she is here?"

Patrick nodded. "I do. She left Scotland believing her brother was imprisoned in the Tower."

"He was charged with sedition for aiding the Pretender," Henry explained.

"Was there proof?" Patrick's clipped words challenged him.

"There was. The boy's stepfather provided me with a letter sent from Mary Gordon."

"May I see the letter?" Patrick asked.

Henry's eyes narrowed. "Why?"

Patrick looked into the thin face and pale, angry eyes of England's king. Assessing Henry's mood, he wiped his face clear of all expression and changed the subject.

"I bring news, Your Grace," he said smoothly. "The Mass for Maggie Drummond's soul will be held tomorrow at noon. 'Tis a bit premature, but we may bring peace between our two countries after all."

The king's eyes gleamed. "Will Jamie take my daughter?"

Patrick nodded. "I believe I can persuade him." He grinned. "When he sees the Princess Margaret, he will need very little persuasion. Give him time to grieve. Our Jamie loved the lass, but he is a canny ruler. He will do what is best for Scotland."

"I would have them wed soon," Henry protested.

"Perhaps a proxy marriage?" suggested the MacKendrick.

Henry rubbed his chin. "I would agree to that. Take my message, MacKendrick." He laughed. "By God, you did bring news."

"There is still the matter of my wife," Patrick reminded him gently.

Underlying the MacKendrick's soft voice was the unmistakable hint of a threat. Henry swallowed and cursed himself silently for sending Cat to Ravenswood. He needed the border lord's support. If Neville had harmed a hair of Catriona's head, it would go ill for England. He risked another furtive glance at the set, implacable face of the Scot and groaned inwardly. There was nothing left to do but tell the truth.

"Catriona is at Ravenswood," he said.

Patrick's eyes blazed a furious silver. For a moment Henry forgot he was a king and feared for his life.

"Why would she be there, Your Grace?"

"'Tis not unusual for a woman to visit her childhood home." Henry knew his excuse sounded weak.

"She came for her brother," Patrick persisted. "Has she seen him?"

Henry squirmed under the flintlike gaze. "I told her Richard had returned to Ravenswood."

Patrick strode to the throne, towering over the thin, frail body of England's king. "You forced her to place herself in the hands of a man she hates and fears." His fingers itched to wrap themselves around Henry's scrawny throat.

"The circumstances were not as they are now," Henry

protested. "Even now, Jamie waits at Newcastle to wrest my throne from me in the name of this Pretender who claims to be Richard of York." His hands clutched the arms of his throne. "You would have done the same thing, MacKendrick. Catriona and her brother share the same bloodline as Jamie Stewart. They are powerful hostages. I merely used the weapons at hand to my advantage."

"You know little of Jamie Stewart." Patrick's voice was filled with scorn. "By God, the man ordered his father killed! He would sell his own mother to the devil if he thought it would benefit Scotland. Bring me the boy," Patrick ordered. "If Cat is harmed, I suggest you make other plans for your daughter. I'll not rest until every trace of the House of Tudor is wiped from England."

Patrick's throat went dry at his first sight of Richard Wells. He was very like his sister. It could have been Cat standing there before him in the small chamber. Richard shared the same slight, proud carriage, the same molding of the face, the same thick, wavy black hair. Only his eyes were different. They were a light, clear amber, the color of aged whiskey. When the boy threw back his head and arrogantly demanded to know why a Scots border lord should have any interest in the earl of Ravenswood, Patrick almost laughed out loud. A man would have to be blind to miss the Stewart stamp on this young noble.

"I'll warrant 'tis something of a shock," Patrick agreed, "but the fact is, your sister is my wife. At this moment she is at Ravenswood, demanding your freedom."

They were standing in Richard's rooms in the Tower. Although not as lavish as a castle chamber, it was by no means an unpleasant place to be imprisoned. A fire burned comfortably on the hearth, and thick rugs and tapestries prevented the room from losing its heat. A large feather bed dominated the available space and several books rested on a table near the door.

Richard's face whitened. "If Cat is indeed at Ravenswood, m'lord, we should be there as well. Neville is a hard man, and my sister has always feared him."

The gray eyes narrowed imperceptibly. What did the boy know? Wiping all expression from his face, Patrick smiled pleasantly. "An excellent idea. We'll leave at once. Cat will be pleased to see you well."

Across a forest thick with marsh and wild game, Richard led the way into the south of England. He set a hard pace, refusing to stop for food or water until the MacKendrick called a halt.

"The horses need refreshment, lad," he said. "They'll not last the journey otherwise." He caught a glimpse of the boy's face. It was pinched and white in the moonlight. Patrick frowned.

"Perhaps you should tell me what is driving you so desperately," he said. "Surely a few hours will make no difference."

"Won't they?" Richard's laugh was bitter. "I prayed for the day when Catriona would leave Ravenswood. Neville made her life a living hell." His face worked and a small, choked sob escaped from his lips. "I could do nothing for her."

Patrick dismounted and called to his men to tether their horses. He walked to Richard's mount and lifted the boy to the ground as if he weighed no more than Isobel.

"Come, lad," he ordered, leading him to the shelter of a thick oak tree. "Sit down and tell me what it is that troubles you."

Richard's lower lip trembled. For a long time he had only himself to rely on. It was difficult to trust a stranger, even one who claimed to be Cat's husband. Still, he thought, it would be a relief to transfer the weight to shoulders far more suited to carrying the burden that had shadowed his young life for longer than he cared to remember.

"It began when my mother was ill," he began hesitantly. "Before that, Neville wasn't actually unkind to us; he just behaved as if we didn't exist. He was younger than Mother. I suppose half-grown children were an embarrassment to him."

Patrick listened intently, encouraging Richard with his interest. The boy's words, halting at first, gathered momentum as he gained confidence.

"I don't remember exactly when my stepfather's behavior

toward Catriona changed," he continued. "One night something woke me. I listened for a long time but didn't hear anything. The next morning Cat didn't come down for breakfast. I went to her room and she told me that she was ill. Later, I found her in the rose garden. She had been crying, but I assumed it was over our mother."

The blood pounded in Patrick's temples and his hands began to sweat, but he kept his silence.

"If you had only known my sister before our father died." Richard's face glowed with warmth. "There was no one like her—no woman at least," he amended. "She rode and ran and laughed like a man. She wasn't vaporish or stupid or ungenerous, and whenever she passed by, people smiled." His eyes were bright with unshed tears. "Ravenswood hasn't been the same since William Neville married my mother." His lower lip trembled. "It wasn't my father's death that made the difference. It was because Cat no longer laughed."

The boy's fists clenched. "He hurt her, MacKendrick. Cat was afraid of the dark. When she defied him, he locked her in a room without even a candle. He did it to break her spirit. When she cried out, begging for release, he would go to her. Sometimes he stayed for hours. Cat was like a shadow of her former self after those visits. She refused to discuss what he did to her." Richard's head dropped into his hands. "I couldn't help her. Even the servants were afraid of Neville. After a while, Cat seemed more like the sister I remembered. It was as if she separated herself into two different people: cold and silent around Neville, and warm and loving during his absence."

Richard's eyes met the MacKendrick's. "Is it possible that she made herself forget that part of her life altogether?"

Patrick nodded. He didn't bother to spare the boy. It was obvious from his tale that Richard understood the enormity of what his stepfather had done. "If the experience is ugly enough," Patrick explained, "a man may put aside what he has seen or done in order to survive. It is entirely possible that Catriona has done the same."

"What will you do to him, m'lord?" whispered Richard.

For a moment something flickered in the hard, gray eyes

of the border lord, and a thin white line appeared around his lips. When he spoke, his words were simple and direct and without compromise.

"Why, I shall kill him, of course."

❧ 27 ❧

A pile of stones that once marked the walls of an ancient monastery dotted the Cornish coast. At the point where St. Michael's Mount juts out of an angry ocean, Mary Gordon stood looking out at the horizon. She was alone. Her vision centered on a small boat coming directly toward her. The wind keened over the dark water and a flock of gulls circled in the gray sky.

A gust of wind tipped the sails of the small vessel. Mary could see two men in the hull. Their oars moved in cadence and, catching the swell of a mighty wave, the boat landed with a graceful surge on the wet sand. The men disembarked and walked toward her.

She bit her lip. Finally, news had come.

"M'lady," the soldier gasped and stopped. Confronted by the fear in those violet eyes, the words he had rehearsed were difficult to speak.

"Tell me," she ordered.

The soldier swallowed. "We were met by several thousand Cornishmen to aid our cause." He stopped to catch his breath. "Then we marched on Exeter but found the city closed against us. His Lordship ordered the gates burned, but the citizens repelled us."

Mary's mind wandered. Was this really she, Mary Katherine Gordon, daughter of the earl of Huntly, on this forsaken strip of English coastline? Had she really ever doubted that another end was possible?

"English reinforcements came from London," the soldier

continued. "The duke fled, leaving the Cornishmen without a leader."

Mary wet her lips. "Where is my husband?"

"He sought sanctuary in the abbey at Beaulieu. The king's forces have surrounded it. Henry has given orders for your arrest, m'lady." He gestured toward the boat. "We have little time if we are to escape."

"No." Mary shook her head. "I am through with running. I go to Henry."

The soldier's mouth turned down impatiently. "I would advise against it, m'lady."

"Nevertheless," she insisted, "I shall wait for the English troops to take me to their king."

Wine flowed in the streets of Exeter. A holiday had been declared. Henry had ridden through the streets, thanking the citizens for repelling the Pretender. Crowds lined the thoroughfares anxious for a sight of their king. They were surprised and disappointed at the thin, graying man who smiled his pleasure through broken teeth.

Two hours later, a hush fell over the crowd as Mary Gordon rode through the fire-blackened gates. Several days before they had seen her husband and rejected his appeal, but they had never seen her. She was granddaughter, niece and cousin to three kings. The paleness of her complexion only enhanced the beauty of her black hair and deep blue eyes. More than one woman smiled kindly and called out an encouraging word. Mary Gordon was married to the Pretender, but she was also a Stewart; and James of Scotland, that fascinating and unpredictable monarch, waited at the English border with an army.

At the entrance to the mayor's house, a soldier lifted her to the ground. The staring crowd parted as she climbed the steps. All sound inside the hall ceased. Slowly, Mary walked to where Henry sat with his nobility and sank to her knees before him.

King Henry had no mercy for traitors, but he was a father as well as a king. The sight of Mary's beautiful worried face gentled him. The Pretender was imprisoned in London. Henry had won the battle. He could afford to be generous to Jamie's cousin.

"Welcome, my dear," he said kindly.

"Thank you, Your Grace." Mary's voice was low and soft, the Scots burr faint but recognizable.

Henry frowned. What should he do with her? Suddenly he knew. "I shall send you to serve my queen," he said.

Mary nodded. "As you wish, Sire."

At that moment the doors opened. Mary did not turn her head, but she noticed that the king smiled.

"Welcome, Sir Andrew," he said. "The lady you asked about is here, after all."

A familiar voice reached her ears and strong hands lifted her to a standing position. Unbelievably, Mary turned to face Andrew Percy. He was older and more handsome than she remembered.

He smiled and the brown eyes twinkling down at her were filled with a warmth she didn't recognize.

Mary colored and looked down. "Hello, Andrew," she said quietly. "Why are you here?"

Andrew forgot he was in the presence of his king and a dozen of the most powerful nobles in England. He forgot that he meant to go slowly, to win her trust and then her heart. She was so lovely and so brave standing there amidst her enemies that he blurted it out all at once.

"I've thought of nothing but you since the day you helped me escape." He lifted her hand to his mouth and kissed her palm. "I was a boy, Mary, with a boyish infatuation." His voice deepened. "Now I am a man."

A cough interrupted him. For the first time Andrew became aware of his audience. They listened in interested silence, hanging on his every word. With a rueful grin, he bowed from the waist and excused himself. Taking Mary's hand, he led her into a small retiring room at the end of the hall and closed the door firmly behind them. His hands resting on her shoulders, he spoke earnestly.

"I know what I tell you is premature and probably cruel as well," he said. "But I cannot wait any longer. Warbeck will be executed. At this very moment Glenkirk is on his way with a message from Jamie. You are to be returned to Scotland unharmed."

The pressure of his hands increased. "I'll follow you if I must, but I would rather you stay in England with me."

Mary was sure she had misunderstood. Her eyes, purple in the shadows, clouded with confusion. "What are you saying?" she whispered.

"I want you to be my wife," replied Andrew. "Please, say yes."

The smile started at the corners of her lips. Within seconds the well of happiness inside her heart had burst and her whole face glowed with an inner light.

"Oh, Andrew," she breathed. Tears brimmed in her eyes and spilled over onto her cheeks. "I know 'tis dreadfully sinful to be thinking of my own happiness when Warbeck is in such trouble." She hid her face against his shoulder. The rich cloth of his tunic muffled her words. "I can't help it. Nothing would make me happier than to stay in England and become your wife."

With shaking hands, Andrew drew her into his arms and buried his face in her hair.

"I'm so pleased about the bairn, m'lord," Mary said, "but 'tis hard to think of Janet as a mother."

"You wouldn't find it so difficult if you saw her," replied the earl of Glenkirk. He had arrived two hours before to rescue Mary from the clutches of Henry Tudor. Imagining that she would be only too grateful to leave England, he was surprised to hear she had other plans. "Are you sure, lass? Janet expects you. She misses you dreadfully and is anxious to show you your nephew."

Mary remained steadfast in her resolve. "Soon I'll have bairns of my own," she said. "Give Janie my love and tell her she'll always be welcome in England."

Alex, looking at the slender beauty before him, marveled at the change in her. Mary was no longer a timid young girl standing in the shadow of her vibrant older sister. She was a woman, and the last several months had changed her irrevocably. He knew her answer was final. Anxious to get on with his task and remove himself from the land of his enemies, he stepped forward to kiss Mary's cheek.

"I have an audience with the Princess Margaret," he said brusquely. "Two days hence, I'm to wed her by proxy for Jamie. Henry wants the wedding to take place immediately. Our Jamie is too canny a king to let such an opportunity slip out of his hands, but Maggie Drummond's death shook him to the core. The princess will not be received in Scotland for at least a year."

Mary smiled warmly. "Take care, m'lord."

Glenkirk bowed and left the room.

Margaret Tudor was too angry to speak. No one, looking at the serene expression on her face, would have guessed that the brilliant sparkle in her eyes was due to a blind, all-consuming rage. For long moments the jewel-bright eyes rested, unseeing, on the man kneeling at her feet.

Alexander Hepburn was nonplussed. Henry's daughter was not what he had expected. Rumor had prepared him for her beauty. Elizabeth of York's bloodlines were strong. The MacKendrick had reported that Margaret also had a keen mind and pleasant manners. Where were they now? Glenkirk wondered. Why didn't the lass speak?

"Pardon me, my lord," Margaret apologized at last. "Your request took me by surprise. Naturally, I assumed my bridegroom would represent himself at his own wedding." The blue eyes were as cold as shards of splintered glass. "How foolish of me to expect such a thing."

"His Grace meant no offense to Your Highness," mumbled Alex.

"No?" With a twist of her hips, Margaret settled back in her chair. "What did he mean?"

Sweat beaded on Alex's brow. His accent was very strong. "I canna' speak for the king."

Margaret's lip curled. "Of course you can." She brushed aside his protest. "If you can marry for him, you can certainly speak for him."

Glenkirk put up his hand. God's blood, but he'd had enough. His mind was not equipped to spar with women whose razor-sharp tongues put a man at a disadvantage. Give him a strong sword and a good horse and he would meet any man anywhere in a fair fight.

"Please, lass," he began. Flushing in horror at his breach of etiquette, he tried to make amends. "Forgive me, Your Highness."

She laughed unexpectedly, and Alex was struck by the clear, melodious sound of her voice.

"You trip over your own words, Glenkirk." She leaned forward, her eyes pinning him to his place on the floor. "Would it be so very hard to tell me the real reason my betrothed sends you in his place?"

Alex waged a war with his conscience. Henry had offered his daughter and James had accepted. Nothing could stop the wedding now. What harm would there be in telling Margaret the truth? She was, after all, a royal princess and would not expect her marriage to be a union of hearts. He wet his lips.

"His Majesty has suffered a great personal loss," he said at last. "His mistress, the Lady Margaret Drummond, was poisoned. She died along with her unborn child."

The haughty, beautiful face didn't change by so much as the flicker of an eyelash. Margaret stood up and walked to the window. Glenkirk was still on his knees. The cold dampness of the stone floor seeped through his hose. Damn the woman, he cursed silently. What was she thinking?

"Thank you," she said after long moments had passed. Her voice was devoid of all expression.

He waited on the floor, his legs cramping beneath him.

She turned. "Rise, m'lord, and take a message to your king." Her expression was remote. For a moment Glenkirk could see her father in the regal, composed bones of her face.

"Tell him that I understand his grief and that the respect he shows the memory of his mistress does him great credit." Her voice lowered. "Tell him also that I accept you as his emissary and I agree to stay in England for the period of a year after the marriage."

Margaret crossed the room to stand before him. She was very close. Never had he seen a woman with eyes so blue and skin so fair. The scent of her perfume distracted him. He couldn't place it.

"Tell him this, Glenkirk." Her voice was as smooth as sandalwood. "I do not hold it against him that he mourns another woman. It rather pleases me that he is capable of such depth of feeling." Her lips parted in a smile that never reached her eyes. "Tell him that I also have a condition: The moment I step across the border, his whoring will stop. I'll not have my husband's bastards populating the whole of Scotland."

Her hand moved to his arm. Immediately he covered it with his own. She had the face of an angel, and Alex was sorely tempted. If she had been other than a royal princess, if he wasn't a man of honor, if Janet and the bairn did not wait for him at Edinburgh, he would have thrown caution to the winds and done what any normal man would do, alone in a room with a beautiful woman.

"If my conditions do not meet with his approval," she continued, "the marriage will be annulled."

She leaned even closer until they breathed the same air. Her voice was the seductive caress of a siren. "You will tell him that for me, won't you, m'lord?"

Glenkirk swallowed. "Aye, Your Highness," he muttered hoarsely. "I'll tell him."

Two days later, after the private ceremony uniting the king of Scotland and Margaret Tudor in marriage, the earl of Glenkirk rode across the moors toward Edinburgh. He was anxious to see Janet and his son. As the hooves of his horse clattered against the cobblestoned streets of the esplanade, it occurred to him that James Stewart had not yet laid eyes on the Princess Margaret.

Alex grinned. Jamie, accustomed to soft and biddable women, was destined for the surprise of his life. With a light heart, he passed through the portcullis gate into the court-yard of the castle.

Ravenswood Manor faced east. The tall gables and slanted rooftops looked black against the setting sun. Pat-rick reined in his horse and momentarily admired the view. No wonder Catriona loved it so. Far from marauding armies, the house had been built for pleasure and comfort. There was nothing of the walled fortress in its graceful lines and delicate architecture. Large, diamond-paned windows caught the dying rays of sunlight. Manicured lawns, green and sweet smelling, surrounded whitewashed brick walls, and in the artistically arranged flower beds roses of every imaginable color bloomed in charming confusion.

There were no sentries posted at the gates. Apparently Neville did not expect him. Patrick's jaw tightened. Sir

William Neville had trespassed. He had dared to lay claim to the border lord's woman. Now he would suffer the consequences. Patrick was past mercy. The remote chance that he would spare Neville's life had died several hours back in the choked confessions and tear-bright eyes of Richard Wells.

Neville's rage, which had abated with a night's sleep and several draughts of cold wine, threatened once again to overcome his reason. Catriona, dressed in a gown of green velvet that matched the incredible color of her eyes, stood before him. The flawless texture of her skin looked very pale against her hair hanging black and unbound to her knees. She looked proud and coldly beautiful.

With a swipe of his hand, Neville knocked the glass decanter to the floor. It broke into a thousand pieces.

"You are very careless with my brother's belongings," remarked Catriona.

"Damn you!" he shouted. "Do you, a mere girl, think to stop me? Where is your mighty lord now, Catriona? Do you really believe he can save you?" He laughed mockingly, his confidence returning. "Perhaps he is glad to be rid of you. What did you tell him on your wedding night when he learned you were not a maid, Lady MacKendrick? Did you lie to him?"

Cat remained silent and Neville smiled with satisfaction.

"Will you be as brave when your husband finds you here alone with me? Can you bring yourself to tell him the way it was with us?"

Her eyes went past him and widened with shock. "It appears you have already told him," she replied coldly.

Neville turned and, for a moment, saw his life flash before him. He briefly considered begging for mercy but immediately discarded the notion.

Patrick MacKendrick stood framed in the doorway. His eyes, a merciless frozen gray, flickered from Neville to Catriona's face.

"If you've harmed my wife, Neville," he said, "I'll kill you now and be done with it."

Neville laughed shortly. "Ah, the mighty border lord comes at last to claim his wife and avenge her shame." He fingered the small dirk in his belt and hoped Patrick wouldn't notice the trembling of his hands. "You presume much, m'lord. I had her first."

Patrick's jaw tightened, and he nodded at Cat. "Are you hurt, lass?"

She shook her head and some of the grimness left his mouth. "This won't take long," he said. "Richard waits outside. Go to him."

Catriona hesitated and he smiled encouragingly. Straightening to her full height, she walked to the door where her husband stood and, for the briefest of intervals, laid her hand on his arm. The look that passed between the two was not lost on Neville. His hands clenched as he watched her leave the room. He waited for Patrick's next words.

"There is something we must settle between us," the border lord said, leaning casually against the door frame.

"Don't be absurd." Neville's laugh was shaky. "I don't blame you for being angry, MacKendrick. A man who finds his wife has played the whore has a right to settle the score. But the fact is, Henry promised Catriona to me. We were lovers before she left for Scotland. I had no idea she would throw me over for bigger game."

As clearly as if it were happening at that moment, Patrick heard once again Catriona's piercing screams. He saw her cold, still body lying on the floor and the scarlet gash marring the flesh of her wrists. The muscles of his face tightened. "Say your prayers, m'lord," he said. "Your fate is sealed."

"How can you be sure I've lied?" Neville taunted.

"I know my wife," answered the MacKendrick. "Nothing on earth would move her to share your bed."

Neville flicked the lace of his cuffs. "You overrate yourself, MacKendrick. She did so last evening quite willingly. Ask the servants if you will. There were no signs of struggle, no tearful protests."

Patrick lifted his sword and moved forward slowly. Neville backed away toward the freedom of the door.

" 'Tis too late for escape," said the MacKendrick. "Make your peace, Neville. Today you will die."

"Would you kill an unarmed man?"

Patrick shrugged. "Armed or unarmed, it makes little difference to me. I intend to finish you."

"For God's sake, man." Neville wet his lips and stepped behind a table. "Allow me the use of my sword. Let this fight be a fair one."

"Very well."

Neville reached for the sword hanging on the wall above the mantel. Pulling it down, he made a sudden dash for the door. Patrick lunged after him, and Neville lifted his sword to protect himself.

Neither man spoke. Neville was small and slight and remarkably agile on his feet. He fought desperately, beside himself with fear. The MacKendrick guarded his strength, seeking only to defend against the other man's thrusts. He parried several quick lunges to his ribs, deflecting the lightning-swift sword that could never quite find its mark.

Patrick fought carefully. His reach was longer. Gradually he forced Neville back against the wall. With a deft movement, he slid his sword past his opponent's defense and pierced his heart with a fatal thrust. Neville fell to the floor, dying instantly.

Swiftly, Patrick wiped his sword on the dead man's coat and walked to the door. "Your master is dead," he said to the frightened manservant who appeared at his elbow. "See to him."

The servant bowed. "Aye, m'lord."

Patrick walked through the long corridor and peered into several rooms. All were empty. He heard voices. The main door of the manor was open. He walked through it and stood on the steps. Catriona was mounted astride his stallion. She wore a riding habit. Richard was beside her.

Patrick grinned. "Were you going somewhere, lass?" he asked.

Cat sighed with relief. "You were an age, m'lord," she scolded. "I feared we would be leaving for Hermitage without you."

The last doubt in Patrick's mind faded away. There had been no possibility of another ending, but Catriona didn't know that. In case of his death, she had planned to flee the country and return to Scotland.

"Shall we be on our way tonight or stay and leave in the morning?" he asked.

Cat looked at the white walls and stately gables of the manor. "I never stopped loving it," she said softly, "but 'tis no longer home." She reached over to place her hand on her brother's. "It belongs to Richard. Later, when he's a bit older, he'll return to claim it. Perhaps the memories of the past few years will have faded by then." She met her husband's gaze directly. "I would rather ride for home."

Patrick swung up on his mount in back of Catriona. "What say you, Richard?" he asked. "Would you like to pay us a long visit?"

"If you wouldn't mind, sir," the boy replied shyly.

Patrick laughed. The world seemed very bright. "I should like it above all things. You'll be happy with us. Hermitage is as fine a place as any to grow up."

Cat bit her lip as she realized Patrick hadn't been home since the fever had claimed so many of his own. Not once had he mentioned Brenna Sinclair. Did he know of her death? Where had he been when the population of Hermitage had been so cruelly diminished? Cat's thoughts strayed to Alison Douglass, and her resentment grew. All was not settled between them. Patrick had a great deal of explaining to do.

Leafy branches brushed at their heads. The foliage was thick and lush, the trees set close together in a seemingly impenetrable forest. Patrick knew they would ride another hundred yards before coming out onto the moor. Catriona's head had fallen against his shoulder. She was asleep. It was after dark and past time to camp for the night.

Lifting his hand, he signaled for his men to stop. Without a word, they slid from their horses, wrapped themselves in their plaids and stretched out on the ground. Patrick threw a blanket to Richard and watched as he gathered an armful of leaves for a pillow. The MacKendrick's lips twitched. It was a good thing the lad had come with them to Scotland. He was soft but he would learn.

Catriona awoke as Patrick carried her to a grassy spot and tucked a blanket around her. Their eyes met and held.

"What is it, lass?" They were far enough from the others to avoid being overheard.

"Is Neville dead?" she whispered.

"Aye, he is dead." His eyes flickered to where the shirt had slipped from her shoulder. Purple fingermarks stained the white of her skin.

She flushed and pulled up her sleeve, wondering what he thought of that other more shameful blemish that she had tried so very long to hide.

His voice was cool, his eyes a cold, implacable gray. "Is there anything else you wish to tell me?"

"No." Cat shook her head. " 'Tis over. He cannot hurt me again."

Patrick's face was as inscrutable as ever as his eyes moved over her. Cat knew by the sudden flickering in the icy depths that he knew all there was to know about those years when she had been at the mercy of William Neville.

The bitter anger in his voice startled her. "I would that he were alive again. A swift sword thrust was too merciful an end."

Cat was very weary. "I no longer wish to speak of it."

Patrick swore fluently. "Why did no one help you?"

"There were only servants and they wouldn't have dared," she replied. "Long ago I found that protesting only gave Neville greater pleasure. I learned to separate myself from it, as if the whole unpleasant deed was happening to someone else. Last night, something changed. I was no longer afraid of him. He knew that and it made the difference." Cat looked at the lean, unyielding face of her husband. She swallowed and summoned the rest of her courage. "We are still very lucky, m'lord. I am alive after all and not so very damaged."

Slowly, the cold in his eyes was replaced by warm laughter. "So you are," he said, "and I'm glad of it. Hermitage needs an heir and I need a wife."

Another man, Cat knew, would have answered differently. He would have comforted her with assurances that never again would he leave her alone. He would have expected her to cry anguished tears and wondered why she hadn't taken her life rather than submit to such shame. Deep in his heart he would have considered her damaged beyond repair and fit only to spend the rest of her life behind the cloistered walls of a convent.

But Patrick was not another man. He was her husband, and his smile brought her great comfort. In his eyes, it was as if she had suffered nothing more serious than a fall from her horse while riding on the moors. It seemed to Cat as if the horrible years after her mother's death had never happened and she was as untainted as any virgin bride on her wedding night.

"Did I ever tell you about Mary, my first wife?" he asked abruptly.

Cat shook her head.

"Do you wish to know?"

Again she shook her head.

"Have you no curiosity?" he demanded. "There are rumors that I knew of the danger the night she died. Some say I deliberately left her behind, hoping she would be killed."

Cat gasped. "I don't believe that."

"Why not?"

"You saved Richard. You came for me. A man who would do that isn't capable of leaving his wife and bairn to be butchered."

His eyes were bright with flickering lights. "Bless you for that. I didn't leave her, Cat. She refused to come with me. Our marriage was a lie from the start. She told me she was with child. After Isobel, I couldn't bear the thought of another bairn carrying the bastard taint." His mouth was grim. "Mary and I were married, and by the time I found out that she lied, the deed was done. I would have made the best of it but she knew I'd wed her only for the child. Her vanity couldn't stomach my indifference. I was away much of the time. In my absence she took lovers, more than I can count. I don't know if the child that died with her was mine." His fists clenched. "But she was still my wife. No matter what her sins, I would have fought to the death to save her."

Cat's cheeks were wet with tears. "Surely no one who knows you could think otherwise," she said.

"It matters not what others think." The tiny flames in his eyes hypnotized her. "You are all that matters, Catriona."

"Why?" Her lips formed the word, but the sound wouldn't come. Her heart pounded and her palms were wet. She wanted an answer, but would it be the answer she needed?

Patrick put his hand under her chin and lifted her face. For a moment, Cat thought he would kiss her, but he did not. His eyes moved from her hair to her mouth. She could feel his hand tighten before dropping away. When at last he spoke, Cat looked into his eyes, unable to turn away as the words, raw and naked with repressed longing, rolled off his tongue.

"From the moment I saw you, there has been no other woman in my heart. I live for the sound of your voice. Your laughter is like music. Watching you mothering my child, caring for my servants, having you in my bed, is all of heaven to me. The touch of your hand, the scent of your hair is like nothing else I've ever known." The lean planes of his face were clear in the moonlight. His voice was very low. "The fire you started inside me will not be quenched, lass. I cannot let you go." He drew a deep breath. "I love you, Catriona. Please believe that I've never said that to another woman."

Incredulously, he saw her flashing smile. "Not even to Alison Douglass?" she teased.

He looked startled. "Most definitely not. Lady Douglass was not the kind of woman a man takes to his heart."

Cat frowned. "'Was,' m'lord?"

"You don't know, do you?"

She shook her head.

Patrick whistled softly. "Maggie Drummond, her sister Sybil, and Alison Douglass are dead, Cat. They were poisoned."

"Dear God!" Her hand flew to her mouth.

"Don't look like that, love." The whiteness of her face frightened him. "It could have been worse. Janet was with them, but she drank little wine. She was spared, but it brought on the babe." He lay down beside her and drew her head to his shoulder. "Glenkirk is more than pleased. The bairn is a boy."

"What of Mary?" Cat asked. "Does she know that she is an aunt?" The warmth of his chest was like a drug. She felt her eyelids drop. Patrick's next words caused them to fly open again.

"By now she must. Warbeck is imprisoned in the Tower and James will agree to marry the Princess Margaret, if he hasn't already. No doubt Mary will be given safe passage back to Scotland."

"Margaret Tudor has agreed to wed Jamie?" Shock widened Cat's eyes. They looked like giant emeralds in her pale face.

"Why do you look like that?" Patrick protested. " 'Tis an excellent match. She is a beautiful woman. Jamie will be pleased. Most important of all, there will be peace between our countries."

"England and Scotland will be at peace, if that's what you mean, m'lord, but there will be no peace at the Scottish court."

"Speak your mind, Catriona. Riddles at this hour are beyond me."

"Patrick, I grew up with Margaret Tudor," Cat said with a chuckle. "She's bonny enough, to be sure, but she's also a wildcat. If Jamie so much as looks at another woman, she'll scratch his eyes out and deny him her bed."

A look of dawning wonder crossed Patrick's face. He began to laugh. He laughed until he was weak and spent. Turning on his side, he gathered Cat into his arms and pulled her close. Burying his face in the silky blackness of her hair, he whispered into her ear. "We shall have to stay close to home, my love. I don't think 'tis wise for you and the fair Margaret to spend a great deal of time together. I had hoped to tame you."

Cat smiled into the darkness. There was no need to answer. He knew she would never play the part of a simpering miss. She turned her head and his mouth came down on hers. Once again the flame within her began to burn, and she had no will apart from the urgent demand of his hands on her body and his lips on hers.

Much later, she touched his earlobe with the tip of her tongue. "Patrick," she whispered.

"What is it, lass?"

"Have I told you that I love you?"

The silence was loud in the darkness. She could hear his deep, even breathing against her throat. Pushing away from him, she sat up. "Don't you want to know if I do?" she demanded.

It was too dark to see his grin, but she felt it. "I already know," he said. "But if you feel the need to say it, I'll not protest."

"Your conceit is boundless." Cat pulled the blanket over her shoulder and turned her back.

Warm hands pulled her against him, caressing the curve of her hip and thigh. "Pull in your claws, Cat," Patrick murmured. "I've known of your feelings for a long time." He nuzzled her neck. "'Tis your eyes, lass. They give you away every time. You can never hide anything from me. From the very beginning, I knew what you were up to." Gently, he turned her to face him. "Look at me and tell me you don't love me."

"I don't love you," she repeated automatically.

He laughed triumphantly. "You see, they are no longer green. Whenever you lie your eyes turn gold." His face was very close. "Tell me you love me, Cat. I would hear it now."

She trembled, but not from the cold. "This isn't a game, Patrick," she whispered. "I'll not say the words because you command me."

"Say what you feel, love." He waited quietly, not hurrying her.

Catriona knew the choice was hers. She wanted very much to tell him what was in her heart. It would not be easy. She wet her lips. "I never knew it could be like this between a man and a woman," she whispered. "You are my life, Patrick. I love you beyond belief."

The stars were bright in the sky above, and in the giant oak branches, an owl hooted. But neither of them noticed their surroundings for several moments.

"I promised Isobel I would return," Cat murmured.

"Aye, she wrote me about her mother's death and everything you'd done for her." Patrick's arm tightened around her shoulders. "I owe you a great deal, my love." He yawned. "What I wouldn't give to be in the library at Hermitage this very moment."

"What on earth for?" Catriona demanded.

"Why, to continue with my reading, of course."

His body shook with laughter, and the outraged exclamation forming on her lips died instantly. She smiled into his shoulder. Tomorrow they would be home. Hermitage would abound with food and drink and merrymaking. The years ahead would see the birth of their children, a new century, and a Scotland ruled by that most stubborn and fascinating monarch, Jamie Stewart. The bards would gather their clans before roaring fires and sing the tale of a lass of royal blood who sailed to Scotland and captured the heart of that fearsome warrior of the borders, Sir Patrick MacKendrick. Catriona closed her eyes and slept.

28

Catriona sat in her favorite chair in the nursery and looked out the window at the brilliance of the sun glinting on the silvery waters of the Firth of Forth. The black-haired baby on her lap sucked noisily on his fist and kicked at the blankets confining his legs. Isobel lay on the bed looking at still another book Janet Hepburn had sent from Edinburgh.

Absentmindedly, Cat stroked her son's tiny head and thought of the message she had received earlier in the day. It was an invitation to the coronation of Margaret Tudor, queen of Scotland. Her mouth turned down in a wry smile. Jamie had finally consented to send for his betrothed. Cat could well imagine the emotions of the haughty Tudor princess when she received Jamie's missive. Not once, in the entire year of their betrothal, had James traveled to England to make the acquaintance of his future wife.

Maggie Drummond's death had had a sobering effect on him. No longer an impetuous, carefree monarch, he had given up his wenching and settled down to the serious business of running the country.

Cat had to admit that Jamie had a talent for ruling. Even the rebellious Highlands, ruled by John MacDonald of the isles, were under the thumb of their charismatic young king. All that was left was to produce an heir. And so, with that in mind, Jamie had sent for Henry's daughter.

The door opened. A gust of cold wind swirled into the room and the fire in the hearth blazed to new life. Catriona turned her head at the same time firm lips pressed against her cheek. It was Patrick. She turned her head to meet his searching mouth. He tasted of rain and clean wind. Feelings, long dormant since the birth of her child, flamed within her. She reached up to touch his cheek. The gray eyes gleamed in response. He knew her well. With a frustrated sigh, he looked over at Isobel.

"How is the reading, lass?" he asked.

"Very well, Da," she replied without looking up.

He looked down at the tiny miniature of Catriona that was his son. "And how is the bairn?"

"Always hungry." Catriona laughed. "I'm afraid he's going to be a monstrous size if he doesn't stop eating."

"Size is an advantage on the borders," Patrick reminded her. "He'll need all his inches to hold on to his heritage." He glanced over at his daughter. "Do you think we can prevail upon Isobel to take her brother downstairs for a bit of sun? It's just come out." He lowered his voice so that only Cat could hear. "I very much want to be alone with you."

Her eyes danced wickedly up at him. "Isobel is a biddable child. If you ask her nicely, I'm sure she'll agree."

Isobel stared at the two of them suspiciously. "What will the two of you do when I'm gone?"

"We'll discuss whether to attend the queen's coronation," Cat replied hastily. "The invitation came only this morning."

Isobel slipped from the bed and held out her arms for her brother. "I did want a sister, but he's really very nice," she proclaimed as she headed toward the stairs. "Perhaps Mary will bring her daughter when she visits."

"I'm sure she will," answered Cat, holding open the door.

"If he cries, give him to Morag—she'll know what to do. And be careful on the stairs."

Patrick closed the door firmly and turned toward his wife. His gray eyes were alight with amusement and something else that made her heart beat faster. She moved into his arms and slid her palms under his shirt, reveling in the feel of the hard, sweat-dampened skin.

He bent his lips to her hair. "Cat," he said hoarsely, "are you sure it isn't too soon after the bairn?"

Her fingers were at the laces of his shirt. "I no longer care," she whispered, her mouth on his chest. "This waiting is beyond anything." Dropping his shirt to the floor, she pressed herself against the lower half of his body. He was stiff with need.

"Holy God, lass," he muttered as her hands removed his belt and found the bare skin beneath. He hesitated no longer. Threading his hands through her hair, he pulled her head back and set his mouth against hers, hard. Her response was like the rush of fire on wind. Their tongues entwined and mated, searching the polished edges of teeth, tracing the smooth line of lips, plunging into the dark, inner softness of mouths hungry for each other.

Gasping for breath, Patrick carried her to the bed, and within seconds, Catriona's clothing was on the floor. He gazed in admiring wonder at the changes childbirth had wrought in his wife's body. Cat was no longer boyishly slim. Blind to everything but the fire in his blood, he buried his face in the valley between her lush breasts and without further preamble thrust deeply into her welcoming flesh.

Catriona gasped. Running her hands over the bunched muscles of his back, she moved beneath him. Her teeth grazed his throat and the dam of his control broke. The pent-up need of three long months was spent at last.

Much later, long after the evening meal was served and cleared away, Patrick lifted himself on one elbow and looked down at his wife. How had he come to the unbelievable good fortune of winning such a woman for his own?

Cat's eyelashes fluttered and he watched as she pushed aside the drugging sleep that follows passion. Her eyes, clear and green as the hills of Hermitage, focused on his face. She smiled.

"What must they think of us?" she asked.

"They will think that the laird of Hermitage will be in good spirits again at last," Patrick retorted. "'Tis difficult being a married man."

"Indeed." Cat looked indignant. "Certainly it is no harder than being a married woman. It was I, after all, who had the bairn."

He kissed the tip of her nose. "So you did, my love." He shuddered, remembering the stabbing fear he had suffered as the hours went by and his son refused to make his appearance. "You did a wonderful job of it. I'd not blame you if you refused to have another."

Her fingers traced the prominent bone of his cheek. "That would mean we could no longer do what we just did. I don't think that would please you at all."

Patrick frowned. "You do want more children, don't you, Catriona?" he asked anxiously.

She laughed, a clear, rich sound like the pealing of chapel bells. "We'll have an entire brood of children, m'lord. I promise you that."

He sighed and rested his head on the pillow beside her. Her hair smelled like roses. "What is this about Margaret's coronation?

"She's to be crowned next month at the cathedral in Edinburgh." Cat stroked the smooth muscles of his chest. "We'll go, of course."

Patrick felt her mouth curve into a smile against his shoulder. "What is it?" he asked, lifting his head to look down at her.

Her eyes sparkled. "I'd give the entire estate of Glenkirk to see Jamie's face when he first lays eyes on Margaret Tudor."

The coronation of Margaret Tudor was the political and social event of the decade. Emissaries from all the courts of Europe were present. Every wynd and close of Edinburgh's dark streets was filled with bodies anxious to catch a glimpse of the royal parade scheduled to march down High Street at exactly noon. Not only was Jamie particularly beloved by his people, he was also young and exeedingly handsome. It was rumored that the princess of England was equally blessed.

The fairy-tale mood of the event permeated every tavern and residence within the ancient city. Wine flowed in the fountains. Ribaldry and drunkenness prevailed. All of Scotland was heady with excitement. The one exception to the merriment was the private apartment of the king himself.

Jamie's dark face was a mask of bored politeness. His eyes were blank and his lips set and hard. The tunic of purple velvet draped across his broad shoulders was lined with white ermine. The crown and scepter of Scotland sat on a table by his side. Only his hands, wide and blunt, showed the depth of his emotion. They were clenched around a wine goblet, the knuckles showing pale through the dark skin.

Patrick frowned. If Margaret saw her new husband this way, she would turn tail and run all the way back to London. Scotland needed this alliance. What was the matter with Jamie? He was a king and it had been over a year since Maggie died.

"Jamie." Patrick spoke softly. "It grows late. Henry's daughter has waited an entire year to meet her husband. She will take offense if she must wait any longer."

The king hurled his goblet across the room. It smashed against the mantel, the delicate crystal shattering and falling to the floor. "Damn Margaret Tudor," he muttered savagely, "and damn this coronation. I want no English princess as my queen."

"'Tis too late for that," Patrick reminded him. "She is your wife, wed by Glenkirk's proxy."

"I don't want her." Jamie's mouth turned down sulkily.

Patrick felt a cold rage rise in his chest. For the first time he saw the man to whom he'd pledged his sword as he really was. He fought to keep his voice from reflecting his thoughts. "Would you dishonor a royal princess?" he asked. "She wanted this no more than you. Margaret leaves her home and family to meet a husband she knows mourns another woman. What would it be like for you, Your Grace, if the situation were reversed? Give the lass credit for her courage, at least. It will be no small thing to have the blood of Margaret Tudor flowing through the veins of your sons.

Think of Scotland," Patrick argued, anxiously watching the sun make its ascent in the sky. "Scotland needs an heir. Do this for your country."

The hardness left Jamie's expression. He stood up and shot a rueful glance at the MacKendrick. "As always, you draw me up short, Patrick. I gave my word to Henry and I will honor it." A bleak look appeared in his eyes. " 'Tis just that I feel as if I have betrayed Maggie."

"Janet told me that Maggie's last words to you were to think of Scotland," Patrick reminded him.

"Aye." Jamie nodded his head. "So they were." He straightened to his full height and reached for the crown and scepter. Flashing a grin at his friend, he asked, "How do I look?"

"Like a king, Your Grace," Patrick replied. "Like the most royal of kings."

"Patrick," James said, resting his hand on the border lord's shoulder, "if Cat were dead, would you marry again?"

Patrick thought of the classic, austere beauty of his wife's face. His stomach clenched. "Of course," he lied. "A man needs a wife."

Jamie nodded. "Thank you, my friend."

With a reassuring grin, the MacKendrick preceded his king down the stairs and into the courtyard. A great roar greeted their arrival, and the royal carpet was rolled across the cobblestones.

Stepping aside, Patrick allowed the king to lead the procession. The gates of the castle were thrown open and the crowds along the esplanade moved aside for the royal party. Head held high, James IV of Scotland walked down High Street to meet his bride.

The woman moving toward him came alone, stepping lightly on the blue carpet with swift, graceful feet. She was too far away for Jamie to see her features, but he knew she was tall and slender, with waving, silvery hair flowing past her knees.

Closer and closer they moved. All of Scotland held its breath. Their eyes were not on their king but on the lovely, fair-haired girl who was his wife. As she passed each curve of High Street, the townspeople stared and a collective breathless sigh escaped their lips. Margaret Tudor was as beautiful as a summer dawn.

Jamie walked until he reached the cathedral doors. There he waited for his wife to reach him. She stopped less than four paces from him, and his mouth dropped open. For a long moment he was speechless. Nothing in either Glenkirk's or the MacKendrick's reports had prepared him for this. Margaret Tudor had the face of an angel. Her skin was rose and white, her eyes the deep blue of the North Sea. Her hair was pale blond, a wash of moonlight over the Valley Tay. From a distance she had appeared slender, but her gown of white velvet hugged generous breasts, a small waist and flat stomach.

For the first time since Maggie's death, Jamie Stewart felt a rush of desire. This beautiful woman was his wife. His heart felt light. He would bed her this very night. He smiled. "Welcome to Scotland, Margaret."

Her lips curved, showing even white teeth. His head swam. Her beauty was dazzling. It was hard to look at her face.

"It has been too long, Jamie." She used the familiar address, her voice low and husky. "If you had ceased your sulking and allowed me to come sooner, your foul mood would have disappeared long ago." She looked directly at him, and her eyes flashed blue fire. "Perhaps the heir to Scotland would even now have made his appearance."

James was startled. A deep red stained his cheeks. His eyes narrowed, and he deliberately raked her figure from head to toe. Many an adversary had cowered before that look.

Margaret lifted her chin and stood her ground. "You don't frighten me, Your Grace. My father is Henry Tudor."

For a long moment, warring emotions battled in Jamie's breast. Amusement won. He threw back his head and laughed out loud. By God, this was a woman fit to be queen of Scotland. What children they would bring forth together. Stepping forward, he reached out and drew her into his arms. Before the delighted eyes of five thousand Scots, he kissed her thoroughly. When at last he released her, her face flamed with color and she swayed against him. He kept hold of her hand and his dark eyes glinted as they bore into hers. "Shall we get on with this, Wife?" he growled. "It grows late and we have an heir to get."

With her eyes bright and her smile tremulous, Margaret Tudor lifted her skirts and walked into the cathedral. Her hand still clasped in his, she knelt before the archbishop.

Anointing her head with holy oil, the priest murmured the age-old words of benediction and placed the crown of Scotland on her shining hair.

She felt her husband's fingers tighten on her hand. Her eyes burned with unshed tears. He was dreadfully handsome. More handsome than even she had dreamed. The feel of his blunt hand, warm and strong as it covered hers, reassured her. She was queen of Scotland. Together they would found a dynasty. She was his wife. Together, they would find love.

Maura watched the images fade from Kate's eyes and knew the exact moment when she returned to the present.

Slowly, the girl lifted her head from the table and looked around, struggling to focus. "I wonder what it would have been like growing up here," she said groggily.

Maura wet her lips and spoke carefully. "Very different, I suppose, from the life you knew."

Kate stared. "Did you know my mother?"

"Fortunately for me, I did."

The cobwebs in Kate's brain were nearly gone now. "Did you like her?"

Maura smiled. "I loved her. She left for America when I was a girl, but I never forgot her. Everyone who knew Bonnie Sutherland was blessed. There was a goodness about her that few people have. That's the reason I sent for her when you were born."

A thought, small at first but gaining in magnitude, wiped everything else from Kate's mind. "Would you say that you know the places here on Cait Ness that she knew best?"

Maura looked puzzled. "It's been a very long time, but I suppose I do."

Kate sighed as if a tremendous weight had been lifted from her. "I need to ask you a favor." Under Maura's bewildered gaze, she lifted her backpack to the table, unzipped the zipper and brought out a small package wrapped in brown paper. "They're her ashes," Kate explained. "Not all of them, of course. That wouldn't have been fair to Megan. Mother wanted her ashes to be scattered on Cait Ness. I've been carrying them around everywhere, hoping for inspiration. So far, nothing's come to me." She hesitated. "Would you scatter them for me? Of all the people in the world, I think she would want it to be you."

Maura lifted startled eyes to Kate's face. Her hand crept to her throat. "Why, I can't, I don't, I—" She cleared her throat. "I don't know what to say."

"Say 'yes,' please."

Maura looked into her daughter's face. She had given this courageous young woman life, yet, except for that, not once had she been there, not for even one of the moments that make a woman a mother. Bonnie had been there instead. Suddenly it was quite clear what her answer must be. "I would be honored," she said simply.

Kate pushed the box to the middle of the table and raised her eyes to her mother's face. "Why didn't you keep me?" There. She'd voiced the thought that had haunted her ever since Bill Brockman confessed her mother's secret.

Maura sighed and looked down at her hands. They were slender and fine-boned, the hands of an aristocrat, except for the years of toil evident in every callused crease. "I thought you should have a family who could give you what I couldn't," she said at last. "I wanted you to have two parents. The life I had wasn't the life I wanted for my daughter. Bonnie and Ken wanted a child desperately. They wanted *you.*"

"Hunter would have married you."

"Yes, he would have, and lived to regret it very soon after. I knew nothing of his life, Kate. I grew up here, on Cait Ness, without plumbing and electricity. I'd never driven a car or used a telephone or even seen a city larger that Lerwick. I would have embarrassed him terribly. My pride was greater than that. I couldn't bear to have him ashamed of me. So I lied. I told him he meant nothing more to me than a night of passion. He believed me and married a woman of his own order. The marriage was a success, I believe. At least everyone says so." She looked directly into Kate's green-gold eyes. "Can you ever forgive me?"

All at once it seemed to Kate as if she could. She knew what it was like to feel exposed, less worthy, somehow, than others around her. What Maura had lacked was confidence, and Kate knew enough about that not to throw stones. "And now?" she asked softly. "Will you still tell my father that he means nothing more to you than a night of passion?"

Maura's eyes gleamed with understanding. "Has anyone ever told you that you're particularly wise for your age?"

"Not until now."

"Well, you are." Maura changed the subject. "What about yourself? I have the distinct impression that a certain young man is not about to return Victoria Sutherland's affections as long as you're in the picture."

Kate's laugh was so clear and spontaneous that Maura's heart nearly burst from the joy of hearing it. "Do you love him, Kate?" she asked when her daughter's mirth had subsided.

Kate's eyebrows drew together. "I don't know—I think so, but I'm not sure." She glanced at Maura. "I feel the strongest desire to see him, right now, this very minute."

"Is something stopping you?"

"No."

"Then go to him. What are you waiting for?"

Kate hesitated. "I've spent so much time reserving judgment. Maybe he's tired of waiting."

"There's only one way to find out."

"You sound as if you want to be rid of me."

"Don't you see, Kate? If it's Niall MacCormack you want, I'll never be rid of you, providing that he wants you as well."

"And if he doesn't?"

Maura stood up and walked around the table to slip her arms around her daughter's shoulders. Resting her cheek on the dark head, she spoke softly, as if all the absent years had never been. "You have a home with me for as long as you wish."

Kate held her breath, the tears close to the surface. Finally she spoke: "Thank you. That means more than you know."

Averting her eyes, Maura walked to the sink and began stacking the dishes. "Run along now," she said, her voice huskier than usual. "You can call and tell me all about it later."

With a quick kiss on Maura's cheek, Kate walked out the door and down the hill toward the village. Dawn touched the hillside, blurring the cliff's sharp edges with a pearl-like, netherworld glow. Wisps of silver streaked the sky, and a gentle tide lapped against the shoreline. Kate's nasal passages burned as she sucked in lungfuls of salt-laced, fish-scented air. Fingering the keek stane in her pocket, she stopped occasionally to search the horizon, to rest her hand against a boulder, still warm from yesterday's sun, to cup the petals of a wildflower, its leaves turned toward the light.

Lerwick and Niall MacCormack loomed ahead. An inner source compelled her. She began to run, and she was still running when she reached the MacLean bed and breakfast. Glennis was up and about as usual. "My goodness, Kate." She wiped her floured hands on her apron. "You look positively radiant. Did everything work out well with Maura?"

Kate ignored her question. "Where is Niall?" she asked breathlessly.

Glennis laughed. "Where anyone would be at this hour of the morning if they didn't have a day's worth of baking to start."

Kate ran up the stairs, two at a time. His door was unlocked, as she knew it would be. Stepping inside, she closed it behind her and walked soundlessly across the floor. He was sleeping, a plaid comforter twisted haphazardly around his body, shoulders bare and brown above the white sheets. The sharp lines of his cheeks were shadowed with a hint of dark beard and his expression was troubled, as if his dreams were not the ones he would have chosen to spend the night with. For Kate, everything was suddenly completely clear. She wanted very much to touch him.

Careful not to disturb his sleep, she dropped her jacket on

the floor and slipped between the sheets to curve her body around his warm back. The heat of their joined bodies and the steady, rhythmic pattern of his breathing worked like a drug. Within minutes she had drifted off to sleep.

Niall stretched and tried to turn, but a soft weight pressed against him. Confused, he shifted his body but the weight followed. Not yet completely awake, he reached behind his back, his hand settling on a rounded and very shapely female bottom. He froze. Wide awake now, his mind leapt to a staggering conclusion: He was in bed with a woman. The implication unnerved him. Christ. What had he done? Last night was a blur, but he couldn't have been that far gone.

Framing a disjointed apology in his head, Niall drew a quick breath, turned around and forgot to exhale. Kate. Kate was here, in his bed. Kate, willing, relaxed, eyes closed in sleep, cheeks pink, hands tucked against his body, lips soft and ready, made for the fantasies taking place in his mind at that very moment.

Giving in to the impulse, he bent his head and covered her mouth with his. She stirred, sighing deep in her throat, and parted her lips for his seeking tongue. When at last he lifted his head, his breathing was quick and shallow. A shock of hair fell over his forehead, and his pupils were large and dark with passion.

Opening her eyes, Kate reached up to push his hair back, grazed his cheek with her hand and felt the swift intake of his breath. Their glances met and held, and the heat of that exchange surged like a current to the deepest part of her being.

He pulled the sheet away deliberately, baring her breasts to his hungry gaze. And when his mouth followed his searching hands, tasting and drawing and bringing her to the edge of trembling desire, Kate gave herself up to the mindless pleasure of his body filling her, urging him nearer, harder and deeper, until there was nothing left to do but close around the rocking, pulsing heat of him and explode.

Later, much later, when the edge of his wanting had dulled, Niall rested his cheek against a propped elbow and looked down at the woman he wanted to wake up beside for the rest of his life. Her eyes were closed again and she had a satisfied, cat-in-the-cream look about her. "Your sister called," he said abruptly. "She sounds lovely. I'd like to meet her."

Kate burrowed close to his chest. "Of course you'll meet her," she said sleepily. "Megan is my family. She'll be here for the wedding."

Niall swallowed, unable to believe he'd heard correctly. "The wedding?"

Kate looked up at him through her lashes. "You did tell me that you loved me and wanted to marry me, didn't you?"

"Yes."

"And you did imply that if I didn't love you back you wouldn't see me anymore, didn't you?"

"In a manner of speaking."

Kate sat up. "Well, I would definitely call this seeing me again."

Amusement flickered across Niall's face. She was so transparent. "I had no choice and you know it. Only a saint would have sent you away."

"Are you saying that you don't want to marry me?"

Niall's gaze rested thoughtfully on the smile lurking at the corners of her lips. He ran his finger down her neck and into the valley between her breasts. "That depends," he said softly.

She felt the delicious aching tension begin to pool once more in her stomach. When she spoke, the words came out in a breathless rush. "On what?"

His hand moved to the swell of her breast and his mouth hovered a mere inch above her lips. "On why you've suddenly decided that you want me."

"It wasn't sudden at all—" Her words were cut off by the firm pressure of his mouth on hers. His hand moved to the back of her head, crushing her against him as he kissed and coaxed and teased the soft skin of her lips, the line of her throat, the curve of her breast, until she no longer remembered anything but the touch of his mouth and hands on her skin, the building heat in her blood and the slow, sweet rise of her passion as it flamed into life beneath him.

"Niall," she said, when the fire had ebbed again, "I think children should be raised by two parents, don't you?"

He rubbed his cheek against the top of her head. "You must stop blaming yourself for what happened in the past, love. It worked out for the best."

"I'm not talking about my past." Her words were muffled against his chest.

"I don't understand."

She pulled away to look directly at him. "You do want children, don't you?"

"Very much."

"I'm not using birth control. I didn't think—I mean, there wasn't any reason to—at least," she amended, "there hasn't been, not for a long time."

"I see." His glance moved from her tousled hair to the pillow behind her. "You know I'll marry you," he said gently.

"Yes." She wet her lips. "I know that you would. But do you still want to?"

"I thought I'd made myself perfectly clear. It was your answer neither of us was sure of."

Color burned her cheeks. "I'm sure now," she whispered.

"Because there may be a child?"

Kate shook her head, refusing to look at him.

He lifted her chin. Gray eyes met green. "Then why?"

The words burst from her throat: "Because I love you. I've loved you from the beginning, only I was too stupid to see it. I have such terrible judgment in men."

The smile that began at his lips finally reached his eyes. They blazed with joy and love and something else that drove the air from her lungs.

"I think your luck is about to change, my love." He brushed her lips with his. "In fact I'm sure of it."

Some time later he asked, "Are you sure you won't mind giving it all up?"

"Giving what up?" Like a cat, she purred against him.

"Your profession, your family, the weather in California."

Kate opened her eyes. "I'm not giving up my family. In fact, I plan on inviting them here as soon as possible. I love my sister, and she is married to a wonderful man. And my nephew is the most brilliant and beautiful child on the face of the earth."

The tiny creases around his eyes deepened with laughter. She wanted children. "You're completely objective, of course?"

"Of course."

His smile faded. "What about your job? A lawyer, for Christ's sake. How can you give up something you've worked years to earn?"

"Because I've found something better." She sat up and tucked the sheet around her. "Seriously, Niall, I've never really enjoyed my profession. I'm terrified of arguing a case in the courtroom. I don't think I'm a people person. Research is my love." Her eyes widened as a thought occurred to her. "Why, I can help you! We'll make a great team. I'll research and you'll write." She bit her lip and looked down. "If you want to, that is."

Niall didn't think he could stand any more happiness. He kissed her nose. "I want to very much."

She smiled, delighted at the prospect of her future. "I even have a suggestion for a topic.

"Tell me."

"I'd like to start with the Sutherland gallery. Hunter has a portrait that I'm intrigued with. The woman's name was Catriona Wells. He thinks that she looks like me. Personally, I can't see the resemblance."

Niall stared at her in surprise. "You're being modest. She's beautiful, and she looks exactly like you." He brushed the hair back from her forehead. "Will you ever think of him as your father?"

Kate thought for a minute and then shook her head. "I don't think so. My parents were wonderful people, Niall, both my father and my mother. I don't think anyone, not even someone with my biological gene pool, could replace him. But I would like to get to know Hunter."

Niall groaned. "I've just thought of something: If we research the duke's ancestor, we'll need to spend time at the castle. I don't think I can do it, Kate. Victoria Sutherland's adoration is quite wearing."

"I have the perfect solution: You'll have to marry me immediately. That way she'll know you're taken."

"Is that a promise?"

Kate pressed her lips to his chest. "Yes."

❧ Epilogue ❧

And so it was, just as I have told it. Niall and Kate were married and it appears that both remain content with their choice. The image in the keek stane has vanished for good and no amount of concentration will bring it back. I've studied enough Scottish history to know that the future of the Stewarts was a tumultuous one at best. Better to leave it, Catriona with her husband and children, finally at peace.

The tea kettle's hiss brought me back to the present. Gray light, dawn's harbinger, filtered through the window curtains. I walked to the window and pushed them back. It was nearly morning and I hadn't slept, but the bone-weary dullness that a restless night inevitably brings had not yet touched me.

Taking my cup of tea outside, I sat down on the step and looked out over the glen, savoring the remote beauty of the island. At night, mists creep into the lower valleys and settle like blankets of smoke, turning everything a bleak colorless gray until morning. Then the sun comes, traveling across the sky, bringing light and life and color back to the land. Now the glens were in their half-stages, divided between darkness and light, void and color, waking and sleeping.

I love the mornings when the world is quiet and the day rises clean and pure and filled with possibility. Perhaps, when the tourists leave, I will move back to Cait Ness. My mother's house is closer to the village than the croft on Foula. Now that I'm older, my need for companionship is greater than when I was young.

Long before my eyes picked out the solitary figure climbing the well-worn path, I felt his presence. Even as a child, before I knew what the fluttering in my stomach meant, Hunter

Sutherland had this effect on me. I stood up and walked down the path to greet him, my smile welcoming, my stride sure as a girl's.

He wore the blue-green Sutherland kilt without a jacket. His crest, bearing the motto "Without fear," was pinned to his full-sleeved shirt. The wind whipped the wool plaid around his knees and pulled the linen tight across his chest. He stood lean and straight, the sharp beauty of his hawk's face as clean as it had been thirty years before. Only the dusting of silver in his hair and the slight gentling around his eyes gave his age away. For a brief stabbing moment, I forgot my pride and admitted to envy. The years are kinder to men than they are to women.

"I thought peers of the realm slept much later than this, Your Grace," I teased him when he stopped before me.

Tiny lights flickered in the green of his eyes when he answered me: "The years pass too quickly to waste in a lonely bed."

I felt the fire in my cheeks and changed the subject. "Have you eaten?"

"No."

"Would you care for breakfast? I've toast and porridge."

He grinned and took my hand in his. "Yes. It's what I came for."

Later, after ladling the oats and pouring tea, I sat down and watched him from across the table, curiosity overcoming my appetite. It was the first time I had seen him eat. Fascinated, I watched as his wide capable hands salted cereal and buttered toast. With a complete lack of self-consciousness, he swallowed oats, bit into toast and drank tea. Occasionally his eyes would meet mine, he would smile and continue eating, his mind completely taken with the meal before him.

Gradually, I relaxed. Beneath the umbrella of his approval, I sipped my tea and eventually managed a bite of toast. By the time he had finished his second bowl of porridge and fourth slice of bread, I had managed to finish enough to sustain me until noon.

Finally he sighed, wiped his mouth and pushed the bowl away. "I haven't had porridge since I was a child."

"You certainly haven't lost your taste for it," I remarked dryly as I reached across the table to clear his plate.

He stopped my hand and lifted my chin, forcing me to look at him. "Don't clean up yet. Watch the sunrise with me and then I'll help you."

I could feel my eyes widen. "With the dishes? Don't be absurd. You've never done a dish in your life."

"You're mistaken. Many a night I go down to the kitchen and help myself to a snack. If I leave the evidence, my housekeeper scolds the cook for setting out an insufficient evening meal. I've no wish to see the poor woman chastened."

"Poor Hunter," I mocked him. "What would it be like, I wonder, to have difficulties such as yours?"

"Why not try it and find out?" he asked casually.

"I beg your pardon?"

The olive-green eyes were steady on my face, and now they were not at all casual.

"Come home with me and find out," he said.

My voice sank to a whisper. "You know that isn't possible."

"Then I'll stay here." Still holding my hand, he walked around the table until he stood looking down at me.

"You can't," I protested.

"Why not?"

"It wouldn't be right. We're not—I mean—What would your daughter say?" I asked helplessly.

He pulled me up so that I stood close to the ruler straightness of his chest. "I've told her about us. I'll admit, she was surprised at first, but not as much as you might expect. She's young, Maura. She was more horrified that two people who loved one another as we did had chosen to spend thirty years apart."

I lifted uncertain eyes to his face. "Did she really say that?"

Hunter nodded. "She did. Lately Victoria has made me very happy."

"I'm glad you're happy," I said.

His hands moved up my arms. Fear and hope mingled together in the husky timbre of his voice. "I could be happier. Make me happier, Maura."

For endless seconds, we stared at one another, Hunter and I. And then I spoke. "Come," I said, slipping my arm around his waist and picking up the package Kate had left on the table. "There is a debt the two of us need to repay, and the sunrise is already here."

AUTHOR'S NOTE

When writing a story set in this period of English-Gaelic history, it is a far more difficult task deciding what to leave out than what to include. I started out believing that I would tell a story of the tumultuous Scottish borders. What better conflict, I thought, than the animosity between an ambitious, powerful, charismatic lord of the borders and an arrogant, passionate noblewoman from the royal English court? When I decided on my setting and began my research, I realized that it was impossible to leave out the personalities of the people who lived their lives in Jamie Stewart's Scotland.

Catriona is an attempt to bring these personalities to life through their conflicts, conversations and actual events of the period. Much has been indelibly written in history. Much is my own interpretation. Many of the motivations and undercurrents that drove these people to behave as they did have been left out due to the limitations of space and time.

James IV of Scotland was an enlightened, intelligent and extremely popular young monarch who, through the sheer power of his charm and force of his ambition, coerced his reluctant country into taking part in the renaissance sweeping throughout the Western world. With Margaret Tudor, he founded a dynasty that was to rule Scotland and England for the next two hundred years. An incredible womanizer with a slew of illegitimate children, he had the misfortune to fall in love with a woman who was of little use to him politically.

History tells us that the grand passion of Jamie's life was Maggie Drummond. Some historians believe they may even have been secretly married. Shortly after she bore him a daughter, Maggie died at a private breakfast with her sisters and several other ladies of the court. Poison was suspected. Jamie was so inconsolable over her loss that he refused to receive his wife by proxy, Margaret Tudor, for one year. He offered Masses for Maggie's soul for the rest of his life. Jamie was actually only fifteen years old when he took the kingdom of Scotland from his father at Sauchieburn. He suffered guilt throughout his life for his part in the murder of James III. For penance, he wore a heavy iron belt, several inches thick, under his clothing.

Janet Kennedy's stormy marriage to the Hepburn is well documented in history. A spirited, intelligent woman, Janet was a distant cousin of the king as well as his mistress for several years. She did bear him at least one child before he gave her in marriage to the Hepburn, earl of Bothwell. The marriage turned out to be a very satisfactory one.

Mary Gordon was really Katherine Gordon, the "White Rose of Scotland," daughter of the earl of Huntley. Janet Kennedy was probably her cousin, not her older sister. Her brief marriage to Perkin Warbeck, the Pretender, ended in his death at the Tower of London. King Henry was so taken with her beauty and loyalty that he gave her an annual allowance and permission to remain at court with his queen. Later she married Matthew, the earl of Pembroke.

Sauchieburn, Jamie's coronation, the uprising at Dunblane, Warbeck's disastrous invasion of England, Henry's reception at Exeter, Mary's loyalty to her husband at Cornwall and Maggie's poisoning at breakfast are all actual events documented by historians of English history.

Catriona Wells—her temperament and conflicts, her family difficulties and her relationship to the Gordons, the Stewarts and the Sutherlands—is fictional, although many elements of the plot closely parallel the stormy courtship of Janet Kennedy and the Hepburn of Hailes.

Patrick MacKendrick is a combination of every border hero I could find, primarily the Hepburn and a bandit of the borders named Rob Roy, who lived much later. The MacKendrick's titles, holdings and possessions, including Hermitage, were held by Patrick Hepburn, the first earl of Bothwell.

No one who climbs the narrow stairs to the turrets of

Stirling Castle and views Margaret Tudor's blurred words carved into the stone wall as she waited for news of her husband fighting at the Battle of Flodden can doubt that Henry's daughter came to love her charming and faithless husband.

The overwhelming and complicated nature of Scottish history, the difficulty of reading faded documents written in Gaelic and ambiguous English, the intermarrying of clans and the varied viewpoints of witnesses to certain events make absolute accuracy for a fiction writer extremely difficult. I have attempted to wade through reams of information to create the story of a fascinating and thought-provoking era. In doing so, I have taken license and hope that those experts in Scottish history will understand that my motive was to write a memorable story.

KASEY MICHAELS